THREE SECONDS OF LIGHT

Joe Fonseca

Copyright © 2024 by Joe Fonseca

All rights reserved. Thank you for buying an authorized copy of this book and for complying with copyright laws by not reproducing, scanning, or distributing any part of it, in any form, without written permission from the author and publisher, except as permitted by U.S. copyright law.

This is a work of fiction. Names, characters, places, and incidents are either the product of the author's imagination or are used fictitiously. Any resemblance to actual persons, living or dead, businesses, companies, events, or locales is entirely coincidental.

Book Cover Design by ebooklaunch.com

Printed in the United States of America

Paperback ISBN 978-8-9911294-0-4
E-book ISBN 979-8-9911294-1-1
Hardcover ISBN 979-8-9911294-2-8
Library of Congress Control Number: 2024914682

A deer in the headlights...

Peaceful driving is difficult. Under normal conditions, you try to stay focused on the road while you watch for other drivers, good and bad. But it gets more complicated when you drive at night, as your thoughts wander and you're tempted to drift off to sleep. Nighttime driving on the Marine Corps Base at Quantico, Virginia, adds a new obstacle with the seemingly endless supply of whitetail deer -"Odocoileus virginianus" or Virginia deer. Their eyes pierce through the pitch-black night on the long stretch of road heading into the FBI Academy, or more succinctly, the Academy. I always felt those deer were the first test for any FBI new agent trainee. Try not to hit the deer on your way in. As I look back at all the Academy new agent training we received, I realize that my classmates and I were the ones who looked like deer in the headlights.

I dedicate this book to them.

FBI Special Agent Joe Fonseca *(retired)*
New Agent Class 98-15

Glossary of Terms

AD - Assistant Director

ALAT - Assistant Legal Attaché

BDU - Battle Dress Uniform

BuCar - FBI vehicle

BuPhone - FBI cell phone

C4 - Plastic explosive

CARDT - Child Abduction Rapid Deployment Team

CAST - Cellular Analysis Survey Team

CFO - Chief Financial Officer

CHS - Confidential Human Source

CIA - Central Intelligence Agency

CIRG - Critical Incident Response Group

CO2 - Carbon Dioxide

COMMS - Method of sending messages

CQB - Close-Quarters Battle

DEA - Drug Enforcement Agency

DecTube - Decontamination Tube

DSL - DNA Sequencing Lab

DWP - Doctors Without Politics

EAD - Executive Assistant Director

EOD - Entry on Duty

EOP - Eyes Only Personnel

ERF - Engineering Research Facility
ERT - Evidence Response Team
ETA - Estimated Time of Arrival
FBI - Federal Bureau of Investigation
FBI HQ - FBI Headquarters, Washington, D.C.
FBI Lab - FBI Laboratory
FTU - Firearms Training Unit
GPS - Global Positioning System
GSP - German Shorthaired Pointer
HQ - Headquarters
HRT - The Hostage Rescue Team
IA - InCit Agent
IBM - International Business Machines
InCit - Invisible Citizen
IRS - Internal Revenue Service
LAT/LONG - Latitude/Longitude
LED - Light Emitting Diode
MCB - Marine Corps Base
MIT - Massachusetts Institute of Technology
NASA - National Aeronautics Space Administration
NGO - Non-Governmental Organization
NSA - National Security Agency
Portal - Position of Remote Triage and Layover
RDS - Rounds aka bullets
SA - Special Agent
SAC - Special Agent in Charge of an FBI field office
SACS - Secure Access Control System
ScentDet - Scent Detection
SCH - Seattle Children's Hospital
SCIF - Sensitive Compartmented Information Facility

SITREP - Situational Report
SORT - Special Operations and Rescue Training
Station - A CIA office in another country
SWAT - Special Weapons and Tactics
TTU - Technical Training Unit
UC - Unit Chief
UFO - Unidentified Flying Object
USUR - Underwater Surveillance
UTL - Underwater Technology Lab
VCMO - Violent Crimes Major Offenders
VPN - Virtual Private Network
WMD - Weapons of Mass Destruction

Prologue

Not long after the National Aeronautics and Space Administration (NASA) was created in 1958, basically a renaming of the previous National Advisory Committee for Aeronautics, a think-tank of scientists and technicians at NASA pitched a funding idea to President Kennedy. The gist: create a monitoring system to watch for asteroids or meteor showers that may come into contact with Earth. This system would utilize powerful telescopes to explore the galaxy, a long way out into space past the Karman line, an imaginary line some sixty miles up, where the Earth's atmosphere ends and space begins. They would collect information on the movement of this space matter having a chance of striking Earth, at any time. This included asteroids or meteors coming close in the future. Years out. Like, light-years out. Hundreds of thousands of light-years out.

President Kennedy bought into the notion, and NASA moved forward, creating a government agency within NASA named Flash Point. The background behind the name came from the fact when asteroids and meteors enter the Earth's atmosphere, they have a flashpoint and then a streak. Idyllically, every asteroid or meteor would burn up on entry. Those flashpoints would be captured, and the trajectory of any possible asteroid or meteor fallout could be relayed to any country impacted by the fallout. Identifying the largest of the space matter and their trajectory would give the human race time to develop a plan to avert our extinction if any asteroid or meteor had even the slimmest of chances of crashing into us. Once identified, Flash Point personnel would categorize the objects by size, their proximity to Earth, the possibility they could hit Earth, and other fun facts. Flash Point would serve as the guardians of Earth's galaxy.

Chapter 1
Replay That

June 13, 1962
2:13 a.m.
NASA's Flash Point Command Center
Alexandria, VA

The technician positioned his feet crisscrossed at a perfect twenty-degree angle and propped on a stool. His arms were symmetrically laid across his chest, and his head was tilted just right so he wouldn't have a stiff neck if he woke up quickly. Ah, the optimal nap.

The type and extent of the high-pitched wail didn't necessarily register right away in the technician's brain. Startled by the alarm - which he was introduced to and had only heard once during the first week of training - he bolted upright and almost fell off his chair. The stool flew out from under his feet and crashed into a computer table. He jumped up and opened his eyes as wide as he could. As quickly as it sounded, it went away. He settled his gaze on the large screen on the wall facing him. The screen displayed a three-dimensional layout of Earth. As his eyes panned back and forth across the screen, he couldn't find any anomaly.

While Flash Point provided many different sounding alerts to signal distinctive trajectories of asteroids and meteors, the particular alarm the technician woke up to only went off if an object entered the Earth's atmosphere. That meant it was super close to Earth. He knew there should have been a different sounding alarm identifying the object much sooner and as far out as millions of miles. Asteroids and meteors don't just show up. This was a glitch. It had to be.

He studied the screen again. There wasn't a blinking light indicating a point of atmospheric entry, and there should have been. Nothing. The screen was perfectly still. He darted across the floor to a set of screens on the console. He typed in his password and accessed the database storing the video playback records. He entered the time he wanted and hit enter. The IBM 7094 computer mainframe began to whir. After approximately fifteen seconds, the large screen on the wall split into two sections, the live view on the left-hand side and the playback on the right. Watching the right, the technician gasped and collapsed into the seat behind him.

A streak of light had raced across the screen, entering the Earth's atmosphere on a downward angle. Almost as quickly as the streak appeared, it disappeared. He guessed the streak lasted four to five seconds. Checking the time, it was exactly three seconds. For this particular atmospheric alarm to be triggered, an object had to be large enough to cause catastrophic damage to Earth. That also meant the possibility of a significant loss of life.

He played the videotape back again. And then a third time. On the fourth go-round, he stopped the playback with the streak at its greatest length. Typing some commands into the computer, the system again whirred to gather the answer. On the small screen on the console in front of him were displayed the latitude and longitude coordinates of 33.950001, -83.383331. Sliding over to the bookcase, he grabbed the "Lat/Long Book," as he called it, and quickly flipped through the pages until he found the coordinates displayed on the computer screen. Athens, Georgia. He pushed himself back to the console and printed off the coordinates. Picking up the phone, he called his supervisor and waited for the hailstorm.

During the next several months, Flash Point technicians and astronomers reviewed the data the computer had collected at the time of the streak and worked at trying to identify it. Most worrisome to everyone at Flash Point was no meteor or asteroid had been located by the Flash Point system further out in space before the streak occurred. After all, Flash Point was created to identify and monitor asteroids and their small meteor cousins so we would have advance notice of any possible impacts.

The President wanted to know why their very sophisticated IBM computer system failed to alert them of an asteroid or meteor's entry if that was *what the streak was.* Some technicians surmised camera angles from the satellites orbiting the earth, which play a part in identifying asteroids and meteors before they enter our atmosphere, froze up for a time. Others joked the streak was an alien entity moving so fast our technology couldn't catch up.

After much debate, they found no answer but concluded the streak was a meteor with a very short tail that had entered our atmosphere and quickly and completely burned up on entry.

The Flash Point personnel, however, would laugh whenever they thought about how close Athens, Georgia, came to being a large, gaping hole.

Chapter 2

Short Weekend

September 7, 2012
11:24 p.m.
Marine Corps Base Quantico
Quantico, VA

Elliott Bell exited I-95 at the Marine Corps Base in Quantico, Virginia, also known as MCB Quantico. A sense of "this is not just another one of those cases" began to cross his mind. Federal Bureau of Investigation Special Agent (SA) Elliott Bell, or Bell, as agents commonly addressed each other by their last names, rubbed his chin thoughtfully, trying to imagine how the calm but serious tone of his supervisor's phone call should be interpreted. And this late on a Sunday night. He ordered Bell to the FBI's Engineering Research Facility, located within MCB Quantico on the grounds of the FBI Academy. And get there fast.

As Bell drove, he looked at his watch - 11:24 p.m. It was dark out, and Bell had yet to pass a car within the base. Bell wound through the dark country roads, passing one shadowy building after another and finally driving around a corner where hundreds of 1000-kilowatt-powered lights announced he was no longer invisible in the woods. Cameras in all positions watched his every move as he continued to close in on the FBI Academy.

The previously posted speed limit of twenty-five miles per hour was reduced to five, and only running lights were allowed as Bell approached the entrance and powered down the driver's side window of his grey 2012 Chevy Tahoe.

"Elliott Bell. Washington Field Office. Heading over to ERF," Bell said as the FBI police officer asked to see his "creds" or credentials.

"Thank you, sir," the officer said, returning his identification. "You know your way, sir?"

Bell raised his eyebrows and leaned out the window enough for the guard to see him more fully. Even though Bell was still in good shape for a man in his late 40s, his true age was certainly made more evident by his brown hair with gray highlights, giving the impression that Bell was nowhere close to being a recent FBI Academy graduate. The officer fumbled, "I'm sorry, sir. I'm sure you -"

Bell rescued him. "Been a while, but I think I can find my way. The first left and then the first right?" Bell asked with just enough hesitation to resemble a boy scout who was not an Eagle Scout yet. He could tell the officer felt embarrassed but thankful for Bell's attempt to move past the faux pas.

"Yes, sir. Good luck."

Bell rolled up his window as he headed towards ERF, wondering if the officer's matter-of-fact "good luck" was more of a prayer than a figure of speech.

Chapter 3
The Engineering Research Facility (ERF)

Bell was not the most tech-savvy agent. He could turn on his computer and cell phone but couldn't be trusted to look at a computer server and figure out the internet protocol. Yet here he was, with nominal technical prowess, driving toward the most closely guarded and defended building owned by the U.S. Government - the FBI's Engineering Research Facility.

The sprawling Engineering Research facility, or ERF, was located on ten acres. It was built some fifteen years or so before Director Hoover died. It was the first building the director built on the land destined to be the home to the FBI Academy, known simply as the Academy.

Hoover never told anyone why ERF was the first building to be erected. But he felt the Bureau, the term Hoover coined for the FBI, needed a scientific workshop to foster creativity from the best minds he could find. And the Academy would be the perfect location. Hoover wanted the FBI to have the most advanced "toys." Gadgets that would be state-of-the-art and so secretive no one would know they existed outside of the Eyes Only Personnel (EOP) assigned to each project.

ERF was not easy to get into. Clearance was granted to only one percent of the FBI's employees at any point in time. Once agents entered their code into a Hirsch Pad and completed a hand scan, depending on who they were, they were granted only so much access.

Most personnel, and certainly every visitor, were never allowed to move past the ground floor.

As Bell drove to the front of the massive ERF building, he thought how nice it would be to have just one weekend off. A meeting at ERF wasn't something Bell had even remotely thought would be on his agenda this evening. Nonetheless, he found a parking spot up close to a side door. Bell locked his Bureau car or BuCar as agents called them and headed towards the ERF side door. Bell pressed his SACS badge to the card reader, punched his eight-digit code, and waited for the hand scan to appear. After his code was accepted, a digital scan pad slid from the wall and rotated downward to a sixty-degree angle. Bell placed his hand over the grid for the scan and waited. After he scanned both his hands, the card reader produced a green light. The door made a loud clicking sound, and the heavy door unlocked. Bell headed inside.

The halls of ERF were brightly lit, not at all like Bell remembered them since he had been there last. Of course, that was during his Academy days, when he was training to be a special agent. The lights hanging from the ceiling produced a soft hum.

Bell moved down the corridor and headed for the ERF wing of conference rooms. Other than the whine of the lights, the only other noticeable sound was that of Bell's wet sneakers on the floor. *Slipping and falling*, Bell thought, *would ultimately make this night complete.*

As Bell walked by several labs, signs on the walls referenced varying sciences, projects, and disciplines - WMD (Weapons of Mass Destruction), USUR (Underwater Surveillance), ScenDet (Scent Detection), CAST (Cellular Analysis Survey Team), Human Growth - pretty self-explanatory Bell thought, then InCit. Bell paused. InCit? He tried to process InCit in his mind but kept walking. What the hell was InCit, Bell asked himself, muttering it out loud.

"Don't give it another thought, Bell," a booming voice shouted from the end of one long corridor, startling Bell just enough to make him seamlessly move for the Glock under his shirt.

"And don't shoot me, you bastard, although I know you would love to get off a few rounds in my direction," the voice continued.

Staring down the corridor in the direction of the voice, the silhouette of a rotund, balding man wearing a suit from the 80s - no, the 70s, had to be - was barely visible as a human being.

"Fuzzy bunny, is that you?" Bell chuckled.

"Yeah, hadn't heard that one in a while," Unit Chief (UC) Stanlislov Eroyee said. "Just get your ass down here. We don't have time to reminisce, and the director is supposedly five minutes out. This room." Eroyee was pointing to a door next to where he was standing.

Bell continued to walk towards the door UC Eroyee pointed to and subsequently disappeared through. Bell walked approximately ten yards when he was startled by another thunderous voice.

"Bell, my man! What the hell have you been doing with yourself lately?" SA David Tracey said. Bell whirled around to see his old classmate walking at a fast clip towards him with a grin on his face stretching ear-to-ear. Tracey kept looking around as his pace quickened even more. What the heck was Tracey doing in ERF late on a Sunday? He just suddenly appeared.

"Tracey?" Bell asked, surprised. "What the hell are you doing here?"

Tracey caught up to Bell and gave him a huge bear hug. The bear hug was a distraction. Bell didn't notice as Tracey placed a small, clear piece of tape with a micro-transmitter on the back of Bell's pullover.

Tracey put Bell back down on the ground. "I hear there's an InCit meeting, and many of my fellow InCit agents are here. I saw you come into the building but couldn't catch up to you fast enough. I did park next to you in the assistant director's spot, however," Tracey said with a broad smile and chuckle.

"Wait, what is InCit?" Bell asked.

"Ah, that's right. You haven't been read in yet. You'll get it all explained to you shortly. Another Eyes Only case, bud. It should be fun!"

"Yeah, I'm heading there now," Bell said with a grunt of annoyance.

He turned and started walking again towards the InCit conference room. Tracey did not; instead, he headed back the way he came.

"You coming?" Bell asked.

Tracey nodded as he continued walking. "I am, but I've got to see a friend first. I'll meet you there."

"Okay. See you soon." Bell had only advanced five feet when he saw a red glare bouncing off the walls and traveling toward him. The infrared dot scanners, Red Ladens, were conducting their routine scan of every inch of the hallways in ERF. Bell had seen Red Ladens in training videos and learned a little of their capabilities. But he had never seen them in action before. They were slowly making their way towards Bell along the narrow hallway of ERF. More to the point, they were floating his way.

They were searching for any anomaly that changed the layout of ERF, from a piece of paper that fell on the floor to an open or unlocked door that shouldn't be to a person who shouldn't be there. They also conducted DNA searches. Permeating your body and running the collected DNA through the ERF computer system, Red Ladens were a failsafe that you were authorized to be in the exact spot they were standing. If someone happened to wander into a particular area in ERF where they didn't belong, the Red Ladens would render the person unconscious by deploying anesthesia.

"Here comes the Red Ladens," Bell said as he looked down the hall towards Tracey and took a position up against a wall. Tracey was leisurely backpedaling as he stared past Bell towards the Red Ladens. Tracey suddenly started to jog away from the incoming Red Ladens.

"Yeah, this happens fairly often here," Tracey said as his voice trailed off. "Hopefully, the Red Ladens don't catch me and knock me out."

That was an odd statement from Tracey. He just said he was an InCit Agent. Why would he think the Red Ladens would knock him out?

Bell turned his attention back to the Red Ladens.

The Red Ladens caught up to Bell, passed through him, and continued down the corridor. Since Bell was still standing, it looked like he was supposed to be there.

Chapter 4

Not So Far Off the Grid

September 4, 2012
11:45 a.m. MST *(four days before Bell's ERF meeting)*
Outdoor Equipment, Inc. (OEI)
Trellis, MT

SA David Tracey tried to sip on his coffee as he drove. Long ago, he gave up cream and sugar in his coffee and went cold turkey - black only. Nothing like a piping hot coffee, he thought to himself. He blew through the hole in the lid to cool it down just a bit. He might not get a sip for another ten minutes. It was that hot.

Earlier that morning, he called his wife from his BuPhone and told her he was still on assignment in the mountains. He also warned her the roof at the lake house had been struck by a tree and that no one should stay there until it was fixed. It was a lie, of course, but Tracey needed to be sure no one showed up unexpectedly.

The parking lot of the OEI store was slowly filling up. The town was crawling with tourists and outdoors folk alike, all hoping to get their fill of the clear air and rugged mountainside. They stopped to shop at the OEI store as if OEI had better gear than any other store. Marketing. That's all it was, Tracey thought to himself. He could buy a pair of waterproof hiking shoes at a discount store for $40, which would do just as good a job as a pair that cost over $200. Marketing. Pure marketing.

Tracey drove into the parking lot and pulled into a spot 100 yards from the front door. For his plan to work, Tracey needed everyone to believe he was in

Trellis, Montana, and trying to hide. He slowly walked from his car and through the front door, making sure each store camera had a good angle of his face. While shopping, he even held up items in direct sight of the cameras. The Bureau would know it was him.

Walking over to the camping gear section, he grabbed a tent and some additional camping equipment, including a propane lamp, a few small propane tanks, a shovel, rope, and a sleeping bag, eventually charging over $700. Shuffling out of the OEI store, he again took his time while passing all the cameras on the way to his car. After he loaded the items in the back of his black SUV, he sat in the spot for a minute, sipping on his coffee that had slightly cooled off.

Reaching into his coat, he grabbed his blackhawk, a Bureau communication device similar to a pager assigned to every Eyes Only agent. The blackhawk was simply a device for texting back and forth. Eyes Only agents could also send pictures and documents on their blackhawks, but they couldn't use it like a phone.

Turning the blackhawk over, he pressed the back panel, slid the cover off, and took both lithium-ion batteries out. He put the blackhawk and the batteries back in his coat pocket and headed out of the parking lot. With his blackhawk disabled, the Bureau wouldn't be able to track him.

Driving west, Tracey covered eight miles on Rural Route #7, passing acre after acre of pure wilderness. No one on the road except one small RV parked on the opposite side with its flashing lights on. Normally, Tracey would have stopped to see if they needed any help, but he had a schedule and plan he had to stick to.

Another six miles down the road, he slowed at a sign for the Beaverhead Municipal Airport and then turned onto its access road. Thankfully, he was driving an SUV as the road hadn't been plowed since the snowfall a week ago. The few cars that had been down the road made a pretty good path for him to follow, and he stuck to it, speeding along to his destination.

After half a mile, he emerged from the tree-shrouded road and continued towards the small tan building housing the air traffic controller. He parked at the end of a row of several cars that had snow on their roofs and looked like they hadn't been moved since the recent snowfall. With ten to twelve inches of new snow expected in the next several hours, Tracey knew his SUV would soon enough look like each of the other cars around his - completely covered in snow. He was counting on it.

He stepped out of the SUV and opened the back doors as he looked around. It didn't seem like anyone was around who would care about his existence. Tracey reached into the back cargo area for his backpack. He opened it to be sure he had what he needed - several strapped bundles of $20 bills, his Secure Access Control System (SACS) badge, some underwear, a collared shirt, a white lab coat, white slip-on shoe coverings, and white hospital scrubs.

Glancing around, Tracey headed towards the hangar at the far end of the runway. Its door was open, and a plane was running with a pilot inside checking his instruments.

Approaching the side door, the pilot noticed Tracey and waved, motioning for him to get on the plane.

Tracey opened the door. Above the noise of the engine, he greeted him. "Hey, good afternoon. You Josh?" Tracey asked.

"I am indeed. You must be Dane?"

"I am sir," Tracey answered, acknowledging the name he told the pilot to expect.

"Okay then, let's get you to Miami. It will take a few bumps and jumps, but I'll get you there. Should take about seven hours."

Tracey hopped in next to the pilot and strapped in. Josh handed him a headset, which Tracey put on.

Josh took a few more readings from the instrument panel and slowly pushed the throttle forward as the plane inched onto the runway. The tower gave them the green light, and the little Cessna sped down the runway and into the sky.

For this plan to work, Tracey would now need a little help from family.

Chapter 5

Covering Tracks

September 7, 2012
11:35 p.m. EST
ERF

Tracey didn't have much time before he would have to explain himself. He also hadn't thought he'd run into anyone he knew at ERF this evening. Let alone his friend Elliott Bell. Bell would certainly be surprised when he learned of Tracey's plans. Tracey was trying to put that reality off for a few more hours if he could. And Tracey had some work to do.

Tracey quickened his pace once he turned the corner out of Bell's sight. The Red Ladens were coming, and he knew he couldn't be found in ERF or anywhere just yet. And he couldn't reveal how he got into ERF undetected either. There might be a price someone would pay for that secret, and the person who would pay the price had no idea they were on the hook.

He continued around the corner from where he met Bell and double-timed it around several more corners before slipping into an empty conference room. Once inside, he left the lights off. The room was dimly lit, the only source of light being the lighted switch plate from an electrical outlet by the door.

Tracey removed his overcoat, shoes, and pants. Underneath, he wore a white lab coat tucked into his pants and white hospital scrubs. He peeled off the lab coat and scrubs and dressed again in street clothes. He put on his overcoat, reached inside the pocket, and took out a pair of white, paper slip-on shoe covers. Over his clothes, he then dressed himself in the white scrubs, white lab coat, and paper shoe covers. He buttoned up his lab coat to hide the clothing underneath, hung his SACS badge around his neck, and headed back into the hall.

He quickly looked in the direction he had come to check on the Red Ladens. They weren't coming his way unless they had gone completely to invisible mode. That was a chance he would have to take. He continued in the direction he originally was walking until he arrived at a door marked "DSL - DNA Sequencing Lab." Under the sign was an 8" x 10" screen. To the left and right of the doorway were small cameras. Tracey turned his head down as he touched the screen, and an appointment calendar appeared with the current month.

To gain access to the DSL, agents had to make an appointment by phone and be added to the calendar using the last six digits of their social security number. You couldn't just stop by and say hello to a friend you knew working there. Ever. But there was one other way to get in. DSL personnel could use their assigned access code. And Tracey had a code to get in. He memorized the code when his friend used it. His friend had no idea, and Tracey never told his friend he saw - actually, heard - the code being entered.

Tracey punched in the nine-digit code, and the door to the DSL clicked open, allowing him entrance to the lab.

Once inside, Tracey could relax, knowing the Red Ladens wouldn't find him. Long ago, the Red Ladens were banned from entering DSL. They were banned after destroying random DNA samples the technicians had left out in various stages of review. The Red Ladens thought the samples were intruders and did what they were programmed to do.

Tracey moved deliberately. He grabbed several vials from the refrigerated coolers and replaced them with vials containing meaningless red and blue dyes, then made his way to a desk against the wall with a nameplate that read "Dana Burnside." Tracey powered on her computer and filled in the information for the username and password - Dana Burnside's username and password. She had been a little too carefree with her password the last time they met, and Tracey never forgot it.

After maneuvering through several layers of files, Tracey found a file with his name on it. He clicked on a few more files and copied a file from one location to another. Satisfied with his work, he logged off. He grabbed a gas mask on the shelf next to Dana's computer and headed for the door.

That was all Tracey needed tonight from ERF. He was there to buy himself time. Time that would allow him to finish what he started only a few short months before. In the next several hours, maybe a day, the Bureau would know he was not in the mountains, and the Bureau would have to reassess everything they thought might be happening.

Chapter 6

The Good, the Bad, and the Weird

As Tracey disappeared down the hall, Bell turned and continued towards UC Eroyee, who had disappeared through a doorway. Loud voices could be heard as Bell drew closer to a conference room. Directly across from the conference room was a doorway with another Hirsch Pad and a sign above it - "InCit Personnel Only," another reference to the InCit Unit. Bell hooked a right into conference room 1450 and entered to find a U-shaped table surrounded by roughly ten people. He headed to the back. *Guess I'm InCit personnel now,* Bell thought to himself.

"What do you make of this?" a voice asked from Bell's left. Bell looked over at a short, middle-aged man.

"Graph, long time, bud," Bell said to Dillard Graph. "Don't know what this is. I did give up a night with Sam Adams to drive here, though."

"Yeah, I'm a bit lost also, and I'm sure it's probably not to give us performance awards." The anxious look on Graph's face wasn't making Bell feel any easier.

Bell slipped into a soft-cushioned, black-leathered chair and let out a short sigh. Bell had a sense no one knew why they were there and hoped to figure it out. Strangely enough, Bell's boss may have been on point when he said Bell would be in the dark as much as everyone else at the meeting.

There were several techies, as Bell liked to call them, sitting at a table in the front. More folks entered and sat up front, some in suits, some wearing battle dress uniforms or BDUs. A couple of folks who entered had on workout gear.

The room was quickly filling up. It seemed like anyone who was someone was arriving for this briefing. Bell continued to worry that, more than the Sam Adams he left on his kitchen table was getting warm, it appeared everyone had a strained, puzzled look about them. And where the hell was Tracey? You don't want to be late for a meeting with the director.

"Feet!" someone yelled near the door. Bureau employees knew when someone yelled "Feet!" it meant everyone in the room was subordinate in rank to who was about to enter, and you'd better stand up, fast. Everyone bolted straight up, and all the banter and noise ended immediately.

FBI Director Lawrence Stillman walked in.

September 8, 2012
12:45 a.m.

The director was wearing a sweat suit and flanked by just a single agent from his protection detail of eight agents. Director Stillman took a deep breath as he paused at the podium.

Starting slowly, he addressed everyone.

"Good morning, everyone, and thank you for coming out so quickly. Please, have a seat."

The director looked out on everyone, panning back and forth.

"When I began as your director several years ago, I knew we would accomplish great things. We. All of us. After seeing some of the programs the people assembled here have begun, developed, and brought to reality, I knew then and still know that greatness exists in the Bureau. I will explain what I am talking about and bring you up to speed on the InCit program you are all a part of."

Finally, there would be an explanation, Bell thought.

"With this assembled group of fourteen support and agent personnel, I will brief four additional personnel today. They are one additional agent and three technicians. Is Special Agent Bell here?" the director asked.

Bell stopped slouching and stood up.

"Sir," he stated with confidence.

"Thank you for being here. You have a lot of questions, I am sure. Let me get started."

Bell sat back down. Oh, he had questions all right. He'd wait his turn.

"I'm going to get right to the point," Director Stillman continued. "We have lost touch with InCit agent #33, or IA33, as you know each other. From what we hear within the Bureau's intelligence circles, there's a greater chance IA33 has gone rogue versus having met his fateful end. He may be attempting to sabotage the FBI or the U.S. government or is trying to sell the InCit technology to someone, possibly a foreign power.

"IA33 has been going through a major crisis in his family. His oldest daughter was diagnosed with a disease a few years ago that was held in check until this past year. She has trouble breathing, and the disease is slowly killing her."

Bell perked up. Did he say disease?

"At the same time, IA33's supervisor removed him from InCit so he would have more time to be with his family. But we mistakenly didn't recover his drone or even turn it off quickly enough. He has been missing with his drone for at least three days.

"We tracked the last message he sent to his wife a few days ago to a parking lot of an OEI store several miles from his vacation home in Montana. She called him in sick to work after receiving the text. She has been debriefed and swears she doesn't know where he is. We believe her."

Bell was paying attention now. His eyes opened wider. His classmate Tracey had a lake house in Montana. And a beautiful daughter who was sick. But Bell just saw Tracey in the hallway.

"We checked the security cameras at OEI, where IA33 entered and purchased a large supply of camping items. We're not sure if he's trying to hide out in the vast forest just outside his home in Montana or if he is trying to throw us off, knowing we would find his last location."

The director paused and looked back down as if trying to collect himself. He began to speak as he lifted his head.

"As all of you know, the president and his staff do not know about this project. As far as we know, no president has ever been told about this project. We want to keep it that way, so we must find IA33 quickly and quietly.

"Okay, for everyone except SA Bell and the new technicians, head to conference room ERF 8. A detailed operation plan has been created individually for each of you. That's all, thank you."

The designated agents got up and headed out as instructed.

The director motioned with his hand for the remaining new folks to move closer to him. Bell stood up and moved to a chair in front of the director. The only personnel left were the director, his one protective detail special agent, one InCit technician, Bell, and the three new techies.

The director began.

"All right, folks. Let's get through this. So, InCit. This project was created following the 1963 discovery of an element, a mineral rock of unknown origin in Stone Mountain, Georgia. Hoover named the element stomonite. Although we don't know where it came from, it is believed to have fallen from space as a meteor.

"I won't give you that whole history. Instead, let me have one of the InCit technicians describe stomonite. Nancy?"

The director waved the technician to the front while he stepped aside.

InCit technician Nancy Lavis began. "The basic properties of stomonite are biological and in rock form. The most unique property of this element is the speed at which it can manifest itself. It spins almost seven times faster than the speed of light. If you're not up on how fast that is, light travels almost 300 million meters per second. At its fastest rotational spin, stomonite becomes invisible. Einstein was close - the speed of light is the maximum speed at which all matter in the universe can travel. Except for stomonite." She gave a little nerd chuckle, and the director joined in.

Bell shifted in his seat. He was trying to figure out if he was being pranked. With all these new words, what he was hearing sounded insane.

"We've been able to harness the speed of that rotational spin and have applied the stomonite to only one type of object over the years - a drone - making the drone invisible under the right applications. For your information, SA Bell, IAs are each assigned one tactical, defensive drone cloaked in stomonite. This drone will follow you everywhere and provide you with an invisible security detail if you will. You will need extra protection due to the dangerous nature of the cases IAs work. SA Bell, before you head out today, you will receive your drone and instructions on how to use it."

Bell didn't blink. He just stared.

From the three new techies, Bell noticed some raised eyebrows, but they genuinely just accepted what they were being told.

Bell was now thinking that the InCit technician and the director were some kind of crazy. Or delusional. Or drunk or on God knows what drug.

Bell shifted in his seat again.

The director nodded in approval as Lavis moved away from the podium. The director flipped through a few papers at the podium. "As I mentioned, IA33's last known location before his blackhawk went dark was in Montana. He and his wife have a lake house there. We've got IA24 making his way there now."

Bell was starting to get inundated with information. Not only was this InCit program a bit much to swallow, but he also had a bad feeling about his friend, Tracey. He had a house in Montana. But again, Bell just spoke with Tracey at ERF, so he wasn't missing. He was in ERF! But still not at this meeting.

"Does anyone have any questions so far?"

Bell couldn't help himself. He raised his hand.

"SA Bell." The director pointed a finger at him.

Standing up, Bell said, "Sir, before we head out, will we be told the identity of IA33 and receive a photo? Also, I don't yet know my IA number. Thank you, sir." Bell sat back down.

"That is a great question, and thank you for asking. You are IA83, the latest addition to the InCit agent program. You will be identified that way in any InCit group texts. As for IA33's true identity, his name and photo have been forwarded to your blackhawk. Also, you have each been removed from the FBI's employee database. As a security measure, all IAs and InCit employees are removed from the employee database so no one can identify them if our system gets breached."

"Thank you, sir, " Bell said.

"Okay, you will find a group text on your blackhawks named 'Rogue.' The IAs in the group text are the IAs you will coordinate with when you head out in the field. I am also in this group, as is my security detail. The name and photo of IA33 are there, so take a look when you can."

Bell couldn't take it any longer. He had to ask the director point-blank if IA33 was his friend Tracey. Too many coincidences existed for it not to be Tracey. And if it was, he had to tell the director he had just run into Tracey down the hall.

Bell raised his hand to interrupt the director. He looked Bell's way, but Bell sensed the director had started talking softer, and Bell was having trouble hearing him. The director was trailing off as he began to point toward Bell, his voice no longer sounding clear. The distance between Bell and the director seemed planetary. It felt to Bell like he had suddenly fallen asleep, like on certain Sundays at church when the priest went a little too long, and Bell would drone him out to enter a homily-induced church coma.

But Bell realized he was still awake but couldn't process what was happening around him. He tried to sit up straight in his chair, and while it felt like he was sitting, he was staring at more of the ceiling than any wall. He was slowly falling and didn't know why. With a heavy thump, Bell hit the floor. Strangely, there was no noise, and Bell felt no pain. He sensed he was now alone, which was stranger still.

Suddenly, all the lights went out. Total darkness. And silence. *What gives?* Bell knew no matter what the explanation was, nothing seemed right at that moment. Bell could see the lights in the hallway were on but were flickering.

Bell forced himself to sit up. He was definitely on the floor. And still no sound. He couldn't hear anyone. Directionally, Bell was lost in the dark. He had no idea which way he had last faced, and now he was struggling with his senses.

What the hell is happening, and who turned out the damn lights?

Chapter 7

Aftermath

Bell grabbed the cell phone out of his pocket. Turning its flashlight on, he quickly pointed it around the room. What he saw next reminded him of crime scenes he had witnessed over the years.

The bodies of the three techies were on the ground next to him. They had fallen out of their chairs. Bell leaned over and flashed the light on the face of one of the male techies. His eyes were completely wide open. He had no expression but appeared to be staring off into space. *Maybe he's alive and is staring off into space*, Bell thought. His face had turned slightly bluish. Bell grabbed for the techie's wrist to check for a pulse. He had one.

Bell then low-crawled in the direction of the doorway to the conference room. Nancy Lavis's body was near the front podium where Bell last saw her speaking. He crawled over to her. She appeared in the same condition as the other techies. He checked for a pulse. She had a pulse as well. And the same blue coloring.

As Bell flashed the light around the podium, the agent on the director's security detail was lying next to Lavis, and the director was lying next to him. Bell decided to check on the director next. He had a pulse as well. A quick check of the security detail agent proved he was in the same condition as all the personnel on the floor. He also looked like Papa Smurf.

Bell stood up and made it to the doorway. The hum of the corridor lights was the only sound he could hear. Weird. It didn't seem so loud before. He didn't even think twice about the low sound after he arrived at ERF. Now, it appeared deafening. He stepped out into the hallway and tried to figure out what was happening around him. Whatever triggered the lights to shut off in the conference room had also tripped the super-sensitive electron-magnetic pulse monitors, which acted as a fail-safe to shut down ERF. The pulse monitors' sensor lights were now flashing in the hallway. As Bell looked to his left out of the conference room, the colorful blur of the Red Ladens headed toward him. Here we go again.

"Is anyone here?" Bell called out. Nothing. Bell thought he heard someone or something coming from the conference room down the hall. Walking over there might clear up what event had just transpired, and he might be able to find help for the director.

First, Bell decided to brace for the Red Ladens. He took three steps across the corridor to the front of the InCit access door. Steadying himself, he grabbed the square black Hirsch Pad box in front of the door with his right hand, out of instinct, waiting for the Red Ladens. That would have been the ultimate irony - called to a meeting in an area he wasn't authorized to access, and he was the only one still conscious.

He lifted his head and steadied himself. Several dozen Red Ladens paused briefly over him before moving into his body. And just like that, almost as quickly as they entered his body, the Red Ladens departed and swarmed into the conference room.

Several seconds later, the Red Ladens exited the conference room and headed down the corridor in the direction where Bell last saw Tracey.

Still pondering why he was the only one conscious, the Hirsch Pad Bell was gripping came to life and lit up. The Hirsch Pad now offered him a chance to enter his eight-digit code. Bell reviewed the sequence that appeared, punched in his eight-digit code, and the "enter" button. A retinal scanner slid open next to the Hirsch Pad. Bell's mind was working so fast that his heart rate began to climb. Why would his access code work on the InCit access door? He hadn't been read into the program yet. And now an eye scan? Whatever the reason, Bell couldn't dwell on it.

Moving to the eye scan, Bell placed his chin in the respective spot and stared ahead. The light blue scan quickly slid from left to right. To Bell's amazement, the bright white door leading to the InCit lab slid open. Bell peered inside. It was an elevator. And darkness. Lovely. And almost as quickly as the door to access the InCit lab opened, it began to close. Bell rationalized that as he opened and accessed the door, he should be able to enter the elevator. Checking on everyone else would have to wait. He needed to see if the elevator would lead to someone who could help him and the others.

Bell eased his way in. Within five seconds of the door having opened, it closed.

Bell had worked countless Eyes Only, highly covert operations, and walked through numerous back doors. He could easily produce a definition for the phrase "Eyes Only." But InCit was quite a step above Eyes Only - if such a thing existed - as no one in the Bureau even talked about InCit. Bell certainly had never heard of it.

Bell stood in the dark as the door clicked shut and a short burst of air released. Bell assumed the area was being decompressed, but for what? His answer came pretty quickly. An orange light above his head began to spin as if he were in a construction zone, casting an eerie orange circle on the floor as he descended.

The movement was smooth - not pulley-driven or grinding like a gear. It was more like the movement of a piston. Like the much-improved state-of-the-art roller coasters developed to replace the clickity-clackity old wooden roller coasters he remembered as a youth. His eyes were beginning to adjust to the dark. He closed them and opened them slowly. He was moving fast enough to wonder why there was nothing to hold onto. But it didn't matter.

Almost immediately, the elevator slowed and stopped.

The orange light clicked off, and the elevator door opened to reveal near darkness. Bell closed his eyes for about ten seconds to help adjust to the obscurity. When he opened his eyes, another sense caught his attention - noise. The sound of muffled voices could be heard in the distance. Bell waited until he could get his bearings and moved out of the elevator. He began to walk towards the voices.

Using the wall as his guide, Bell headed down a hallway that he realized was slowly proceeding downhill, and he could see a light up ahead. After about ten yards, Bell came to an open door on his left, the source of the bright florescent glow. Bell could hear several voices, and one was female. They were in a heated discussion but didn't seem to be arguing. Above the doorway was a sign: "InCit Command."

Given the night he had endured so far, Bell decided to draw his firearm. He began to "slice the pie," a room-clearing technique of slowly inching forward from a position of cover or concealment to gradually see what was in front of him, several degrees at a time. Bell crept further into the middle of the hallway while beginning to peer through the doorway, his firearm up and in front of him.

At first, Bell saw microscopes, test tubes, and other technical-looking equipment. Bell safely assumed this was a lab. He continued to move slowly in the hallway, with his firearm sweeping the open doorway. He saw a male techie wearing a white lab coat, making his points like he was born in Italy - speaking with his hands. Bell continued to pan into the lab. Standing next to the male techie was a female in a lab coat. She looked to be about sixty-five years old. She was listening with a frustrated look and her arms crossed about her chest. She didn't seem to be having whatever he was dishing out, and she appeared to be the boss.

A few more degrees of slicing the pie and Bell picked up a third techie, a guy who looked like he was twelve years old. He stood by listening and agreeing with each of the opinions the two techies presented. The third techie had to be an intern, acting like he didn't want to get fired.

Bell held his position. He listened for any other voices. It appeared to be a safe environment. He gave it another minute and was curious enough to hear the conversation. He holstered his Glock and stepped through the doorway.

"Does anyone know where I can find the bathroom? I drank *wayyyyyy* too much water tonight." As usual, Bell couldn't help the attempt at humor.

The older male techie startled and jumped. All conversation ended as Bell's entrance thoroughly confused everyone except the intern.

"And who the hell are you?" the female asked, taking a step backward.

"I actually live next door and was just trying to find the bathroom, I swear." Bell chuckled to himself.

"Listen, smart-ass. You are in an Eyes Only area, so you better be cleared to be here, or you're not going to be cleared for anything except prosecution."

"Sorry. It's been a crazy past few hours. Elliott Bell. I was sent here tonight to be debriefed on some emergency and would have been enlightened to that event, except the lights went out before the director could explain what was so urgent."

"That doesn't explain how you got down here. Access to this lab had been cleared only for InCit personnel," the female techie continued. "And I don't remember ever seeing your name as one of those persons. So again, how'd you get past the door?"

Bell figured she probably couldn't take any more jokes, so he tried the truth. "I must admit, I'm a little surprised myself. After the lights went out in the first-floor conference room and the Red Ladens didn't take me out - twice - I knew my blood had been entered into at least the DNA database, allowing me access to ERF. As I steadied myself in the dark by the doorway to InCit, I grabbed the Hirsch Pad, and my palm print was recognized. The numbers generated on the pad and lit up. I entered my code, and the door to InCit opened. The rest is history. So here I am, feeling like I'm part of the Inquisition." Bell said.

"I have no idea why I'm here or what the hell InCit is all about. But we do have to find out if everyone upstairs is okay. I left the director and several others unconscious in a conference room. There also may be others out cold in the conference room down the hall from there."

The male techie spoke next. Extending his hand, he approached Bell.

"Doctor George Gaeber, biochemical engineer assigned to ERF and the InCit program. Nice to meet you. You can call me George," he said, smiling broadly.

Bell reached out and shook Dr. Gaeber's hand.

The female techie crossed her arms and tilted her head sideways while looking at Dr. Gaeber. She then turned her attention to Bell.

" Dr. Sidney Parker. You can call me Dr. Parker," she said, raising her eyebrows. "This is my lab."

The intern reached out his hand and looked toward Bell but never made eye contact.

"Eric," the intern said, likely because he thought he should give his name and not because he wanted to. He seemed scared of his own shadow.

"I just graduated from Cal Poly with a Master's in chemical engineering. This is my second week here."

"It's nice to meet you all," Bell said.

Dr. Parker turned to Eric. "Call the security unit and see how everyone is doing upstairs."

Eric ran to his desk like he was being chased by a bear and called security.

Bell looked at Dr. Parker. "Now, maybe someone can tell me what is going on. I've never seen a tougher lab to gain access to. And what the heck happened upstairs?"

"That's the funny thing, Elliott. InCit, in and of itself, isn't meant to be seen," Dr. Gaeber said without blinking an eye. "It stands for Invisible Citizen."

Chapter 8

InCit

Dr. Parker motioned for Bell to follow. As Bell entered the lab, he took stock of all the lab materials. Nothing special, Bell thought. Five walk-in freezers lined the back wall, each with a red and green light above it. All the red lights were illuminated above each freezer. On the right end of the walk-in freezers was a door.

As they approached this door, Dr. Parker asked, "Did the director mention a new element?"

"Yes, stomonite. He mentioned it being found and the FBI recovering it but not much else."

"So, the director gave you a quick but insufficient explanation of how we found stomonite and why it's what we consider not only the rarest material on Earth but by far the most valuable. And dangerous. So, let me give you a more in-depth story.

"Stomonite, as you may have learned from the director, was discovered in and named after Stone Mountain, Georgia, in the early 60s. At first glance, stomonite looks like a piece of granite that makes up the majority of the rock formation of Stone Mountain.

"An eight-year-old girl from Virginia was on vacation camping with her parents in Stone Mountain and picked up what she thought was a pretty black rock. She kept it in her backpack and took it on the plane as she headed home. The girl was playing with the rock in her seat on the plane when the rock suddenly jumped from her hand and struck a man behind her in the forehead. The man had been leaning over the back of the girl's seat. The man fell backward into his seat. The rock returned to the girl's hand almost as quickly as it had left."

"As it turned out, the man had concealed a subminiature camera in his hand and was snapping pictures of the little girl."

Dr. Parker continued to talk as they walked from room to room. "The FBI was waiting for him when the plane landed. They discovered the man wasn't as innocent as he tried to make them believe. Two years prior, he had been arrested for being a "Peeping Tom," standing outside his nine-year-old neighbor's bedroom window. The man had a similar camera with him at the time when he was arrested.

"The historical moment for us here in InCit, and why this lab exists and has had a part in many of the Bureau's successes over the past 50 years, happened a week later: there was another incident with the girl from Virgina."

Dr. Parker stopped walking. She had caught Bell's attention, and he listened with interest. "The girl had taken the rock to school as part of her project on what she did over the summer. One of the class bullies took the stone and played "keep away" from the little girl. That's when things got weird. The bully tossed it between his hands and threw the rock toward one of his friends. In mid-air, the rock reversed course and struck the bully square in the head. It knocked him out. Just as quickly as it had left her hand, it returned to the girl's art project lying on the table. Not your average rock. And it makes you rethink the "dumb as a rock" moniker."

"Does this rock have a defense mechanism? Why did it never decide to attack the girl?" Bell asked, trying not to sound skeptical.

Dr. Gaeber opened his mouth to answer Bell, but Dr. Parker cut him off.

"The main theory just about everyone got behind was the stomonite attacked based on being able to sense a person's ethical behavior. You were safe if you had good intentions. It seems a bit pie-in-the-sky to theorize this way, but it would explain why the little girl's assailant on the plane and, subsequently, the bully at her school were attacked. Neither of them had good intentions. So, the stomonite would not bond with the assailants. It also proved why the stomonite bonded with and protected the little girl. She wasn't evil. The stomonite's loyalty appears to lie with the first true, good-intentioned person who handles it.

"After the incident with the child, the FBI reviewed the data more closely. We pinpointed the exact location in Stone Mountain where the meteor landed. The geological makeup of the soft earth surrounding Stone Mountain was noticeably depressed on the side where the little girl found her rock. Thermal imagery showed a gorge under the ground approximately two hundred yards wide. Traces of stomonite lined the entire length of the gorge to the final resting place of the stomonite, fifteen hundred yards down. The theory, again, is the stomonite was so hot and traveled so fast when it entered the Earth's atmosphere that it was invisible. The sides of the gorge where the stomonite was found were smooth, indicating the stomonite was in liquid form when it entered the earth, easily piercing the ground around Stone Mountain. It cooled as it entered the ground and returned to its rock-hard form. We were able to mine over 80,000 tons of Stomonite.

"To prove the theory about its properties, we experimented on stomonite for over three years in this lab. Five agents ultimately survived the tests to become the first InCit Agents, or simply "IAs." These IAs were each given a number and known by this number as long as they remained in the InCit program. The first five InCit Agents were known as IA1 to IA5."

They passed into a glass-enclosed lab that didn't have any equipment in it. There were tables and a lot of dents in the glass. Bell tapped on the glass. Not glass. Hard plastic, it seemed.

"What is this made of?" Bell asked.

Sheepishly, Dr. Gaeber said, "Twenty-two-inch, clear graphite mixed with the same organic compound protecting the outside of ERF - a combination of spider silk and the teeth of the limpet, a marine snail living on the bottom of the ocean whose teeth are comprised of the strongest biological material ever tested. As stomonite is the rarest material on Earth and the most unpredictable, we wanted a secure location to escape to should we ever need to protect ourselves from it. The dents in the graphite resulted from our tests when we threatened the stomonite with lasers and forced it to attack us. The stomonite couldn't get through it. We named this small section of InCit 'The Panic Room.'"

Dr. Parker took over. "As the scientists continued to work with the first five IAs, they made startling discoveries. When placed in a protective chamber - similar in make-up to the twenty-two inches of Lucite plastic that you see surrounding this room - the stomonite lay still, allowing us to analyze it. But the stomonite, while visibly projecting no state of motion, was vibrating ever so slightly. The scientists then agitated the stomonite by using a laser beam on it. As soon as the laser hit the stomonite, it jumped up quickly and disappeared. The stomonite didn't attack the container it was in. It just disappeared. The scientists examined the container using ultraviolet light, among other things. As soon as the room went dark and the UV light was switched on, the stomonite could be seen in the same spot it was before disappearing. It hadn't moved one iota, but it seemed to be spinning. Using some extremely sophisticated equipment we borrowed from the asteroid/meteor-monitoring agency named Flash Point, and subsequently NASA, the stomonite was measured by the Bureau scientists and found to be spinning seven times faster than the speed of light. The stomonite made itself invisible as a defense mechanism."

"Is it alive?" Bell asked.

"We don't believe it is alive, but it displays properties of decision making, like something alive. But, we assume, only to lash out to protect itself or the human it binds with.

"We can only guess what stomonite is made up of. Stomonite has no earthly qualities. Not one ounce of it. It's an element from outside our atmosphere."

Bell's mind was racing. He had so many questions.

"Can the stomonite be destroyed?" Bell asked.

"Yes, but not easily. We'll explain later," Dr. Parker said.

They continued to walk past the clear graphite lab. On the other side, Eric could be seen making his way to them. He was grinning and had his thumb up in the air.

They had been standing outside a door made half of metal on the bottom and half of glass on the top. Dr. Parker worked the Hirsch Pad and held the door open for them. They all stepped through the doorway and stopped in what looked like a decontamination airlock. No one moved as they waited for Eric to reach them. Eric subsequently made his way into the airlock as well.

"Red Ladens, Elliott." was barely out of Dr. Gaeber's mouth when the tiny red balls flooded the airlock from tiles in the ceiling.

Most ERF labs kept Red Ladens in "hunt mode" and illuminated so they could be seen, giving agents time to prepare to be temporarily paralyzed. But Red Ladens could remain invisible, cloaked in stomonite and not illuminated. They could hunt or strike in invisible mode.

The Red Ladens hovered over and then passed through everyone. They retreated after five seconds.

"Good Lord, how many fail safes are there for this lab?" Bell asked, with a hint of "Enough is enough."

Doctor Parker raised an eyebrow. "You will learn the InCit lab isn't like any other Bureau space you have ever accessed."

Over the years, it seemed like every new case Bell was read into was like no other case. Yet, they all had similar beginnings and endings - someone did something incredibly stupid or evil, forcing the FBI to end or capture them and contain whatever they released onto the world.

Dr. Parker finally took a break to acknowledge Eric's return. "Your thumbs-up must mean good news. Would you like to fill us in?"

"Security is tending to everyone. No one was seriously harmed except to have been knocked unconscious by some form of gas that was fed into the conference rooms. The director was taken to the hospital for further evaluation to be sure he's fit to make decisions."

"Good," Dr. Parker said. "Now, Elliott, can you tell us why the director was reading you in on InCit?"

"I don't know the whole story. But we were being tasked with finding a rogue IA agent - IA33. I'm flying blind. I have no idea where IA33 might be, although he has a home in Montana and was last seen near there. I have a good idea who IA33 is, but it's just a guess. It might be my friend David -"

Dr. Parker wasn't interested. Her mind was somewhere else as she interrupted Bell.

"Check your blackhawk, SA Bell. The missing IA name is in there. The director sent a text out to all the IAs involved. He's the one who will verify if IA33 is your friend.

"I'm still trying to wrap my head around how much money the stomonite would be worth. I haven't seen a method yet where we've been able to re-code the stomonite to another agent's DNA. If we could, that process would have to be done in this lab, using our technology. So how could IA33's stomonite be worth anything to anyone?" Dr. Parker asked out loud to no one in particular.

Bell certainly didn't know the answer or what she was talking about. But in just his short period being around Dr. Parker, he concluded she would get to the bottom of it.

"You're the expert, so I suspect you'll figure it out," he said.

Dr. Parker gave Bell a look, suggesting she agreed. "I've worked on this project far too long to let it go sideways now.

"We're not going to get anywhere standing around lamenting the issue, so let's head into the lab and run some scenarios. And I guess it is time for you to get your stomonite assigned to your DNA, SA Bell, or I guess I should say IA Bell now." Dr. Parker smiled.

"So, how do I get my DNA stoned?" Bell said, looking around and laughing like a teenager. "Get it? Stomonite? Stoned?" Bell asked, grinning ear to ear as he looked around at everyone. Dr. Parker was not amused. Dr. Gaeber chuckled. Eric just looked at Dr. Parker for approval.

"Dr. Gaeber will get you set up," Dr. Parker said after rolling her eyes. "This process will take about an hour or so. We have to start with the sample of your blood we have on file." Dr. Parker grinned, but Bell had no idea what she was talking about.

"My blood sample? When was that again?" Bell asked.

"Hold on a second. Let me take a look at when that was exactly," Dr. Parker said as she began to type into a computer on the table. After a few keystrokes, she stepped back and reported what came up.

"The day you were given your shots before you left for the Philippines. If you remember, we took a blood sample from you in the event you went missing while on your overseas assignment."

"Oh, yeah, right. I forgot the Bureau saves our blood samples even after we return, so we don't have to provide another one for future assignments."

Dr. Parker said, "We don't just keep the sample. We regenerate your blood sample, so we have enough on hand to give you a transfusion of your blood if we have to ship it somewhere else in the world."

Bell wanted to say something about that little piece of info about his blood being regenerated. But he didn't understand how or why they did that, so he wasn't going to crowd his brain with something that seemed like it could be a benefit to him.

"I didn't ask Eric to look into whether or not ERF is on lockdown. If we are locked down, you won't be able to get out, SA Bell. We need to get you over to your drone and on your way. Let me go check on the lockdown." Dr. Parker left them and walked towards her office.

"Well, this was fun," Bell said with a huge smile. They all laughed.

The group began to have small talk about sports, the weather, and how cold it was going to be at Quantico in the next few months. While they talked, Dr. Gaeber looked past Bell towards Dr. Parker's office. They all noticed his stare and turned to look. Dr. Parker was on the phone and holding up a thumbs-up sign. They all clapped softly in appreciation as Dr. Parker emerged.

"Okay, good to go. ERF is up and running. I'm going home to get some sleep. I'll be back early in the morning." She looked at her watch. "Even though it's already early in the morning."

She shook her head as she walked away.

Chapter 9

Time to Fly

September 8, 2012
2:37 a.m.
Firearms Training Unit (FTU)
The Academy

It was warm for a September morning in Quantico. Maybe seventy-five degrees. The sky was clear, with a few clouds and billions of stars.

Bell and Dr. Gaeber walked out the side door of ERF and towards Building 5, Bay 5 of FTU, the Firearms Training Unit. In the distance, Bell could hear the Hostage Rescue Team (HRT) practicing near their compound on the Academy grounds. Bell could also see several ambulances' lights moving toward the Academy's entrance.

As they walked. Bell said, "Hey, doc. Can I ask you a question about the stomonite?"

"Absolutely. What do you want to know?"

"Why is all the stomonite in rock form? Can't you pulverize it and turn it into a liquid or dust? Or something more malleable."

"Not a bad question. The simple answer is that we only found it useful in rock form. But remember when you asked earlier if anything could destroy the stomonite?" Dr. Gaeber asked. Bell nodded.

"To date, the only successful process was sonar. We bumped up the velocity of a sonar wave to almost ten times the normal sonar wave frequency and threw it at pieces of stomonite weighing almost twelve tons. It didn't destroy it, but the stomonite did break apart into multiple pieces. We turned the sonar frequency down and kept trying it on different sizes of stomonite until we broke off pieces in five-ounce sizes, similar to the size, shape, and dimension of the rock the little girl found at Stone Mountain. Anything smaller in size wasn't possible. The stomonite disintegrated and became useless."

"So, if someone learned that sonar could destroy the stomonite, all they would have to do is emit a high enough sonar frequency to destroy any IA's stomonite, leaving them vulnerable?" Bell asked again.

"Indeed," Dr. Gaeber said. "To counter this, the InCit folks worked on developing a way to negate the effect of sonar's waves bouncing off the stomonite, especially at those higher levels that destroy the stomonite.

"Metallurgists in the Underwater Tech Lab or UTL on ERF's second floor had already been working with the military on a technology that would make submarines invisible to sonar. The technology involved covering the submarine with sound-absorbing, perforated rubber tiles. When the sonar wave hits the tile, it is absorbed by a spongy material within the tiles. There is no return signal. The sonar wave is absorbed, dissipated, and delivered as a small puff of air. The UTL created and named the material Sonar Protection, or SoPro for short.

"There is no patent. The technology is only known here at ERF. We distributed the SoPro to the military but didn't reveal the results of the adaptive traits. In other words, we gave them the answer to how they could make submarines invisible to sonar, but of course, they don't know what we are using the technology for - protecting the stomonite.

"You're going to watch me insert your DNA into a little silver tube made of a magnesium alloy 'discovered' in a Chinese lab by a Chinese double agent working for the FBI. Think of this little silver tube as if it were a small submarine. The SoPro lines the outside of the silver tube and performs the same function as it does on the outside of the submarine. The stomonite is shielded."

"Wow, nice," Bell said, nodding his head.

"So, the magnesium tubes and SoPro don't affect the stomonite's function as a protector or weapon?" Bell asked.

"None at all."

Bell and Dr. Gaeber passed the indoor firearms ranges. Located at the far end was the Special Operations and Rescue Training Facility (SORT). All new agents and subsequent agents training for overseas assignments trained there in firearms and agility concepts. They were put through the wringer, is how Bell thought of it.

Bell and Dr. Gaeber walked down the corridor between the two SORT obstacle courses.

"You ever been to the end of the course, SA Bell? And I mean the *END* of the course?" Dr. Gaeber asked with raised eyebrows.

"I'm going to have to say I haven't made it *that* far, Dr. Gaeber," Bell answered with his head slightly turned downward.

As they came to the end of the corridor, they stood in front of a pair of steel doors with louvers on the bottom. A sign was attached to the doors, which read "Mechanical Room." The doors were secured with an X-10 electron-mechanical lock. This type of lock was used on high-level safes and doors where more than Top-Secret material was kept. Bell had never noticed these doors before. He guessed it was because when he was training in SORT, he had all he could handle just trying to pass the damn course.

"Right this way, SA Bell," Dr. Gaeber said with a smile.

Dr. Gaeber walked to the door and turned the dial on the lock. After several back-and-forth movements to obtain seven numbers, Dr. Gaeber grabbed the large handle next to the lock and pushed it downward. He pulled the door open, and a slight "whoosh" of air escaping could be heard and felt. Dr. Gaeber entered, and Bell followed him.

They began to walk down a small corridor leading to another door and an X-10 lock. Dr. Gaber unlocked the door, and the Red Ladens floated in and did their thing. Once they finished, Dr. Gaeber and Bell continued to a door leading to a second room. They entered the room.

They were now in another well-lit lab. Two stainless steel tables and a few chairs occupied the lab. On the far wall were two computers and some accessory equipment attached to them. A half dozen shelving units on wheels were stacked neatly with Pelican cases, molded plastic cases that seal with an airtight and watertight gasket. Directly in the middle of the room were two reclining chairs.

"Except for the stainless-steel tables, doc, this could be my living room." Bell laughed as he spoke.

Dr. Gaeber countered, "You mean except for the drones and the rarest material on Earth."

"Okay, there is that," Bell said matter-of-factly.

They both smiled. Dr. Gaeber started walking towards a computer station at the far wall.

"Have a seat. I'll be right back. I've got to find your blood sample, and then we can begin."

Dr. Gaeber typed in a few commands into the computer. He studied the screen for a few seconds and then headed towards a second circular-lock doorway just to the right of where Bell had found a seat. Dr. Gaeber entered the airlock and exited with a whoosh through the doorway.

Bell sat comfortably in one of the blue recliners when Dr. Gaeber returned several minutes later. He had his feet up and his shoes off.

"Okay, roll up one of your sleeves. I would suggest whichever arm you don't shoot with," Dr. Gaeber said as he began to rifle through drawers and cabinets, retrieving needles, gauze, and other lab instruments. He also grabbed a small silver tube containing a sample of stomonite from a safe secured by an X-10 electron-mechanical lock.

Bell rolled up his left sleeve. Dr. Gaeber grabbed a chair and rolled over to Bell.

"Here we go," Dr. Gaeber said with confidence.

The whole process took about thirty minutes. Dr. Gaeber took a sample of Bell's blood and compared it to the sample they had on file to be sure Bell was who he said he was. Then Bell's blood - his DNA - was injected into the silver tube. Ten seconds after that introduction, they watched as the clear light on the top of the silver tube went from no light to green light. The process was complete. The stomonite sample had successfully bonded with Bell's DNA.

"The stomonite thinks you're a good guy, I guess." Dr. Gaeber laughed.

"Okay, one step down, one to go. To quote Al Pacino: 'Let me introduce you to my little friend!'" Dr. Gaeber laughed like a fifth grader. Bell just chuckled. It certainly didn't take much to get Dr. Gaeber going.

Dr. Gaeber placed Bell's silver tube on the table and walked over to the shelves of Pelican cases containing the drones. Every case had a cable lock on it with a blinking sensor. Dr. Gaeber placed his fingerprint on one case and waited for the light to turn green. Once the cable was unlocked, Dr. Gaeber removed it and secured it on the shelf, locking it back into itself. He took the Pelican case, walked over to one of the stainless-steel tables, and placed the case on top.

Inside the case was Bell's Drone. The drone was approximately 2 feet long by 2 feet wide. It had a smiley face on the front, and the silhouette of an M4 rifle etched on each side. Pretty cool design, Bell thought.

"Come over here so I can give you a tutorial on your drone," Dr. Gaeber said as he waved Bell over with his hand. "Grab a chair, too."

The drone had four legs. Bell watched as Dr. Gaeber executed a pattern of pushing the legs in until the drone lay flat on the table. The drone instantly turned on when the last leg closed.

For the next forty-five minutes, Dr. Gaeber explained the capabilities of the drone. He also added Bell's silver tube of stomonite into the slot reserved specifically to carry the tube. Bell was shown how to turn the drone on and off, the reload mechanism for the .223 magazines, and what not to do. More importantly, Bell was given a set of twenty or so commands he could use to control his drone.

After the tutorial, Bell rolled down his sleeve and stared at his new toy. He took a deep breath as he contemplated what he was about to begin. He lightly patted the drone like it was a dog. And it was similar to a dog. But with a bigger bite.

"You're good to go, SA Bell, or, should I say IA83?" Dr. Gaeber said as he leaned back in his chair. They both smiled.

It was time to fly.

Chapter 10
Friendships are Born

1998
Miami, FL

Tracey's neighbors were all pretty down-to-earth. The neighborhood, Osprey Landing, was located just seven miles from the FBI Miami field office and had only 125 homes. Tracey and his wife Trina wanted a small subdivision. They didn't want to run into a never-ending line of residents at the pool or otherwise.

They purchased a home in the middle of a cul-de-sac, and Tracey would often wave and say hello to his neighbors. But the Traceys never had them over for parties to catch up on the news or for any other social event. They all just kept their distances. There was one neighborhood family, however, who would become their closest friends.

Athan and Stella Kratos lived directly next door. Athan's family had been in the U.S. for two generations, emigrating from the island of Mykonos, Greece, in the early 1920s. They came to the U.S., as many did in those years, to live the American Dream. They lived through the Great Depression and survived because of Athan's grandfather, Phillip Kratos.

Phillip came to America as a recently graduated high school student. He attended the University of Pennsylvania as an engineering student of geological studies and became fascinated with the oil industry. Entrepreneurs like Rockefeller, Hunt, and Getty were the names that stirred his imagination.

Athan's grandfather worked for a small oil company outside of school. He wanted to learn how to make the drill bits that were used to drill for oil. A professor in one of his first classes demonstrated how drill bits broke, and they couldn't drill down far enough to reach some of the oil. He wanted to create a better drill bit. While working for the small oil company, Phillip Kratos designed a drill bit that uniquely staggered diamonds, allowing the drill to carve out more stone. At least, that was his theory. He needed to get the drill bit idea patented. So, Athan's grandfather took all his earnings from the job and hired an attorney. At age twenty-one, Phillip Kratos patented a drill bit that may or may not work.

As he researched oil companies and tried to decide whom he could trust not to steal his patent, Phillip was drawn to the story of J. Paul Getty and how, in 1916, two years after he graduated from college, Getty became a millionaire. So Phillip introduced himself to Getty in a short letter stating: "Mr. Getty, you and I will find all the oil on Earth. I have a device that will make you rich." He provided his address and waited for a response.

The rest was history. Getty sent a car a couple of weeks later, and Philipp was whisked away to Texas to meet the young millionaire. After a month of arranging legal documents, the drill bit Philipp had designed would remain his, and Getty would use it. Philipp and J. Paul Getty became the closest of friends and business partners.

Over the next decade, Philipp's drill bits performed as effortlessly as Philipp had theorized. The Getty Oil Company used these drill bits to reach new depths of oil ore exploration. And wealth. For Philipp's part, the drill bit design, he was given a salary and stock options in the Getty Oil Company.

Ten years after signing his contract with J. Paul Getty, Philipp sold his shares in the Getty Oil Company and formed his own company, Kratos Exploratory, Inc., headquartered on the Greek Island of Crete, where most of Philipp's extended family still lived.

The drill bit his grandfather designed and created is what set the Kratos name apart from other drilling companies. It was technologically more advanced and could drill some 45% further down than the other oil company drill bits. Kratos

Exploratory evolved into Kratos Oil & Shale Company and became a multi-billion-dollar conglomerate.

As a direct result of his grandfather's ingenuity and intellect, Athos and his family were wealthy.

✦✦✦

May 2010
The Tracey residence
Miami, FL

Over time, Tracey and Athan organized many family cookouts in their backyards. They installed a gate in the fence that separated them so they could each access the other's backyard. Often, they would text each other that one or the other was having a beer on their back deck and to come over for one.

When their two oldest girls decided to throw a dual party for their 16th birthday, the dads planned a backyard barbecue to celebrate. Gone were the days of ordering a pony to ride or the traditional bouncing inflatable. Now the party activities were cornhole games and lawn darts, and the gifts were made of paper with numbers and zeros.

This birthday party Tracey and Athan threw for their oldest daughters would be the most expensive they had ever organized. Both girls were about to enter their junior year of high school. Upperclassmen now. They thought they were the coolest thing since walking out the door with their driver's permit. Tracey didn't have an opinion either way. They were teenage girls. Most of the time, they weren't human-like. At least not when you compared them to boys, anyway.

Tracey contracted with the popular band from his daughter's high school - *The Will Bees* - to play for three hours. The lead singer told Tracey he came up with the band's name. He was certain that one day they "will be" successful. After hearing them, Tracey thought they had a chance. They were good. And the $300 for the three-hour gig might be the cheapest anyone would ever pay to get them to play.

While Tracey and Athan watched the high school kids listen to the band and generally have a good time, Tracey flipped burgers and chicken.

"So, how's the fracking business?" Tracey teased Athan, aware that Athan's business dealt mostly with oil and less with gas.

"Ha, we're blowing up the Earth and taking names as we go," Athan said as he tipped his beer to his lips. "Just like you guys, I'm sure." He looked off into the distance.

"We're doing okay, though," Athan said, resigned. Tracey picked up on it.

"Just okay?" Tracey asked as he glanced at Athan and continued to flip a couple of hamburgers.

"Yeah, we have a few issues here and there, and the bottom line this year is down about 40% from last year. We have too many oil fields that aren't producing as they have for the past eighteen to twenty years. That drop in oil production has led us - all kidding aside about fracking - to invest more energy in finding and developing gas reserves."

"Dang, a 40% drop can be tough on the bottom line, yes?" Tracey asked.

"Like you can't imagine," Athan said as he finished a beer. He leaned over and opened the cooler, grabbing another. "You need one?"

"Yes, indeed," Tracey said as he chugged the last inch of his beer and tossed it in the trash.

"We're talking about some layoffs and some oil well closings. That could result in a reduction of 15% of our workforce. The board meets weekly to discuss new revenue streams, and the cuts are constantly being discussed. I'd have to do most of the laying off and closing of facilities myself. So, everyone left will hate me when their friends are let go."

"Wow, sorry, bud. Sounds like you have your hands full. What about exploration into fracking or other possible oil reserves?" Tracey asked.

"We have committed another sixteen million dollars to R&D to see if we can gently ease into the fracking industry, but historically, we've only kept 4% of our yearly earnings in gas. We never thought we'd be at this point, considering fracking the number one option to stay afloat, even solvent. When we talk about oil reserves, we own the rights to the Deep Blue Oil Fields in Alaska, and there are potentially huge oil reserves in the Russian Urals we jointly own with our Russian partner ComCore. Plus, we have a lease agreement that expires in two years to drill for oil in the Fools Gold Oil Fields under the Norwegian polar ice cap. But that won't melt any time soon. Thus, its name."

"So, there are options, but it looks like you have a roadblock everywhere you turn?" Tracey commented as he put down the spatula and moved to his smoker to check on the pork.

"Yes, we do. Last month, we were forced by the board to meet every week. My team reviews options every morning. We'll try anything."

"I wish I could help you somehow, buddy. The only thing I know about oil is it's black, right?!" Tracey said, trying to get his friend to laugh.

Athan smiled and chuckled halfheartedly. "You never know. Maybe you can. Don't you have access to some high-tech FBI gadgetry that could help us? Why don't you check and see what you have lying on your desk," Athan said with a wry smile and wrinkling of his eyebrows.

Tracey smiled and checked the temperature of the pork butt. He then closed the smoker and moved back to the grill. As Tracey continued moving the food around the grill, he thought about Athan's last comment and the toys the Bureau had at their disposal. Boy, the Bureau could certainly influence the capital markets. He wondered, for a second, how he could help Kratos Oil & Shale Company as he stared off into the sky.

Tracey snapped out of it, laid the spatula down, and grabbed his beer. He smiled as he shuffled over and sat with his friend to listen to The Will Bees.

✦✦✦

July 2002
ERT Training
Crime Scene Photography Class
The Academy

In early 2000, after Bell had two years in the Bureau and was officially off probation, he signed up for the FBI's crime scene unit, the Evidence Response Team. ERT was made up of hand-picked agents and support personnel. Membership was based on reputation - agents had to be hard workers who paid attention to detail.

Once selected for the team, agents would be sent away for weeks to train on general crime scene processing - lifting latent fingerprints off every surface from wood to skin, from toes to fingertips, vacuuming for trace evidence in a car, and securing drug samples. They would work in every environment. Agents would hone search techniques in the heat of the Arizona desert or at one of the FBI's secret facilities, such as the iced-over underwater facility in Alaska.

Bell decided long before he joined the Bureau that he enjoyed taking photos. Once a member of ERT, he was selected to be the team member responsible for taking crime scene photos. To hone that craft, the Bureau sent Bell to various training courses. Bell had now photographed more than eighty crime scenes throughout the world.

After two years on ERT and four years in the Bureau, one of the advanced photography classes Bell was selected for was a training course called an "In-Service," held at the Academy in the heat of July. Bell would learn much about taking quality photographs. He also met several agents and support personnel at that In-Service whom he would come to call some of his best friends in or out of the Bureau, including his closest Bureau friend, Special Agent David Tracey.

Bell first met Tracey at the Academy's watering hole, the Board Room. At first, he thought Tracey was obnoxious, yelling and whooping and hollering at all the women. On one trip walking back from the bar, Tracey backed into Bell while carrying three beers, spilling them all over Bell. Tracey immediately apologized to Bell and offered him a beer.

The two reveled in the Board Room for a few hours that first night. Bell didn't know what to make of Tracey by the time he left for the evening, but he had changed his mind about Tracey being obnoxious. Bell was fairly confident Tracey was eccentric but harmless, to others at least. And Tracey sure could drink his fill of beer.

The next day, Tracey and Bell were assigned to the same class, Basic Latent Fingerprinting. They were paired together for over a week and completed the course with the highest grade. They would remain close friends as their Bureau careers continued.

Chapter 11
Bring on the Budderballs

Eyes Only projects created by the U.S. Government existed long before Hoover began to use them in the Bureau. The U.S. Government realized research on top-secret projects needed to be seen and known by only a select few. The Venona Project and Manhattan Project, programs created to decrypt messages sent by the former Soviet Union and the atomic bomb, respectively, conducted vigorous research with the results used in the U.S.' favor during World War II. They were all "Eyes Only," limited to a handful of knowledgeable individuals and a few head honchos.

Hoover's Eyes Only agents, selected for their ability to improvise and complete the hardest tasks without fail, only numbered around 400, give or take a few, at any time. If one of these Eyes Only agents had cause to be removed from a program - they died, were fired, demoted, or retired from service - another Eyes Only agent, already identified on a short list known by very few at the top of the FBI's management team, would be chosen and added to the database.

The FBI worked earnestly on several Eyes Only projects in the 1940s underneath the warehouse building at Quantico, what is now ERF. The success of the Red Ladens project was an example of one of those Eyes Only projects.

The project was created by FBI scientist Dr. Joshua Budder, one of the first scientists to work on the stomonite project with Dr. Parker. In the early 1970s, Dr. Budder led a covert team of scientists at ERF, under Hoover's direction, who were able to complete automated chain-termination DNA sequencing. It was difficult and time-consuming. But whatever Hoover wanted, he managed to get. And what Hoover ultimately wanted was for Dr. Budder to work on creating a

DNA-driven security system that didn't rely on humans and their ability to screw things up.

Hoover ultimately set a policy that no Eyes Only agent would be identified using their name. Instead, their DNA sample would be entered into the Eyes Only database and only by a scientist within the Eyes Only project that the specific agent was working on. Every director following Hoover has adhered to the same protocol.

This DNA-driven security system would only need to rely on humans for one reason - to add a person's DNA sequence to the database. The complete security system, consisting of eye and hand scans and other identity verification protocols, vigilantly assured every employee was where they were supposed to be within the most top-secret Bureau facilities.

Dr. Budder experimented with different amounts of stomonite dust. He mixed it with various elements to see how the stomonite would react. His goal was to create an air-based security system of drone-like balls. When combined with the right combination of hydrogen gas and helium and surrounded by the stomonite mixture, the balls could travel as fast as Dr. Budder required. An added feature of the balls was they contained anesthesia that would render a person unconscious if their DNA was not in the system and recognized by the balls. And the stomonite would serve as a protector for the balls. Dr. Budder named his creation "Budderballs."

Dr. Budder gave Hoover a show-and-tell one day at ERF and demonstrated how the Budderballs worked. Dr. Budder had a techie stand on a section of padded flooring as he released the Budderballs from the overhead air ducts. They were approximately three-quarters of an inch in diameter. And invisible. Almost immediately after Dr. Budder released the Budderballs, the techie crashed onto the floor in an unconscious heap. Hoover clapped in appreciation. He was pleased – the techie, maybe not so much.

Hoover ultimately tasked Dr. Budder with making the Budderballs visible as well. He wanted the Budderballs to be seen by employees at ERF so the employees knew they were always around. In other words, don't try to enter an area if you weren't read into that area. Just keep moving. That gave agents ample time to lie down instead of falling.

Dr. Budder ultimately worked on and created a mechanism so the Budderballs would be seen. He made them red, a badass way of saying, "Red, you're dead" -ish.

The FBI decided to use the Budderballs in 2011 to hunt down Osama Bin Laden. The thought was the Bureau had an invisible bloodhound they could unleash on the world without anyone knowing. At least the bad guys would never realize it.

The Budderballs, cloaked in stomonite, caught a ride on a military cargo plane and were unceremoniously dropped out the back end at 20,000 feet. Deployed in Pakistan, Sri Lanka, and along the Tibetan border, they were on their own with a programmed directive to search for only one particular strand of DNA. The Budderballs wandered through some four million square miles of the Middle East, hoping to find Bin Laden's DNA profile.

As they traveled through the atmosphere, the Budderballs located a DNA match to Bin Laden in a small doctor's office in Skardu, Pakistan. Years earlier, the Bureau learned Bin Laden coordinated terrorist attacks against Western culture from the basement of this doctor's office at a time when Bin Laden was trying the nerves of every Western leader. However, Bin Laden had not been seen there in over six years, and it made sense he wasn't hiding in plain sight.

This doctor employed some half dozen personnel, including two doctors who were in charge. These two doctors were the brother and sister of Bin Laden. A third doctor was from a small country in South Africa, whose identity was unknown as the name and passport he used while living in Pakistan were fraudulent. He worked for Doctors Without Politics. Unfortunately, the events unfolded so quickly at the doctor's office that his true identity was never known.

The doctors used liquid nitrogen and frozen three liters of Bin Laden's blood in case the terrorist needed an emergency medical procedure. Bin Laden had the rarest of all blood types, AB-negative. With only 1% of the population possibly able to provide a transfusion for Bin Laden should he ever need it, the doctors and his family decided this was the safest and most secret way to be able to save Bin Laden's life should the need arise.

Storing Bin Laden's blood sealed the fate of the doctor and his personnel when the Budderballs found the blood sample and alerted the FBI. In turn, the intelligence was passed to the U.S. military. A day after locating the blood sample, all major news outlets reported an explosion in Skardu, Pakistan. The explosion was identified as a drone strike conducted by the U.S. after intelligence sources - i.e., the Budderballs - reported terrorist collaborators and, possibly, Osama Bin Laden was in that doctor's office. The drone strike was not a stomonite-laden strike, of course. Simply the average Predator drone that detonated upon impact. The South African doctor, his family, the entire medical staff, and twenty-seven people outside were all killed.

The South African doctor who was killed, Dr. Salan Repuso, never heard the explosion or suffered a painful death when the drone hit the building. His last moments alive were spent watching a TV report describing how the U.S. was getting closer to locating the world's most wanted terrorist.

Unfortunately, they missed Bin Laden. But the hunt was on. They were closing in.

Several days later, when the Budderballs finally tracked Bin Laden down to a safe house in Abbottabad, Pakistan, the Navy SEALS did the rest. At the end of that fateful day, as the world's media and the powers-that-be spoke gallantly of a "courier" who led the SEALS to Bin Laden, little did anyone know the courier was an invisible ball created by the Bureau.

Based on the success of the Budderballs from the raid on Bin Laden's compound, they were renamed Bin Ladens and, subsequently, Red Ladens.

Dr. Budder was not very pleased.

He did get promoted to Unit Chief, however.

Chapter 12

Closer to a Plan

January 18, 2012
8:30 p.m.
The Kratos residence
Miami, FL

Tracey and Trina headed to the Kratos' place for a Saturday evening game of cards and cribbage. Tracey brought a new bottle of Bombay East gin, some tonic water, and limes. Trina contributed her usual bottle of white wine. She could easily be persuaded to open a second bottle provided by Stella later in the evening.

"Ding-dong, the neighbors are here," Tracey said as he rang the doorbell and let himself in.

"You guys aren't naked, are you?" He laughed out loud.

Athan came around the corner from the kitchen dressed in shorts and a T-shirt. "This is about as naked as you're ever going to see me," Athan said, chuckling.

"I guess you don't know about the camera I installed then!" Tracey shot back with his usual FBI humor.

"Ha. You wish."

Stella yelled out she was in the kitchen, and they all made their way through the foyer towards the great smells coming from within.

"Wow, whatever you're cooking smells great," Trina said.

"I'm making meatballs for the girls' volleyball match tomorrow. Were you making something or providing drinks?" Stella asked Trina.

With a sudden look of surprise, Trina said, "Oh crap! I forgot about that. Looks like I'm bringing drinks."

Tracey and Athan made their way to the bar, and Tracey added his bottle of gin to the large selection of alcohol Athan had assembled.

"I brought some kaffir limes, too," Tracey said. "They're so much more flavorful than the run-of-the-mill limes."

"Nice. That's my favorite lime. Gin and tonic then for both of us."

Athan expertly plopped two glasses down and filled them to the rim with ice - they had to be full of ice - and added some of the Bombay East gin and a sufficiently fat slice of lime before stirring them completely. Athan then added a couple of extra ice cubes and slid one glass to Tracey.

"Cheers," Athan said as he clinked Tracey's glass.

"Cheers, bud," Tracey added.

Athan took an unusually long swallow of his gin and tonic. Tracey looked over at him and tried to brush it off.

"You like the kaffir lime, I see," Tracey joked.

"It's been a long week. I've been under a lot of pressure. I know you understand what pressure is, too, so you know what I mean when I say I need to unwind," Athan said with a heavy sigh.

"The industry still down?" Tracey asked.

"Yeah, and we didn't get good news on our fifth most cost-productive oil well in the Gulf of Mexico. That well's oil flow generates less income than it costs us to operate. We're going to shut it down in the next few weeks.

"Then we had some young economist in a meeting last week tell us we should try to drill now on our leased property in the polar ice cap in Norway and not wait until 2040 or so when there should be a more favorable time to drill for oil there. He said the time is now. We all looked at him like he had three heads."

"Is what he suggested not possible?" Tracey asked as he sipped on his gin and tonic.

"It's not that it's impossible. In theory, if we located a favorable point to start drilling, we believe we could reach what could amount to billions of gallons of oil. The Norwegian polar ice cap is believed to contain over 13% of the world's untapped oil reserves. The value of even twenty billion barrels of oil would sustain our company for the next two generations, conceivably.

"Our oil production problem is two-fold. Where we have leases - in the middle of the ocean, where no country has a claim, and in Norway - there are still regulations on drilling. We can't just start drilling through the ice as it could cause dire consequences for marine life, or so we are constantly told by marine biologists and every environmental group in the world. So far, no government or world policy group has allowed us to start drilling. Greenpeace alone would send ships and cause problems for us. That drilling could take years.

"The second problem is the ice is still just too thick. The workaround to both scenarios is if a mother-nature-made opportunity occurs, such as a crack in the ice allowing for safe drilling, we could get our drills going. Or if technology is developed that allows for some non-evasive, non-eco-killing drilling. We're just not sure how that looks right now. Hell, if I were invisible, I would quietly go and drop a little C-4 down a hole and blast enough ice out of the way to suggest Mother Nature caused the hole. Then we could drill. Doesn't the Bureau have something we could use?!"

"Ha!" Tracey laughed out loud as he took another sip from his drink.

Athan had no idea how right he was.

As Tracey's smile relaxed, his brain floated an idea of how easy it would be to send in his InCit drone with a little C-4 and carve out a small hole in the ice for his friend. Just as quickly as he thought it, Tracey dismissed the idea.

"Maybe that little geek of yours you've mentioned with all the ideas will come up with something else that will help, bud," Tracey said to Athan.

"He certainly better come up with a new idea soon," Athan said as he began to shake his head. "We've only have so much financial wiggle room left."

Trina yelled out from the kitchen area that they had some samples of the meatballs if Tracey and Athan wanted to try them. They both headed towards the kitchen. Tracey thought about the financial wiggle room comment.

The thought of the InCit drone crept back into Tracey's brain.

Chapter 13

Heading to Trellis

September 8, 2012
3:20 a.m.
Outside ERF

Now that Bell had his drone and was as much of an InCit agent as he could be, he sat in his Tahoe under the bright perimeter lights of ERF, trying to digest everything he had seen and been told. The ambulances were gone, and it was again quiet in front of ERF. What next? He sat still. The only movement interrupting Bells' thought process was the occasional appearance of the green beacon shining from the top of the ERF roof-top antenna. Green was good. All was secure.

The incident with the lights going out and everyone left unconscious still bothered Bell. Since the building was green, all was back to normal. But why were they knocked out, and why was Bell spared? And where did Tracey go? His head was starting to hurt.

Bell grabbed a couple of ibuprofen pills from his armrest, swallowed them, and settled into his seat. He pushed his head back onto the headrest, unzipped his pullover, and contemplated his situation. As his pullover made closer contact with the back of his car seat, he heard a soft rustle, like he'd sat on something. He leaned forward and turned around but saw nothing on his car seat. Bell switched on the interior lights. He grabbed the back of his pullover and tried to turn it to his front to see if something was stuck on it. That proved difficult in the small space, and he couldn't see the pullover close enough using the dim interior lights.

Bell opened the door and stepped out of the Tahoe. He took off his pullover.

"What the ....!!"

A small piece of transparent tape was stuck to his pullover. He pulled it off. Upon closer inspection, he ran his thumb over an embedded transmitter glued to the tape. How the heck did that get stuck on him?

Looking at the tape and transmitter, Bell could tell the transmitter was Bureau-made. Unlike transmitters the Bureau designed to be used inside electronic devices, like a hand-held radio, this transmitter was crafted to be hidden in objects you wouldn't think contained a transmitter. It was small, only one-half inch by half inch, with a gel-like substance covering it. Then it struck Bell - this transmitter was meant to be inserted inside the body. It was a tracking device or delivery system. Bell recalled a time when he had received a similar implant before departing for an overseas mission several years ago. The tracker he was implanted with was a fail-safe in case he was kidnapped or went missing so he could be traced. But again - why was one stuck to his pullover?

As Bell began to put his pullover back on, another sobering thought shot through his head. Bell remembered back to when he saw Tracey earlier that evening. Tracey was adamant about giving Bell a bear hug. Could Tracey have planted the transmitter on Bell? And if he did, why? Whatever the reason, Bell couldn't dwell on it. He tossed it on the ground and stepped on it. He'd tell the director about it later.

Bell quickly got back in the truck. He had more important things to do, like texting his wife and alerting her he was about to be unreachable for some time. It was a text similar to those he had sent many times before.

Bell reached under his seat and yanked on what looked like a piece of the driver's seat. A velcro-ripping sound followed. Bell's hand reappeared with a small black device that looked like a smartphone, only half the size. Named a "blackhawk," the device would normally operate off any radio wave and transmit short and long bursts of radio waves in the event of an electromagnetic pulse. The blackhawk transmitted from any number of satellites orbiting the Earth. It was to be used simply for text messages when there was a breakdown in FBI operations or a major electronic failure that knocked out cell signals. Bell figured the events of the last few hours counted as a breakdown in FBI operations. Stability was a major problem at this point.

Bell turned on the blackhawk. He used his thumbprint on the initial screen of the blackhawk and then a quick infrared scan of his right eye. After the blackhawk powered up, a short beep told him he had messages. Bell would get to the messages later. He pulled up his contact list, found the small icon bearing his wife's picture, and started to text.

"Made it to work - weird hours babe - got to take a road trip - may have to stay overnight for two days or so - call you when I can."

That was really all Evelynn had to see. She often got texts like that and managed to get through those texts by believing Bell would take care of himself.

After texting his wife, Bell thought about calling his supervisor, but he realized his SAC or someone in the director's office would let his supervisor know he was on a case.

And that would be all his supervisor would be told.

Bell clicked his way over to the messages. He saw the "Rogue" group. There were two messages. The first message was sent a few minutes after Bell had arrived at ERF. It was from the director. The text had no subject line.

Bell clicked on the message. It was short and to the point.

"IAs - work fast and diligent - you can't give IA33 the benefit of the doubt just yet, so be mindful of your surroundings - IA33's picture is attached - his name is David Tracey."

Bell almost dropped the blackhawk. He kept staring at the words and his friend's name as the director had typed it. It was surreal. He'd suspected Tracey, but having it confirmed brought a shock and dread he wasn't prepared for.

Bell quickly thought back to the bear hug from Tracey earlier. Did Tracey plant the transmitter because Bell was about to be read into the InCit program? Or did Tracey need someone in InCit to get information covertly?

Bell switched to denial mode almost immediately. He couldn't believe his friend would go rogue.

Bell was aware of Tracey's vacation home in Montana, and the director stated earlier that IA33 was last seen at his vacation home in Trellis, Montana. But Tracey was in ERF a few short hours ago. Bell wasn't hallucinating that fact. They talked, for crying out loud. If only Bell had been able to tell the director he saw Tracey at ERF before all hell broke loose.

Bell moved on to the second text. It was also from the director and sent before the meeting as well. This text had a subject line - "IA Bell - Your Orders." Bell opened the text. It read:

"Head to the InCit lab - they'll give you an overview on InCit - then head to Trellis, Montana - HRT will give you a lift - Tracey may still be hiding there." The Director ended with a final directive.

"Use your navigator and get with IA24 - he will head to Tracey's house with you - rein Tracey in - good luck."

Bell had already accomplished the meet and greet with the InCit folks. That part of the director's instructions was completed. But Bell wanted to reply *right away*. He wanted answers. What was Director Stillman's physical status? Was he or anyone else hurt? And the obvious question - *where* was the Director?

And Bell didn't have a navigator.

Bell began his text. "Understood sir but I ran into IA Tracey here at EFR several hours ago! - also located a transmitter stuck to my coat - please advise." Bell hit send.

Bell took it all in. He didn't have any more thoughts. Everything was too upside down at the moment. Bell looked over at his drone in the Pelican case. What the hell was he now involved in? Cool? Sure. Way past dangerous? Absolutely.

Bell squirmed in his seat like a kid at the dentist's office. It was painful. He waited for what he thought would be an immediate reply from the director. Nothing. And there was no one else he could tell. His orders came from the director, and he answered only to the director.

After fifteen minutes of being the most patient IA he could ever hope to be, Bell said, "Screw it," and started the engine. He placed his blackhawk in his pocket. Then he reached under the seat and repositioned the Velcro covering for the blackhawk.

Tracey could be on his way to Montana by now. It was possible. And maybe the director had already known Tracey was somewhere near ERF but assumed he would head back to Trellis. Bell didn't know. All he knew was the ibuprofen hadn't kicked in yet.

The questions would have to wait. Bell had a ride to catch. He had to find his friend somehow.

Bell backed out of the parking spot at ERF and headed out the gate toward the HRT compound. He was overloaded with all the information he had to digest in the last several hours. It wasn't unusual to be thrown head-first into the unknown with his job. Bell learned many years ago that life in the Bureau, each day, changes quickly. He could count on that. And it made for a great job. Then there were days where he would shake his head - like today - and remember this is the way of the Bureau. He lived for it. But now he had to perform a task unlike any other - arrest a fellow FBI special agent.

As he passed the Jefferson Building, the main entrance to the Academy, an HRT helicopter conducting early morning operations whizzed by him. Bell watched the helicopter fly away with two HRT operators dangling a leg out the left side. They were heading towards HRT. Bell hooked a left and drove past the cafeteria, firearms unit, and outdoor track before turning right into the HRT compound. The gate was down, so he slowed and approached the intercom by the gate. After producing his creds at the screen, the anti-vehicle barriers lowered, and Bell was directed around to one of the buildings towards the back of HRT's compound.

Bell jumped out of his Tahoe and immediately heard the whirring of the rotors on one of HRT's UH-60 black helicopters. They would fly him quickly over to the Critical Incident Response Group, or CIRG, in Fredericksburg, Virginia, a short fifteen-minute ride. Once at CIRG, Bell had the ultimate ride lined up on the Bureau's Gulfstream V jet.

The Bureau's Gulfstream V didn't have the normal amenities of a full-sized galley. And instead of seating up to eighteen passengers, the FBI's Gulfstream only had seating for eight people. All these modifications allowed for a lighter plane, a maximum flight speed of 652 miles per hour, and a maximum range of 8,500 miles.

With the two-hour time difference, the smooth-flying Gulfstream would cover the 1,900 miles to Montana in under three hours.

Bell would be in Trellis around 5:00 a.m. MST.

Chapter 14
Diamond-Blackfan Anemia

The overwhelming majority of FBI agents work hard - some raise a family and possibly get by without certain things because they can't afford them. Most entry-level special agents in the FBI follow a certain routine - they get up five days a week, or sometimes every day if they're working a big case, and do their jobs. The beauty of the daily life of an FBI agent is there are no two days alike. The job was the ultimate varietal. It made it easy to go to work every day. Tracey felt this way.

David and Trina Tracey had two beautiful girls, April and Savannah. Like any parents, they would do anything for their girls. They stuck up for them when they were ridiculed. They counseled them to make good decisions. And they felt the pain their children did when they were hurting.

But it was even worse when a child couldn't fight for themselves. David understood that. At 13 years old, April was diagnosed with Diamond-Blackfan anemia or DBA, a rare blood disorder in which the bone marrow didn't make enough red blood cells to carry oxygen through the body. The diagnosis came out of the blue since DBA was a disease normally identified in infancy or the first several years of a child's life. Before the diagnosis, April didn't exhibit any uncomfortable symptoms, such as fatigue. She also wasn't born with any known physical defects associated with DBA, such as smaller ears, droopy eyelids, a smaller head, and others.

The DBA stayed in check for the most part, but as she entered high school, her body started rejecting all the medicine she was taking to be that "normal enough" kid. Her lungs couldn't get enough oxygen for her to breathe.

Then the Traceys learned April's lungs were deteriorating. Every day, her blood received and delivered less and less oxygen to her organs. The doctors told David and Trina their daughter would most likely need a full-time oxygen tank by the time she was in her early 20s. And worse still, by her late 20s, oxygen tanks wouldn't help her anymore as her lungs wouldn't function. It started to look less and less likely that April would live into her mid-30s.

When April was first diagnosed with DBA, both David and his wife were immediately checked to see if they carried the mutated DBA gene. The testing revealed neither David nor his wife passed the gene to April. His daughter was in the group of 50% of children who didn't inherit the condition from a biological parent. Researchers had no idea what triggered the genetic mutation. David blamed himself anyway.

The only known cure for DBA was an Allogeneic stem cell transplant. To complete the Allogeneic stem cell transplantation, abnormal cells were replaced with healthy stem cells. This method would boost red blood cell production. It was a last resort, attempted only after all other treatments hadn't worked. Most healthcare providers wouldn't cover all the costs of the transplant unless the patient had more than the basic coverage. But the Traceys couldn't care less about the costs. They signed April up for the procedure. And they prayed. And they prayed some more.

Finally, after more than a year of waiting and one day after April's sixteenth birthday, Tracey's healthcare provider approved the Allogeneic stem cell transplant. It was the belated birthday present of all belated birthday presents. They were ecstatic. April was apprehensive, but she knew it could save her life.

Three days after turning sixteen, April packed some clothes and her favorite nine pairs of shoes, a pair of slippers, two phone charges, her laptop, and a picture of her family and boarded a plane with her mother and father bound for Seattle Children's Hospital (SCH). The Traceys chose SCH after researching how successful the hospital was with curing this disease and its proximity to their house in Trellis.

Tracey told himself it had better work. He knew it could be April's last option.

Chapter 15
Family Matters

Evelynn Bell was used to not seeing her husband, sometimes for several days. When Bell started working for the FBI, she had difficulty sleeping when Bell was out on an arrest or search warrant. As the years passed, though, if she didn't get a call in the middle of the night saying he was on his way home, she learned to sleep more soundly. She was less worried that anything bad had happened or would happen. Of course, Bell figured this was because he had increased his life insurance to a couple of million dollars, but maybe not.

All joking aside, Bell knew Evelynn began to trust the squad Bell was on in Knoxville as an adrenaline-pumping, hyper-safety-first squad. Later, as a supervisor in Washington, D.C., Bell removed all doubt he would be involved in dangerous arrests, as his job consisted of meeting after meeting with other paper-pushers. Not even when he stepped down from his supervisory position at FBI HQ in 2011 to become a regular special agent working counter-terrorism in the FBI's Washington field office was he likely to be in harm's way.

Evelynn heard the short chime come from her phone. It was plugged into the wall and lying on her bedside table. She was in almost full REM sleep and had to think about whether she had heard anything. Sitting up in bed, she waited for a couple of seconds, and the familiar ringtone she had assigned to Bell's blackhawk number chimed again. She yawned and reached over for her phone.

She quickly read what her husband had written. She hit "Reply" and typed back, "No worries. Don't stay up too late. Be safe. Let me know how it's going in two more days if you can." There was nothing else she needed to say.

✦✦✦

September 8, 2012
6:10 a.m.
Dr. Parker's office

Dr. Parker sat at her desk, staring at her coffee. The steam from the cup lulled her into a trance to the point where she wasn't thinking about anything. She told herself when she poured the coffee, she would take a minute and think about nothing. Daydream. The steam was just so soothing to look at. And at 6:10 a.m., her head already hurt.

She wasn't a big fan of Advil, Tylenol, or any pain reliever. But right then, a little pain relief might help. Before she could figure out where some medication might be in the office, a "whooshing" sound let her know someone had entered the lab. She snapped to attention and looked out her office to see a female lab technician enter through the air-locked doors leading from the only other entrance into InCit from the underground parking garage. As this entrance fed directly into the section of InCit containing opened samples of DNA, everyone coming through that door had to be decontaminated upon entry. The technician headed down the decontamination tube or "DecTube," a ten-foot enclosed walkway leading from the entrance into a decontamination room.

Dr. Parker moved the computer mouse on her desk, and her screen immediately came out of sleep mode. Her wallpaper image of a kangaroo with a headset on its head, roller-skates on its feet, and stepping out of Apollo 11 onto the moon lit up her screen's background. She typed in her password, a task she completed more than a hundred times daily.

Her priority that morning, as it had been for the past several days, was to figure out what was happening with IA33's - SA David Tracey's - DNA. Dr. Parker had never spent a great amount of time in her days as the Unit Chief of the InCit Lab trying to figure out how to undo an IA DNA link to stomonite. Until recent events unfolded, procedurally removing an IA from the InCit program went smoothly. Every previous IA had their DNA sample withdrawn from the InCit database by the InCit team, and the stomonite assigned to the particular IA was weighed and recovered when they departed. It worked that way no matter what the circumstances were when they left - if they quit the Bureau, quit the program, were suspended, fired, retired, or died. Their sample of stomonite retired with them, never to be linked to another IA's DNA.

The protocol for retrieving the stomonite and removing the IA's DNA from the InCit database was clear and unchanged since Dr. Parker became the caretaker of the InCit program. At different locations, a combination of Dr. Parker, an assistant director, the director, the IA being removed from the program, and a random computer-chosen IA located within 15 miles of the IA being removed would each receive a text on their blackhawks. The text would contain a phone number and GPS coordinates for a location where the IA leaving the program could drop off his drone. After receiving the text, both IAs would call the computer-generated phone number and identify the GPS coordinates sent on their blackhawks. The computer would verify the IAs were calling in on their Bureau cell phones or a dedicated landline assigned to the Bureau. Once verified, a "kill code" would be sent, and the departing IA's stomonite and drone would be taken offline. The IAs would then meet, and the drone and stomonite would be returned.

While the process seemed lengthy, considering the steps it took to execute a kill code, it did work smoothly, Dr. Parker thought. The redundancy of having all the kill codes sent, the distance between the personnel involved, and the need to call on a Bureau phone were to ensure that no one could assemble - or take hostage - all the personnel needed to execute a kill code. If a subject thought they could take out a member of the assembled group, so a kill code could not be completed, they would have to know the exact location of each person and correctly guess who the computer's randomly selected IA would be. Not impossible, but highly improbable. With only 83 IAs, a subject could theoretically get to all the IAs.

Because IAs were located all over the world, however, it was unlikely - a near zero percent chance of happening.

Dr. Parker, with the director's authority, or the director on his own, could also bypass those protocols to shut down any drone immediately using a kill code of all kill codes, the "ultimate kill code." None of the IAs knew of the ultimate kill code. It was used only when the drone shutdown had to be "right now," immediately. Dr. Parker or Director Stillman could click a few buttons on their computers, and the drone was dead to the IA. The ultimate kill code gave Dr. Parker and the director total control to disable the drone if the Bureau ever needed to.

This ultimate kill code had only been used twice, and it was due to some extreme circumstances. And Tracey's disappearance was one of those circumstances. The director authorized Dr. Parker to execute the ultimate kill code for Tracey's drone several days ago, removing Tracey's DNA from the InCit database. Or so they thought.

Dr. Parker assumed Tracey still had the stomonite and deactivated drone in his possession. However, she could no longer track Tracey on the InCit world map to help her locate the items. He must have turned off his blackhawk and removed the batteries. She was frustrated.

Dr. Parker navigated through several folders and finally found Tracey's DNA sample. She clicked on Tracey's DNA profile and read through his DNA analysis from the past three years. Each year, IA's have a random sample of blood taken to make sure the InCit program has each IAs DNA sample in the computer. No one in the InCit program believed an IA, or any other InCit personnel, could alter his/her DNA. Dr. Parker figured she would check to rule out the absurd.

Each short tandem repeat of Tracey's DNA looked normal. She wanted to compare each year's sample to be sure they belonged to Tracey. So, she began by looking at Tracey's 2011 sample. It was identical to his original sample taken in 2010. When she compared Tracey's 2012 sample to the original, however, the sample was marked "not verified" by the computer. This meant no technician within the InCit lab verified the authenticity of the DNA sample.

Dr. Parker clicked on the lab notes section to read the history of the 2011 DNA sample. It appeared Tracey had the sample taken at the FBI's office in Coeur d'Alene, Idaho, approximately 125 miles from his mountain vacation home. That was in February 2011. That sample was verified by the InCit lab. The more recent sample was added in September 2012. It was from the current week. The notes stated, "entered but not verified."Ced. Dr. Parker was puzzled. Why hadn't it been verified? And why was a sample of Tracey's DNA entered into the system this week?

Dr. Parker opened up the FBI's DNA computer program. She selected Tracey's DNA profile from 2012 and entered it into the search engine. Two different names popped up on her screen in a couple of seconds.

"What the...," Dr. Parker said out loud to herself.

She continued to read. The first name was Tracey's. His entry on duty date or EOD date was listed as 8/30/98. That was correct. His field office was noted correctly. His participation in the InCit program was also confirmed. No surprises there.

The second name was Dana Burnside. With a puzzled look, Dr. Parker sat back in her chair. Wait. Where had she seen that name before?

Dr. Parker jumped forward and grabbed the computer mouse. She switched screens and clicked on the Bureau employee database. Typing in the name Dana Burnside, she hit enter. Up popped Physician's Assistant, PA, Dana Burnside. Female. Location: ERF, Surgical Unit, DSL. What the heck was wrong with that picture? How could a PA with the ERF Surgical Unit have her DNA crisscrossed with Tracey's? It was certainly crisscrossed when the data was entered. It had to be a mistake. Dr. Parker knew it wasn't possible that Tracey's and PA Burnside's DNA were identical. Well, unless they were identical twins, and then it was more than likely they had the same DNA. But on top of it, they both worked at the FBI. Nope. Not probable.

Dr. Parker clicked over to the DNA database and typed in Dana Burnside. Her file came up, and Dr. Parker read through it. Born in Montana, she graduated twice from Johns Hopkins University, first with a degree in nursing and subsequently with a master's degree in physician assistant studies. Following her residency, she worked as an emergency room physician's assistant at Walter Reed Army Medical Center. She wrote on her application for the job at Walter Reed she wanted to "help save the lives of veterans who put their lives on the line for their country."

Burnside worked at Walter Reed for two years and subsequently, at twenty-nine years old, applied to become an FBI agent. This was getting interesting, Dr. Parker thought.

Burnside appeared to be moving through her class at the Academy when her dream of becoming an agent was stopped dead in its tracks following an accidental discharge of her gun at the firearms range. Dr. Parker clicked through her medical file to read the report on that accident.

FTU noted in its investigation that Burnside was with her squad of new agent trainees at the firearms range and had just finished firing on a paper target. As she moved to holster her weapon, her fingertip caught the trigger, and she fired a round directly through her holster and into her right leg. The bullet entered the top of her thigh, hit her femur, and ricocheted through her leg, missing her femoral artery by the slightest of margins. The damage caused to her leg and nerves was severe.

Burnside underwent three surgeries within eight hours that first day. She would undergo six surgeries in all over seven months. She lost almost 35% of the muscle in her right leg. Burnside's potential career as a special agent in the FBI was done. She would never pass the rigorous physical fitness test.

At the same time, the Bureau needed staff for their ERF Surgical Unit. Burnside saw this as a new career opportunity and accepted a position as a physician's assistant within the ERF's Surgical Unit. She subsequently moved to DSL.

After spending a few more minutes reading through Burnside's file, Dr. Parker was no closer to figuring out why Burnside's and Tracey's DNA was the same or why Tracey's DNA was not verified. Was it just mislabeled?

She took a sip of her coffee and immediately made a face as she realized the coffee was now lukewarm and only slightly above room temperature. She swallowed anyway. Yuck. She stood up, walked over to the small microwave in her office, and shoved the cup inside. This would undoubtedly be the first of many coffee warm-ups she would perform today. It was a daily occurrence.

The microwave beeped, and she removed her cup of coffee.

Dr. Gaeber had returned and was entering the DecTube. He would head for the decontamination room next.

Dr. Parker was at a loss. Not something she was used to. Something had to give.

She picked up the phone and decided to call FBI HQ Personnel. Maybe if she looked at the personnel files of both Tracey and Burnside, she could figure something out.

Chapter 16

I Have a What?

Tracey was thirty-five years old when his father passed away. He inherited his father's assets even though his father never thought he had amounted to much and didn't consider himself wealthy. The Trellis property notwithstanding. And his mother would always tell him the estate was not complicated and not to hire an attorney. She even had transfer deeds for their houses signed and notarized, ready to be filed in the land records. Sell everything else, she told Tracey. They were simple folks. And Tracey was the only child. At least, that's what Tracey had always thought. When he visited his parents two years earlier on his thirty-third birthday, just before he received his appointment to the Academy, Tracey received the heart-stopping news he had a sister he never knew.

Tracey's father and mother sat him down that afternoon in their backyard. At the time, his father's health had greatly deteriorated. He was confined to the wheelchair he would be in for the rest of his life due to neuropathy that made it impossible for him to walk. Tracey's mother cared for his father's daily needs. She was a saint, as most mothers were. But there was one time she described when she had a very unsaintly relationship.

Tracey had heard all the jokes about kids being born and not looking like their father. He even cracked a few of those jokes with teammates in high school. The joke was their mother must have "gotten it on," "done the deed," with the milkman. In Tracey's case, it was true. His mother had an affair with their milkman.

Over time, his mother and father had reconciled this indiscretion, and the milkman jokes would come out from both his parents. Tracey never really knew why they kept up with the jokes about the milkman being his father, but adults never made sense to kids. Parents always seemed like aliens anyway.

It turned out the milkman was more than just a milkman. His name was Landon Burnside. He went to high school with Tracey's mother and later became the family's insurance agent. After a chance run-in at the grocery store one day, Tracey's mother and Landon innocently went out for coffee to discuss insurance needs for Tracey's family. A short time later, Tracey's mother invited Landon to explain his insurance products during a "lunch-and-learn" at her job, a paper supply company. After too much alcohol at the lunch-and-learn, they found themselves in a hotel. Thus, the unsaintly behavior.

To add a little extra to the "you have a sister" bombshell, his mother also told him his sister was his fraternal twin.

Landon didn't want to raise two kids. So, right or wrong, the determination was made that Landon would raise their daughter, and Tracey's mother and father, as he knew his father to be, would raise him.

As complicated as his parents made hiding who Tracey's real father was from him, all Tracey wanted to know was who his sister was. His parents swore they had not stayed in touch with her or Landon over the years, except they knew Landon had died several years ago.

In time, Tracey would look for his sister.

✦✦✦

June 2003
Miami FBI field office

Tracey leaned back in a conference room chair while he ate his lunch. He was in his fifth year working for the FBI. After the usual bickering among squad mates about whether they would watch Jerry Springer or the news, the consensus was to watch Springer. The Springer show they started to watch that day featured an episode of separated twins finding their twin after years of searching. Tracey almost choked on his sandwich. It was a sign. His sign. The thought of his lost twin sister came rushing back into his consciousness.

Tracey headed to his desk and clicked open the internet to begin his search. He started with the information he had - a birth certificate with his parents' names signed by a doctor. After a couple of hours, Tracey had narrowed down the "milk man" and his sister to one of two possible families still living in the U.S. Five minutes later, Tracey found his sister.

From what Tracey was told by his mother, his biological father, Landon Burnside, had lived in Providence, Rhode Island, but was deceased. Tracey learned through his research Landon had two sons and a daughter. Landon's daughter was named Dana. She was the same age as Tracey. A Johns Hopkins University graduate, first with a degree in nursing and second with a master's degree in emergency medicine. Her current employment: U.S. Government. This fact immediately caught Tracey's attention.

He searched the internet and located a work profile for her. She stated in her profile she was a medical technician and listed the same two degrees from Johns Hopkins University. She currently works for the U.S. Government. The profile didn't indicate which agency in the government she worked for, but she listed her current location as Washington, D.C.

Hot damn.

Tracey felt good. He believed he had found his long-lost twin sister.

He couldn't wait to give her a call.

After thumbing through several databases, Tracey came up with six possible phone numbers for Dana. He dialed the first one. Without even ringing, a message said the phone was no longer in service. One down, five to go. He dialed the second number and reached a hair salon in Washington, D.C. They had never heard of anyone named Dana. He was zero for two. On the third call, his heart jumped a beat.

"This is Dana."

Tracey froze for a second. Or two. Or three. He hadn't written anything down for a good interview like he'd practiced hundreds of times.

"Umm, yes...umm, I'm looking for my - I mean for Dana Burnside," Tracey finally blurted out like a nervous high school-er asking to borrow the family car.

"This is she. Can I help you?"

Tracey knew she worked for a government agency. But he didn't know which one. He figured he would try a little white lie and see if she bit.

"I hope so. This is Special Agent David Tracey with the Federal Bureau of Investigation. I'm hoping you can - " That was as far as Tracey got before Dana cut him off.

"Ha, so formal. You know, most folks only say FBI." She chuckled. "What office are you in?"

"I'm in the Miami field office. I'm hoping you could answer a few questions regarding possible fraud we discovered over at your unit." He held his breath.

"In ERF?" Dana shot back immediately. Bingo. Tracey was in.

If she could have seen Tracey's face, she would have seen him change from a ruddy complexion to one Casper would be proud of. *Did she say ERF? As in the Engineering Research Facility at the Academy? No freaking way*, Tracey thought. Could she possibly work for the Bureau? Or was this ERF meant for some other government agency? It had to be the Bureau.

"Indeed, ERF," Tracey continued with the ruse. "I'll be up your way next Friday and am wondering if we can meet, possibly over at Quantico somewhere. The fraud appears to have started in your unit, so we're keeping this hush-hush for now."

"Umm, sure. Of course, I'll have to call down to the Miami and make sure you are who you say you are. Why are you handling this from Miami? Shouldn't this be a headquarters unit that handles the Academy?"

"Because we received the complaint from a retired agent, we can work the case. HQ knows about it, of course. We keep them up to speed. And no worries about calling to check on me. Dial away," Tracey said and afterward regretted how stupid that sounded. Dial away? Duh.

"When you call me back, let me know a good time next Friday and a spot, maybe for lunch? I'll meet you there."

"Ok, sounds good," Dana said.

They both hung up. Tracey sat back in his chair and rocked back and forth. Was he finally going to meet his twin sister, and she had no idea he existed? Or did she know he existed but didn't bother to find out where he was over the years?

He'd soon have his answers.

Tracey and his sister finally met a week after speaking on the phone. They ate lunch at the Subway restaurant at MCB Quantico. Their conversation was simple and laid back. Dana detailed her shooting accident at the Academy years before while training to be a special agent and how she ended up instead working in the Surgical Unit at ERF and was now in the DSL. And Tracey gave her a rundown of some of the cases he had worked on in Miami. Tracey and Dana sat and talked for more than an hour.

Tracey found the nerve midway through their lunch to bring up the fact they were siblings. Halfway through his explanation, Dana held up her hand to stop him. She already knew. Her father told her a few years before he died.

Both Tracey and Dana were happy to have finally found each other.

A year after their Subway lunch, Tracey was again at Quantico for a week of training on the latest techniques to investigate white-collar crime. While he was at the Academy, Tracey called his sister to see if she wanted to have lunch. Dana readily agreed, and they subsequently met and had lunch in the ERF cafeteria.

After lunch, Dana gave Tracey a tour of her lab, the DSL. She had a surprise for Tracey. On the elevator leading to Dana's lab, Tracey was introduced to the Red Ladens for the first time. When Dana told Tracey what the Red Ladens were capable of, he chuckled until he noticed Dana's expression suggested she was serious. Once the Red Ladens had passed, Tracey questioned why he wasn't knocked unconscious. Dana explained how she added his DNA from the blood sample he provided as a New Agent Trainee into the Red Laden database. He would have access only for that day. But that wasn't the surprise.

When they arrived at the DSL, Dana was required to type in her numbered password on the Hirsch Pad. After she entered the last number, she hit "Enter" and quickly started to push open the door. She nearly slammed her head into the door, however. The Hirsch Pad beeped a solid tone and produced a red light, indicating she had entered the wrong sequence of numbers.

She entered her numbers again and once again didn't wait for the green light but went to push open the door. Again, the door didn't open, and the same red tone suggested she entered the wrong numbers for a second time.

She stared at the Hirsch Pad, reciting the numbered password out loud. Loud enough for Tracey to hear it. And remember it.

She entered the numbers. Finally, a green light lit up the pad, and the door clicked. She pushed the door open into the unit.

Once inside the lab, Tracey took it all in. It wasn't a big room as far as labs go. The room was maybe 30' by 30'. Stainless steel tables were everywhere, covered with various scientific instruments that Tracey didn't recognize.

Dana walked over to a small desk with a computer and sat down. "Come over and grab a seat," she said to Tracey.

Tracey followed Dana and maneuvered a rolling chair to the side of Dana's desk.

"This is the surprise I mentioned," she said.

Tracey looked at her and shook his head just a little bit sideways, partially closing one eye.

"I'm afraid to ask you just what this surprise might be, especially sitting in this lab after those dancing red balls invaded my private parts," Tracey said with a laugh.

"Oh, don't be a baby!" Dana said. "This will be for your benefit if you someday decide to come on board with any of the upper echelon, Eyes Only cases or join a team that goes overseas. The deal is this: I'll take your blood sample and stick it into the database as your DNA profile in a file we call "Prospective Eyes." Then you won't have to waste time coming here to give a blood sample. This was my idea a few years ago, and management didn't hesitate to give me the green light. My blood sample is also in there even though I have no desire to travel overseas at any time soon."

Tracey thought that was cool.

"Unfortunately, I couldn't use the small amount of blood you provided as a New Agent Trainee for the blood sample to get you into the Prospective Eyes program. I need a little more blood than that. I'll need a small blood sample to enter into the computer and a test tube amount of blood we can save. So, roll up one of your sleeves."

Tracey complied, and Dana proceeded to draw a full test tube of Tracey's blood, squeezed a drop on a glass slide, and softly placed the slide on a tray that slid into the computer. After several whirs and beeps, the process was complete, and Tracey's DNA was added to the Prospective Eyes group of agents. She labeled and placed Tracey's test tube of blood in one of the refrigerated units in her lab.

Tracey and Dana talked for another thirty minutes before they said their goodbyes. Dana walked Tracey out of the lab, up the elevator, and out the doors of ERF, waving to him as he left in his Bureau car to head back to his class at the Academy.

They vowed to stay in touch more than just once a year.

figured that was his location. Bell continued to look at the screen. He couldn't be sure, but there was a solid green dot that looked to be within ten clicks of his position. A portal? Other solid green dots appeared on the screen further away from his location. Bell stuck to what little he had learned in the InCit lab - solid green is safe. He would head for the nearest solid green dot and pray it was portal 17.

Bell made his way to the edge of the airfield and pulled out onto the small country road.

He never noticed the black Ford Bronco Tracey had parked at the airport the day before. It was completely covered with snow.

Chapter 18
The Cat's Out of the Bag

September 8, 2012
8:45 a.m.
ERF

Dr. Parker sat at her desk, sipping her coffee again. She waited patiently for the Personnel Office to send her the medical files for Tracey and Dana Burnside. She tried to relax, knowing she had barely slept the night before. Then, her computer chimed, indicating she had a new email. It was from the personnel department. Three files were attached to the email - Tracey's medical file, Dana Burnside's medical file, and a chart with several pages containing the DNA profiles for both Tracey and Dana Burnside. Dr. Parker continued to sip her coffee as she clicked on the chart with Tracey's and Burnside's DNA profiles. She compared them side-by-side. She noticed the anomaly right away. There was no difference. She slowly withdrew her coffee cup from her mouth and placed it back on the desk. The DNA profiles were identical for Tracey and Dana Burnside.

Dr. Parker then clicked on Tracey's Bureau medical file. The latest and last entry indicated the director had authorized the removal of Tracey's DNA from the database to disable his InCit drone. That made sense. The entry just before this removal of Tracey's DNA from the InCit program was one adding Tracey's DNA profile to Dana's DNA folder. This entry was also from two days ago and made by Dana Burnside from within DSL. This didn't make sense. But it did explain why no one in InCit had verified it.

Dana Burnside replaced her DNA profile with Tracey's DNA profile. Why? And what the hell happened to Dana Burnside's DNA profile?

She clicked over to the personnel files for Tracey and Dana and put them up side by side. Reading through each one, she learned they were both born in a small town. It turned out to be the same small town. Their dates of birth were the same, and they had the same mother. But different fathers?

It hit her all at once.

David Tracey and Dana Burnside were twins.

But why the different fathers? There was also no reference to them being related as siblings in each of their files. What gave?

Dr. Parker passed this info to the director and the InCit management team.

And someone had to let Bell know.

✦✦✦

September 8, 2012
6:15 a.m. MST
Trellis, MT

Bell worked his way down the two-lane highway. His heart raced a little, even though he felt certain he wouldn't find Tracey in Montana. He knew Tracey couldn't have gotten there quicker than Bell, as they were simultaneously at ERF a short time ago. And Tracey didn't have access to the speedy Gulfstream as Bell did.

His navigator was open on the dashboard. The red dot indicating his position continued to blink red as he moved closer to the portal, which should be portal 17.

Portals were Positions of Remote Triage and Layover constructed by Director Hoover in the early '60s. Originally set up as safe houses in light of the Cold War with Russia, portals would provide locations for hunkering down and planning a counter-strike if the U.S. was attacked. After the Cold War, it made sense for IAs to utilize the portals as a location where they could gather to assess situations that became untenable at any time of national or world crisis.

Unmistakably nondescript and dotting the countryside all over the U.S., portals were created beneath small homes that seem to have just sprouted up from the ground where they stood. Most didn't appear occupied, and there was hardly any sign of life. They sat at odd angles to main roads and always needed a good coat of paint. Often, a dog strolled through the front yard as old run-down cars lined the driveways. And the weathervane always squeaked. Nobody ever oiled the weathervane, Bell thought. Ever. It irritated him. Thankfully, no one takes notice of these isolated, single-family homes as access points for the FBI's InCit Program.

Inside a portal, an IA would find supplies, recover if wounded, and communicate with other InCit personnel in the InCit command center and anywhere in the world. They were highly secure and always remote. And if the director needed to conduct a meeting post-haste, an IA would make it to a portal as quickly as possible.

The only lights for any distance were the headlights from his Tahoe. Bell then checked his blackhawk. Nothing. He thought it was odd that IA24 had not responded to him. Given the nature of the case they were both working on, IA24 should have at least responded he *got* the message.

The road ahead appeared to end in a grove of trees and at a cross street. The navigator told Bell to take a right turn at the cross street, which he did. His map indicated he was a half mile from the portal. Bell passed a small farm on the right and a small "Come & Go" convenience store just after that. Lights were on in the store, but no cars were in the parking lot.

Bell was thirsty, but he didn't want to stop. The portal would have something to drink. Hopefully.

At three-tenths of a mile from the portal, Tracey drove up to a car parked on the same side of the road. It was a black Chevy Malibu.

The car didn't look broken down, but it was unevenly parked with three wheels off the road. It looked like the driver just bailed out. The Montana license plate looked odd. There wasn't a number prefix to indicate the county in Montana where the car was registered. Usually, only government cars had that quirky nuance. Bell decided to check it out.

He pulled over and in front of the car. He turned off the Tahoe, placed his navigator in his coat pocket, and exited. He began to walk towards the Malibu. It was eerily quiet. As Bell reached the side view mirror on the driver's door, he sensed someone was watching him. Bell slowly looked at his surroundings without deliberate movements to indicate he was scanning. He didn't see anything. Bell then peered into the driver's seat. The keys were still in the ignition. Bell noticed a black object partially hidden beneath the driver's seat. The back seat was empty.

He opened the driver's door. Bending over, he discovered the object was a blackhawk. So, this *was* a BuCar. And not only a BuCar but one belonging to an Eyes Only agent with an assigned blackhawk. Was this Eyes Only agent an IA? It made sense since it was parked a short distance from a portal. But still.

Bell knew Eyes Only agents could access their accounts using another agent's blackhawk. Blackhawks functioned like small computers. They needed to be powered off and then back on again. Subsequently, a new login could be performed, like accessing email from the library or a friend's computer. There was one major difference - any IA logging in would also have access to the texts belonging to the IA originally assigned to that blackhawk. This feature was helpful, especially in an instance such as this, where the IA couldn't be located.

As Bell stood outside the Malibu, he flipped open the screen and expected to power the blackhawk on. But the blackhawk was already on. And the security functions had all been disabled. *Not smart*, Bell thought to himself. *Why would the agent disable the blackhawk's security protocols?* Anyone could then read Top-Secret data.

Nonetheless, Bell worked his way to the text messages and clicked on the latest of several unopened messages. The message had been sent "To IA24" from an unidentified number, or at least a number that didn't start with the same first six numbers as the other IA numbers did. So, this was IA24's blackhawk.

"Find the dog first," the message read.

Curious. Bell had no idea what the heck that meant. Contacting IA24 to ask for an explanation was now difficult. It appeared Bell was holding IA24's blackhawk. And this was most likely IA24's BuCar.

Bell needed to check his blackhawk and see if IA24 had sent him a message. Bell grabbed his blackhawk from his coat pocket and powered it up. After adding his credential numbers and password, the screen popped up with one text message. It was from IA24. Jeepers, finally, IA24 texted him. Bell clicked on the text message. He read it quickly and again before finally looking away from the screen.

"The sentry at portal 17 is not responding. Not sure what's up. Use caution."

Bell hated not knowing what was going on. He needed to get to the portal sooner than later, though.

He walked to the front of the car and touched the hood. Cold. While Bell stood outside IA24's BuCar with his hand on the hood, he again wondered why IA24 had abandoned his BuCar and left his blackhawk behind, with its security turned off no less.

Bell's next thought would have to wait.

Chapter 19
Unexpected

The sound that a gun's firing pin made when it was pushed into the back end of a bullet cartridge wasn't something anyone ever heard. Guns just operated for the most part. As a shooter, you believed it would function as anticipated. The internal mechanics weren't usually given a second thought. The time difference between when the firing pin hit the bullet cartridge and when the cartridge and bullet separated was insignificant if one was trying to count. An accurate timing is not reasonably possible. And as the speed of a .223 caliber bullet was faster than the speed of sound, the term "bang, bang" was fairly accurate.

That's why Bell never heard the firing pin.

The bullet entered Bell's right wrist, making the smallest of holes. But the exit wound was a cavity an inch wide. With a tumbling effect, the bullet continued moving as it exited Bell's wrist, ripping the top off his gun holster and missing his Glock and his crown jewels by millimeters. The round ended up in the dirt in front of him. If the round had hit a thicker part of Bell's arm, he would have ended up with a larger exit wound and much more damage. Of course, the shot could have been just as accurate as intended.

The backside of Bell's wrist was a mess. He surmised the round went through his wrist without striking the largest of his wrist bones, as that pain would have been intense. The pain was tolerable, but it hurt. Bell immediately fell to his knees. His right shooting hand was now inoperable. Bell didn't waste any more time thinking about what happened to the agent and his car on the side of the road and switched into survival mode. Finding out who the hell was shooting at him was first on his priority list. As he reached inside his coat for a handkerchief, he moved to the front fender and tire and crouched down. He wrapped the handkerchief around the wound and pulled the ends together with his teeth. Looking up slightly, the engine block would be his new cover and concealment. If he remained low enough, he'd be shielded from more rounds. From the trajectory of the shot, he figured the shooter was at least 100 yards away. The shooter was probably still watching Bell's location through the rifle sights or binoculars, so trying to move from his cover would certainly draw more fire. Bell checked his wrist. The bandage he made was working. He had at least stopped most of the bleeding, but the pain was becoming a little more intense. His right hand was useless. He tried to squeeze it and stopped immediately as the pain made him wince.

Bell had to get out of there and fast. He was a sitting duck. He turned his attention to the keys in the ignition. Based on the angle of the shot, Bell surmised any subsequent shots would come through the front windshield. He could jump into the car, start it, back up, and hopefully survive any windshield glass fragments the additional rounds would cause. He knew a bullet coming through the front windshield would fragment less than a side window due to the layering of the windshield glass.

Bell went for it. He rolled to his right under the driver's door, and a second round hit the pavement to his left, narrowly missing his right foot as he rolled. The shooter must have moved to a higher vantage point, as Bell's foot was barely visible when he rolled. That complicated Bell's plan. Now, it seemed the shooter was shooting down into the car instead of across. His head was throbbing from the pain, and the handkerchief was almost completely soaked through with blood. While he might not bleed out, he could certainly pass out, which would be just as deadly.

With a quick move, Bell pulled himself partially into the driver's seat floorboard. He reached up with his left hand and turned the key in the ignition. The car started immediately. Before Bell could pull himself fully into the driver's seat, a volley of shots rained down on him from overhead and into the rear seat. A thought then hit Bell - could it be an InCit drone shooting at him? There was no way a human being could move that fast and not be seen or heard. If it was an InCit drone, it must be invisible and in protection mode. But where the hell was the IA that the drone should be protecting? From the crash course Bell just received from Dr. Gaeber, he knew the stomonite wouldn't let the drone kill Bell. Bell also wasn't being hostile towards an IA, and he was an IA himself, for God's sake! Two things a drone was programmed to account for. Although, he could be shot again in a non-lethal location. That *was* a drone directive. Incapacitate. Not kill. Great. It was time to stop thinking about getting shot again and get the hell out of Dodge.

Bell pulled himself into the driver's seat and closed the driver's door as the next volley of bullets hit the pavement outside. Bell wasn't hiding anymore. He debated for a second he ever was. He sat up, rammed the gears into reverse, and floored the pedal. The Malibu shot backward at an angle, and the car righted itself with all four wheels now on the road. Bell wasn't sure why the text instructed the agent to send the dog first, but he had to lose the drone, and the portal was his best chance to survive.

Bell stamped on the gas pedal and headed towards portal 17. As he drove, he removed the navigator from his coat pocket. Portal 17 appeared to be less than a tenth of a mile away. And the drone, or whomever wasn't firing at him anymore.

Thank God.

Bell was surprised he didn't take any more rounds if it was a drone shooting at him. He was more than ecstatic he didn't, though. The shooter seemed to have remained behind at the location where he was initially shot. Bell never saw the shooter, but he didn't doubt it was a drone. Since every IA drone could be cloaked in stomonite, it wouldn't be seen anyway. An IA could uncloak the drone to add ammunition or service it, but otherwise, it remained invisible. Additionally, an IA could use the stomonite assigned to his drone to configure the area of coverage, altering the range of the drone and setting its flight pattern from 150 yards away to just above the IA's head. There were many other commands available for controlling an IA's drone.

As he drove, Bell tried to wrap his mind around what had happened. Bell was now in the InCit database. The drone would have updated immediately with Bell's DNA profile as soon as Bell's drone came online at the Academy. But why was this drone trying to incapacitate Bell? It wasn't random. No way. Stomonite was loyal to a fault and had never failed over the years. The drone seemed to be protecting the Malibu. Could an IA command a drone to protect a BuCar? Was the IA still near the BuCar? Hurt or dead? Bell didn't know any of those answers. He realized, however, that more important issues had to be immediately addressed.

Bell checked the navigator. A counter appeared and was counting down quickly. Bell was less than 500 feet away from portal 17. Three hundred feet. On the left. A white picket fence ended, and a driveway began. The navigator beeped loud and long, and a green light hovered on the screen over a small, light gray, single-story home just in front of him.

Bell turned into the driveway.

Chapter 20
Man's Best Friend

Bell kept the car running in case he needed a fast retreat. He looked around but saw no movement of any kind. He rolled the window down a few inches. There was no sound except the occasional bird calling out. Bell was willing to accept a little peace and quiet, but a barking dog would put his mind at ease. Somewhat. A barking dog meant a living, breathing sentinel. That meant the portal most likely wouldn't have been compromised in any way. No barking, however. Ugh.

Unlike a family's dog, a sentinel was trained from birth to bark for only one reason - the presence of an IA. The Sentinel Program was created on the basic principle that a friendly dog, one that didn't look like a killer and didn't bark, was a dog that wouldn't need to be killed by anyone thinking it was a threat. And that made for a successful program. The sentinels served as an early warning system. In the forty-five years of the program's existence, only two sentinels died of anything other than natural causes - one by a postwoman distracted by a phone call and another by a drunk driver who crashed into a portal, running over a sleeping sentinel in the front yard.

The scent of all eighty-three IAs in the InCit program was known to every sentinel. They were trained to wait and notify the sentry through any number of signals if someone approached the portal who shouldn't be there. These alerts were captured by the portal's highly technical notification system. Peeing on the mailbox post by the road triggered an alert a car was coming down the driveway. The sentinel's urine was the trigger. Picking up one of the small footballs hidden away in the bushes to play with was another trigger, along with rolling in a small clover patch. All the triggers set off an alarm inside the portals and were meant to give the portal personnel time to react.

Bell checked his wrist. The bleeding seemed to have stopped. He knew it would become increasingly more difficult to use his right hand as time went on, so he wanted to be sure the bleeding had stopped while he still had some range of motion.

Bell needed a new bandage to keep the wound clean. He leaned over and opened the glove compartment. Shoving several small replacement automobile bulbs out of the way, a throwaway camera, and some pepper spray, Bell located a chamois cloth neatly folded up in a square. Bell grabbed the chamois and, using his left hand, placed it between his teeth. He ripped a six-inch wide strip off the cloth. He formed a slipknot and worked it over his right wrist, stopping below the bloodied handkerchief. He lightly tied the new cloth bandage under the handkerchief and removed the handkerchief. The blood had already started to clot around the wound. Bell noted the exit wound on the back of his wrist was barely holding on to a tiny piece of a forearm tendon. Bell pushed the piece of the tendon back into the opening and sucked up the pain. He pulled the cloth down over the wound.

Bell glanced outside the car and looked down the road again, slowly scanning it and the sky around him. No movement. He grabbed the bloodied handkerchief. If it was a drone that shot at him, he wanted to test the drone's range and eyes. He grabbed the handkerchief and crumpled it into a ball before tossing it out the window. It landed about five feet from the driver's door without incident. Checking the side view mirror, Bell thought he saw a flash of something in the sky about seventy-five yards out. He kept watching for another flash. After two minutes of staring alternately into the side-view mirror and the rear-view mirror, Bell decided he was safe enough to leave the car.

He turned off the car but left the keys in the ignition. He wasn't going to struggle with that again. Taking a deep breath, he checked his rear-view mirror and slowly pushed open the driver's door. He waited. Nothing. With his left hand, he unholstered his Glock and stepped outside. It was even quieter than when he sat inside the car if that was possible. Bell stepped around the door towards the front and stopped at the front driver's side headlight. Looking back towards the road, he saw no movement and heard no vehicles. His right hand was throbbing again. He tried to use his right hand to steady his left hand and the handgun he now held with it.

Now, where the hell is the sentinel, Bell thought to himself. No dog. That was a bad sign. The sentinel was either dead or sleeping. Bell was hoping for the sleeping dog. Bell loved dogs, and he needed to see a friendly one.

As Bell walked towards the house, he noticed only one car in the driveway. It looked like it had several bullet holes in the back window. His eyes weren't as good as they used to be, but he wasn't losing his mind. There were bullet holes. While he kept his eye on the car with his peripheral vision, he slowly approached the front porch. He reached the bottom stair of the porch and was just about to step up when he heard the faint sound of a James Taylor song playing somewhere inside. He noticed the front door had received two neatly placed bullet holes just above the door knob. There were no other bullet holes Bell could see, and the front of the house didn't appear to have any additional signs of a firefight. Bell waited and scanned the front of the house again. There was no movement, which was good since Bell had zero concealment and even less cover. He was a sitting duck.

As he continued up the steps, he heard a muffled whimper. He took one more step and was about to move onto the top stair when a more defined whine came from under the porch. Bell stopped, backed down to the ground step, and stared straight ahead, waiting for any movement. Out of the corner of his eye, he saw something move to his right, under the porch, and he shifted his gaze and Glock in that direction. His eyes traced the outline of an animal about four feet long. That would fit the description of a sentinel. But why was the sentinel hiding?

Bell gave out one quick short whistle. The animal then began to low-crawl towards the end of the porch. Bell slowly brought his Glock up to his chest and drew a bead on the spot where the animal would emerge. A dog's head leaned out at the end of the porch and looked directly at Bell. The dog's ears immediately went down. From the way the dog's body was shaking, Bell could tell its tail was wagging. He assumed this was the sentinel. Bell holstered his weapon and knelt as the sentinel crawled from under the porch.

The sentinel was a beautiful, all-liver-colored German Shorthaired Pointer. It was a female. She limped towards Bell, trying not to place any weight on her right front leg. As she neared Bell, he could see her foot had been bleeding. Bell remained crouched with his hand out, and the sentinel continued towards him, wagging her tail.

What worried Bell was the sentinel didn't bark when she saw him. She still hadn't barked. He then realized this sentinel might have been hurt before the sentry could have introduced her to Bell's scent. Or even worse still, the sentry was incapacitated. And given those scenarios, if she had been outside for the last twenty-four hours, she wouldn't know his scent.

Even more problematic was that InCit personnel inside the portal watching him would think he wasn't an IA as the sentinel didn't bark. Unless he could figure out a way of identifying himself, he was likely to get shot by friendly fire.

Given the day he was having so far, Bell was leaning towards the theory of getting shot.

Again.

Chapter 21
Approaching the Portal

The sentinel struggled as she walked but finally made her way over to Bell. Bell rubbed the sentinel's head while she licked him. Her collar said "Fallon" in a fancy script.

"Good girl, Fallon," Bell said softly.

As advanced as the Bureau was, they had not yet trained dogs to talk back. Bell continued the conversation anyway.

"What happened to your foot there, little girl?" he asked.

She let him reach for her paw. Bell turned the paw over slightly, and Fallon let out a little squeal and pulled her paw back slightly. A piece of glass was stuck in her pad. Bell pulled the glass out slowly, and very little blood came out. Bell let go of her paw and stood up. She continued to lay on the ground.

As he looked at Fallon, Bell remembered the text message on IA24's blackhawk - "find the dog first." Maybe Bell was supposed to help the dog. Once he was convinced the portal was secure, Bell would certainly help Fallon.

Bell wanted to check out the car in the driveway before attempting to access the portal. He turned to his left and started walking towards the side of the house and a 2000-style Ford Taurus.

The car was parked somewhat haphazardly and crooked. Just like he had found the Malibu. Bell walked up to the back of the Taurus first and heard the faint sound of a chime indicating one of the doors was open. Inching closer, he saw the driver's door was ajar, and the window was rolled halfway down.

He unholstered his Glock again with his left hand and carefully approached the car from the rear. The interior light was off. He crept closer with his Glock out in front and pointed towards the back seat. He cleared the back seat and the front seat as well. The car was empty.

Bell noticed the keys were in the ignition, the source of the constant chime. The interior light was off. The car battery wouldn't last much longer. He reached in, took the keys out of the ignition, and placed them on the front seat. He continued slowly walking down the driveway with his Glock out, checking the windows along the way. Everything looked normal. Still cautious, he continued towards the back of the house. When he reached the back corner, he carefully did a quick peek and performed this movement a couple more times. Confident nothing was out of the ordinary, he moved around the corner.

Bell scanned the two first-floor windows in the back. They were intact. He turned his gaze towards the garage. The double doors of the detached garage were wide open, and Bell could see it was empty except for a tractor parked on the right side.

Bell quickly turned his attention back to the rear of the house. Something about the back door was out of place. The outside screen on the back door was closed, but the wind blew the mesh screen back and forth, and Bell could see it was torn. The inside door was solid on the bottom and didn't appear damaged. But the top half of the door was glass, broken and jagged glass. On the ground directly below the door was a pile of broken glass. He'd found the probable source of Fallon's injury.

Bell's next task was going to be tricky. He had to enter the house and see if any InCit personnel were present. If no one was home, he needed to review the cameras in the portal command center to see what the hell happened. And Bell still wondered why no one had tried to contact him since Fallon didn't bark.

Bell was slightly uncomfortable now, thinking there could be a threat inside he had to deal with.

Chapter 22
What Happened Here?

Circling to the front porch, Bell found Fallon sleeping on the landing. Bell gripped his Glock firmly with his left hand as he approached the front door. He nudged open the screen door with his right elbow while keeping his Glock approximately ten inches in front of his face at eye level. Holding the screen door open with his hip, he reached for the front doorknob, trying to twist it with his right hand. Nope. He had almost no strength in that hand. He transferred the Glock to his right hand and leaned into the door as he twisted the doorknob with his left hand. As the door opened, it immediately hit him: the smell of death.

He reached for the tee shirt under his long-sleeved shirt and brought it up to cover his nose. It hardly helped. He pulled his shirt back down and began breathing out of his mouth. Bell transferred the Glock to his left hand and slowly inched into the house. As he entered, he realized there was no cover to shield himself. He was in a living room with a couch, TV, chairs, and a fireplace. The best he could tell, the smell seemed to be coming from his left at 11 o'clock. He quickly cleared the living room and continued walking towards the smell, Glock extended.

A bathroom appeared on his right. Bell used his foot and pushed open the door. Empty. He moved a few more feet and stopped. He was about to enter the kitchen. He saw a foot lying just inside the doorway. He walked even slower as he led with his Glock in front of him and entered the kitchen. Immediately, he came upon the source of the putrid odor.

Lying on the floor to his left was the body of a white male who appeared to be in his early sixties. Bell kept his Glock in front of him at eye level as he panned the room for movement. None. The room was clear. It was clear of anything living anyway.

Bell listened for any movement coming from inside the house. It was quiet, and there were no signs of life, but he decided to clear the remainder of the house anyway. He stepped over the man on the floor and continued through the kitchen. Bell finished clearing the first floor using the same room-clearing process he used in the front room and bathroom and slowly headed upstairs, clearing two upstairs bedrooms, closets, and a bathroom. Empty.

Even without using his right wrist, Bell's right wrist was throbbing. He holstered his Glock. Looking at his right wrist and the cloth bandage covering it, the blood had started to dry. That, at least, was a good sign. He wouldn't bleed out and die.

Next, he needed to identify the man lying on the floor in the kitchen. If the dead man is a sentry, Bell's navigator would recognize him as one.

Bell also thought a face mask couldn't hurt. God, it was a crazy bad smell in there.

Bell headed towards the front door.

Chapter 23
Almost a Great Meal

June 3, 2012
Miami Dade High School
Miami, FL

The softball pitch came in at fifty-eight miles per hour. It was a curve ball. The catcher knew the runner on first base would take off as soon as the ball hit her catcher's mitt. It was just a smart softball play to steal second base. And there was a runner on third base. The opposing coach figured with a high degree of certainty he could get his runner safely to second since the catcher had to watch the runner at third before deciding to throw down to second. Often, the catcher would fake a throw to second and hold onto the ball before throwing it back to the pitcher.

The catcher caught the pitch after it dipped down in a curving motion. She stood up and fired down to second base. April was ready on the mound. She ducked down after she pitched the ball to appear to let the throw go all the way to second base. But before the pitch, her coach yelled, "Jupiter! Jupiter!" That meant the catcher would throw towards second base, but the pitcher would cut off the throw to the shortstop, the original intended recipient. The plan was to catch the runner on third in a rundown if she tried to run home or took too big a lead off base.

The catcher threw the softball like it had been shot out of a gun. As the ball started to pass the pitcher's mound, April stood up and snagged the ball, quickly looking towards third base. The runner had taken a short running start down the baseline. That was all the distance April needed. She turned and fired the ball to the third baseman. The runner took off for home plate. The third baseman caught the ball from April, stepped onto the dirt infield, and threw quickly to the catcher. The runner was called out by three feet. Great play. Game over.

David and Trina stood up, whooping and hollering at how the game ended.

"Great play! Way to throw it, April!" Trina yelled out.

April looked at her parents and gave them a thumbs up as she and her teammates gathered around her near the pitcher's mound. But not before April put her mask back on. She knew to be careful following her last DBA procedure.

That procedure involved April completing the stem cell transplant at Seattle Children's Hospital. She remained there for five months. Now, her red blood cell count was normal, and she had no signs of DBA. April's senior year was a joyous blur. She joined the debate team and made All-State. She also took second place in the science fair for her exhibit on football player concussion protocol, play-related head blows, and their relationship to chronic traumatic encephalopathy (CTE).

She made it through her senior year unscathed from the DBA, and her future was full of promise.

+++

Traffic wasn't too bad when the Traceys drove away from the school. Several cars in front of them were driven by other girls on the softball team, and they were busy honking their horns in excitement following the win.

The Traceys made it home uneventfully. They unloaded from the car, and Trina headed into the kitchen to stir the crock pot of beef stew she had been cooking all day. Grabbing a spoon, she took a sip of the gravy, shaking her head in enjoyment. It was good, she thought. They would like it.

David headed upstairs to change out of his work clothes and into some shorts and a T-shirt. On his way, he peeked into the room of his younger daughter, Savannah, where she was busy watching a video on nutrition. She was taking notes and crunching on a celery stick.

"Hey, kiddo. Getting some homework finished?"

"Hey, Dad. Yeah, nutrition class. It's a pretty good class. I figured I'd eat healthy while I watched the homework video."

" Nice. We'll be eating in about 10 minutes. Mom made something that smells pretty darn good. I think it's rabbit stew."

Savannah swiveled around in her chair as she stopped crunching on the piece of celery. She raised her eyebrows and frowned. "Real funny, Dad."

"Just saying, you never know. At least tell me you've seen Madeline's rabbit in the past few days?"

Madeline was Savannah's best friend who lived down the street. She had a pet rabbit.

"Definitely not funny, Dad."

"Ten minutes, okay?"

David chuckled as he walked away.

Savannah made a sound of agreement with the ten-minute warning and turned back to her video.

David changed quickly and started to head back downstairs. The girls' shower was still running. April took the longest showers. David's water bill reflected this fact. He screamed into April.

"Ten minutes until dinner, April! Your skin will look like a slice of jerky if you don't get out soon." No answer. He figured she heard him. She didn't think he was funny, though. She used to think he was funny. She was growing up, and he needed new jokes. He continued down the stairs and into the kitchen.

"Smells great," David said to Trina as she dug a bowl out of the cabinet and began to make a salad.

"I'll bet it tastes good. It's been cooking all day. Beef stew. I may have sampled a little, so I may take my bet." She and David laughed.

David picked out four sets of utensils from the cutlery drawer and walked over to the dining room table, setting them down with some napkins. As he started to walk back into the kitchen, he could still hear the shower water running. He'd give April a few more minutes.

Meanwhile, Savannah made her way downstairs. "Wow, that smells good, Mom," she said.

"Hope so," Trina said.

Trina grabbed her spoon again and took the cover off the crock pot. She dipped the spoon into the crock pot, blew on the sample, and slurped loudly like she knew David would do if he had been testing the stew.

They all laughed.

"Needs a little pepper, maybe," Trina said.

"I think so too, Mom," Savannah quickly responded. Too quickly.

Both Trina and David turned their heads towards Savannah.

Savannah smiled and sheepishly looked down at the floor. "I may have tried a few spoonfuls in between nutrition videos."

They all laughed again.

April had certainly blown by the ten-minute warning by at least two minutes. David walked over to the bottom of the stairs. The shower was still running.

David had enough. He took the stairs two at a time and walked to the bathroom door. He knocked with enough force to jolt her out of her hot-water-induced steam bath.

"Hey. April?"

Nothing. His annoyance suddenly left. Now, he was getting worried. He tried the door handle. Locked.

"Trina, can you come up here, please?"

Trina walked around the corner from the kitchen and looked up the stairs at David.

"What's up?" she asked.

"April's not answering. Can you get in there?" David's voice was urgent and sharp as he nodded towards the bathroom door.

David feared something was wrong. He wasn't sure why, if not just because April wasn't answering him.

Trina bounded up the stairs, grabbing the railing as she went to gain speed. She got to the door and was about to knock. There was no time for that. David lunged forward with his foot, kicked the door handle, and the bathroom door swung open. Trina gasped.

David hadn't yet turned around to look. "Is she clothed?"

Trina cried out. "Yes, she is, and she's on the floor!"

David turned quickly to see his daughter lying almost face-down on the floor. She was by the tub with her softball uniform on and one sock halfway off.

"April!" David and Trina yelled at the same time.

Trina reached April first. She rolled April over. "She's warm, and she's breathing."

"Savannah!" David shouted to his daughter as he ran to the top of the stairs.

Savannah appeared in the doorway to the kitchen and looked up.

"Call 911 right now. Tell them your sister has passed out, and we need an ambulance!"

"What?"

"Savannah! Do it!" David screamed back.

"Okay, got it."

Savannah ran to the kitchen counter and grabbed her phone. She dialed 911 and told the operator what her father had said. The ambulance was five minutes out.

David and Trina attempted to diagnose what was wrong with April. Trina felt April was burning up with a fever, so she grabbed a washcloth and ran it under cold water. She applied it to April's face and forehead while David kept his finger on her wrist, checking her pulse. He noticed she had a small cut on her lip.

Savannah appeared in the doorway of the bathroom. "Oh, God! What happened?"

"We don't know," Trina said.

At that moment, April began to open her eyes. She looked around the room but appeared to have trouble focusing. "What's going on?" April weakly asked.

"Hey, kiddo. You seem to have passed out," David said.

"I did?"

"Yes, you were lying on the floor with one sock almost off. Do you remember anything?" Trina asked.

"I remember sitting on the tub, and I started to take my socks off. But I don't remember feeling light-headed or falling."

"How are you feeling right now?" David asked.

"My head hurts a little, and my --," April said as she stopped and felt the cut on her lip. "My lip hurts. Is it bleeding?"

"Not now. It was when we got to you, but it's stopped," Trina said as she continued to wipe April's forehead with the cool washcloth.

David thought that was a good thing. A clotting wound was good news since April had been through so much with low red blood cell counts.

The ambulance was loud and came to a screeching halt in front of their house. Neighbors looked out their windows to see what was going on. The paramedics ran out of the ambulance, grabbed the stretcher from the back, and pushed it quickly to the front door. They rang the bell repeatedly.

"Savannah, let them in," David said.

Savannah ran downstairs and subsequently led the paramedics up to the bathroom.

They wasted no time getting up the stairs. David and Trina backed out of the way as the paramedics took April's temperature and her pulse and asked her a few questions. David and Trina filled them in on her stem cell transplant and her overall health since the transplant. Given that history, the paramedics felt it was best to get April to the hospital to let the doctors take a look at her. The Traceys agreed.

✚✚✚

After several hours in the Miami hospital, there was no good news. The tests revealed April's red blood cell count had dropped below 70% of what it should be. And it was continuing to fall at an alarming rate. Given the fact she had already completed a full stem cell transplant in Seattle, it was decided her oncologists in Seattle should discuss the next course of action with them.

Within twenty hours of pitching her team to a softball win, April, David, and Trina were on a flight to Seattle.

Chapter 24

Do You Believe in Miracles?

June 5, 2012
Seattle Children's Hospital
Seattle, WA

David and Trina sat in the same bright conference room at the Seattle Children's Hospital where they previously received the wonderful news of April's successful stem cell transplant. It seemed unfair they could now possibly receive bad news regarding that same transplant in the same cheerful conference room.

The doctors confirmed the Miami results. April's red blood cells were breaking down due to a new cell mutation. They weren't sure if the mutation was cancerous, and it wasn't anything they had ever seen. April was producing red blood cells at a slower than 1% rate. The doctors couldn't stop the degrading of April's red blood cells. It was only a matter of time before she would need to remain in the hospital and receive round-the-clock blood transfusions.

Sitting across from David and Trina was April's oncologist, Dr. Binch, and two additional oncologists, a relatively young black male and an older white female. After they gave David and Trina the news, they pledged to continue working on a cure. But it didn't look good.

Trina started to shake a little, and she began to cry. She tried to maintain her composure, but within thirty seconds, she was sobbing completely.

After a few more words of encouragement from the doctors and condolences that April's health had deteriorated, the doctors stood up and headed for the door. David and Trina remained for a few more minutes, then stood up and followed.

The young, black doctor remained at the doorway as the other doctors left. Trina thanked him again. She wasn't sure what she was thanking him for, but she did anyway. She moved towards the elevators, concentrating on putting one foot in front of the other. She wanted to get back down to April.

David was the next-to-last person to leave the conference room. As he started through the threshold of the conference room, the same young oncologist lightly touched David's arm. He turned around.

"You coming, David?" Trina asked as she stepped into the open elevator.

"Yeah, yeah. Hey, let me talk to Dr. -," David began.

"Dr. Undulee," the young doctor said.

"Go and see April. I'm right behind you."

Trina nodded and let the elevator door close.

David and Dr. Undulee walked back into the conference room. David sat down as the doctor closed the door behind them. He sat across from David and folded his hands in front of him.

Dr. Undulee spoke very softly. "What I am about to tell you, I will never say I told you. We have to first agree on that, Mr. Tracey."

David couldn't care less about a promise he was about to make. "Absolutely. We never spoke. You never even spoke at the meeting."

"Very good. By way of a short background, when I was in my fifth year at Duke University Medical School, I met a friend, a fellow fifth-year student, during residency. His field of study in medical school and following graduation was bone marrow diseases.

"When we graduated, I came here to SCH, and he went to his homeland in Africa, the small country of Jafaire, a relatively young country. Jafaire is located in a war-ravaged area of Africa near the Somali Sea. His family were refugees in Jafaire and moved there with the help of the United Nations and many other countries. Possibly, you are familiar with this country's history?"

"I do know a little of the history of Jafaire, yes," David said.

"Well, my friend, Dr. Henry Embuke, had been working on a bone marrow procedure while still in medical school. His procedure included manipulating small amounts of a nuclear isotope, which he combined with a toxin to stop mutated cancer cells from over-producing red blood cells. Slowly, over a five-to-six-week period, the mutated cancer cells shriveled up and died. There was nothing for them to mutate with. They were blocked from attacking the red blood cells. They starved themselves to death."

"You mean to tell me your friend has found a way to cure cancer?" David asked, wide-eyed as he leaned in closer.

"Unfortunately, no. There was no way to know if more mutated cancer cells were in a person's body as all the tests were done in a lab setting, in a test tube. And after two to three months, the effect of the nuclear isotope in the lab setting wore off, and the cancer came back."

"So, why are you telling me this?"

"Mr. Tracey, have you ever heard of Dr. Embuke's sister, Chisomo Embuke?"

David nodded his head slowly.

"Then you know she is the President of Jafaire. She was stricken with DBA like your daughter. Although it was later in her life, she also had a stem cell transplant, and similar to your daughter's stem cell transplant, it only worked for a short period.

"While she was in remission, she was elected President of Jafaire. The people overwhelmingly elected her. The citizens were never told, however, before the election or afterward, that President Embuke had DBA and had been extremely close to dying." Dr. Undulee paused before he continued.

"You must understand that President Embuke is in every sense of the word the 'people's choice.' There is stability in Jafaire and, for the most part, in that region because of her and her policies. The Embuke family didn't want the world to know about her health issues for fear they would consider President Embuke physically unfit to lead them and, thus, condemn the election."

David shifted into an even straighter position in his chair.

"Dr. Embuke began treating his sister as a last resort, hoping to save her life. President Embuke received two months of transfusions with the nuclear isotope and toxin mixture. Although she was substantially breathing better in the first twenty-four hours following her transfusion, she was extremely sick for the next few weeks. She was not improving as Dr. Embuke had hoped."

"I remember seeing reports focusing on why no one had seen her in public in some time," David said.

Dr. Undulee continued, "The world was concerned there had been an assassination attempt."

"I also read several classified bulletins discussing the possibility of a coup attempt by poisoning," David said.

Dr. Undulee nodded. "But after the initial few weeks, she began to improve. Three years later now, President Embuke is alive, and her DBA has been cured. Her red blood cell counts are normal and remain so. Dr. Embuke's research worked."

"So why isn't this procedure known worldwide? At the very least, the cancer doctors would love to get hold of Dr. Embuke to have him continue his research and possibly cure cancer. He can't be far off from finding the cure."

"Let me ask you a question: do you think the pharmaceutical companies would react positively if they learned of his research? Do you think they would welcome him with open arms, knowing they would lose possibly trillions of dollars when no one needs their drugs anymore to treat the side effects of cancer?" Dr. Undulee let that thought sink in for a minute.

David *hadn't* thought about that. He was solely in "cure-April-mode."

"I guess that is very probable," David said as he stared at the floor.

"I believe my friend will help your daughter. If you give me your phone number and email, I will email this information to my friend. I am confident he will help you.

"As I am sure you have already guessed, his procedure is unknown to anyone except me and his family. And the cost of the transfusion will be substantial. Once Dr. Embuke left the government-regulated hospital that provided him with nuclear isotopes and other ingredients, Dr. Embuke had no choice but to arrange to buy all the transfusion components on the black market to save his sister."

David couldn't wait to answer. "Right now, I would like to get in touch with your friend and see where this goes. My daughter's health is my first concern. I'll figure out the payment part."

David and Dr. Undulee traded phone numbers, and David gave Dr. Undulee his email address as well. He thanked Dr. Undulee and left the conference room with a sense of purpose.

As the doors to the elevator opened, David's burner cell phone vibrated, indicating he had a text message. He flipped open the phone. The message was from Athan.

"How's the trip going? Any good news?"

David looked away from the text message and sighed. He thought about his reply to Athan. In the recess of his brain, an idea shot forth. He would later consider it the most life-changing decision he would ever make. He remembered his cook-out conversation with Athan the previous summer. And how they joked about trading Bureau technology for oil exploration and saving Athan's company. Could that be an option? Could David ask Athan for the money to help him? And would David go to jail for the rest of his life after he completed what many would consider traitorous behavior?

So many things to consider. David wasn't even sure how he could help Athan. First, he had to figure out how to bring up the conversation.

He texted Athan.

"Hey, bud. We just met with the doctors. We were given some pretty promising information. I may need a loan. Seriously. Can we chat when I get back?"

David hesitated for a moment. Actually, for almost a minute. In his mind, he saw his daughter's face. She was smiling. He then quickly saw her face in pain when she was lying on their bathroom floor and when she was at the hospital. She needed this miracle. Screw it. He hit "send."

David tried breathing again. He just needed to sit down and take it all in. And figure out how he would tell Trina.

If he would tell Trina.

Chapter 25

Working Out the Plan

August 11, 2012
7:00 a.m.
The Tracey residence
Miami, FL

Three short beeps coming from the kitchen indicated the coffee was brewed. It was 7 a.m. on Saturday. Tracey had already showered and toweled off. He grabbed a T-shirt and jeans from the bureau and quickly dressed. Trina was still in bed. She liked to get an extra hour of sleep at least one day on the weekend.

Tracey hoped his conversation with Trina the day before hadn't kept her up all night. He told Trina only enough of a story to let her know he was arranging a procedure for April that could cure her. There was no need to tell Trina everything. She would lose her mind. And he definitely couldn't tell her about the drone.

Tracey quietly opened and closed the bedroom door and headed down the hall to April's room. He peered into the open room. She was asleep. The room was eerily quiet. Thoughts swirled in his head. This was what it would sound like if April were not there. Lately, it seemed he was only a few seconds away from either yelling or crying.

April's health was declining. The folks at SCH were working on finding something to slow down the deterioration of her red blood cells. The reality, he knew, was April's time on earth was rapidly fading. He needed to arrange the surgery, and soon, before it was too late.

He walked away from her door and headed downstairs. After pouring himself some coffee, Tracey sat down at the desk in his office. He pulled open a drawer and selected one of the many "drop" phones - untraceable back to him - he stored there. It was time. He had to talk to Athan. He had devised what he thought was a pretty good plan, and now Athan had to hear it.

Part of his plan involved taking his InCit drone offline, but he still needed to be able to use the drone. Tracey was a little worried he couldn't pull off the disappearance of his InCit drone for the period he needed.

Tracey opened his Signal account on the drop phone and texted Athan. "Hey, can you chat? It's Tracey."

He took a sip of his coffee and waited for a reply. Before he could finish his sip, Athan replied.

"Yup. What number?"

Tracey texted back. "In person."

Athan immediately replied. "I'm home. Come on over."

Tracey grabbed another one of the drop phones. He checked to be sure it had a battery and a charging cord and stuck it in his pocket.

Tracey was a firm believer in drop phones. He would occasionally buy several drop phones at various little mom-and-pop stores. Drop phones, when activated, would be set up on a no-name network that didn't require a valid identity to set up.

Tracey liked using "Santa Claus" and famous people as a username to activate a drop phone. Tracey would only use each drop phone once, sometimes twice, if the scenario called for it, such as in a foreign country. The goal was to avoid creating a pattern with common users. Tracey was careful to buy the phones in a store while wearing a disguise - sunglasses, a wig, and usually a hat. Sometimes, he was an old man with a cane. On one occasion, he ventured down the aisles in the ladies' section wearing a very long dress so he wouldn't have to shave his legs, a wig, and sunglasses. He thought about wearing a bra with some "double Ds" standing at attention, but he figured that would be a stretch, figuratively, and he would stand out.

He chose the small stores since they had few or no security cameras that could reasonably catch a shot of his face. And he never bought drop phones from the same store twice or when he was on assignment, so no one could trace them back to his travels. Tracey made the phones *mostly* untraceable.

For good measure, and just in case he needed another drop phone or two for any reason, he grabbed two more drop phones from the drawer.

Tracey had one stop to make before heading to Athan's house. He was Savannah's ride that morning for drama club practice. He grabbed his coffee and headed back through the kitchen towards the stairway. Taking two stairs at a time, he reached Savannah's door and knocked softly. He could hear music playing. She opened the door with a toothbrush in her mouth.

"Your chauffeur is here, kiddo," Tracey said as Savannah pushed past him and into the bathroom. She gave a thumbs up.

"I'll be downstairs. You want something to eat before we go?"

Savannah spit and turned to Tracey.

"How about a bagel, egg, and cheese? But this time, Dad, skip the burnt part of the bagel." Savannah smiled. Tracey gave her a thumbs up and headed to the kitchen.

While Savannah finished getting ready for practice, Tracey prepared her breakfast without burning the bagel and set it down with a glass of her favorite juice, grapefruit. It wasn't Tracey's favorite, though. He sat at the counter and waited for Savannah while he thumbed through his BuPhone and read the world news.

After five minutes, Savannah appeared with her book bag, wearing shorts and a "Macbeth the Musical" tee shirt. Tracey and Trina had taken Savannah to see the play the previous year. They managed to sneak out before the end of the play and buy the shirt for her as a Christmas present.

"Mom tells me you're up for the lead of Mame Dennis in *Mame*," Tracey said.

"Yeah, I'm not sure I like the music I have to sing, though. It's like oldies or something."

"That musical was created in the 60s, kiddo." Tracey laughed. "You probably won't get any Kelly Clarkson songs to sing."

"Yeah, I guess not. I hit the notes okay. The tunes are just different, but I do like the play."

"You are the best singer at your school, so I expect they wouldn't hesitate to give you the lead role."

"That would be nice," Savannah said as she gulped down her grapefruit juice and grabbed her bagel sandwich.

"Let's go, Dad. I can eat on the way." Savannah slung her book bag over her shoulder and started for the front door. Tracey got up and followed her, taking his keys and his drop phones.

"Right behind you."

✦✦✦

Twenty minutes later, Tracey walked into the Kratos home. He slowly began the conversation with Athan.

"So, I have conducted quite a bit of research since we returned from Seattle following April's last doctor's visit. I've been concentrating on learning as much about the bombshell of a miracle that exists for April. Bear with me."

Athan didn't move in his chair. He sipped his coffee, listening intently to a story that might require alcohol early in the morning.

"The gist of it is this. You know, the doctors at SCH informed us that April's red blood count is spiraling downward. There's nothing the doctors at SCH, or any other doctors in this country, can do for her."

Athan may have only been on his first cup of coffee, but he was awake enough that his eyes flew open when Tracey said, "Doctors in this country."

"When we were leaving the meeting with April's oncologists, one of the doctors, who had not said a word during the meeting, grabbed my arm. He startled me. What he had to say was about to change our lives.

"The doctor brought me back into the conference room. It was just the two of us. He told me he believed there may be a cure for April. He told us about his close friend from medical school, a research doctor, who spent countless hours researching the same disease April has. He wanted to cure his sister, who also had the disease. And he found a cure, albeit in the lab. The vaccine, administered as a transfusion of her blood, had never been used on a human being. A lot of risks were associated with his sister being injected.

"She was dying, though, so she just went for it, and within twenty-four hours, she was on her way to being cured."

Athan took another sip of his coffee. Tracey had his full attention.

"This doctor who found the cure for DBA lives overseas. His credentials are impeccable. He's not someone I have to think twice about whether or not he can help April."

"Does the U.S. government know about him?" Athan asked.

"No, they don't. And neither will you or where he's located. That will be the simple story you will give should I ever get caught with what I am about to suggest we do."

"Okay, it sounds like you've been working on some scenarios. Let's have it."

Tracey laid out the plan. A plan he developed with Dr. Embuke. He told Athan enough of what he would need to know to consider the plan. That plan included traveling to a small country halfway around the world. The total cost included an anonymous donation to the SCH as a research fee of two million dollars. The doctor who would perform April's procedure requested it. The remaining costs are for medicine, flights, and possible bribes. And the total: three million dollars.

"I know it's a lot of money, and this might be too much to ask for. I'll explain in a minute what I can do in return to help your company's financial situation."

Tracey finally paused, wanting to hear what Athan had to say.

"What do you think so far?" Tracey hesitantly asked.

The sunlight was trying to pierce through the blinds in Athan's home office. Athan sat back in his chair. He said nothing. He rocked a little bit, then reached back to the desk and took his coffee cup, blew a little bit on the contents, simply for effect as the coffee was far from being very hot anymore, and took a slow sip. He continued to rock in his chair with the coffee cup in his hand. Athan remained silent. Thinking.

Athan swung around to his desk and put his coffee down before he spoke to Tracey.

"Three million, huh? If you're asking me if I can get my hands on that much cash without alerting folks at the company, I can do it. Our research and development budget is 20 times that amount. I'll take it from there and come up with an explanation. I know this is to help April, obviously, but what would the FBI be able to do to help my company?"

Tracey moved back a little in his chair. He had just realized with all his excitement he had inched his butt to the front of the chair. He must have looked like a dog with rabies the way he was talking to Athan. Tracey was so frantic he probably even spit on Athan without noticing.

"Let me explain the thousand-yard view of a program I'm part of that can help you with your polar ice cap issue. I have a plan for the oil fields you own the leasing rights to under the ice cap, which could save your company. And no one would be the wiser as to how the oil fields "all of a sudden" became accessible to you."

"The Bureau will let you use this technology for a consumer project?" Athan asked with a confused expression on his face. He chuckled softly.

"Not exactly. I'd be risking quite a bit. At the very least, my job would be at stake. Possibly my freedom for the rest of my life if the Bureau doesn't believe me," Tracey said, looking down slightly.

"No way," Athan said as soon as the last words came out of Tracey's mouth, and he sat back in his chair.

"There is no way you can risk that much. I won't be a part of that."

Tracey shifted forward again in his chair. He had an equally quick response.

"Is your daughter dying, Athan? We both know that answer. And I have never been so sure of anything. This plan will work, and it requires very little from you. Also, the Bureau won't be coming after you. You won't have to worry about lying to the Bureau about anything. You're simply loaning money to a friend and not sure how you'll be repaid. That's your story."

"When it's all over, the Bureau will never know we worked together to accomplish what we both needed to do. I'm all in. I need you to be all in and completely on board. What do you say? And if you don't think my plan is viable, I'll scrap it and find another way."

Athan sighed heavily and then took another sip of his coffee. He almost spit it out as it was less than lukewarm. He moved forward and placed his coffee cup back down on the desk. After a pause from Athan that seemed like an hour but was only ten seconds, Tracey had his answer.

"Ok, let's do this. What's the plan you're risking your life for?"

Chapter 26
The Only Way Out

Tracey wasn't delusional by any stretch of the word. He knew the path he was going down in lending his drone to Kratos Oil & Shale Company could lead to an unhappy ending for him. He had been entrusted as one of only a handful of FBI Agents to be part of the Eyes Only program and even a smaller number of agents selected to guard those secrets. And he was about to tell someone outside of the FBI about a program that could produce invisible objects.

Tracey consoled himself with the fact Athan didn't know stomonite was the mineral that powered the drone, so in a way, the InCit program was still a secret. The technology, anyway. Tracey wasn't about to give that up. Not to anyone. He didn't need to. The drone just had to work as Tracey said it would.

For the next eight hours, Tracey laid out the plan for Athan. They discussed how the drone pilot program worked and how it could burrow down through the ice in the polar ice cap fields at a depth that could force the ice to break apart and thus allow for oil exploration. Environmentalists and legislators would never know it was a man-made device that caused a small explosion and would be led to believe it was Mother Nature. The Kratos Oil & Shale Company should then be able to press on and move forward with drilling. The environmental concerns would be minimal or much more manageable.

To fly the drone, Tracey would have to give Athan access to the drone's remote program. It would be limited, restricted access. Athan would be given certain commands to fly the drone to exact coordinates and perform these specific tasks. That was it. And the drone would fly to the ice cap unseen by anyone. Attached to the drone would be a small, powerful drill and one of the Kratos drill bits. Once the weather conditions become optimal, the drone will use the drill and burrow down to a certain depth. The drone would then release the package of explosives, exit the hole, and, once clear, they would be detonated. Immediately following the discharge, the drone would be recalled back to Miami. As far as the world would know, it would appear to be a naturally occurring break in the ice caused by, let's say, global warming.

He gave Athan a drop phone and explained how the phone was not assigned to anyone. It was untraceable so long as Athan followed Tracey's outline for using VPNs and other dark web browsers.

After thanking his friend, Tracey left around 4 p.m. and headed home. He was feeling confident about his plan and getting his daughter the medical attention she needed to live.

Although Tracey was fond of saying, "a true secret was best kept among one person, not two," he found himself in direct contradiction with that. Tracey was now in no-man's land. He couldn't necessarily turn back. He needed the financial payout from Athan. And his InCit drone would deliver him the financial answer he needed to save his daughter's life.

Athan wanted to save his company and, thus, his family's livelihood. Kratos Oil & Shale was the world leader in oil exploration, and that reputation pushed Athan mercilessly to do one thing. Maintain that reputation and solvency.

Tracey and Athan had similar needs, but different for sure.

Their plan now had a starting point, What they both didn't know, however, was another player was about to enter their game. That player wasn't looking to save a child's life or a company's bottom line. That player wanted the power that came with riches. No cost was too great to achieve such a goal. A little revenge wouldn't hurt either.

Tracey would be thoroughly caught off-guard.

Chapter 27
Jafaire, Africa

Tucked away on the easternmost side of the African continent is the small country of the Democratic Republic of Jafaire. It is roughly the size of the state of Connecticut. Containing just about 6,000 square miles, Jafaire is the smallest country in continental Africa.

Jafaire has a short history. It was formed from the conclusions reached during a United Nations think-tank group studying world peace. In 2009, portions of land from three large countries caught up in a twenty-plus-year civil war were annexed to create Jafaire. The U.N. sought to create a country that would be a haven between the warring countries. And Jafairians would only consist of refugees from those three war-ravaged countries.

The eastern border of Jafaire runs completely along the Somali Sea. With the Boriman Mountain Range encircling the remainder of the country, Jafaire appears like an almost completely circular land mass from the sky. Some say it looks like a pumpkin pie from satellite imagery due to the entirety of the land's orange-brown, swirl-like composition surrounded by crust-like mountains. The color of the land is due to the dry environment.

The U.N. oversaw a mostly civil exodus of people from the three warring countries. Approximately six million refugees flooded into Jafaire when it was created. All the world powers assisted in some way, shape, or form. Whether it was for the construction of housing and schools, food supplies, electronics, etc., the world came together to put Jafaire on the map and hopefully survive. Tent cities were formed initially while housing was being built. The people struggled in the first few months, but it was an improvement over where they had come from.

There was one glaring concern Jafaire encountered as it tried to sustain itself into the future - there weren't many options for creating a gross domestic product. It is surrounded by mountains that demographically protect it from potential adversaries and the theft of its only produced export - semi-precious metals found inside its border at the bottom of the mountain range. And as it turned out, Jafaire was sitting on the largest chromium deposit in Africa. These semi-precious metals, mostly consisting of chromium and iron ore, initially provided 100% of Jafaire's gross domestic product. That deposit could sustain Jafairians for generations to come. However, extracting the ore was time-consuming and costly. The Jafairians needed a more readily available export.

Despite the concern for additional exports, the most pressing need for Jafaire was a sustained water source. Living conditions depended on it. Producing crops demanded it. But the current climate conditions made it impossible. Jafaire received very little rainfall, and the mountain range wasn't high enough to produce enough water to support the citizens or grow crops. The land was hardscrabble and desert-like.

To help out, the U.N. council awarded drilling contracts to several water engineering companies. It was apparent, however, that after several months of tearing up the land, there wasn't enough water to adequately supply the population of Jafaire.

The U.N. then developed a new plan and built a desalination water system that tapped into the Somali Sea. The water system proved to be highly successful. Jafaire solved their water problem with a method that was not only energy-efficient but also environmentally sustainable.

The abundant water supply also provided a product for export to similarly water-deficient African countries. The income generated by the water export helped Jafaire create infrastructure programs, sewer systems and plants, affordable housing, and other first-world developments.

Over the next few years, Jafaire thrived. The country started to show signs of a developing society, with supermarkets, clothing stores, and schools. Two large world banks opened in Jafaire - French bank BNP Paribas and Bank of America. The two largest banks in the world, both Chinese, wanted to establish bank centers in Jafaire. The U.N., however, voted not to allow them a bank license simply because they were fearful China would try to take over the country.

That seemed like a reasonable assumption.

Chapter 28
Destiny's Child

After a year and several months of organizing land rights and setting country boundaries, the U.N. oversaw Jafaire's first presidential election with ballot monitors and peacekeepers. Six candidates were running for president. The U.N. considered these candidates to be the best choices to rule Jafaire.

The election ran smoothly. Given the media outlets ran negative stories about whether there could be a valid election running up to the day of the election, it was a breath of fresh air to see just how smooth the election turned out. The ballot totals were just under 98% of the registered voter population. It was a record for voter turnout. In any country. Ever.

Ms. Chisomo Embuke was overwhelmingly elected as the first President of Jafaire in June of 2009, with nearly 78% of the vote. Chisomo translates to "grace."

President Embuke was born in Vista Porto in the 1950s before it became one of the warring countries next to Jafaire. Her father, Amari Embuke, was an oil executive for Exxon. He gave time and money to Vista Porto. His philanthropy was unmatched by anyone, including the country's ruling class. His immense salary covered more than his family needed to survive and prosper. So, he gave half of his salary to build schools and a solid infrastructure of roads. The Embuke family was revered. But they were humble and remained out of the public eye.

Because her family was part of the upper class, President Embuke grew up in Vista Porto with a somewhat sheltered life. She was driven to school, socialized with wealthy friends, and only played on sports teams from the private schools.

Known to her friends as Chiz, Chisomo Embuke was stressed out, however. She wanted to attend school with girls she met while playing soccer and tennis at the local park. She was down-to-earth and believed in picking up trash when she saw it and giving spare change to anyone holding their hand out. She was pure of heart. She "hated being gated," was her common mantra. Her parents explained she was a kidnapping target, and they had to be security conscious. That is why she lived with so many security protocols. Her driver was armed, and he was her protection. But, again, she "hated being gated."

Chisomo learned to love Vista Porto for the natural beauty it contained. Vast plains of dry earth were home to some of the most beautiful animals in the world. She went on school safaris not to gaze and gawk at the wildlife but to serve as an ambassador to protect them and help them thrive without interfering in their natural habitat.

She created a recovery habitat for the black rhino, an animal hunted almost to extinction. Out on the plains and backed by corporate donations, other animal hospitals and recovery centers were built because of her. For her efforts, when she was a junior in high school, she was selected as a top ten "Young African Difference Maker."

She was destiny's child.

Chapter 29
The Miracle Worker

President Embuke's father knew some pretty powerful and exceptional people. Several of the COOs of the banks and corporations in Jafaire were his classmates at Yale. He golfed with athletes from many professional sports and sat on several distinguished company boards of directors.

One of his closest friends was a hematopathologist, Dr. Kagiso Ajugo. Dr. Ajugo had lived in Vista Porto for most of his life. His parents moved to Vista Porto from Nigeria when they were children. His father was also a doctor, and he was highly respected.

The Ajugo family moved to Vista Porto to help the poorest of the poor in a war-ravaged country. They lived a simple life, ate simple meals, and attended local schools. They blended in with society. As was the norm, however, in a country constantly in a state of upheaval, frequent bombings and skirmishes killed many civilians. And Kagiso Ajugo knew this first-hand. One afternoon, when Kagiso was eleven years old, his father and sister were killed when an errant grenade exploded in the marketplace in Vista Porto. His sister was nine. His father was 40.

Years later, Dr. Ajugo, his mother, and his two brothers continued to live in Vista Porto despite the weakened economy and constant fighting. Like his father, Dr. Ajugo provided health care for the country's poor. It was a noble role to play in society. Dr. Ajugo supplemented the paltry pay he received from the warlords by dedicating his studies to curing diseases related to bone marrow.

As a family friend, President Embuke's brother, Henry, would talk at length with Dr. Ajugo about medical school. He was Henry's inspiration when he left for the U.S. to study. After seven years at Duke University Medical School, Henry graduated as a hematopathologist in the top five of his class.

Once Henry graduated from Duke, he contacted Dr. Ajugo and inquired about working with him in Vista Porto. Henry wanted to go home to help those in need as Dr. Ajugo had done. Dr. Ajugo was happy to have Henry work with him. He had long hoped to set up a clinic in Jafaire and asked Henry if he would open it for him. Henry gladly accepted.

Henry took on this task in earnest. He worked out leases and arranged the delivery of equipment. He hired staff and opened the satellite clinic approximately eight months after coming home to Jafaire.

✢✢✢

June 11, 2012
Dr. Henry Embuke's clinic
Lingos, Jafaire

Dr. Embuke and Dr. Ajugo would hold early morning video meetings once a week to review patient charts and discuss updates in the world of bone marrow research. One project Henry never discussed, however, was the research project he had developed while in medical school. Only five people knew of the results of Henry's research project - Henry, President Embuke, his father, his mother, and Henry's closest friend in medical school, Dr. Sefu Undulee. Dr. Undulee was sworn to secrecy. He told no one. That was until he met Tracey.

Henry arrived at work every day just as the sun was rising. He liked the deserted streets as he drove. He would park down the street from his clinic so patients who needed easier access could park in front. After opening the doors, he would come back outside with a handmade sign that read "Wheelchair Parking Only." He placed it on an orange cone out front in the road.

Henry turned the lights on and made for his desk in the back, as he did each day. He switched on his computer and then headed for the coffee pot. While he waited for the computer to come alive, he added several scoops of Sumatra coffee to the wire filter basket and placed it back in the pot. He grabbed a bottle of Jafairian filtered water and poured it into the coffee reservoir. He hit "brew" and returned to his desk.

He sat down just as the screen lit up, asking for his password. He placed his middle finger over the fingerprint scan, and the computer seamlessly unlocked. Clicking over to the internet, he brought up his email and stood up to get a cup of coffee. Before he could look away, he noticed one particular email subject line all in caps. It was marked "URGENT - MUST READ NOW!" and was from his friend in the U.S., Dr. Sefu Undulee.

Henry sat back down. The coffee would have to wait.

Clicking on the email, Henry started to read, stopped, and started again. He wasn't sure he was correctly reading what his friend had emailed.

"Henry ... hello, my friend. Sorry, I haven't written in a while," the email began.

"I start to write or call, and then life happens. I know you understand. Hopefully, you are enjoying your successes and your family.

"I needed to let you know sooner than later about a conversation I had last week with the father of a dying girl. I know what you're thinking right now before you even read further. But remember, we are doctors with a duty to help those in need.

"I sat in on a meeting with a family whose daughter is stricken with DBA. Advanced DBA. So advanced that her stem cell transplant recently failed. New mutations we can't explain shut down her immune system again. Her red blood cells are attacked by mutated cells, unlike cancer cells. They don't completely overproduce the red blood cells as the cancer does but only attach to them, drawing out all the oxygen. She is at 70% capacity and losing about 1% capacity every other day. Prognosis: she only has about four months to live. Does this mutation sound familiar to you?

"I know we both were sworn to secrecy regarding your research. And I have kept my word on that - until now. I was overwhelmed by the plight of this young girl. I told them about you. But I haven't given them your contact information. It is up to you now.

"Please consider them and their daughter. If you decide to help, call or email the father. His contact information is below. He is anxiously waiting for a reply from you. I will also tell you - he is an FBI Agent. He can keep this secret. I feel that in my heart.

"I miss my friend, my brother for life. Be safe. Peace. S"

Henry sat back, competing thoughts racing through his head. Anger. Fear. Hope. He hadn't heard from his fellow resident partner in over a year. Sefu was busy at SCH, and he was glad for him. Sefu was a smart guy and a good doctor. And an outright stellar human being. Henry didn't have to wonder why Sefu would give up his secret research.

Henry couldn't wrap his brain around the thought of using his research to help someone outside his family. Everyone knew why the success of his research was sworn to secrecy, to keep it hidden from the world. Once that veil was lifted and the world learned Dr. Embuke was close to curing cancer, death threats, blackmail schemes, and even possible kidnapping attempts would certainly occur, targeting Dr. Embuke and his family. And there was the fact that the Jafairian President hid her illness. How would the Jafairian citizens react to that? Impeachment? She was elected as a "healthy" president. Would they have voted for her if they had known she was sick? These were too many questions for Henry to handle all at once.

This cure for DBA, so far 100% effective, could change the world. And the possibility it could cure cancer was imminently promising. Jafaire would become a destination, an oasis, for people to be saved. That was Henry's logic. But the dark side of human nature always lurked in the background. Someone would misbehave and become financially motivated. Henry firmly believed that. And any potential cure would be held hostage, ransomed to the highest bidder.

However, the new anomaly with April's red blood cells now had his full attention. Had he missed something in his DBA research that could someday affect his sister's cured DBA further down the road? Oh, God, that would be terrible.

Henry's head hurt. He sat back. Then he started typing.

The coffee pot had beeped long ago.

His coffee was ready.

Chapter 30
The Enemy Within

July 2010
Jafaire, Africa

President Embuke's most daunting task was prioritizing the most urgent needs of her fledgling country. She wanted to be sure there were schools and a healthy economy for all citizens. She created a cabinet of advisors, much like the U.S., and held weekly meetings to address the needs of the citizens. And a little luck never hurt.

A year after President Embuke was sworn in, she received a frantic call from the Australian water company that was adding additional piping to the desalination plant. While they were bulldozing a swath of land to lay a stretch of pipes, the bulldozer "nicked" what appeared to be an oil deposit.

Within two hours, the well was capped, and Jafaire now had another product they could export. Yet this newfound wealth would come with enormous threats, especially from the warring nations surrounding Jafaire, which now knew there was oil in Jafaire. There would be plans to steal the oil. And all that Jafaire had earned in its short history could be wiped out. President Embuke needed to figure out how she would protect their new resource.

There was no requirement from the U.N. to immediately set up a national defense in Jafaire when it was formed. But President Embuke was working on it. For starters, Jafaire received military hardware from the world powers. The Jafairian Army and Navy built four small military bases and controlled the border by creating outposts and checkpoints. Jafaire could adequately defend itself.

To lead her military and serve as Jafaire's Defense Minister, President Embuke appointed a four-star general who had retired from the Vista Porto Army several years prior, General Dule Repuso.

General Repuso was the oldest of three brothers. His youngest brother, Salan Repuso, became a doctor. Dr. Repuso was an idealist. He believed in supporting the less privileged by redistributing wealth in proportionate amounts depending on the size of each family. He wasn't sold on capitalism and thought the underprivileged always suffered. After graduating from college in East Africa, Dr. Repuso received funding from worldwide medical sponsors. He used the money to travel to the poorest of the poor in Africa, providing free health care where he could. After several years of traveling thousands of miles on his continent, Dr. Repuso joined the group of doctors called Doctors Without Politics or DWP. DWP was created to physically heal people.

General Repuso's middle brother, Destal Repuso, grew up as a shepherd. He loved sheep and brought them home safely every day. He remained in Vista Porto following his graduation from high school and, ironically, took a job at the local butcher shop, helping to cut up and deliver meat products.

Because the Repusos were all born in the bordering country of Vista Porto, they were all eligible to become Jafairians. General Repuso and Destal Repuso jumped at the chance. They renounced their citizenship in Vista Porto and were two of the first hundred thousand citizens of Jafaire. Dr. Salan Repuso did not eagerly assume the same chance for a new beginning. He continued to travel the world, helping the less fortunate.

General Repuso was aggressive in his approach to defending Jafaire. He instructed his subordinates to create a leadership course for all soldiers. The soldiers didn't need to pass the course, but they would understand how superior officers made decisions. He believed that would lead to less distrust of the officer ranks. Although many junior and inexperienced officers were accidentally killed from lack of experience during training, General Repuso wanted to continue the program. The president didn't hold the program in as high esteem, canceling it after six months.

General Repuso was also harsh when doling out punishment. Soldiers were lashed. Food was withheld. He ran the military like a dictatorship, not what President Embuke envisioned. His tactics were so aggressive that President Embuke canceled all but a few of his programs. She then scheduled weekly meetings to go over the military. She reigned him in. Somewhat.

She unknowingly created an enemy within.

Chapter 31
Clean Up on Aisle 3

September 8, 2012
7:15 a.m. MST
Portal 17

Bell pushed open the front door and was met by Fallon. She wasn't whimpering anymore. Bell patted her head as she continued to lay on the front porch.

Stepping off the porch, he walked over to the Malibu and grabbed the keys from the ignition. He hoped this BuCar was stocked with crime scene supplies similar to how he stocked his own BuCar. Bell headed to the back of the car and opened the trunk. Bingo. He found an evidence kit with disposable gloves and masks.

He grabbed three pairs of latex gloves and a mask and closed the trunk. He would always take three pairs of gloves into any crime scene - one for him, a second in case the first pair got ripped or got so full of whatever it had to be changed out, and one for the rookie agent who forgot a pair.

Bell closed the trunk and headed back to the house, fixing his mask in place while he walked. He adjusted his fingers inside the bright blue latex gloves and walked to the kitchen and the man lying on the floor.

The man was on his side. Blood had pooled on the left side of his face, which had been closest to the ground. Blood always pools to the lowest point, leading to the condition of hypostasis the man was now in. There was a bullet hole in the back of his head. The exit wound was just in front of his right eye. Bell turned the man over. He also had two bullet wounds in his chest. This was an execution, as the two chest wounds would have done the job.

Bell leaned over the man and grabbed his wrist. The skin was pale and loose. It was starting to separate from the bones in his wrist. Nice combo. Given his state of decomposition, Bell guessed the man had been dead for several days. And he was casting a smell that would lead an amateur to puke within seconds.

Bell first clicked through several options on the navigator and made his way to its finger scan component. A screen with different choices of fingers lit up on the screen. Bell now realized the man's hand served simply as a bag, a repository for the bones that used to form his hand. It appeared part of the ulna arm bone had slid down as well.

Bell grabbed the man's wrist and brought the navigator down to the man's thumb. Squeezing the man's thumb, Bell felt the bone inside shift completely into the man's wrist. It felt like squeezing a tomato without it squirting all over the place. If he was a sentry, all the man's fingerprints would be in the system. Bell reached more carefully for the distal phalange where the man's index finger should be.

As the bones tried to separate, Bell was ready and kept several bones in the tip of the man's finger. Unsure which phalanges he had managed to grab, Bell held fast and pressed what used to be the man's index finger against the navigator's glass. The machine read the fingerprint, whirred, and finished.

Almost immediately following the fingerprint scan, a short chime indicated the results were being sent. The screen then flashed a small picture of a man in his late 60s, and next to it, his name, Travis Keith, Sentry, Portal 17. It was tough to make an ID by simply looking at the man's face. There was, however, a small mole with a single hair protruding from the man's face in the picture on the navigator. Bell turned the man over slightly, and the mole was found in the same spot as the picture of the sentry's decomposing face.

Bell stood up and took off his latex gloves.

He felt confident the dead man in the kitchen was Mr. Keith, portal 17's sentry.

But how'd he end up dead on the kitchen floor?

✢✢✢

Bell stepped over Keith's body. He learned in his short InCit briefing that the access point for entry into a portal's lower-level command center was almost always in the kitchen. It would be hidden in plain view. Behind a switch plate. Under a set of dishes. As an on/off switch in the laundry room. Something big enough to hold a Hirsch pad and scanner.

After several minutes, Bell located the Hirsch Pad. It was next to the refrigerator and disguised as an electric can opener. He turned the can opener around and snapped off the back panel. After typing in his security code, he pushed "Enter." The eye scanner under the Hirsch Pad slid forward and upward to receive Bell's eye. A quick light flashed. The machine whirred and blinked green. Bingo.

The countertop next to the refrigerator began to fold in and then up against the wall. The refrigerator slid three feet to the right, exposing an elevator behind it. Bell entered the elevator.

The door closed, and Bell almost immediately started to descend. He unholstered his Glock again and took a position behind the right panel of the door so he could shoot if he had to with his left hand. He needed to be ready if the portal command center had been compromised. After a seven-second descent, the elevator stopped, and the door opened.

Bell peered quickly into the brightly lit room. After several quick peeks, he glimpsed a small filing cabinet he could use for concealment. He hunched over, quickly exited the elevator, and took about eight steps to the cabinet. He saw no movement as he made his way there. Raising his Glock to his chest, he backed up enough to lead with his Glock about ten inches in front of him, just enough to peer over his gun sights.

In front of him was a large conference table with about ten chairs around it. Multiple screens hung on the walls with green dots. Bell knew the dots to represent the location of all the InCit agents. He scanned the command center again. No movement.

Grabbing a chair near the back wall, he sat down with a vantage point to see anyone who might try to enter from the elevator. It would give him a better chance to defend his position.

Bell sat still, looking at the board on the wall with all the lights. He didn't bother counting all the lights to see if they amounted to the 83 IAs. 82 at this point. He trusted the board. He had bigger issues.

He moved closer to the table. A keyboard sat in front of each chair, but there were no computer screens. He grabbed a keyboard and pushed the "Enter" key. Immediately, a computer screen slid upward.

Bell grabbed the mouse and logged into the computer. Only a few desktop icons were available for him to choose from. They were labeled "Portal 17 Access," "Portal 17 Cameras," "IA Triangulation," "Sentinel Notes," "HQ Command Center," and "Active Ops."

Bell knew he had to figure out what had happened at this portal, which the computer desktop also confirmed was number 17. The cameras should give him some idea. He double-clicked on the folder "Portal 17 Cameras."

The folder opened to reveal almost a dozen more folders, all identifying camera locations in and around the portal. Bell started with a camera identifying movement from the furthest distance to the portal. He located several folders he believed would be helpful: "Street View," "Driveway," and "Rear."

Inside those folders were videos from each day, in 240-minute increments - four hours for each video. There had to be a way to search for what would most help him. Bell navigated back to the desktop and double-clicked on "Portal 17 Access." He right-clicked on the top of the folder to find 1,100-plus videos dating back three months.

A search option in the top right corner allowed Bell to search for a specific category based on movement, time of day, Hirsch Pad entry to the portal command center, etc. Bell typed in a date range going back seven days from and including the current date and time. He had several filter options to narrow down his search to view just what he wanted to see. He checked the boxes for "Movement Outside" and "Sentinel Contact." He figured he didn't need to see all the other videos of Fallon stretching or peeing in the yard.

A more manageable list of seventy-three videos popped up in his search. It was still going to be arduous. As each video was four hours long, changing the playback speed to three times faster than normal would speed it up quite a bit.

Bell didn't have much time, and he had to know what happened at portal 17. So, he dug in and opened the first video from seven days before.

Chapter 32
No Turning Back

September 4, 2012
6:30 p.m. EST
Kratos Oil & Shale Company, Corporate Headquarters
Miami, FL

Tracey landed and made his way to the Kratos Oil & Shale headquarters. The Bureau certainly had no idea he was working with Athan, so the meeting with Athan went undetected. Tracey now had to get the drone moving to the polar ice cap.

For fear of collateral damage, Tracey programmed an avoidance code into the drone, a non-collateral damage code. Any object that came close enough to threaten the drone - within 300 yards - would be avoided. Side-stepped. Tracey wanted to be sure the drone would not hurt anything on its way to the target. It would maneuver away from potential threats, such as airplanes.

The only sound made by the drone amounted to a soft hum. And you had to be fairly close to the drone to question whether or not you heard that. Otherwise, the drone flew steadily at 145 miles per hour, undetected. The drone clipped along, maintaining an altitude of 14,000 feet to accommodate landscape changes. It flew straight across the ocean.

The drone was capable of flying at 185 miles per hour. But attaching both the extra battery to keep the drone charged for another sixty hours and the drill mechanism added weight and reduced the drone's speed. The drone had to travel over fifty-four hours to complete the trip to the Norwegian polar ice cap. Once it landed, it would be placed in low battery mode. The drill would be ditched over the ocean when the mission was complete, and hopefully, the extra battery would get it home.

Athan and Tracey - mostly Athan - monitored the drone's flight. In addition to the drill mechanism, the detonation package was attached to the drone. It was clipped in place by a remotely operated steel clasp. Athan would control the remote activation to release and detonate the package when necessary.

When creating the explosive charge, Athan configured it so no remnants would remain once it detonated. No reference to anything man-made having created the explosion would be found within the polar ice cap. The ice would melt, and any detonator or remnants would wash away into the ocean. Athan was used to these detonation packages since he'd used them to cap oil wells. Most importantly, it would appear like the explosion occurred naturally.

Tracey sat still in a chair across from Athan, who was sitting at his desk. He said nothing. Tracey was so caught up in this operation with Athan that he hadn't stopped to think about how close the Bureau was to finding him. They certainly had realized they couldn't track him anymore. Hopefully, the Bureau was under the impression that Tracey had been kidnapped and taken hostage and was planning a rescue mission. And his drone had been compromised by bad operators and not Tracey.

He decided to check the security system at the house in Trellis and see if the Bureau had been there yet.

He grabbed the drop phone he had given Athan off Athan's desk and flipped it open. He would leave this phone with Athan so they could stay in touch. For the hundredth time, he made sure his location was turned off. He clicked on the VPN and logged onto the command room's wireless router. Using The Onion Router, he headed into the Dark Web. His location would be shown to the world as Rio De Janeiro. He then opened the application for his security system.

Before he could turn on any camera at the house to check a live status, he received several notifications that the cameras had picked up movement yesterday after he went offline to the world.

One notification came from the camera fixed to his front door aimed at a forty-five-degree angle off the door into the front yard. He clicked on the video attached to the notification. It showed two deer walking through the yard.

The only other notifications came from a camera hidden in a birdhouse Tracey had constructed for a family of downy woodpeckers, camouflaged and attached to look like a door. This birdhouse camera was fifty yards from his front door, aimed above Tracey's house, and positioned to detect motion only at the second-story bedrooms.

He clicked the videos and watched as more than a dozen birds flew past the bedroom windows.

The Bureau would figure out Tracey wasn't in Trellis. As he started to turn the notifications for the security system off, Athan interrupted his train of thought.

"Hey, you alive over there?!" Athan yelled to Tracey.

Startled, Tracey jumped a little and looked up from his phone. He smirked.

"Yeah, just checking the cameras at my lake property to see if I've had any visitors," Tracey answered.

"And?" Athan asked.

"Just the deer. We're still good."

He closed the phone and placed it back on the desk, forgetting to turn off the security system notifications that would continue to be forwarded to the phone.

"The good news is no precipitation is forecast on the weather radar for the next thirty-six hours. Once the drone lands, we'll only need seven hours until it's dark, and I can trigger the charge. So, we're looking at forty-three hours to blast off, if you will."

"Okay, great," Tracey said.

"Have you heard anything more from the research doctor?" Athan asked.

"I did receive an email through the account I created to set up the surgery. April's doctor sent an email that he was traveling home this week, and he verified he received an email from Dr. Undulee about your donation. That anonymous donation to SCH from your offshore bank account will clear tomorrow. He also sent me the coordinates for his clinic where April's procedure will be done."

"It will work, my friend," Athan said confidently. Tracey shook his head very slowly. He wanted to believe it.

Tracey leaned back in the chair. He'd remain at Athan's corporate office for several days before executing the next part of his plan at ERF.

Chapter 33
Nice to Meet You Doc

September 7, 2012
11:45 a.m. (UTC +2.00)
Jafaire, Africa

The Boeing 777 exited the clouds without a bump and descended to the Jafaire International Airport. The plane banked smoothly to the left and evened out its flight path to prepare for landing. After touching down, it taxied for a few minutes before coming to rest.

It was 11:45 a.m. Jafaire time. Tracey was now six hours ahead of Miami and Washington, D.C. If the Bureau had since figured out how they were traveling to Jafaire from Reagan National Airport in D.C., then the gig was probably up. The authorities would be waiting for them at the gate when they deplaned.

Tracey stood up and let the last passengers go before he moved into the aisle. He grabbed both the backpacks as April pushed herself up by the armrests and leaned into the aisle. Tracey reached for her, and she slapped his hand.

"Oh, there'll be time for your help, for sure. But right now, I want to feel like I can at least do something physical on my own," April said to Tracey without looking at him. She started down the aisle, and Tracey smiled to himself. Tracey realized they both had no idea what was in store for them.

After walking the jetway, April and Tracey emerged at Gate 4. Almost immediately upon exiting the jetway, two men approached them, one pushing a wheelchair. *April is going to love this,* Tracey thought.

"Mr. Tracey?" one of the men asked.

"Yes, hello. I'm Mr. Tracey, and this is my daughter, April."

"Very nice to meet you, and welcome to Jafaire. We have arranged a wheelchair for Miss April. It will look more normal than if we only greeted you here. Please."

The man pointed to the wheelchair and motioned for April to sit. April didn't fight it and sat down in the wheelchair. The men turned and started to head away from the gate.

So far, so good. They were there to help them. The Bureau hadn't located Tracey yet.

Upon arriving at the customs exit, Tracey handed their passports to the man and waited with April. They passed through customs without any trouble.

Next, they made their way outside, where a black van was waiting. The van had the sidestep lowered by the curb, ready to accept the wheelchair. The man wheeled April onto the sidestep facing forward and strapped her into a seat belt. The driver locked the doors, and off they went. The two men from the gate remained behind and continued their duties.

Tracey settled into the seat next to April. He stared ahead and sized up their driver. He was a young black male with a medium build, wearing a T-shirt and a NY Yankees baseball hat. Good Lord, Tracey thought. Did he have to see a Yankees hat after traveling halfway around the world? How about a Florida Marlins hat? Would that be too much to ask?

"Yankees, huh?" Tracey blurted out.

The driver looked back at Tracey and smiled.

"Yes, very, very good team. They are America's team, yes?!"

Tracey didn't have the heart to debate him. He quickly twisted his head and lips with an indifferent "Sure.".

The driver continued to beam a big, broad Eddie Murphy *Coming to America* smile.

"My name is Amir. If you need anything, please ask. I can stop anywhere you like along the way."

"Thank you, Amir. We'll let you know. We're just ready to get to the clinic to start the procedure," Tracey said.

Tracey looked at April, who had her eyes closed. She nodded in agreement.

As Amir made his way out of the airport, the busy roads turned into a single-lane highway with street lights dotting the side of the road every tenth of a mile. Tracey stared ahead and could see mountains in every direction. The satellite image of land surrounded by mountains on three sides and the water on the fourth side immediately came to Tracey's mind. Tracey took it all in.

For this plan to succeed in Jafaire, everything had to come together without a hitch. And April only had this last week of summer vacation off before the school year would start. Tracey didn't want to call attention to her missing any days at school if he could help it. Notwithstanding Tracey's concern, the school knew April had an illness, so she had a little wiggle room to take some sick days at the beginning of the school year if needed.

Tracey continued to calculate how far they had traveled after leaving the airport. They had driven at a moderate pace and had traveled only two miles when the skyline of downtown Lingos, the capital of Jafaire, started to appear in the distance. It didn't look like Times Square, but Jafaire was growing. The city was home to several medium-sized, high-rise buildings, and they all looked brand new.

Amir made his way from the city outskirts to its main artery. The city was alive with a noticeable amount of hustle and bustle. They came to a roundabout similar to the Arc de Triomphe in Paris. Amir entered at the 6 o'clock location, circled right, and exited at 11 o'clock.

A few blocks later, Amir turned down a side street containing several medical buildings. Tracey immediately noticed a tan-colored military Humvee, probably one donated by the U.S. military, parked within twenty yards of the corner. As they went by the Humvee, Tracey noted the vehicle was "occupied two times," a term he used to indicate two people were sitting in a car. There was a driver and an occupant in the passenger seat. They seemed intent on staring straight ahead. They didn't even look at their van as they passed.

Amir continued down the street another 500 yards and began to pull over to the curb. Several orange cones were in front of the spots reserved for two handicapped vehicles. Amir gave one short honk, and a nurse came running out and grabbed both the orange cones. Amir pulled into one of the two parking spots.

After parking, Amir exited. The nurse was already at the side of the van, opening the doors for Tracey and April. Amir reached inside and pushed the button to begin unfolding the automated sidestep. Thirty seconds later, it was fully extended.

Before April could be wheeled out, a young man in doctor's scrubs exited the building.

"Mr. David Tracey. Welcome. I am Dr. Embuke." Dr. Embuke extended his hand as he walked towards Tracey.

"What a pleasure it is to meet you, Dr. Embuke," Tracey said as he grabbed Dr. Embuke's hand and shook it with utmost respect. "I am so pleased we are here."

"We are happy you have traveled to see us, and we can't wait to help with the beginning of the rest of your daughter's life. And where is the star of this show?" Dr. Embuke asked, smiling as he peered around Tracey and into the van. Amir turned April's wheelchair towards the van's doorway and began rolling April onto the sidestep.

"Hello, Dr. Embuke. I am so happy to meet you," April said as she raised her hand in greeting.

"Hello, April. The pleasure is mine. I am glad to welcome you to my country. Your trip was okay?"

April nodded, as did Tracey. Dr. Embuke smiled and bowed slightly.

"Let's begin then, shall we?" Dr. Embuke said as he waved his arm towards the clinic door.

Amir lowered the wheelchair to the curb as Tracey moved in to push April. But Amir insisted again, so Tracey stepped aside as Amir wheeled April into the clinic. Dr. Embuke's nurse was the last to enter. Tracey noted she locked the door behind them and turned around the sign indicating "Open" and the hours they were open to reflect "Closed." Her name tag read "Talia."

Amir wheeled April towards the back and into a triage room. Dr. Embuke's nurse returned and thanked Amir.

"Okay, April. I'd like you to head to the changing room just beyond the closet door on your left. Here is a patient top and bottom."

April inspected the clothes. "Oh, cool. Much better than the hospital gowns in the U.S. that show your butt," April said, smiling, as she made her way out of the wheelchair with the clothes and headed for the changing room.

Tracey smiled.

Amir started to turn for the front door. "Mr. Tracey. I will wait for you and April and take you back to the airport when you are done."

"You're going to wait here at the clinic?" Tracey asked.

"Of course," Amir said with a smile.

"Overnight?"

Amir nodded his head in the affirmative and bowed slightly.

He is getting paid handsomely, Tracey thought.

If Tracey only knew.

Chapter 34

The Devil is in the Details

September 8, 2012
9:15 a.m. MST
Portal 17

Bell continued to pour through the portal's Street View videos. The three-times fast-forward button was helping Bell get through the videos quicker than he thought he would. As he worked his way through the first five videos, he stopped to look at the size of each one. The majority were exactly 2MB in size. He figured those videos had no extra movement, so he ignored them and started in on the larger ones. He hoped the greater size meant something was happening, more than just the mailman filling the mailbox.

He found nothing out of the ordinary from seven days prior through early morning the day before. The same camera angle started becoming monotonous. And then he almost missed it.

He clicked on the sixty-sixth video. At six minutes in - of course, "666," it would have to be the devil's number - he watched as a car drove from left to right in front of the portal and turned down the driveway. It was the same Ford Taurus currently sitting in the driveway. Fallon immediately appeared on the screen. She had been sitting under the porch in the spot Bell found her. She ran out about three feet and stopped. Wagging her tail, she stood still. But she didn't bark. After a few seconds, she sat down. As Bell watched, Fallon looked down the driveway to her right and stood up again. And she barked. So, the Ford Taurus was occupied by someone who was an IA or InCit personnel, possibly the sentry. What happened next made Bell's heart race a little.

A white van entered the video frame. It careened off the road and barreled down the driveway toward the direction of the Ford Taurus. Fallon kept wagging her tail.

Bell fast-forwarded the video. At the thirty-second mark, Fallon was still wagging her tail and began to walk towards the driveway. She barked one time and walked off-screen. Bell switched over to the Driveway camera for the same time frame. There was one video. Bell hit "Play" and watched the melee that followed.

Four men, all dressed in black, wearing masks and carrying AR-15s, jumped out of the van. The brake lights on the Ford Taurus went on briefly and then off. A man exited the Ford Taurus and looked behind him at the men jumping out of the van. He ran towards the back of the portal. Bell could tell the man was the sentry, Travis Keith.

The four operators started shooting at Keith as they walked down the driveway in a slightly staggered and offset, single line, one behind the other. By their movement, Bell could tell they had some close-quarter battle training or CQB training. They walked in unison, slowly, with purpose, constantly moving forward. Their rounds struck the rear window of the car. They missed Keith by a wide margin, which made Bell think maybe they weren't well trained. Keith didn't look back as he continued running.

The operators didn't look twice at Fallon. She did her job. She wagged her tail. She walked to the mailbox, barked again, and took a pee. She then lay down on the grass by the road. But why did she bark at the operators? She knew to bark only if someone in her presence *was* an IA or InCit Personnel.

Two of the operators peeled off and moved to the front door. The third and fourth operators continued down the driveway. Bell switched back to the Street View video. As the first two operators approached the front porch stairs, the lead operator fired two rounds into the front door. They bounded up the front porch stairs and through the front door in a blink of an eye.

Bell switched back again to the Driveway video. The other two operators continued towards the back of the portal.

Bell switched to the Rear camera. He watched as Keith fumbled with his keys and dropped them. Leaving them on the ground, he used his elbow to break the glass on the top half of the screen door and then one small glass panel on the inside door. Keith reached in and unlocked the door, making his way inside. The pursuing operators made their way down the driveway. They paused at the rear corner of the house. The third operator turned his head slightly to the right, apparently speaking into a headset. They continued to hold their position. The fourth operator turned and made his way to the garage.

Bell clicked back and forth between the Driveway and Rear videos. He saw no further movement from the driveway as the two operators who entered the front door remained inside. He watched as the third and fourth operators continued to the back door and proceeded into the portal.

Bell clicked off that video and moved to the next one. Forty minutes into the following video, all four operators came out the front door with their weapons lowered. They slowly jogged over to the van and jumped in. The van backed out and headed down the highway, away from the direction they had arrived.

Bell now had a lot of questions answered, including the sentry making his way back into the house after coming under attack. He never made it to the portal command center, however, as was evident from his body lying on the kitchen floor. The operators may not have known there was a command center. If they did, they never went down there either. Unfortunately, the sentry didn't have time to alert HQ that the portal was under attack.

Bell finished watching the videos up until the time he arrived. What Bell didn't see was equally as alarming. There was no evidence in any of the videos to indicate IA24 had made his or her way into the portal. So where was the IA whose drone attacked him? And where did that IA's drone go? And why did Fallon bark? Bell would have to find those answers elsewhere. He had to get a move on.

The date on the video for the attack was September 5th. That was around the time Tracey went off the grid. Bell had to get to Tracey's lake house. Maybe he would find Tracey there, holed up in some secret room Tracey built for a scenario like this. It wouldn't be unlike Tracey crafting something like that.

Little did Bell know Tracey was 7,000 miles away and in just as bad a situation.

Chapter 35
All Systems Go

September 7, 2012
7:30 a.m.
The Kratos residence
Miami, FL

Athan continued typing on his laptop. He needed to check on the drone's location. It should be relatively close to the polar ice cap. His heart was pounding.

He moved his cursor to check on the flight speed of the drone. It was motionless. It had touched down. He clicked again for an update on the current weather conditions at the polar ice cap and, more specifically, at the exact location where the drone was sitting. All was good, all within the weather parameters they needed to trigger the explosion, get the drone out of the area, and back home. The clock in the upper-right corner of his computer screen was counting down - 5 hours, 45 minutes, 12 seconds until it would be dark and he could execute the plan.

Athan sat back in his chair. He folded his hands behind his head and took a deep breath. He still couldn't believe this was about to happen. Athan dreamed for a minute about the phone call he would make to the board of directors, telling them there had been a mother nature type of explosion at the polar ice cap, specifically where their oil drilling rights were. Their company might be saved for that reason alone. But Athan knew it wasn't a done deal just yet. A lot of help from Mother Nature was still needed. And, of course, the drone had to perform as they hoped.

Athan took the burner phone Tracey gave him out of the side drawer. Tracey told Athan he would be six hours ahead of him. He flipped it open and turned it on. The battery read 4% remaining. He'd charge it soon enough. The phone prompted him for a password, and he typed "Savedin2012." He thought it was appropriate. He opened the message folder. There were still no messages from Tracey. Tracey was supposed to text him "All good," but only if it was all good.

He texted.

"You on schedule? I am." He sent the text and waited. After ten minutes of ghosting, Athan closed the phone and placed it back on the desk. He wasn't sure what was going on, but he trusted Tracey.

Something must have come up.

Chapter 36
Blindsided

Behind the glass in the prep room, Tracey could see Dr. Embuke washing his hands. Nurse Talia tied a mask around his face and cross-tied his scrubs.

April's procedure would take a similar amount of time as a stem-cell transplant, four to six hours. As Dr. Embuke successfully sped up the process in the lab setting, he used the same method on his sister. His sister's procedure was completed in just under four hours.

April would be awake for the entire procedure. Her blood would be taken out in intervals, processed, and re-introduced to her system. The success of Dr. Embuke's procedure eliminated the need for a full transplant of each cell, as was required in a stem cell transplant. As Dr. Embuke reintroduced the newly cured blood cells, they would replicate immediately and begin to kill the bad cells remaining in April's blood, providing the same outcome as if April's blood cells were removed and directly treated outside her body. That was the major reason the procedure was reduced to under four hours. In addition, although Dr. Embuke's sister felt nauseous for several hours after her procedure, she began to feel stronger eight hours after the procedure. Tracey was counting on a similar outcome as each hour on their schedule to get back home was very much accounted for.

While Tracey continued to think about the procedure, April emerged from behind the glass in the triage room directly in front of him. She proudly displayed her new hospital uniform, twirling around for all to see.

"Bam! Do I look stylish or what?!" April said as she slowly did a 360 like a runway model.

"Oh, that is so you," Tracey said as he nodded his head up and down. "Fits like a glove. And no butt crack." April chuckled as she pushed her fanny in the air in agreement with Tracey.

She sat back down in the wheelchair and waited.

Dr. Embuke pressed a panel on the inside of the room, and the door opened. April was now in a vestibule similar to those at the InCit lab and FBI HQ. A short burst of air shot down from the ceiling. April jumped at first, startled by the blast. She looked out at Tracey. Tracey yelled out: "Decontamination. You're good."

After one minute, the air dissipated, and the interior door opened to where Dr. Embuke, nurse Talia, and a second nurse were waiting for her. They walked her to a bed in the middle of the room. April stepped up on the stool next to the bed and lay down. Dr. Embuke walked to the window and looked at Tracey, giving him a thumbs-up and slowly turning the blinds down.

Tracey assumed that was it for him, and he couldn't do any more until April emerged a new, healthier person. He prayed that would be the case and headed towards the waiting room in the front of the clinic.

When he arrived, he first noticed Amir was on his phone talking to someone in Arabic. Tracey took a chair across from Amir, with his back to where he left April and a direct view of the front door and the street outside.

Amir ended his call and looked up at Tracey. "Your daughter is starting the procedure, yes?" he asked.

"Yes, the procedure has started, Amir. God willing, this will all go smoothly."

"I shall also pray to Allah, Mr. Tracey. We will double our efforts!"

Tracey smiled. Certainly couldn't hurt, he thought.

Tracey removed the drop phone from his front pocket. He wanted to see how things were going with Athan and the drone. As Tracey flipped open the phone, he was just about to turn it on when he heard a key enter the front door, and the door unlocked. Tracey's heart jumped a beat. He didn't have the warm fuzzies about who could be entering. Tracey quickly closed the phone and shoved it down his pants. He looked up, and before he could get out of his seat, a half dozen

Jafairian soldiers entered with handguns out and pointed at Tracey. Amir stood up and quickly walked out the front door as if he were invisible, and they didn't see him. But of course, he wasn't. They'd seen him but did not attempt to stop him. Something was going to happen, which Tracey wasn't expecting. He knew that for sure.

Following closely behind the last soldier who entered was an older soldier with no weapon. He was definitely in charge, Tracey thought.

"Special Agent David Tracey?" the man dressed in his military best uniform asked. He didn't wait for a response but continued.

"I am General Dule Repuso. You and I are going to conduct a little bit of business. For your daughter's sake."

Chapter 37
The Unplanned Meeting

As his soldiers stepped aside, General Repuso sat across from Tracey. Amir left so fast that he never told them Tracey had a phone. And Amir's rapid departure could only mean he was in on whatever this was. Tracey never saw whatever this was coming, and he was pissed about that.

General Repuso put his elbows on his knees and leaned towards Tracey.

"Let me ask you, Special Agent Tracey, why are you here?"

Tracey knew he had to answer. He also knew it was worth trying to fake it for a while and see how far he could go.

"My daughter is receiving a transfusion for a blood disorder she was born with. The doctor is with her right now, completing the procedure."

General Repuso nodded his head as he pursed his lips.

"DBA, correct?" the general asked Tracey.

"Yes," Tracey simply stated, trying not to act surprised.

Tracey was starting to get a little worried. As far as Tracey knew, only Dr. Embuke, his resident friend from the U.S., President Embuke, and her family knew of the research Dr. Embuke had completed.

"How do you think the procedure is going?" General Repuso said out loud.

Tracey never took his eyes off the general. He didn't believe the general cared one way or the other about the procedure.

"Seeing as the doctor hasn't come out yet, I'm hoping that's a good sign," Tracey answered evenly.

None of General Repuso's men had left the room, so unless the general had a mole on Dr. Embuke's medical team, then Dr. Embuke probably didn't know what was going on in his waiting room.

"By my calculations, the good doctor - you do know he is the brother of our president, by the way, yes?" the general interrupted for Tracey to reply.

"I do, yes," Tracey said.

"The procedure should take approximately four hours, maybe a little more. That's how long you have." The general was looking directly at Tracey.

Tracey waited. He wanted to know immediately what he had four hours to wait for. But he said nothing.

Just as he was about to ask, the general spoke.

"Would you be surprised to know I am aware your FBI has a technology that can render objects invisible?"

That was certainly blunt. How the hell did he know that Tracey thought to himself, but he kept a poker face.

"Yes, I would be surprised if the Bureau had that technology. If we did, I'd be even more surprised you knew about it," Tracey said. Then he shifted his leg and crossed one leg over the other, leaning back in the chair to deflect the question and hopefully hide his surprise at the general's interrogation.

Tracey figured it was worth a try to feign ignorance, but he knew the general knew something about InCit, somehow, though he might not know the name of the program nor the actual technology. God, hopefully, he didn't know that. But how did he know about any of it?

"Are you surprised, though, Special Agent Tracey?" the general continued. He wasn't looking for Tracey to answer and continued.

"If you know a little bit of our history, you know we were lucky enough to strike oil a few years ago, and this natural resource gave notice to the world that Jafaire could discover more oil and compete as one of the richest oil-producing countries in Africa and, I dare say, the world. Our infrastructure is growing, our citizens are thriving, for the most part, and we are starting to be regarded as a major exporter of water and, to a lesser extent, oil."

The general paused for a few seconds as he stared at the ceiling.

"One of my brothers believed I would always become the leader of the warring country we fled from, Vista Porto. Are you familiar with this country on our border, Special Agent Tracey?"

"I am," Tracey answered. Following the daily briefings at FBI HQ, Tracey was more than familiar with President Embuke's rise to power as the overwhelming choice of the people in Jafaire and her status as a beloved leader. And how she invited citizens of Vista Porto to become Jafairians. Tracey had done substantial research leading up to his trip with April. He knew a little of General Repuso's background but not a lot. And he never expected to meet him under any circumstance.

"That plan didn't work out, and I never became the leader of Vista Porto, which is for the best anyway. Instead, I sought an opportunity within Jafaire to lead the military. President Embuke's father was my steadfast ally and spoke highly of me to the president. She appointed me to this position, and I am grateful." General Repuso eyed Tracey with a calculating look that chilled him.

"But she doesn't let me lead my troops, not really. I must go through her for every military exercise. My budget rests on her decision alone. She has recently cut the number of active-duty military, re-assigning the young soldiers who have completed their military duty to work in engineering and other business enterprises. This hurts our military strength and appearance. It is not good. We are always at odds as to how to lead this country forward. And I want this country to be more. Bigger and better. And feared by others."

Tracey just listened. He didn't know where the conversation was going, but the general had set the stage to suggest he didn't support the president.

"That same brother warned me a couple of years ago not to accept this position to head Jafaire's military. He believed people should govern, without arms, together as one big, strong family. He believed in providing for those less fortunate in every aspect of life - if you couldn't grow crops, work your neighbor's land with them and receive your fair share. Suppose you had no skills to work as a teacher. Then, sharpen pencils and clean the classrooms. My brother was a doctor. He practiced with the same mindset - he used his skills for the poor. But he was leaning too far into socialism. And communism would not be that far behind. He and I disagreed on this. But we loved each other as brothers do."

Tracey noticed the general said his brother "was" a doctor. Did he change careers, or was he dead? Tracey didn't have to wait long for the answer.

"Your government was fairly intent on finding Osama Bin Laden, weren't they Special Agent Tracey?"

Tracey re-positioned his leg and carefully weighed what answer he should give.

"We were pretty determined, and we succeeded, as you know."

The general initially appeared to be satisfied with the answer. Tracey watched as the general's lips tightened and his eyes widened.

"On April 29, 2011, the United States launched a drone that struck a small doctor's office in Islamabad. Your government thought they had finally located Bin Laden in this location. The so-called 'intelligence' was they located his DNA there. I'm not sure why your government thought this, but they did. Have you ever heard of this drone strike?"

Tracey, of course, had been briefed on the strike as all Eyes Only agents received the daily intelligence briefings. And every member of InCit knew of the creation of the Red Ladens and how they got their name.

"I do remember hearing about many strikes in Islamabad, general. That one strike, in particular, I am not any more aware of than any of the others," Tracey lied.

The general stood up. He slowly walked towards Tracey.

Tracey could tell he was not happy, maybe with Tracey's answer, or he was coming to the crescendo of his story.

"Dr. Salan Repuso was one of the doctors killed that day when the Americans obliterated most of the city block. He was working with children who had been deformed following the many U.S. drone strikes in the area. Does the name sound familiar, Special Agent Tracey?" the general asked loudly as he drew within two feet of Tracey's face.

So, the general's brother was killed by a drone strike meant for Bin Laden. Tracey didn't budge in his seat. He wouldn't appear unnerved and give the general the satisfaction of making Tracey feel bad about his brother, who was in the wrong place at the wrong time.

The general was certainly blaming the U.S. for his brother's death. Specifically, the general appeared to be blaming the FBI.

Chapter 38
Born to Command

The Repuso brothers were close because they grew up in one of the harshest environments on earth. The humid climate, disease, inconsistent water supplies, and the constant strain of civil war made daily life difficult. Even going to the town market was an arduous task. They had to remain vigilant at every turn.

For safety, the brothers traveled in numbers. They would walk together whenever possible. Rival warlords had an unwritten understanding that they would not kidnap their enemies' children. At least not all of them at once. Given the possibility, the Repuso family felt it would be safer if the boys traveled together and would be less likely to be kidnapped and held for ransom. Of course, the more realistic theory was that their enemies would take only one of the boys if they were found in the market together. Either way, the Repuso brothers survived childhood.

When he was growing up, Dule Repuso made himself known as someone to be trusted. The warlords liked Dule because he would quickly do as he was asked, and he never said no or asked questions. He just followed orders. Whether carrying a little paper bag to a man in a tribe some two miles away or running to get some of the "dintalee," the tribal alcohol, for the warlord and running it back to him, Dule accomplished it.

Dule Repuso never doubted he would be a soldier when he grew up. He finished near the top of his primary education classes. When he turned seventeen, he had the choice of leaving Vista Porto and heading to college in Cape Town or staying and defending his country. He chose to stay.

He rose through the cadet ranks, and with each month of proving himself, he earned the respect of his fellow soldiers and leaders. He gave up rations of food when others missed their turn in the food line. He volunteered for all the dangerous training assignments, including learning how to handle explosives and defuse them. He could shoot straight as an arrow and piled up accolades.

He later graduated first in his military class and earned the rank of captain at the prehistoric age of twenty. For the next seven years, he commanded young troops, some of whom were his friends from school. He saved lives and took the lives of enemy soldiers. When he turned twenty-eight, he was promoted to Junior Chief of Staff to the General commanding Vista Porto's military forces.

It was under the tutelage of this general that Dule Repuso learned how to lead. He continued to lead by example. He was smart when dealing with the soldiers - those same soldiers who would die defending their country. He grew to be respected and loved by his countrymen.

When his mentor was assassinated while eating lunch in a daylight ambush, Dule Repuso was promoted to general and selected unanimously to lead the Vista Porto military. He held this command for the next thirty years.

He survived more than a half dozen attempts on his life. Many attempts came in the same manner as his predecessor saw, with ambushes and attempts at blowing up his vehicles. Many soldiers died protecting him.

All in all, the general was considered very successful. And President Embuke wanted a successful military.

Chapter 39
Finding Answers

September 8, 2012
11:00 a.m. MST
Portal 17

Bell headed back up the elevator. He wanted to be sure Fallon had enough water and food until the Bureau could get a team out there. He wasn't sure how long she had been without either. Exiting the elevator in the kitchen, he rummaged through the cabinets until he found Fallon's dog food. Located in the sink was her clean food bowl. He filled the food bowl and headed out the front door with it.

Fallon was sitting on the ground next to the front stairs. Bell showed her the food bowl and motioned for her to follow him. They walked down the driveway, now engulfed in shade, and he placed the food bowl down next to her water bowl. Grabbing the hose next to her empty water bowl, he filled it to the top. Fallon continued to wag her tail as she began to eat. Bell patted her on the head and headed towards the IA's car in the driveway. She would be okay until the team got there.

He needed to exchange IA24's car for his Tahoe, but he was concerned a drone was still monitoring it. He certainly didn't want to take any more gunfire. But he needed to retrieve his drone.

He jumped in and reached into the glove box, grabbing another cloth he had seen earlier. Gingerly, he unwrapped the bandage on his right wrist. It didn't hurt as badly as a few hours before, and the bleeding appeared to have stopped. Bell replaced the bloodied bandage with a new one, slowly backed out of the driveway, and returned to his SUV.

It was in the same spot. He drove thirty feet past and turned around, coming in behind. He parked parallel to a half dozen trees. Maybe they would provide him some cover from getting shot again. This was the part he hoped wouldn't be too dicey. Similar to when he sat in the portal driveway, he took the bloody bandage in his left hand and placed it in his lap. He carefully lowered the driver's window and grabbed the bandage with his left hand. As he threw the bandage out the window, he ducked down onto the front seat. Nothing. He sat up slowly and opened the door. He put both feet on the ground and waited. Still nothing. He then inched out of the car and hunched over. He realized the drone could have easily moved around to the driver's side of the car and opened up on him, but he saw nothing. Most importantly, no drone fired at him. He walked quickly to his vehicle and got in.

Bell reached into his pocket and turned on the navigator. The red light was blinking, again showing him his location. The portal he had just left was still green. A further confirmation that Mr. Keith had not been able to reach out to headquarters and let them know he had visitors.

Bell turned off the navigator and put it back in his pocket. He reached under the seat and grabbed his blackhawk. He turned it on and waited. When the screen popped up, he had two new messages. Thank God. One message was from the director, and one message was from his wife. He clicked on the message from his wife.

"Hope the work trip is going smoothly. I haven't heard from you, so I'm going on vacation with the kids without you. Hope you don't mind! We'll be gone for a few days, and I'll call you soon. Love you, and be safe."

Bell understood the message – his wife figured out he may be having work difficulties and the family may be in increased danger. So, she was taking the kids and driving out to the location previously set up by Bell and Evelynn as a haven. That location was a small beach cottage they rented in Key Largo. It would take her just under three hours to get there by plane. She would pay for the rental through the Venmo account she and Bell had set up in the dog's name years ago. She always thought it was fun to set up, and she laughed about Trigger Bell's Venmo account. She never really thought they would use it. She found out over the years, however, it became useful. She wouldn't be tracked there.

Bell then clicked over to the director's text.

"ERF is secure - No one hurt - I was quarantined, so no contact with anyone - have you made contact with portal 17? - I sent HRT to Tracey's place ahead of you - no sign of him - we did not know he was in D.C. - looking for him here - the transmitter was probably Tracey's - not sure why he would place it on you - update when you're available."

At the moment, Bell was grateful for two things: his wife and kids were fine, and the director was alive.

Bell began to type a reply to his wife.

"Work is okay - take a few more days on vacation - meet you there. Love you."

He wasn't going to tell his wife he got shot. Too much to explain, and he didn't have time to type that in a text. She'd be mad at him for not telling her, but it was better she didn't have to worry about him at the moment. His wife would know Bell told her he needed a few more days before it was safe for them. And while he didn't think they were in much danger, better safe than sorry was a good plan.

Bell didn't fully know what he was dealing with, and if the Bureau had spies within, then there was a slight chance they knew Bell would be trying to stop them. He had to tell the director.

Bell typed a text back to him.

"Good to see your text sir - portal 17 was attacked - command center not compromised - sentry dead - will need cleanup - 4 subjects 2 days ago gone now - was shot in the wrist but okay - moving to Tracey's place - not sure if anyone in the Bureau is involved - Bell clear."

He didn't wait for a reply text from either his wife or the director. He turned the blackhawk off and put it in his pocket. Punching in Tracey's address on the SUV's navigation screen, he drove off.

As Bell headed down the country roads, the elevation changed slightly and became more mountainous. Gradually, the surroundings became populated with thicker tree lines, and Bell could no longer see across miles of terrain. He drove approximately fifteen minutes until the navigation system announced he had arrived at Tracey's house.

He switched the map off to concentrate on his surroundings. A gate in front of him was shut and had a chain draped around it. There was no lock. Bell slowly rolled up to it. He got out and walked up to the gate. Removing the chain, he pushed the gate open and jumped back in.

Slowly, he continued down the road, looking in every direction for any sign of his Bureau counterparts. He saw nothing as he drove approximately a half-mile down the road.

Finally, he reached an opening in the woods, revealing a house and a lake just beyond. He decided to park there and carefully approach on foot. Bell also wanted to be sure he had backup if needed, so he exited the front seat and opened the rear door, grabbing the Pelican case with his drone.

After a few minutes of fumbling through powering up the drone on his own and practicing commands, Bell set the drone to invisible mode. He realized his commands weren't the best yet, and he'd have to get better at directing his drone. His first command sent the drone into a nearby tree when Bell tasked it to "hide and seek." He realized the command didn't mean to become invisible and find any threats. Bell took several deep breaths.

"Close distance," Bell whispered. The drone made its way back to within fifteen feet of Bell.

He grabbed his Glock - again with his left hand - and, keeping it by his side, he closed the Tahoe door softly and walked towards the house. He could hear the soft buzz of his drone behind him. When he came to the end of the wooded area, he paused before walking into the exposed open area. All was quiet.

Bell waited approximately five minutes. After seeing no movement, he made a quick beeline to the back deck. He waited by the stairs with his gun in front of him. There was no movement. His drone followed, still at the "close distance" of fifteen feet. He cautiously walked up the steps and moved to the corner. He holstered his Glock and, reaching into the inside pocket of his jacket, he found his small pen flashlight and removed it. Turning on the flashlight, he placed it gingerly in his right hand and again unholstered his Glock with his left hand. He walked around the side of the house and stopped underneath the windows so he wouldn't be seen if anyone was inside. He then continued to the other side of the deck. Still no movement. He checked the back door, and it was locked.

If HRT had already been there, like the director said in his text, Bell figured no one was home. It would be okay to break in. Backing up a step, he kicked in the front door handle. The door slammed to the back of the wall and started back towards him. He stuck his foot in the threshold to stop the door from closing again and pushed it open slowly. Standing still, he waited again for any movement. Nothing. Bell eased his way inside. Gently cradling the flashlight in his right hand, he cleared his way through the first floor, stopping at the stairs to the second floor. The drone followed. He waited and listened. Again, there was no sound. Slowly, he crept up the stairs and then cleared the upstairs in the same manner. The only sign of anyone having been upstairs was a broken window in the master bedroom. On the floor next to the bed was a burn mark indicative of a flash-bang grenade being set off - HRT's entry point. He then started back downstairs.

"Tracey!" Bell yelled. "It's Bell. If you're here, come on out. HRT's gone. It's just me."

Bell waited for a few minutes. Nothing. He moved to the kitchen area and shouted the same greeting, but still nothing. The director was right. Tracey was not there.

To be sure, Bell sent the drone on a hunting expedition.

"Detect."

If Tracey was there and Bell missed him, the drone would find him and alert Bell. The drone headed into the living room to begin its search.

While the drone did its thing, Bell surmised Tracey would have the house wired with a covert video security system. Bell certainly would have if he owned the place. And Bell would have that system capable of monitoring remotely. So would Tracey, which meant Tracey could figure out Bell was in his house.

After rummaging through several kitchen drawers, Bell found a notepad and a Sharpie. He wrote:

"CALL ME" and added his drop phone number. He left the kitchen and slowly walked around the house, stopping every few feet while displaying the note he had written. After about fifteen minutes inside the house, Bell went outside. His drone was now back at his side, having found no one.

Bell stopped in a few dozen areas in the yard, presenting the same note. If Tracey had any security cameras set up, he would see Bell's message.

After thirty minutes, Bell went back into the kitchen. He was thirsty and realized he was starting to get dehydrated from the wound. He grabbed a glass, filled it from the tap, and drained it twice. Looking for something more soothing, he opened the fridge and was glad to see a half dozen beers. Eagerly reaching for one, he cracked it open and took a few sips as he sat at the kitchen table.

Casually reaching into his pocket for the navigator, he turned it on. Unfortunately, it showed no nearby portals. The closest one was portal 17 he had just left.

He powered off the navigator and returned it to his pocket, alternately removing his blackhawk from a different pocket. As the blackhawk turned on, an alert indicated two new messages. Again, from his wife and the director.

From his wife: "Glad you're okay - will spend extra time on vacation - chat soon."

His wife understood. Bell then opened the director's text message.

"Good job - get to a doctor - sorry about the sentry - will secure #17 - IA24 delayed but will reach out - will update you with a new plan."

Bell called out to his drone. He certainly wouldn't get the simplest of commands wrong.

"Ground. Uncloak." The drone lowered itself onto the kitchen table and uncloaked from being invisible. Its rotors stopped turning. Bell patted it like a dog and laughed at how improbable his day had been. Bell took another sip of his beer and burped. It felt good.

Chapter 40
We're Leaving

September 7, 2012
1:00 p.m. (UTC +2.00)
Dr. Embuke's clinic
Jafaire, Africa

The general got up, and his men did likewise, keeping their guns at the ready and trained on Tracey. The general walked to the front door of the clinic and looked out. He didn't say anything for about a minute. It was starting to get a little busier on the road outside as more cars and buses went by. Tracey didn't know what type of convoy the general and his soldiers arrived in, but their presence was possibly causing a scene outside the clinic. Tracey figured additional soldiers were outside, stopping anyone from walking directly in front of the clinic, as no one had passed the front door since the general arrived. April was about thirty minutes into her procedure. She still had at least three and a half hours to go. The general abruptly turned around as if he heard something coming from the back where April was. Sure enough, as Tracey looked to his right, the second nurse walked out and greeted the general with a hug.

"Hello, Father. Everything is going just as the doctor had hoped with the procedure. Do you need anything else from me?" she asked.

Tracey raised his eyebrows at the familial title. Things were making sense. The general did have someone on the inside. Tracey would have done it the same way. Get a source on the inside, and they could learn just about anything. Tracey stared at the nurse's nametag. "Mariama." He'd remember her name.

"Hello, my dear. I do not need anything from you right now. Just keep me informed as you get close to the end. I think Special Agent Tracey here will help me with my request, and he and his daughter can be on their way soon enough," the general said as he looked over at Tracey.

"Does that sound good, Special Agent Tracey?" General Repuso asked.

"I'll help you if I can," Tracey said.

"Oh, you most definitely can," the general said.

"But nothing bad better happen to my daughter; I can also tell you that. You might think you have the upper hand right now -". The general cut him off.

"Save your idle threats, Special Agent Tracey," the general said without looking at him. Instead, the general focused on his daughter and put his arm around her. Tracey was happy to be underestimated.

"Nothing will happen to your daughter. She will complete her treatment and be ready to go as soon as I get what I want. As you can see, I have someone here who will keep me updated on her progress," the general said as he smiled at his daughter.

Nurse Mariama hugged the general again and retreated to the back of the clinic.

General Repuso motioned to his soldiers to grab Tracey and head out. With a flourish, the general went out the door, following two soldiers. Tracey was helped to his feet by two other soldiers. As he started through the door, Tracey turned and looked back towards the rear of the clinic, where he had left April lying on a bed. They couldn't see each other, and she had no clue what was happening. Tracey hoped it stayed that way.

With a soldier in front of him and one behind him, Tracey was marched through the door and told to turn to the right. After walking approximately two yards, he noticed Amir sneaking back into the clinic behind him. Tracey kept watching him as Amir appeared to lock the door and move away from the view of the street.

Tracey was led to a tan Humvee and forced inside. It was probably the same Humvee Tracey had noticed earlier when they arrived at the clinic. As soon as he sat down, one of the soldiers put a zip tie around his hands and sat next to him. A second soldier entered from the opposite door and sat on the other side of Tracey. A caravan of Humvees then departed from Dr. Embuke's clinic.

Approximately ten minutes later, the caravan approached the entrance of a compound. The building Tracey first noticed appeared to be a government building of some type surrounded by an eight or nine-foot-high wall. A barricade slowly lowered into the ground as they approached two massive metal gates, Once the barrier was completely down, the gates swung open. The caravan entered the compound and pulled around the back of the building.

Tracey was led upstairs to the general's office. It was decorated with war memorabilia and photos of the general with world leaders, including several former U.S. presidents. There was even a picture of the general and the current U.S. president. Tracey was ordered to sit down on a couch. Another couch, several chairs, and a table faced him. The soldiers remained beside him, and several others appeared and lined the walls. After approximately five minutes, the general walked through the doors with a coffee in his hand, followed by a man and woman carrying trays of coffee and food. They placed the drinks and food on the table by Tracey and departed.

Walking over to Tracey with his coffee, the general sat down across from him and smiled. He motioned to the soldiers to remove the zip ties on Tracey's hands. As they cut off the zip ties, the general spoke. "I certainly hope you understand the position you're in here. My men have been instructed to shoot you should you decide that escaping was in your best interest."

"I understand, General. I'm not stupid."

"Good to hear that. And I would never say that you were stupid, Special Agent Tracey. Knowing what you have accomplished so far in getting here, I would assign you the highest level of intelligence. Now, please, have a cup of coffee and something to eat." The general motioned to the tray of coffee and food. "It is going to be a long couple of days, and I want to make sure you and your daughter are comfortable."

"Thank you, General," Tracey said as he reached for a cup of coffee and a croissant-looking pastry. Tracey figured he wasn't about to be poisoned since the general wanted something from him, and he needed to keep his strength up so he could continue to think. He also knew any sign of disrespect would not be taken lightly by the general.

It was better to play the game than not.

Chapter 41

Tunnel Vision

Tracey and the general ate their pastries in silence. No discernible noises were coming from anywhere inside or outside the building. It was just quiet. The soldiers stood at half attention, maintaining their shoulder weapons at the ready. Either way, Tracey knew things were about to get ugly in Jafaire based on the general's current actions, and Tracey was afraid it was because of the Bureau's technology. That fact was still not sitting well with him as he wondered how the general learned about the drones. Once Tracey had enough to eat, he figured he would start the conversation.

"So, General, can you tell me how I'll be able to help you?" Tracey asked before taking another sip of his coffee.

The general didn't answer right away. He continued to sip his coffee and reached for a second pastry. Sitting back in his chair, the general made soft sounds indicating he was enjoying his pastry. He smiled dryly as he finished his pastry and nodded to one of his assistants waiting patiently ten feet away. She walked to him and took his plate as the general wiped his hands clean of the crumbs. He sat back again, took a sip of his coffee, and looked at Tracey before he spoke.

"I know your daughter is sick, and I'm sure that's why you came up with this plan, Special Agent Tracey. Parents want the best for their kids. We will do anything for them. I understand. I'd try to save my daughter at all costs, too."

The general uncrossed his legs and placed his coffee on the table. "Let's talk business, Special Agent Tracey. You have something that I not only want but I need. If I am to make this country great - and I mean abundant in its riches - I need protection from outside sources and the technology to be successful.

"Oh, and before you try to lecture me on how Jafaire already has all of these high-tech weapons to protect our borders, let's not forget that almost all our military technology is military surplus. Except for your country's missile detection system, the rest is just cast-off military garbage from first-world countries.

"Our borders are fairly secure; I will give you that. But our true enemies will come from within, from those pretending to be our friends and those who can cross our borders with impunity to steal our resources or who might already be here. I want to be protected against those things I can't yet know."

"Like you?" It was probably not the best response from Tracey, but he felt good saying it. The general ignored him.

"The president trusts too many people. Someone is going to take advantage of her kindness. We need to be ready," the general continued.

"She trusts you, doesn't she?" Tracey asked again, just trying to piss him off.

"Not enough," the general said. "The world will see that my view as a military strategist is more sensible than hers. I do not want to sit and idly wait for someone to steal our oil reserves or any minerals we mine. I know how to deal with the warlords I grew up with. And their children, who have now taken over some of those positions, are a desperate bunch. They don't have the oil or minerals we have. They fight every day to have food. The world seems to have abandoned them. These countries certainly envy Jafaire. I am intent on not letting that envy destroy us." The general leaned back in his chair and slowly looked at the ceiling.

"What exactly do you think I have in the form of technology?" Tracey asked, squinting a little bit.

"Ah, let's get to it then, Special Agent Tracey. You have been fairly patient.

"Three years ago, Jafaire was selected by your FBI to send one of our military commanders to your FBI National Academy. We sent a close friend of mine, a colonel whom I grew up with in Vista Porto."

"The colonel loved her time there. She studied with other U.S. law enforcement officers and foreign military colleagues in her class. For ten weeks, she trained and learned quite a bit. She learned something from all the material she gathered, but nothing would become more important than what she saw one day at your firearms range. It was something none of the students were supposed to see. Or should I say, didn't see?"

It was clear the general had learned of the InCit program somehow, and he was about to tell Tracey how that came about.

"After a couple of hours of shooting weapons on your firearms range, a military helicopter, which the colonel later learned was carrying members of your Hostage Rescue Team, flew fairly close to the students on the range. Several operators fast-roped down from the helicopter and continued into the woods nearby. But it is what happened next that caught everyone's attention."

Tracey thought no matter what he would hear next, it was about to be the Bureau's fault the world would learn of InCit - not his.

"The colonel watched as a drone flew next to the helicopter, hovered next to the rope dangling from the bottom, and then disappeared. At the same time, another operator began to make his way down the rope. As he did so, bursts of what my colonel presumed were blanks were fired within ten feet of the operator's head. Everywhere the operator turned, aiming his weapon, the shots rang out from above his head. It was clear the operator did not fire any shots, however.

"Strange, wouldn't you agree, Special Agent Tracey?" the general said sarcastically.

Tracey's face was expressionless. "One of your colonels witnessed something at our firearms range at the FBI Academy, and you all of a sudden think we have some secretive technology? And one that you think I know exists?" Tracey asked, with an air of "you're crazy."

"I'm sure you are aware of the phrase 'loose lips sink ships,' aren't you, Special Agent Tracey?" the general asked.

Tracey nodded his head.

"I'm sure you know what happens when people have too much alcohol to drink. That phrase becomes even more important. Your Boardroom pub at the FBI Academy is a great place to socialize. For me and my colonel, it will prove to be providence for us. You see, the day after the incident, and after quite a few drinks, one of my colonel's National Academy special agent counselors decided to brag about what he worked on. Guess who that counselor might have been, Special Agent Tracey."

Tracey was starting to feel like his own worst enemy. He remembered his time as a counselor for one of the FBI National Academy classes and that episode the general described. He also remembered getting very drunk in the Boardroom, but he didn't remember bragging about anything. Could he have been the loose lips agent? Was the leak going to be his fault after all?

The general continued, "Your 'loose-lips' agent explained he was on a special team with invisible drones. The drones served to protect the agents and could sense danger. I would love to know how a drone senses anything, Special Agent Tracey."

"And you believe that?" Tracey asked with a matter-of-fact attitude, suggesting the general was crazy to believe what he said.

General Repuso looked at one of the guards and raised his right hand, waving at the guard to bring him something. The guard left and returned quickly, carrying a manila folder. The guard handed the folder to the general, who took it and sat back in his chair.

Tracey didn't want to seem apprehensive. He was a bit on edge, though, wondering what the general had in the folder. Tracey shifted very slowly in his chair and took a sip of coffee.

The general opened the folder. He thumbed through the documents contained inside. He smiled and smirked every time he turned to another document. Tracey had to admit: the suspense was killing him. He slowly sipped his coffee, suggesting nothing the general could say would cause his heart to beat any faster than it already was. He would be wrong, though.

The general then took a photo from the folder and leaned towards Tracey. He started to give it to Tracey and stopped. He placed it back in the folder and instead handed that to Tracey.

"Some of our better work, I think you will agree, Special Agent Tracey," the general said as he sat back in his chair. "See if you recognize the man in the photos as one of your teammates who commands an invisible drone. You can see in the pictures why he agreed to help us. Well, for that reason and the safety of his family and friends."

Tracey opened the folder. What immediately struck him was the folder contained only photographs. All the photos were the same size, 8x10. The first photo depicted a man and woman having sex in what appeared to be one of the Academy dorm rooms. The man *was* an agent on the InCit team, but Tracey couldn't place him by name. The next set of photos included a photo of his house and a photo of him and his family getting into their car in the driveway. There were also pictures of Athan and his family, Athan at his house, and driving his car. Several photos were of Tracey with Athan, including Tracey walking into Athan's corporate headquarters and up Athan's driveway.

Tracey flipped through a torrent of photos quickly after that first bunch. A few other photos that stuck out were shots of him and April boarding the plane in the U.S. and of them both going through customs at the Jafaire airport. One photo, probably meant to piss Tracey off, was a photo of Amir giving a thumbs-up to the photographer as Tracey and April got into the van at the airport.

Tracey's first reaction was anger. He was mad at himself for not noticing he was being watched in the U.S., let alone Jafaire. As none of the photos were of Tracey inside the Academy, he was going to believe for the time being that the general did not have a mole working for the FBI. Even if Tracey was followed as he drove towards the Academy, and he didn't notice the tail, the FBI security cameras would have picked up a surveillance team belonging to the general long before they got close to the Academy on the back roads of Quantico. That was probably why the general did not take the chance.

Tracey tilted his head with an air of indifference. "You appear to have followed me and my neighbor. Okay, so what? I'm not sure why you would surveil me, but you did. I'm curious - why are there no photos of me after I went off the grid?

Was it because you knew the FBI would find your surveillance team if you had a team?"

"No, we just had enough information on you and your friend, and it was no longer necessary to follow you. We also installed bugs in your friend's home and work to keep track of you both. As a bonus, we listened to some great conversations." The general smiled.

Tracey shrugged as if he didn't care. But he was now worried about what the general heard. "None of this proves anything, general. You have me in the company of my friend many times. We're good friends. I'm not sure that the world cares about our relationship. There is no secretive plot to blow up the world."

"Oh, I'll get there, Special Agent Tracey." The general put his hand up and waved to his assistant as he again gave a verbal instruction. She walked to his desk and picked up a laptop computer, which she quickly handed to the general. He placed it on the table and used his fingerprint to access it. After several keystrokes, he turned the laptop around to Tracey.

"Hit the play button if you would."

Tracey leaned forward and hit the play button. An audio file began to play with the two voices recognizable to Tracey. They were of him and Athan. They were meeting in Athan's home - talking about how Tracey would help Athan with his problem, and Athan would help Tracey with his.

There were several more files. The most damaging was the audio file from Athan's command center at his corporate headquarters. That one was dated three days before. Tracey then realized the general knew at least the fact Tracey had some technology from the Bureau he was using to help Athan's company. But the general had no clue about the technology behind the drone, even though he now knew Tracey had control of a drone.

Tracey would have to think fast with an explanation that would appease the general, so it would look like Tracey stole the drone and had no idea how it worked. That would be why he was in so much trouble with the Bureau. Yeah, that would have to work.

But Tracey had to be careful with what he said.

And he desperately wanted an update on his daughter's procedure.

Chapter 42
The Demand

Tracey casually placed the folder with the pictures on the table and sat back on the couch.

"Congratulations, General. You managed to follow an FBI Agent. We pride ourselves on picking up on surveillance, so you have that going for you and your team." Tracey clapped his hands very slowly and softly.

"But what do you think I know about any of this technology, and what do you think I can do for you?"

"Well, I'll go along, for now, believing that you don't know exactly what technology powers the drone, making it function. That is a possibility. But you do have a drone assigned to you. I am sure of that as you admitted it to your friend. What I also know is you have prepared a plan with your friend that involves your blowing up a portion of the polar ice cap, using that drone and the FBI's technology, for him to salvage his company and you to save your daughter. You will give me access to this technology first. In exchange, you'll have my silence regarding your arrangement with your friend. And most importantly, you and your daughter can be on your way."

Thankfully, the general didn't press Tracey on the technology that powered the drone. The stomonite's existence was safe, for now. But the general knew Tracey had access to the drone from the bugged conversations at Athan's home and work.

Tracey could only think about how he could get his daughter out of there safely. He wasn't so concerned about himself anymore; just that the procedure was successful and she would survive and live a long life. And in that moment, he came up with a plan. He would try it on for size and see what the general thought.

"Okay, General. Let's say I can get you that technology. First, it would take a day or so for me to get it here. While you wait for its arrival, I would consider it a sign of good faith if you would allow my daughter to leave before you have your hands on it. Her procedure will be done in a couple of hours, and if it's successful, her recovery period is only twelve hours or so. Let her go home."

The general recrossed his legs and crossed his arms. He didn't say anything. He just looked directly at Tracey. After a few minutes, he said, "I'm listening. What are you suggesting?"

Tracey slowed down his thoughts to get it all out accurately. "In under two hours, if my calculations are correct, my daughter's procedure will be complete. The doctor suggested she remain in his clinic for twelve hours following the procedure so he could monitor her for complications. He doesn't believe there will be any, but it's to be safe. Once she has passed that twelve-hour recovery window, you will allow her to board a plane and return to the United States. You can have one of your associates travel with her to Paris before she flies on to the United States.

"Your associate won't need a Visa to land in France. The French will ask them to return home to Jafaire. You take care of my daughter getting safely on her flight, and the technology will be here in Jafaire shortly after that. I, of course, will remain here as your hostage." Tracey stopped for a breath and let it all sink in for the general.

"But what will stop you from telling me you won't give me the technology after your daughter is safe, Mr. Tracey? It appears your death is of no consideration to you, and quite honestly, to the world, it would seem like I had kidnapped you."

"Agreed, that would be a reasonable thought. However, I have no way of contacting anyone at the Bureau. My only contact is with my friend and my wife. Seeing as how you put together a team to follow me around, and we never knew it, you are probably as capable of killing my family and my friend's family.

"Once you have the technology, I will depart Jafaire and return home. No one will know I was ever here. I am sure your contacts at the airport have made you aware I am traveling on an undercover passport. I will advise the FBI that I lost the drone and was trying to find it and get it back before I got in trouble. I will accept whatever consequences come my way from the U.S. government. Should the world find out Jafaire ended up with our technology after I say I have lost it, that is on you and not me."

The general didn't say a word. His facial expression remained the same.

"That's an interesting scenario, Mr. Tracey. Let me think for a moment."

The general leaned back in his chair. Tracey reached for a water bottle, feeling like he had just saved the world. He knew the general might alter the plan he came up with, but for the time being, he felt better about April's survival. And that was all that mattered to him. He had a second plan he would have to execute simultaneously. The general wasn't going to be informed of that one, however.

One plan at a time.

Chapter 43
The Clock Starts

After a minute, the general straightened up and grabbed his water from the table. Tracey had to hand it to the general - he kept his cool.

General Repuso leaned back with his bottle of water and then spoke. "I have you bent over a barrel here. It is my play, not yours. Here's what you are going to do. I believe you can access the drone you spoke of with your friend. You are going to divert that drone to me here in Jafaire. You can blow up the polar ice cap on your own time and find another way. I don't care about that. You have twenty-four hours to get me the drone. Figure it out. Once I have it, you and your daughter will be free to leave."

Tracey didn't hesitate to respond. "You'll have me and my daughter killed the moment you have the drone. I'm not stupid, as you have already said, General. No one knows we are here. Not even my friend or wife. You'll have me divert the drone through my friend, and then you'll kill him, too, once you have it. That's what I would do anyway. Safer that way, right? My friend's accidental death, I'm sure, would also be arranged."

The general said nothing. He didn't even move.

"I'll get you the drone. But in exchange for me. Period. Otherwise, my daughter and I will die here, and you get nothing. My friend expects to hear from me in -," Tracey paused to look at his watch, "- just under 40 minutes. If he doesn't, he knows to abort and destroy all evidence of our plan. The drone will be flown back to the FBI, and they'll always wonder what happened to me and my daughter. But I won't be treated like a traitor. Quite the opposite - the FBI will try to find out what happened to me, and they won't stop until they do. Your little overthrow plan will have to take a different route. If you can live with that, be done with it and do what you must to me and my daughter."

Tracey tried not to swallow. He was bluffing out his ass. He didn't want to be the cause of his daughter's death after everything they had gone through. He grabbed his water bottle and stared at the general, hoping to look confident.

The general also drank from his water bottle and finished it. The assistant immediately came over, took the bottle from him, and offered him another. He accepted it and waved her away without looking at her, staring directly at Tracey the whole time.

"Okay, Mr. Tracey. I can live with these terms. How exactly are you supposed to contact your friend, Mr. Kratos?"

Tracey began to reach into his underwear. Two soldiers immediately pointed their weapons at him.

"You're good at following people but terrible at securing prisoners," Tracey said, not to aggravate the general but to prove a point. He slowly raised his left hand as he continued reaching into his pants with his right hand for the drop phone he had hidden there.

"The best place to put contraband when you believe you are about to be searched. Everyone is afraid to grab the crotch of the same sex. I was counting on that."

The general was not amused by this lack of attention to detail as he glanced at the two soldiers who had accompanied Tracey in the Humvee. They averted his gaze.

Tracey chuckled to himself as he removed the phone. Once the general saw the phone, he motioned for his soldiers to stand down. They lowered their weapons and returned to their posts.

"May I have the phone, please, Mr. Tracey?"

Tracey leaned over to the general and handed him the phone.

The general turned it on and passed it back to Tracey once he saw the request for a password. Tracey obliged, entered the password, and handed the phone back to the general, who began to search through the device. There was only one text message. It was from Athan, asking Tracey if he was on schedule. But that was all. It was quickly apparent to the general the phone was simply a one-way communication device with only one contact. The number didn't even have a name assigned to it. There wasn't much the general could use against Tracey there.

Tracey wasn't a fool. He had been extensively trained and knew not to name anyone as an identified contact in a drop phone. Additionally, Tracey bought the drop phones they had been using years before. Neither Tracey nor Athan's phones would come back to either of them. Athan knew to destroy the phone at the first sign they were exposed. They even had a predetermined location where Athan would separate the phone into pieces and destroy it by placing them in several different watery graves.

"Only one message between the two of you, I see?" the general said.

"Yes. We agreed only to use the phone to communicate once I arrived in Jafaire. I am sure he is anxious to hear from me. And afterward only to communicate the final part of the plan."

"Blowing up a piece of the polar ice cap, I presume?" the general asked.

Tracey nodded his head.

"Let's send a text to your friend then. And for your sake, do not send it until I've had a chance to read what you wrote." The general handed the phone back to Tracey.

Tracey thought for a moment how he could make Athan aware he was being held against his will and that all their lives were in danger. He started to type immediately to make it seem like he *wasn't* thinking of that plan. But he was typing and deleting at the same time while he thought of one.

Once Tracey sent the text, Athan would have no reason to believe it wasn't Tracey who was sending the text. Tracey began his text;

"Hit a snag - Need our friend here for a short period first - Need it here in 24 hours or less - Will explain later - Send to these coordinates."

Tracey passed the phone with the text message visible to the general for his approval. He read the message and nodded his head in agreement. He then said something to his assistant, who left the room. She returned quickly with a piece of paper, which she handed to the general. The general looked at the paper and then handed the paper and the phone back to Tracey. "These are the coordinates. They will lead the drone directly here to my building."

Tracey carefully typed them into the text message. Before hitting send, he handed the phone back to the general with the piece of paper. General Repuso nodded.

"May I?" the general asked, his thumb hovering over the send button.

"By all means," Tracey said. The general hit send and closed the flip phone before placing it in his pocket.

"Now, let's check with the doctor and get an update on the procedure."

Tracey managed a small sigh. His thoughts were centered on getting his daughter safely back to the U.S.

Strangling the general was a close second.

Chapter 44

Not the Best Cavalry

Tracey's lake house
Trellis, MT

Bell knew he had to get to the hospital. But he so wanted to finish his beer. And he had to connect with IA24. He'd give IA24 a few more minutes and then head to the hospital. Right on cue, his blackhawk beeped to indicate he had a new message. Bell opened the blackhawk to find a text from the same number Bell found in IA24's blackhawk telling Bell to "find the dog first."

"IA83. IA24, Jerry Cranset here. A car accident delayed me. I'm ok. Director knows. He relayed you're at Tracey's house. I'm ten minutes out. Blue Tahoe."

Bell was confused. He drove IA24's car at Portal 17, and his car hadn't been in an accident. This wasn't adding up. Maybe there was another rogue agent on the InCit team. Bell decided he better prepare for a confrontation.

Bell took another swig from his beer and began to type. "No worries - See you in a few." Bell hit send. He looked at his wrist. The bleeding had stopped, but Bell didn't know if the wound was infected. And he certainly didn't want to take a chance if it was. He had to get to the hospital and get his wrist sewn up. However, he'd wait for IA24 or whoever was on their way.

Looking at the drone, he smiled slightly. Bell would have his backup for sure. His smile quickly faded to a look of "Oh, shit" as he suddenly realized he had not fully charged the drone's battery as Dr. Gaeber had instructed.

Bell stood up and, as best as he could, given his injured right wrist, grabbed the drone with both hands before turning it on its back. He had to turn it off to charge the battery. He managed the correct sequence for folding in the drone's legs and turned it off. He then opened the bottom panel and grabbed the charging cord for the battery. It would take thirty minutes for the drone to be fully charged. The drone would then have forty-eight-plus hours of fly time.

He reached for his beer and took what he hoped would be the last, long swig. Before he could finish his beer and charge his drone, he heard a door close outside. If it was IA24, that was quick and certainly less than ten minutes. Either IA24 couldn't estimate time worth a dime, or someone else had arrived before IA24. Bell stood up and only managed three steps towards the kitchen door when a gunshot rang out, followed by three more. All the rounds came barreling through the glass of the kitchen door and embedded in the opposite wall.

Bell wasn't a person who swore often, but at the moment, it seemed appropriate as he yelled, "Are you fucking kidding me!"

Bell's beer slipped out of his hands and onto the floor, and that pissed him off even more. One round narrowly missed his right arm. That would have just made his day. Who the hell else could be shooting at him? As Bell contemplated where he could turn for better concealment and cover, he wondered if IA24 had made his way down the driveway. If he had, then IA24 would have been able to engage whomever or whatever was shooting at him. Where the hell was the cavalry? And he sure picked the wrong time to charge his drone's battery.

Bell crouched down and moved away from the cabinets. Slowly inching backward, he grabbed his drone as he went. He made his way to the kitchen doorway leading to the stairway for the second floor. He paused. He didn't hear any movement. He quickly panned from right to left and stood up. He didn't see any movement. He decided to head up the stairs to gain a tactical advantage and get his drone back online. So long as whoever was shooting at him wasn't above the first floor or in a helicopter, Bell would be much safer.

After climbing the stairs quickly, he turned at the top and listened. Nothing. No movement. He then moved across the stairway and into the opening of a bedroom. Again, waiting to hear any movement downstairs and hearing none, he quickly walked towards the window to get a view of the driveway. Once at the window, he noticed a blue Tahoe in the driveway. IA24 said he had a blue Tahoe. What the hell? If this was IA24, why was he trying to kill him?

A sickening second thought entered Bell's mind as he again remembered the text from IA24, which said he would be there in ten minutes. Only about one minute had elapsed since he sent his text message, and he heard the car door before the rounds came through the kitchen. Either IA24 was woefully inept at calculating distance or was closer than he suggested when he texted Bell. But why would IA24 suggest it would take him longer to arrive than it did? Then it struck Bell. Was it IA24 who just texted him, or was it someone else?

Bell placed his drone on the ground. He quickly maneuvered the drone's legs back in place and hit the power button. The drone's rotors spun, and the drone started upward. Bell felt relieved.

"Secure perimeter," Bell whispered. The drone started out the bedroom door. And just as quickly, fell to the ground. The battery was dead. Bell shook his head slowly. He'd have to address the threat by himself.

This day was getting better and better.

Before Bell could entertain any more thoughts of IA24 being a mole, he heard the pressure of glass breaking downstairs. Somebody had stepped on a piece of glass in the kitchen. Bell carefully moved to the bedroom door and unholstered his Glock, training it on the stairway.

From downstairs came a loud booming voice.

"IA Bell. It's IA24, Jerry Cranset. Are you here? I heard gunfire as I pulled up. You okay?"

Bell was very certain all the rounds Cranset said he heard came through the door *at him*. And Bell knew he heard the car door close just before the rounds went off. This Cranset guy would have seen the shooter or was the shooter. And he didn't say he saw anyone. He had to be the shooter. Bell decided to play along.

"You don't mind if you come to the base of the stairs with your gun holstered and your hands up since we've never met before?"

"Oh, no problem there. I'm holstering and walking to the bottom of the stairs now."

Bell could hear the crunch of glass in the kitchen as Cranset walked towards the bottom of the stairs.

"Hey, I'm here at the bottom of the stairs. I'll keep my hands up until you see me, how's that?"

Bell slowly peered out of the bedroom doorway. He kept his sights down the stairway as he walked with his Glock out in front. Standing at the bottom of the stairs was a white male, approximately 6' 2" tall and nearly 200 pounds. His hands were in the air, and he wore black camo pants and a long-sleeved black shirt.

As Bell began to lower his Glock, he said, "Sorry to have to do that, but I didn't know who was coming in, and we've never met."

"No worries. I completely understand," Cranset said. "You threw me for a scare there. When I heard those rounds, I was afraid of the worst."

Bell wasn't buying his story. This guy, Cranset or not, had to be the shooter. "No, I'm good. The first round just narrowly missed me, and then I retreated upstairs. Did you see any cars coming or going?"

"No, I didn't see anyone. I just heard the rounds as I drove up."

He was flat-out lying. Bell wanted Cranset to believe he was on board with that story, so he holstered his Glock and started walking down the stairs. Cranset lowered his hands slowly and rubbed the top of his head with his left hand.

After walking down the stairs, Bell said, "I didn't even get to finish my beer." He faked a small laugh. "Why don't you grab a couple of beers from the fridge, and we can sit and talk? It's been a crazy day."

"Sounds like a plan," Cranset said.

As Cranset turned and walked through the kitchen towards the refrigerator, Bell noticed the handgun in Cranset's holster was not a Bureau-issued Glock .40 caliber. It looked like a Sig Sauer. That was enough to convince Bell something wasn't right with Cranset. Bell reached across and over to his holster with his left hand and took his Glock out again.

"Why don't you stop right where you are."

Bell's Glock was trained directly on Cranset's back. Cranset turned around quickly, and with complete surprise, he jumped a little.

"What the ..?" Cranset said, clearly surprised and angry. "Why would you draw down on me?"

"Let's just say I don't believe a single word you've said. I'm not even sure you are IA24."

"And why not?" Cranset asked.

"For starters, I heard your car door close ten seconds before the rounds started coming through the door. And since you said you didn't see any other car when you arrived, nor the shooter, it was pretty simple to deduce your car was the one that pulled up right before the rounds were fired. So, tell me I'm wrong?" Bell glared at him.

Cranset hesitated with his answer just long enough for Bell to know he was right.

"Look, whatever you're thinking, you're wrong," Cranset said. "I came down the driveway and heard the shots. That was it."

"And I'm saying you're lying. Where are your creds? And your badge?"

"My badge is under my shirt if you want to see it."

"No, don't move, and keep your hands up. Where are your creds?"

"In my pocket. My back pocket."

"Which back pocket?"

"My right pocket."

"Then use your left hand and reach behind you and grab your creds."

"This is completely unnecessary. But I'll do it to make you feel at ease."

Cranset slowly took his left hand and worked his way around to his right back pocket. As he did so, Cranset slowly turned his body diagonally, placing his right side toward Bell. In one quick movement, he reached with his right hand for the weapon in his holster. Bell didn't hesitate. He fired two quick rounds, one hitting Cranset in the upper shoulder and the other striking him in the chest. Cranset never fired a round and dropped his gun as he fell to the ground, moaning in pain. His gun bounded off to the side, out of his reach.

Bell covered the distance between him and Cranset quickly. He leaned down and picked up Cranset's Sig Sauer. Cranset continued to moan as Bell placed the Sig Sauer in the small of his back. Turning the man sideways, Bell took a black wallet that looked like FBI credentials out of Cranset's right rear pocket and opened it. FBI Special Agent Jerry Cranset. Just great. Bell took a deep breath and let it out.

"I'm going to call an ambulance. Hang in there."

Bell dialed 911. He told the operator he needed an ambulance right away. And to bring the police. Bell wanted Cranset handcuffed in that ambulance on the way to the hospital. Bell wasn't taking any chances.

"Okay, the ambulance is on its way. So, you want to tell me what's going on here?" Bell demanded.

Cranset moaned several more times before speaking. Bell grabbed a towel off the stove and applied it to Cranset's chest. He was bleeding pretty badly.

"You have no idea what's going on with the InCit program. I can tell you our country is not the only one that knows about InCit. And your friend Tracey is working to help overthrow a country with the Bureau's InCit technology."

"And how do you know that?" Bell asked

Cranset's breathing was labored. He shifted slightly on the floor but remained on his back.

"I met Tracey when we were both National Academy counselors last year. He and I quietly discussed the InCit program once we realized we were both IAs. Later on, he sat down with the National Academy students in the Boardroom, drunk as shit, and wouldn't shut up about the InCit program. I got him out of there and took him to his room. From what a few other counselors told me, the idiot didn't remember anything the next day or that I took him to his room. I wasn't so lucky."

Cranset took a deep breath.

"When I left Tracey's dorm room, a female National Academy student from some small African country rolled her pretty blue eyes and started flirting with me. Before I knew it, I was in her room, getting drunk and ultimately having sex with her. Later, I found out she had a hidden camera. They had me.

"Because that dumbass Tracey told everyone in the Boardroom I was also on this 'special team,' her country assumed I had access to a drone. A week later, I got a package of photos of me having sex. Then three men cornered me at a coffee shop and pointed out the pictures were the least of my problems." Cranset took a breath and continued to speak slowly.

"They said they would kill my family if I didn't help them steal the InCit technology. I told them I was a junior agent and didn't have access to the technology. They believed me but forced me to find someone with access and to steal their drone. I tried to convince them it wasn't possible, but they gave me a month to figure it out. I didn't know what to do." Cranset coughed up a bit of blood. He was closing his eyes more frequently, and Bell feared he wouldn't make it.

"Luckily, I ran into your buddy Tracey again several weeks later at an InCit team meeting. Tracey seemed a bit off-base. He mentioned that InCit was such a great program that could help so many people that he wished he could share the technology with others. I passed his thoughts on to the men who had followed me and suggested Tracey might be a good target. So, they began to surveil Tracey and bug locations he visited and people he was associated with."

"So, why didn't you tell the director about Tracey's frame of mind if you were concerned? You and your family would have been kept safe."

"And have them take that blabbermouth Tracey out of the InCit program, leaving me back in the spotlight with these strangers?! I don't think so. I needed Tracey to take the fall, and no one would have ever known about me."

Cranset was breathing very slowly now and closed his eyes.

"Hey, stay awake! I'm going to get you out of here and to a hospital. Heck, I have to get to a doctor myself. I got shot by a drone near portal 17." Bell held up his right hand with the tourniquet around it.

Cranset opened his eyes slightly and looked at Bell's hand.

"Sorry about that. That was my drone. I put it on Protect Mode and had it guard my car where I left it."

"That was your BuCar just before portal 17?"

"Yes. I left it there and got into a van with the foreigners as we drove up to portal 17."

"Then you know what happened at portal 17?"

"Yes, I was told to work with several of their operators to secure portal 17. They wanted access and were going to blame Tracey since no one could find him. He became the perfect patsy."

"Who killed the sentry?" Bell asked as he applied pressure to Cranset's chest.

"That sucked. The sentry wasn't supposed to be there. We only went to the portal because we saw him driving away from the house. But the sentry turned around on the road, and we missed it. He was getting out of his car as we pulled into the driveway. They chased him into the house and killed him before he could get himself or us down to the portal command center.

"As bad luck would have it, my password was not yet entered into the system at headquarters for this mission, so I couldn't access the portal command center. We left without gathering any information about Tracey's whereabouts."

"Why didn't you simply give them your InCit drone?"

"Remember, I told them I was too junior an agent to have a drone, and I would get the technology to them without the drone. They never knew my drone was with me the whole time."

Bell nodded his head. "Exactly. I would think a plan for the drone to take them all out would have been possible, though," Bell said without looking for an answer. "You should have killed the sentinel to make it look like strangers simply stumbled upon the portal. I watched the video of the attack. I wondered why the sentinel barked when four masked individuals walked down the driveway. You were one of the masked operators, and the sentinel knew you were an IA."

"I know. I just couldn't kill the dog, though. That's why I sent the text to my blackhawk. I saw you in town and knew you were heading to portal 17. I hoped you would stop at my car. I wanted you to 'find the dog first' to be sure she was alright."

Cranset coughed. A little blood came out. "And again, sorry about the drone."

Bell was mostly unmoved by Cranset's little speech.

"But it's okay to kill me?" Bell said with disgust in his voice. "Why didn't the drone keep shooting at me? I drove off in your BuCar and returned it to the same location."

While he waited for Cranset to answer, Bell walked over to the cupboard and found a glass. He filled it with water and leaned down to help Cranset take a sip. Cranset was laboring even more now. Bell had to get him out of there. He didn't hear the ambulance yet.

"In Protect Mode, the drone will remain where it's placed. It wouldn't follow you when you left. I don't know why it didn't shoot at you again when you returned. Maybe something was blocking its view."

"When I returned, I parked your BuCar close to several trees. That may have saved me from taking another round.

"Why *did* you try to kill me?" Bell asked as he gave Cranset another sip of water.

"What you don't know is Tracey is not in the U.S. If I killed you, it would appear that the madman overseas he is working with killed you. It would keep the Bureau looking for Tracey even longer. No one would know it was me. That's all I cared about. I'm sure you already picked up on the fact I didn't use my Glock to shoot at you."

"I noticed that. It was the deciding factor in my mind to draw down on you. So where is Tracey then?" Bell asked.

Cranset didn't answer right away. He swallowed and tried to answer. "Why - - don't - - you - - ask - - Ath- -," Cranset began slowly saying each word as he coughed up blood and grimaced. Cranset closed his eyes, and the grimace on his face faded away to nothing.

Bell placed his hand on the blood-soaked towel. Cranset had lost a lot of blood.

"Stay awake, dammit!" Bell shouted, lightly slapping Cranset's face. Cranset didn't even flinch.

"Why don't I ask who? No, no, no!!!" Bell shouted. He felt for a pulse. Nothing. He tried again, but still nothing. Cranset was dead.

Bell released the pressure he had been applying to Cranset's chest. There would be no need to handcuff Cranset to the gurney in the ambulance.

What a shitty day. Bell wanted a do-over.

Bell could make his day a little better, though. He was taking a ride to the hospital when the ambulance arrived. His wrist was starting to throb again.

He didn't want to end up like Cranset.

Chapter 45

The Mission Changes

September 9, 2012
8:30 p.m.
Kratos Oil & Shale Company, Corporate Headquarters
Miami, FL

Athan's heart was pumping so fast he could see his shirt rising and falling. He pushed his chair backward, stood up, and almost immediately sat back down. He quickly stood up again. He was trying to understand what he had just read.

Athan had no reason to believe it wasn't Tracey texting him. It was a text from the only phone that knew Athan's drop phone number concerning their plan. They had gone over it many times - only use the drop phone and only call or text if the original plan was in jeopardy or you lost something, like the detonation codes for the drone or access to the computer. Anything along those lines. Athan quickly realized the reason for the text; "the plan was in jeopardy." But Tracey had a request. What the hell? Tracey's text was worded so evenly. Was it made under duress? Tracey was clear, though - only use the drop phone if you lost something or the original plan was jeopardized.

Tracey surely had faith that Athan could get this done. Good God, Athan hoped so. He knew a lot of people were counting on him. April's life depended on it. Tracey's life most definitely depended on it. Hell, Athan's livelihood depended on it. Now, he had to cancel the drone's current mission and send the drone to Tracey, wherever that was.

He slid his chair under the desk and flipped open his laptop. He clicked over to his VPN and made sure it was on. He opened his secure TOR browser for added anonymity and security and tunneled his way through forty or so networks before opening up the drone flight program. The video feed sent back by the drone reflected the same status. All systems were operational. The drone had nestled itself down between two small ice formations. There was still no precipitation to worry about. The green status light was illuminated. It would be completely dark in three hours, and they could detonate the charge. Damn it. That would now have to wait.

Athan worked his way over to the launch file. The drop-down menu gave him a host of different choices. He clicked through the selections and started to re-route the drone. Tracey's instructions included latitude and longitude coordinates. He decided to look up the actual address for these coordinates before he changed the drone's flight plans. When the results came back, Athan stared at the screen dumbfounded. The coordinates came back to a country named Jafaire. He was puzzled. Where the hell was Jafaire?

Athan plugged in the address and the coordinates for the destination. A picture popped up of a government-looking building on the edge of Lingos, the capital city of Jafaire. As Athan kept reading, he learned the building was the headquarters of the Jafairian Defense Ministry. Was Tracey helping the country of Jafaire first before he blew up the ice cap? Athan had no idea.

He clicked back over to the drone's hardware profile and flight speed. The distance the drone would travel, from the Norwegian polar ice cap area of Austfonna to Jafaire, was just around 7,700 miles. He calculated it would take the drone approximately fifty-two hours to get to Jafaire. That was a long way. And Tracey told him he needed the drone in 24 hours. It looked like the drone would be late.

Athan clicked on a few more buttons, and the drone released the package of explosives and the drill mechanism as if the plan was still on track to blow up the polar ice cap. He had to be sure not to hit the countdown to detonate the explosives. He managed not to.

He then double-checked the coordinates Tracey sent him. Athan assumed that Tracey needed the drone for an important reason. He hesitated for a second, with his hand pausing over the "send" button, and then clicked the send button, and the drone now had its new flight plan.

The drone's camera then displayed a live video of the drone ascending from the snow tunnel where it lay in the snow and ice. When it reached the surface, it began its new flight path. The drill, drill bit, and package of C4 were no longer attached. A new countdown appeared at the top of the page. Eighteen hours, twelve minutes. A whole hell of a lot faster than Athan had calculated. Losing the extra weight of the drill, drill bit, and C4 greatly adjusted the flight speed. Maybe it would get to Tracey in time.

A few buttons lit up as it departed the polar ice cap. One button turned green from red, indicating the drone was now invisible. Another button indicated "RDS (30/30)." Athan had no idea what that button meant.

Tracey, however, was counting on that specific indicator to be accurate, a reflection of the number of .223 rifle rounds the drone was carrying and right at capacity. Tracey knew he would need every round.

✦✦✦

Thirty minutes before Dr. Parker executes the kill code

Athan stood by his office window and stared out. It was starting to rain. He could see the guard booth and the guard sitting inside reading the paper. A bus made its way down the street as it took on passengers. A few cars traveled in each direction. The world was oblivious to what Athan and Tracey were doing. Athan wondered if the world would approve of their plan. But he knew it didn't matter what the world thought. He was helping his company and saving a friend's daughter's life.

Athan walked back to his desk and sat down. He moved the mouse cursor on the computer and brought up the drone program. A graphic showed the drone was in flight to its new location. The counter said eighteen hours, seven minutes, thirty-seven seconds, and counting. The video camera on the drone shut down when it was at full speed, so Athan couldn't see what the drone was seeing. All Athan knew was what the screen indicated: the drone was moving at 205.3 miles per hour. That was faster than the speed the drone managed on the way to the polar ice cap. It wasn't carrying anything extra, and favorable winds had to be pushing the drone forward.

As Athan continued to wonder how they would succeed at their plan, he decided he should let Tracey know when he could expect the drone. Powering on the drop phone, it vibrated quickly and gave off a short beat. There were several messages. He flipped open the phone and saw several text messages, none from Tracey and all from one wireless address. Athan had no idea who the text messages were from.

He decided to text Tracey that the drone would be there in roughly 18 hours. After updating Tracey on the ETA, he went back to the messages.

The subject line on the first message said: "Activity Detected." The two lines of text stated, "Your security system has detected activity in the following location - Trellis Birdhouse." And there was a video file attached.

Athan figured it was a spam message, but how would anyone know this drop phone number? Tracey only recently activated it, and as near as Athan could tell, Tracey hadn't used any Bluetooth or wireless on the phone at all. They were both turned off. While he scrolled down, he thought again about the "Trellis Birdhouse." Didn't Tracey have a place in Trellis? Maybe this was no coincidence, and it had something to do with Tracey's property in Trellis. As was the case with Athan lately, he thought, "Ah, screw it," and he clicked on the video.

What Athan heard and saw next almost caused him to retch. He heard the slow whirl of helicopter blades grow louder and louder until a helicopter with men dressed in military clothing hanging over the side approached what Athan assumed was Tracey's lake house. Lights were shining from both sides. The men were looking for something or someone as they moved their flashlights from side to side. After rising to about fifty feet, the helicopter stopped, the lights switched off, and it flew away. What the hell was that? Athan wondered.

Back at the main screen, he counted sixteen more messages. They were sent several hours after the first one. He clicked on the next message and then the attached video. Athan watched as a man with his gun drawn approached the back door of the house. Athan had no idea it was Bell. Athan watched Bell enter the house.

The next several videos showed Bell clearing the house. One video appeared to come from a camera in the kitchen. Another video appeared to have come from the living room, and yet another video showed Bell at the top of the stairs. As Athan tried to figure out why he had received these videos in the first place, he watched as Bell walked throughout the house carrying a piece of paper in front of his face. Athan found the right button and zoomed in on the note. On it was written, "Call me. Drop phone. 401-401-4101." Athan figured the man knew Tracey could access his security feed and would call him after seeing the videos. Athan copied the phone number down.

Athan then watched in disbelief as Bell battled it out with Cranset, and the EMTs took Cranset away, leaving Tracey's house silent.

After viewing the last video, Athan slowly sat back in his chair. He sighed heavily and thought about all the videos he had just watched. He closed his eyes. And then the phone beeped again. Another message? Athan grabbed the phone, but it *wasn't* a message. Shit. The beep was an alert the phone's battery was about to die. Athan scrambled to the wall behind his desk and plugged the phone into the charger. Too late. The phone had turned off, but it was charging.

He didn't think there was any rush to turn the phone on as there were no new messages. Athan would wait until the phone was fully charged. He'd get to it later. But not soon enough to warn Tracey.

It wouldn't be until the next day before Athan turned the phone back on. And that would be too late to see the most recent text notifications from the drone's software program alerting him the drone was now offline. The ultimate kill code from Dr. Parker did the job.

Tracey wouldn't know his help wasn't on the way.

CHAPTER 46
Another Cleanup, Different Aisle

Bell could hear the sirens as the emergency and police vehicles barreled down the road leading to Tracey's lake house. He got up off the floor and slowly walked to the door. When he reached the door, he waved outside to the EMTs who had arrived and jumped out of the ambulance.

"Up here, guys." The police officers exited their cars as well.

The EMTs quickened their pace and bounded up the stairs with their gurney. Bell held his badge out for them to see.

"FBI Special Agent Bell. There are no threats in the house. On the floor in the kitchen is FBI Special Agent Jerry Cranset. He took two rounds. One to the chest." The officers slowed their pace once they heard Bell identify himself and mention there was no danger to deal with.

The EMTs raced inside and immediately began to work on Cranset. Bell followed them. After about three minutes, both EMTs stopped and shook their heads, signaling he hadn't made it. Bell could have told them that.

The EMTs inspected Bell's wrist and changed out the bloodied cloth, re-wrapping the wound with a new gauze dressing. They suggested he should go to the hospital with them. Bell simultaneously explained to the officers what had occurred. Mostly. Rogue agent, unhappy with the FBI, etc. They took down some notes and told Bell they would get their report to him to review and sign. Bell told them ERT and an FBI shooting team would be on scene soon, and they would be handling the investigation and crime scene. The officers agreed to remain until the FBI teams arrived.

The EMTs reached down and picked up Cranset, putting him on the gurney. They maneuvered him out the door and carried him down the stairs and into the ambulance. Once Cranset was strapped in, they again urged Bell to visit the hospital for further treatment. Bell convinced them he could drive and promised he would follow right behind them. The EMTs reluctantly agreed and drove off.

Bell went back inside and recovered his drone. It was lying on the floor just outside the upstairs bedroom where he left it, visible as it had no power source. He grabbed a pillowcase off a pillow in the upstairs bedroom and stuffed the drone inside so the officers wouldn't see it. He walked out the kitchen door onto the deck, looking around as he went. What a mess. But clean up wasn't on Bell.

Bell prayed there was a security camera in the house somewhere, and Tracey saw what happened over the last few hours. And, hopefully, Tracey saw Bell's signs to call him.

Glad to leave the house behind, Bell followed the ambulance to the hospital. When he arrived at the hospital, he parked his Tahoe near the emergency room and wirelessly plugged his drone into the Tahoe's power supply. He waited one minute for the drone to receive enough power for Bell to turn it on. Once on, Bell commanded the drone to "Cloak," and the drone remained on and invisible. Remembering the command Cranset gave his drone to protect his BuCar, Bell barked out "Protect Mode" and headed into the emergency room.

Bell described his wounds to the front desk staff, and then a female doctor and nurse began to examine him. They took several X-rays and asked Bell follow-up questions. Bell provided mostly truthful answers. Of course, there was no drone involved in the shooting, only a random shooter Bell never saw. And that was somewhat true. After the doctor reviewed the X-ray film, she gave him her observations and a course of action. "Ok, Special Agent Bell. You were pretty lucky. The round missed almost all of your wrist bones. It nicked the side of two wrist bones, but you'll never feel anything different once it's fully healed. It was a through-and-through. Unfortunately, it is not all good news. The round managed to slice through a small tendon across several of your wrist bones. I'll sew this tendon back together. However, your ability to squeeze moving forward will be diminished." The doctor poked at the wound softly with a pair of forceps. "We're going to numb the area with a little local anesthetic and get some stitches in there to secure the tendon back in place for you."

"Thank you, doc. How long will it take to sew me up? I do have something super important to get done."

"We'll get the local in place here right now, and it should take around three minutes to get numb before we can stitch it up."

"Save the three minutes, doc. Just stitch it. I honestly have to get a move on."

The nurse and doctor looked at each other quickly and shrugged.

"Okay then. Let's do this."

The doctor and nurse worked together for about 15 minutes, stitching in and around the wound on Bell's wrist. Bell's mind wandered off while they worked, thinking about his friend and how it would end. He didn't even think about the pain of the needle as his hand had been throbbing so much it didn't matter to him anyway.

"Done," the doctor announced. "It looks good. You alright?"

"Fine," Bell replied. "Thank you both."

Bell looked over at the mini-surgery the doctor had just performed. As far as Bell could tell, he looked all stitched up. His hand was now throbbing just a bit more. "Any chance I could get a few ibuprofen for the road?" Bell asked as he hopped off the hospital bed.

The doctor smiled and went off to retrieve some ibuprofen for Bell. When she returned, she gave Bell a few pieces of advice. "Change the bandage every day. Change it more frequently if you notice any seepage of blood or a build-up of puss." The doctor reached into her coat pocket and handed Bell gauze, tape, and some antibiotic ointment. "Do you have any questions for me?"

"When can I use my right hand to shoot again?" Bell asked, smiling broadly.

"Guess that depends on your pain level, Special Agent Bell," the nurse said as she and the doctor laughed. Bell smiled at them.

He rolled down his sleeve as he walked. The pain in his wrist was bearable, so he tried to squeeze his right hand. Okay, that hurt. Maybe he wasn't ready for that exercise just yet.

Bell signed the release forms and headed out to his BuCar.

As Bell entered the Tahoe, he looked down at his drone lying on the front passenger seat floorboard. "Uncloak," Bell barked out. Making itself visible, Bell could see the side of the drone, and the solid green light told Bell it was fully charged. He left the hospital feeling a little bit relieved.

He reached under his seat and grabbed his blackhawk. He also grabbed his navigator. He had to get to a portal to use a secure phone line and call the director. Consulting the navigator first, portal 17 was now further away from him. The next green blinking light indicated the closest portal was fifteen miles north. He would head towards that portal.

Bell then turned on his blackhawk. After it powered up, the blackhawk beeped to indicate messages were waiting. Bell saw he had one text message with several replies. The original text was from Dr. Parker. Bell was cc'd on a text she had sent to the director. He read her text.

"Mr. Director. I have uncovered that IA Tracey switched his sister's DNA profile with a copy of his. Long story, but he has a twin sister who works in ERF. No one knew this fact. So, we have only deleted one of SA Tracey's DNA profiles."

Bell re-read the text. Three times. What the hell was she talking about? She had to be wrong. Bell would know if Tracey had a sister. He just would.

Bell then read the reply from the director. "Great work - remove SA Tracey's additional DNA profile from the InCit database."

Dr. Parker's reply. "Done. The drone should now be disabled. I'm sending you the sister's information for debriefing, sir, on the secret side."

"Good - I'll text IA Bell - he is at IA33's lake house." That was the last text between the director and Dr. Parker.

Bell's head swirled with what he had learned from Dr. Parker's text. He was trying to make sense of it all. Was it a ploy? If so, for what purpose? Then it hit Bell.

From what Cranset said, Tracey was the architect of this plan, whatever it was. So, Tracey knew he would lose access to the drone when he went off the grid, and management would know something was up. An ultimate kill code would have been initiated, and Tracey's DNA profile would have been removed from the InCit database. The drone would've immediately shut down. That would be the protocol.

Tracey, however, must have shut the drone down earlier, as soon as he put his plan into action. And somehow, Tracey changed his sister's DNA profile with his DNA profile in the computer system, hoping they wouldn't figure out he had a sister. Tracey turned the drone back on using his sister's DNA profile. Tracey was more than likely still operating his drone. If he was, Bell had to give Tracey credit. He did his homework. But he would still receive a failing grade.

✦✦✦

Several hours now removed from the polar ice cap, Tracey's drone flew along directly toward Jafaire.

And then it wasn't. It just stopped. Midair.

The two fishermen pulling in their fishing nets had no idea what created the splash just off the bow of their boat.

Tracey's drone had received the ultimate kill code and slowly sank to the bottom of the Tyrrhenian Sea.

Chapter 47
Killing Time

General Repuso's office
Lingos, Jafaire

The phone rang on the general's desk. His assistant immediately took two steps to answer the phone, and the general waved her off. He looked at the caller ID before answering and smiled. He spoke in English for Tracey's benefit.

"Hello, Amir. How are things going at the clinic?"

The general listened as he nodded his head and looked over at Tracey.

"Wonderful. That is good to hear. I will let Mr. Tracey know. I'm sure he will be happy to hear the news. Keep me informed. We are still on schedule."

The general hung up the phone.

"Mr. Tracey, you will be happy to hear that your daughter's procedure is completed. The doctor came out looking for you two times, but Amir put him off, so he and your daughter are none the wiser about our arrangement. We should be able to keep it that way.

"I am going to give you your cell phone for a moment. You will call Dr. Embuke and tell him you are sorry that you got caught up talking to an American stranger you came across at the coffee shop who was also from Miami. Also, tell him you booked a hotel room at the Hotel Tralfor so you could shower. That is where you have been resting and where you will be returning to while you wait for your daughter to recover. Dr. Embuke shouldn't be suspicious of that story. Tell him you are sorry for making him worry. Of course, you should ask him how your daughter is and when you can see her."

"I can do that," Tracey said. He was more relieved than his facial expression let on about his daughter's status. He needed to keep his head about his plan to leave the country with his daughter.

Tracey dialed the number the general already programmed for him. As he waited for Dr. Embuke to pick up, he could only think of April and her resting comfortably. After two rings, Nurse Mariama picked up the phone.

"Hello, this is Nurse Mariama." Tracey put his hand over the mouthpiece and quietly mouthed to the general it was his daughter, then handed him the phone.

"Hello, Daughter. I am going to have Mr. Tracey speak to the doctor. Could you get the doctor and say he is calling?"

"Absolutely. Just one minute."

The general handed the phone back to Tracey. "He should be on in just a minute. Remember what we talked about."

Tracey nodded his head and waited for Dr. Embuke. After a minute or two, Tracey could hear someone shuffling their feet as they approached the phone. The receiver clambered off the desk. It was Dr. Embuke.

"Hello, Mr. Tracey. I was worried when you were not in the waiting room. Amir said you went for a walk. That was a very long walk!"

"Yes, sorry to worry you, doctor. I met up with an American who used to live in Miami for some time, and we talked for quite a bit. Then I rented a room at the Hotel Tralfor to take a shower. How is my daughter doing? Can I see her?"

"She is resting nicely. You can see her anytime. We are now in the window of her twelve-hour recovery period. We will monitor her closely, of course. If it looks like her time frame for recovery can be moved up a little, I will let you know. She is a fighter, and her defense system is strong, with the only exception being the DBA. When will you stop by?"

"Hang on just a second, doctor. Somebody is at the door here at the hotel."

"General, the doctor is asking when I will return," Tracey said with his hand over the phone. The general started to answer, and Tracey loosened his grip on the mouthpiece. *God, let the doctor hear the general's voice.*

"Tell the doctor you can be at the clinic in an hour. Your conversation will be that you will head back to the hotel following that visit to get some sleep as you wait for your daughter to recover. Remember, Mr. Tracey, that my daughter will be watching your every move and listening to your conversation. I would suggest you don't try to outwit me."

Tracey gave the general a thumbs-up with his left hand as he removed it from the mouthpiece.

"Dr. Embuke, I should be by within the hour if that will be okay. I'll then head back to the hotel and get some rest while my daughter recovers."

Dr. Embuke hesitated. Had he heard the general on the phone as Tracey had hoped?

"That is perfect, Mr. Tracey. Just knock on the door outside, and my nurse will let you in. Amir is also here, and he may get to the door to let you in before she does."

"Thank you, Doctor. See you soon."

As Tracey finished saying, "See you soon," the general looked away and snapped his fingers at his assistant. That was all the time Tracey needed.

Tracey closed the flip phone and dropped it into his lap. He'd secure it the next time no one was looking.

"So far, everything appears to be working as planned, don't you agree, Mr. Tracey?" the general asked, looking back at Tracey. And just as he uttered those last words, Tracey's drop phone beeped in his lap with a new message. Shit. There goes that plan.

"Before we head over to see your daughter, let's see what that message says." The general motioned to the phone in Tracey's lap and smiled dryly.

What a dick. It was worth a try.

The general read the message from Athan indicating the drone was eighteen hours away.

Chapter 48
How Can I Help?

As Bell drove away from the hospital, he checked his navigator. It indicated he was still headed toward the next portal. But he was unsure of what to do now. Tracey was not at his lake house, and from Bell's deduction, Tracey probably still had access to his drone. But where the hell was he? As Bell thought again about Tracey's location, and what Dr. Parker had found out, his drop phone rang. The screen read "Blocked" with no numbers visible. Typically, Bell wouldn't answer those phone calls, but after the last few days of craziness, he figured anything might be possible. And no one knew this drop phone number except for a few choice folks - including Tracey - so maybe it was something helpful.

"Hello," Bell answered. There was silence.

"Hello," Bell said again.

"Hello. My name is Athan Kratos. I am a close friend of Special Agent David Tracey."

Bell slowed down a bit. He sat straight up in his seat.

"Okay. How did you get this number?" Bell asked, puzzled.

"It's an interesting story. But I promise you I will get right to it."

"Before you say anything, do you know where Tra-, I'm sorry, Special Agent Tracey is?" Bell asked.

"I think I do know where he is. And I can give you all that information."

"I'll tell you what. Call me back in ten minutes because I'm on the road and driving to a location where we can talk privately."

Based on what Bell knew so far from Cranset, there was a chance his BuCar was bugged. Bell knew the next conversation he had with this guy Athan had to be conducted in a secure location, like a portal.

"Sounds good." Athan hung up as did Bell.

Bell looked at his navigator. Portal 18. East. 8 miles. Perfect.

Hopefully, that portal was not compromised in any manner.

Chapter 49
Recovery Room

Dr. Embuke's clinic
Recovery room
Jafaire, Africa

It had been a couple of hours since Tracey's drone went for a swim. However, Tracey believed it would be only sixteen hours before his drone arrived. It had also been several hours since April's procedure. She was awake and thumbing through songs on her phone as Nurse Talia concentrated on the readouts from the machines April was plugged into. Dr. Embuke brusquely walked into the room. April saw him coming and took off her headset.

"Hello, April. Good to see you are wide awake and alert. How do you feel?" Dr. Embuke asked with a smile.

"I don't know about the 'wide awake' part, but I feel good," April said as she smiled back. "I am still a little groggy, but other than that, I feel like I can run out of here." Dr. Embuke laughed out loud. "That is great to hear. I just spoke to your father, and he will be here within the hour."

"That's good news. I'm anxious to see him. How do you think the procedure went, Doctor? Do you think I'll be in recovery for the full twelve hours?"

"So far, your vitals are very strong. Your recovery in these first several hours has been impressive. You have a strong defense system, although you might not think so, given your history. Because of that defense system, your recovery should be quicker. Your red blood cells are now producing at a near-normal pace, and we both know that is good for combatting DBA.

"When your father arrives, I will bring him to see you. Hopefully, we will get you out of here sooner than later and back to your home in the U.S."

"That's the best music to my ears," April said, motioning to the headset in her lap. Everyone laughed. She closed her eyes and lay back to get some more sleep.

"Keep an eye on her for me, please," Dr. Embuke said to the nurses but to no one in particular. I'm going to my desk to check my emails. I will be back shortly with her father once he arrives."

The nurses nodded in approval and turned back to their computers. Dr. Embuke headed out of the recovery room and over to his office.

As Tracey had hoped, Dr. Embuke *had* heard the general in the background when Tracey called. He was sure it was the general. But why would April's father be with the leader of Jafaire's armed forces?

Dr. Embuke entered his office and headed over to his computer, He logged in, opened the last email from Dr. Undulee, and replied.

"Hello, my friend. I wanted to tell you that I conducted the procedure on Mr. Tracey's daughter. She is five hours into her recovery and appears to be healing. Like my sister, the transfusion may save her life. I am curious if you know if Mr. Tracey had any thoughts of visiting our armed forces while he was here in Jafaire. Or did he ever mention he would meet with anyone in Jafaire other than me? Let me know as soon as you can. I have had a curious situation arise. Be safe, my friend. H."

After Dr. Embuke sent the email, he headed to the coffee pot. He poured himself a cup and put it in the microwave. It was long past the time the coffee pot had shut off. As he watched the cup turn inside the microwave, he realized that Amir was still in the waiting room. The microwave beeped, and he grabbed his cup of coffee and headed towards Amir. Maybe Amir had some answers. He would have to proceed carefully.

Dr. Embuke opened the door to the waiting room. He noticed Amir sitting against the wall in the same seat he was in earlier. Amir looked up and immediately smiled.

"Hello, Dr. Embuke. How are things going in there with Mr. Tracey's daughter?"

"The procedure appears to be a success so far, Amir. She is done with the procedure and is well into her recovery now. Hopefully, we can get her out of here soon. She has a stronger immune system now."

"That is wonderful news," Amir said with the biggest smile.

"Amir, let me ask you a question. Did Mr. Tracey say he was meeting anyone else while he was in Jafaire?"

Amir's smile disappeared. "Why do you ask, Dr. Embuke?" Amir said as he put his phone in his lap.

"It seems strange he left and knew where to get a hotel room. He has been gone for so long."

"Oh, not to worry, Doctor. He is a smart man. I am sure he is doing fine." Amir gave a thumbs up. Dr. Embuke slowly nodded as he looked away and headed back in.

Dr. Embuke sat down at his desk with his coffee. He thought Amir's answer was a bit contrived. Something was up. Dr. Embuke felt it. A quick call to his sister, the president might clear things up, but then he would have to tell her he broke his promise never to perform the procedure again. And then they would both worry.

They would worry their whole family could be targeted for death by the pharmaceutical companies, the same companies that stood to lose trillions of dollars if their drugs were no longer needed to stem the advance of a disease possibly cured by Dr. Embuke.

On the other hand, morally, Dr. Embuke wanted to save lives.

It was a dilemma he didn't wish on anyone.

Dr. Embuke let out a sigh. He sat back in his chair and slowly sipped on his coffee.

Chapter 50

There and Gone

The general stood up and left the room while Tracey remained on the couch. After several minutes, he returned with two additional soldiers following him. He entered the room and walked over to his desk while the soldiers remained at the door. The general spent another fifteen minutes writing something by hand, then clicked something on his computer and began to type. A few minutes later, he stood up and walked over to Tracey.

"Okay, Mr. Tracey. I am sorry we are leaving later than we told the doctor, but I had to finish a few things. Please, let us leave and see your daughter. I am sure you would like that."

Tracey smiled. "Yes, I would very much like to see my daughter."

"Let us go then," the general said as he waved his hands, motioning Tracey to make his way to the door. Tracey walked ahead of the general and followed two soldiers as they led him toward the same stairway he had used earlier. Once they descended the four flights of stairs, they emerged outside, and Tracey was directed into the same Humvee he arrived in. The general entered a Humvee two cars ahead of Tracey, and they headed out again as a caravan.

Following almost the same route they took when leaving Dr. Embuke's clinic, the caravan again approached the clinic. It took approximately twenty minutes. They stopped as they turned the corner to Dr. Embuke's clinic, and the general called his daughter.

"Hello, my dear. We are just around the corner from you. I will send Mr. Tracey to the door with the instructions we discussed earlier. Please let me know if he doesn't follow those instructions and appears to be planning something suspicious." His daughter responded and hung up. The general closed his phone. The driver exited and opened the general's door. He climbed out and approached Tracey's Humvee. The same soldier opened the door to Tracey's Humvee, and the general leaned in.

"You are going into the clinic by yourself, Mr. Tracey. I caution you not to try anything. My daughter will know if you do, and then we will have a situation."

"Don't worry, General. I'm not planning on doing anything to put my daughter in harm's way. You have agreed to let her go home, and I will stay here while we wait for the drone to arrive. That's the deal. I'm sticking to it."

"Very well, Mr. Tracey. You have my word, and I believe I have yours."

The general backed up, and the soldier next to Tracey exited the vehicle. Tracey jumped out. He began to walk to the clinic. He quickened his pace when he turned the corner, away from the general's view.

He wanted to see April.

Chapter 51
Speak to Me

Trellis, MT

Bell barreled down the road at seventy-five miles an hour as the navigator indicated he was only three miles away from portal 18. Two miles down the road, he exited the highway. After turning down several dirt roads, the navigator chirped, indicating he was within 500 yards of the portal. Bell approached a white picket fence and could see the house a short distance away. He took a right and headed towards it.

It was a very non-descript small farmhouse, similar to portal 17. No cars were in the driveway, and the doors on the small red barn next to the house were closed. He didn't see a soul.

He pulled down the driveway and stopped. Turning off the engine and looking to his left, he saw a beautiful golden retriever wagging its tail. Hopefully, this was a sentinel, so stepping out of his Tahoe wouldn't get him shot. Bell opened the door and got out. He stood for a few seconds before moving closer to the golden retriever. The retriever barked and wagged her tail. She came up close to Bell. She stopped and licked his hand, then walked away. About fifteen yards down the driveway, the dog lay down. Good, Bell thought to himself. If someone is inside, they would know he was an InCit agent, and he would not be attacked with any luck.

Bell walked up the front porch and rang the doorbell. The screen door was in place, and the inside door was open. From inside, a female voice yelled for him to come in. Bell opened the door and walked into the house.

"I'm in the kitchen," the same voice called out.

Bell continued through the house, peering left and right until he finally arrived at the kitchen. A woman with an apron on was mixing ingredients in a bowl. She turned around as Bell entered the kitchen.

"I suspect you need to get below?" she asked as she turned back to the bowl.

"I do, thank you."

"The keypad's in the back of the coffee maker. Just push the can opener out of the way."

Bell walked over to the can opener and moved it aside. He then turned, grabbed the coffee maker, and slid its back cover off, revealing the hidden Hirsch Pad. Bell punched in his numbers and completed the eye scan. Immediately after finishing the eye scan, the table to his right folded against the wall to make room for the refrigerator as it rolled to the exact spot the table had been. A fake wall now slid open, just like in portal 17.

The two doors for an elevator opened, and Bell stepped in. Following a short seven-second ride down, the door opened, and Bell exited to a brightly lit room. The room reminded him of the bright InCit command center at ERF.

"Hello?" Bell called out. Nothing. He assumed as much. Bell headed over to a desk and sat down. He turned to a computer and started to log in. He had only hit a few keystrokes before his drop phone rang. He immediately answered it.

"Hello."

"Yes, sir, this is Athan again calling back."

"Okay, Athan. Perfect timing since I just got to a secure location. Let's get to it then. You said you knew where Special Agent Tracey was."

"I do. Special Agent Tracey gave me a phone and sent me two texts. In one text, he gave me certain coordinates to send him a piece of equipment he had assigned to him. Those coordinates come back to a country in Africa named Jafaire. In the second text, he asked when the equipment would be in Jafaire."

Bell knew of the country Jafaire. But Tracey was there? And he had this Athan guy sending him a piece of Bureau equipment? That was probably his drone.

"Okay, so you're telling me Special Agent Tracey asked you to send him a piece of his equipment and that he is in an African country named Jafaire. That about sum it up?"

"Yes, that's exactly it," Athan said.

"What was the equipment you were sending him?"

Athan hesitated. The hesitation told Bell all he needed to know. He was about to hear a lie, but since Athan had reached out to him, Bell hoped it would be close to the truth.

"I have no idea what the equipment is. He just gave me the coordinates and told me to hit a few buttons in a computer program he gave me."

What Athan was saying is possible. IAs did have the ability to control their drone with a computer program. He would cut this guy some slack until he could find more information.

"Special Agent Tracey has been missing for almost five days now. We are worried about him. Do you think somebody has done something to him, and that's why he's not reaching out?" Bell asked.

"I don't know," Athan said. "I hope nothing bad has come to him, of course. He is my friend."

Bell would have to figure out later how this guy knew Tracey. For now, time was of the essence in finding Tracey and, more importantly, where the hell the drone was.

"What is your last name, Athan? And I never did find out how you got my phone number."

"I would rather not give you any more information about me. I'm calling you because of other text messages I received on the same phone Special Agent Tracey gave me. The message redirected me to click on videos from what appears to be a security system at the Tracey vacation home in Montana. One of the videos was a video of you displaying your phone number and asking Special Agent Tracey to call you."

So, the video worked, Bell thought to himself. Good.

"Okay, do you know if Special Agent Tracey has any other phone?"

"I know he has at least one phone. That's the phone he used to text me the coordinates."

"Okay, give me the numbers for the phone he gave you and the one he is texting you from," Bell said, and Athan complied. "Thanks, Athan. Stay by the phone. I'll get back to you if I have more questions." They each hung up.

Bell's mind began to race. He opened the computer and typed in some broad research questions regarding the country of Jafaire. He learned everything that Tracey probably knew about the country's short history. Knowing the Bureau, if Bell mentioned Tracey was in Jafaire, the U.S. military would swarm into Jafaire to find him, and the gig could be up for the InCit technology and Tracey. Bell was torn. He wanted to help his friend, but his loyalty had to remain with the Bureau.

Even worse, Bell wasn't sure that Tracey was planning something more than just traveling to a foreign country. But why did he need his drone? Or maybe he was being held hostage. Tracey could still be in trouble, and it might not be his fault. There were too many thoughts.

Bell grabbed his drop phone. He dialed the number Athan had given him for Tracey. It took a few moments for the call to go through.

Once it did, Bell wasn't ready for the person who answered it.

Chapter 52

Intercepted

General Rapuso was startled by the unfamiliar ring of Tracey's phone. The general stopped typing and reached across his desk for the phone. As he picked it up, he saw it was a number originating from the United States. The general contemplated not answering the phone but was curious about who it might be. He figured it was Tracey's friend helping him deliver the drone to the general.

"Hello," the general answered with a simple greeting.

Bell froze. It didn't sound like Tracey. He needed to hear the person speak before he could be sure. He decided to test the person on the end of the line and get him to speak.

"James! What the heck are you doing?" Bell waited.

"This is not James," the general said. "I'm sure you know that, though. Is this Special Agent Tracey's friend in the U.S.?"

Bell held his breath for a second. Tracey was definitely in trouble. There is no way Tracey would have given up his drop phone unless physically he was unable to answer it. Okay. How to handle this, Bell thought. He decided to see if he could get some answers.

"It is, yes. And I always call Special Agent Tracey "James" because of a joke I played on him years ago. Who is this?"

The general seemed to believe Bell's quick response. "Very good. And your name is?"

"My name is Athan. Who are you?" Bell asked again. The general ignored his question.

"Special Agent Tracey is not available. He is checking on his daughter following her procedure. He should be back in the next hour and a half or so. Can I have him call you back?" The general was unsure what this man Athan knew about the Bureau's technology. He would have to ask Tracey more about that when he returned.

"Okay, that will be fine," Bell said. "If you could have him call me back when he returns, I would appreciate it."

"I can do that for you, Athan. And what is your last name?" the general asked.

Bell didn't hesitate. "You won't tell me who you are, but you ask quite a few questions. I don't think that's necessary right now."

"My name is General Dule Repuso. I am the head of the military forces in Jafaire."

Bell froze for just a moment.

"Nice to meet you on the phone, of course, General," Bell replied. "I'll wait for Special Agent Tracey to call me back. Thank you." Bell hung up without a reply from the general or giving up Athan's last name.

Now what? Tracey *was* in Jafaire from everything Bell could put together. And his daughter was there with him. And he wasn't able to answer his drop phone. Bell could see no other way to spin it. Tracey might be in over his head.

Bell switched back over to the computer in front of him. After typing in several addresses and searches, he found several pages about General Repuso. Bell read how the general was a survivor of civil wars and had risen to his position when Jafaire was created. Bell didn't understand why Tracey would be working with him, however. And certainly, Tracey couldn't be giving this general the InCit technology. And why was his daughter there with him? Bell needed to call Trina for answers. It was early morning, and she was always up before the sun.

Bell grabbed his Bureau cell phone and looked up Trina's number. Bell knew the Bureau would have bugged every electronic device belonging to Tracey or his family. He would be careful what he said to Trina on the phone to protect his friend and family. And all without getting in trouble himself, of course, as he was tasked with finding Tracey. He would have to get her off the phone and to a video call where he could write out his thoughts as he did for Tracey at their Trellis home.

Bell dialed Trina's number. After three rings, Trina picked up.

"Elliott?" Trina said quickly, sounding surprised.

"Hey, Trina. I suspect asking you how you're doing would have an obvious answer?" Bell asked.

"To say the least." That's all she got out. She started crying. She muttered a few words that Bell couldn't understand. It was his opportunity to get her to switch over to video.

"Hey, I'll tell you what. Why don't you grab your laptop and head outside for some air? Call me back on video, and we'll start again."

"Okay, that would be good," Trina said between sobs. "Give me a few minutes."

"Sounds good." Bell hung up. He moved his chair back to the computer, opened an internet browser, and waited for Trina's call. A few minutes later, Trina called him back, requesting a video call. Bell clicked on the video button.

"Hey there. How's the fresh air?" Bell said with a tone of "There hasn't been breathable air in Miami since the 20s."

"Ha, ha. You know there isn't any fresh air left in Miami." Trina managed a smile. So did Bell.

"Hang on for one second, Trina. Let me get some coffee." Trina nodded as she sipped on her cup of coffee.

Bell was only feigning getting a cup of coffee. He moved to another set of drawers in the conference room and grabbed a stack of paper and a black Sharpie. He wrote on one of the pieces of paper: "Your house is probably bugged. Follow my lead. Act natural." His next note read: "Get some paper and a pen."

Bell pushed his chair back to the computer screen as Trina sipped her coffee. She looked at Bell and said, "I might have to get more coffee." She managed a weak smile, and they both laughed.

"I've got mine now. I'm good," Bell said as he held up the first piece of paper. "Your house is probably bugged. Follow my lead. Act natural." He put his fingers to his lips to suggest she not say anything. Trina read the note and put her coffee down with a surprised look. Bell then gave a thumbs up and started a straightforward conversation so she could continue the ruse.

"Are you still taking your coffee with more cream and sugar than there is coffee?" he asked with a laugh. Bell held up the second note.

"Oh, you know it!" Trina exclaimed as she squinted her eyebrows and moved closer to her computer screen to read the second note Tracey put up.

As Trina stood up and walked away, she kept the conversation going. "Hang on one more second for me. I think I'll pour a bit more creamer than usual in my coffee today. Be right back." Bell watched her move out of screen view.

Trina returned with a pad of paper and a black marker. She held them up to the screen so Bell could see them. Trina had already written on one piece of paper, "What the hell is going on?!" Bell again held his finger to his mouth and continued his scripted conversation.

"Hmm. Creamer good with a little coffee in it?" Bell joked as he continued to write out his next note. He held it up to the screen.

"Open your safe. Grab a device that looks like this. It's red." Bell drew a picture of a small electronic-looking device about the size of a kitchen sponge. It even looked like a kitchen sponge. Bell couldn't draw and would never be confused with Van Gogh.

"I told you coffee is always good with creamer," Trina said out loud. Then she blurted out, "What the heck? Hang on a second. I think that was the doorbell. But this early?"

"Hey, be safe going to the door. You want to bring the laptop so I can see who is at the door?" They were both playing the game now. Trina knew what to do. She was an FBI wife, after all.

"No, I'll scream out if it's bad." Trina laughed.

Bell knew Trina was making a beeline for the safe, opening it faster than she ever had. In a flash, she was back.

"Well, it seems Savannah decided to change her alarm to a sound similar to a doorbell," Trina said. "Go figure. She's all set now. She has soccer practice in an hour."

Trina held up the red piece of equipment for Bell to see. He was ready and held the next note for her to read: "Turn the volume as low as it can go on the computer." She did. Next note: "Turn the device on, button on the side." She looked at the screen and smiled. After finding the button, she clicked it to the on position. She kept reading Bell's notes. "Scan the computer. Tell me if the unit beeps." After several passes over the computer, Trina wrote back: "No beeps."

Bell wrote back: "Take Savannah to practice." Trina gave a thumbs up.

Bell kept up the appearance. "So, how does she like soccer?" Bell asked.

"She likes it, but she hates getting up so early. I keep telling her she won't improve unless she works hard and puts the time in. She thinks that means I believe she isn't good. Too funny."

Bell laughed as he held the next note to the screen: "Take your laptop. Find a quiet place after you drop her off. Video call me back on this number." Trina gave a thumbs up.

"Let's talk later. I've got to feed her before we head out, or she won't eat anything for hours."

"Okay, that sounds good. We have to talk about Tracey, okay? I'm growing concerned, and I hope you can help me find him."

Bell held up one last note: "Take the electronic device with you. Scan the car before you call me back."

Trina read the note and gave a thumbs up. It was a good way to end the call if they were being monitored.

"Okay, Elliott. I'm so worried I can't think. I'll call you back in a little while."

They both gave a thumbs-up and ended the call.

✛✛✛

As she slowly pulled away from the school, Trina watched Savannah jog towards the soccer field. She thought about how the conversation was going to go with Elliott. It would be nice if he gave her some good news, but she wasn't getting her hopes up.

Trina pulled into a convenience store parking lot. A few cars were in front, but none on the side. She pulled around back and got out with the scanner. Walking around the car, she aimed it at every part she could see. No beeps. No bugs. She got into the car and completed the same task on the interior. Again, no beeps. No bugs. Good. She opened her laptop and dialed Bell's number. While she waited for Bell to answer, she looked around to see if she had been followed. Clear. Bell answered. His face popped on the screen.

"Hey, Trina. I forgot to ask you earlier how your car was doing. I know you've had some problems with it."

"It's good. We can talk. I scanned it inside and out. No beeps."

"Perfect," Bell said.

"I had to be sure there were no bugs near your computer or outside. The Bureau has most likely wired the inside of your house without you knowing it, so they are probably listening to all your conversations. Try not to think about that when you get back. Don't look for or move any bugs you notice, or they'll be alerted you're looking for surveillance. Just act natural. Even after what I am going to tell you."

"Okay," Trina said dejectedly.

"I received a call from a man about an hour ago who says he's David's friend. His name is Athan. Do you know who he is?"

Trina's eyes opened a little bit. "Yes, that's Athan Kratos, our next-door neighbor."

"How well do you know him?"

"Our families are good friends. We usually have dinner with them once a week. Our kids have grown up together, and our oldest daughters are best friends. Why? Do you think he has something to do with David's disappearance?"

"I don't know if he's responsible for David's disappearance, but he knows where David is. I think he and David may be working on something together, and unfortunately, it may be tied to some of the Bureau's technology. Can I ask you what Athan does for a living?"

"Athan is the head of the Kratos Oil & Shale Company. I'm sure you've heard of them. They're one of the largest oil companies in the world."

"I do know the name. How long have you been friends with them?"

"Just about from the day we moved into our house. Some days, Athan and David are inseparable. They cook on the grill every weekend and hang out doing guy things. What do you think they're mixed up in?" Trina backed away from the screen, a little in disbelief.

"I don't know, but Athan called me and said David might be in trouble and that he was overseas."

Trina put her hand to her mouth. Her head was swirling. She began to tear up. She quickly thought of April. "And April?" Trina asked, assuming Bell knew David was with April.

"What about April?" Bell asked, squinting his eyes and feigning ignorance.

Trina immediately realized Bell might not know Tracey was with April. She took a deep breath. Bell sat still, apparently waiting to see what Trina would reveal.

"David promised me he would handle this and that I shouldn't be told too much. I have kept my end of the bargain. But now, there are two lives at stake here."

"Okay, take your time, and tell me what you know."

Trina moved closer to the camera.

"You know, of course, April has DBA. And we have traveled down many roads with her, looking for a cure. Over the years, April has had some success with certain procedures. After a treatment at the Seattle Children's Hospital a year ago, she was in remission. But it turned out that the process she went through did not cure her. We went back to Seattle for more testing several months ago.

"While we were there, we met with her medical team. The doctors told us April's condition was now terminal. Following that meeting, David was approached by one of the oncologists. He took David aside and told him he had a doctor friend living in another country. This doctor had cured his sister or someone who had DBA. It was a medical miracle. David arranged to take April to that country to see if the procedure would work for her. He said there would be risks getting April there and back, but he would handle most of it. All I had to do was fly April to Washington, D.C., a few days ago. That's the extent of what he told me about his travel plans. And now you're telling me he might be in trouble, which means April is equally at risk." Trina broke down and just started crying.

Bell let Trina have a moment. Then he said, "Okay, I'll see what I can find out. Meanwhile, let's not talk unless we use a video call. And I can prompt you with a piece of paper and notes you can read if necessary. And if you're at home when we speak, head out to the patio again. Does that sound good?"

"Yes, thank you," Trina said, relaxing a bit.

"We'll talk again when I find out where David is, okay?" Bell said confidently.

"Okay. Thank you, Elliott. Bye."

Bell hung up and sat back in the chair. What in God's name had Tracey gotten himself into? No wonder the Director wanted this taken care of quickly and quietly.

This wasn't a good look for the Bureau.

Chapter 53
How's the Patient?

Seven hours after Tracey's drone was scuttled
Lingos, Jafaire

After walking the final couple hundred yards, Tracey approached the door to Dr. Embuke's clinic. He tried the handle. As he had assumed, the door was locked. Tracey tapped gently on the door, and Amir appeared from inside, wearing the same big smile he had when he greeted Tracey at the airport.

"Welcome back, Mr. Tracey," Amir said, bowing slightly.

Tracey ignored him and looked past Amir towards the inner office and recovery room where he'd last seen April.

"My daughter is still in recovery, I assume?" Tracey asked as he stared at Amir.

"I believe so," Amir said. "Let me call the doctor for you." Amir could sense Tracey was not thrilled to see him. He motioned for Tracey to come in, then locked the door behind them. Picking up the waiting room phone, Amir spoke with someone. Tracey assumed it was the general's daughter. In Arabic, Amir spoke briefly with the person before hanging up.

"The doctor is on his way," Amir said as he bowed slightly again and sat down on the opposite side of the room from Tracey. Tracey took a seat and continued to glare at Amir.

Amir quickly looked outside and then back at Tracey. "I am sorry, Mr. Tracey, but I had no choice. If I do not do as the general asks, my entire family will be put to death."

Tracey continued to look directly at Amir. He wanted to mete out some form of retribution on Amir right then and there. Tracey shrugged and calmly spoke to Amir.

"Your fate is also my fate now, Amir. I guess we're in the same boat."

As the two waited, Dr. Embuke entered, followed closely by Nurse Mariama. It appeared Nurse Mariama had orders from the general to go everywhere Dr. Embuke went.

"Hello again, Mr. Tracey!" Dr. Embuke enthusiastically greeted Tracey with a broad smile and his hand outstretched. Tracey shook the doctor's hand.

At that moment, Tracey had a bad thought. What if he had been so blind-sided by the chance his daughter's life could be saved that he overlooked the possibility Dr. Embuke could be involved with the general? No way. Dr. Embuke wouldn't overthrow his sister. Tracey snapped out of it.

"Your daughter is doing wonderful. Let's go see her."

Tracey walked with Dr. Embuke and Nurse Mariama to the recovery room, where April rested. When they entered, April's eyes were closed. She opened them just as they reached her bedside.

Tracey grabbed her hand. She smiled at him.

Dr. Embuke said, "Right now, April, you are at a 78% oxygen recovery rate. Your oxygen recovery rate when the transfusions ended was 72%. Your numbers are climbing very fast. Your recovery is happening at a much quicker rate than my sister's did. You are younger, so that helps."

Tracey and April both sighed a huge sigh of relief.

"You are doing better than I could have imagined. Your levels are almost normal. Let's give it another three or four hours and see where we are. If your oxygen levels go up another 10%, you will be at 88% oxygen level. With those numbers, you can travel home. And earlier than expected."

"That's great news," Tracey said.

"Yes, it is. Mr. Tracey, will you go back to the hotel to wait? You may relax here if you wish."

"If you don't mind, I will sit here since it may only be a few hours before we can head home. I know April and I would both like that."

"Very good. Would you like a cup of coffee while you wait? I also have some water in my office."

"Yes, thank you. I would love some coffee." They both started walking away. After several feet, Dr. Embuke stopped abruptly and turned around. "Would anyone else like a cup of coffee or bottled water?" he offered.

"I could use some water," April managed with a smile. Dr. Embuke gave a thumbs-up and started to walk away again.

Nurse Mariama volunteered she could get the water for April and headed out with them.

The general's daughter wasn't letting Tracey out of her sight. But Tracey was hoping to get Dr. Embuke alone so they could talk.

Once in his office, Mariama headed for the refrigerator to grab the water bottles for her and April.

"How do you take your coffee, Mr. Tracey?" Dr. Embuke asked.

"Just black, please. Thank you." Tracey put all thoughts of Dr. Embuke being involved with the general out of his mind. He had to trust him. And he needed to talk to him alone.

Just then, the clinic phone rang outside of Dr. Embuke's office.

"If you wouldn't mind, Nurse Mariama, could you see who that might be? Be sure to tell them we are working on records management and will be closed until next week." Nurse Mariama hesitated for a second and then nodded and said, "Yes, Doctor," as she stood up and headed for the telephone. It was Tracey's chance. He had to take it. There wouldn't be much time.

"Dr. Embuke, I need to tell you something very quickly. My daughter and I are in danger from your armed forces leader, General Repuso. Are you aware Nurse Mariama is his daughter?"

Dr. Embuke put his coffee down and stared at Tracey. "Does this have anything to do with the conversation I overheard when you called earlier today? And yes, I am aware Nurse Mariama is General Repuso's daughter. My sister helped get her this job as a favor to the general."

"It has everything to do with that conversation, and I was hoping you heard the general on that phone call. General Repuso is going to try to overthrow your sister. Don't ask any questions yet. Just listen. After April began her procedure, the general and his soldiers were let into the clinic by Amir, and they took me away to the general's headquarters building.

"The general told me he was planning a coup, and he wanted me to provide him with a certain top-secret FBI technology to assist him with that coup. The technology does exist, and I have access to it. He forced my hand and told me my daughter and I - and my family and friends in America - would die if I didn't arrange for the technology to be delivered to him."

Dr. Embuke just stared. His mouth was slightly open. They both looked out at Nurse Mariama, who was still on the phone.

"I have arranged for the technology to be flown here, and the last calculations suggested it should arrive in the next eleven hours or so." Tracey looked at his watch. "Maybe a little under eleven hours now."

"I told the general he does not get the technology unless my daughter is on a plane on her way back to the United States. I will stay behind as collateral to make sure the technology arrives. He has agreed to these terms and arranged for April's flight to France and then on to the U.S. Once you tell your sister of the coup, she cannot do anything, however, until my daughter is safely out of Jafaire and on that connecting flight to the U.S."

"I don't know what to say," Dr. Embuke began. "How much time do we have?"

"You tell me, Doctor. Can April be ready to go in two hours if her oxygen levels reach 88%?"

"Yes, April can safely travel at that oxygen level, and her body should produce oxygen like a normal, healthy seventeen-year-old in no time."

"That is great news."

"Okay then, what do you want me to do?" Dr. Embuke asked. "And when should I tell my sister?" He looked past Tracey and to the other end of the clinic, where Nurse Mariama appeared to be wrapping up the phone call. She would be heading back to them shortly. Tracey had to get the plan out fast.

"I will sit in the waiting room. Amir will call the general, and I will either get picked up and taken to the general's headquarters or remain in the waiting room and see if April's status is good enough for her to depart. If we're good to go, April and I will head to the airport, and I will make something up for April as to why I have to remain here. The general's man will accompany her, and I'll wait for the delivery of the FBI technology. When it arrives, I should be able to get out of Jafaire using that technology. But I will need a plane ride home. Do you think your sister could help me with that?"

"I will ask, but I am sure she can help," Dr. Embuke said, nodding as he looked at Tracey.

"Great. Alert your sister when I head to the airport with April. The president will need a secure location for the next twenty-four hours to protect herself. I believe the general won't make a move on the palace and your sister until he has the FBI technology anyway.

"After we leave here, the rest of the day is yours. Remember that the general's men will most likely follow you around town. And assume they have your phones bugged, so be careful."

"I will, thank you. This will work."

Tracey was about to continue when Nurse Mariama walked in. "What should work, Dr. Embuke?" Nurse Mariama asked while tilting her head sideways. They hadn't heard her walk up on them, but Dr. Embuke didn't skip a beat.

"The plan for getting oxygen on the planes for April to travel to the U.S. That shouldn't be hard at all. I will need your help to organize it, Nurse Mariama."

Nurse Mariama seemed to be okay with that explanation. Tracey hoped so. Tracey stood up to leave.

"Let me get out of everyone's hair. I'll wait out front for someone to check back with me in the next several hours."

Tracey hoped Nurse Mariama didn't question whether or not Dr. Embuke knew of the plans her father had in store for the country. He hoped it would stay that way until Tracey could get his drone and execute the next part of his plan.

Both Dr. Embuke and Nurse Mariama gave Tracey a thumbs up, and he headed out.

Chapter 54

New Orders

Bell began frantically clicking through databases. He needed to get a handle on how Tracey left the U.S. without being tracked. The first thing he looked at was the Bureau's undercover database. He logged in and clicked on several folders before he got to the folder for InCit agents with last names between the letters S, and Z. He found Tracey's folder and clicked. Bell scrolled through all the documents relating to Tracey and found he had no undercover pieces of identification.

Bell moved over to the State Department database and logged in. He entered Tracey's name, and his official Bureau passport came up. He clicked on that passport. The results indicated that Tracey's last official travel was two years before when he traveled to Yemen. The picture was of Tracey, and his passport was issued in his official Bureau name.

Bell switched to the airline database and entered Tracey's real name and all of his alias names. Who knew: maybe Tracey obtained a passport in his real name, but surely, the Bureau would have caught that. Bell hit enter, and the computer indicated it was working on his request.

Thirty seconds later, the results came back negative. Bell then decided to run a phonetic search on Tracey's name so that any name similar in sound or spelling to David Tracey would be identified as a potential hit. Bell checked off several boxes and hit enter. Once again, the computer digested the request and came back with one result: a similar phonetic match for a traveler named "Dana Tracey." The name was close, but not Tracey. It then struck Bell. He remembered the text message from Dr. Parker. Wasn't Tracey's twin sister's name Dana? But she had a different last name.

Bell clicked over to the State Department database again. He typed in Dana Tracey and waited. The results came in. Bell almost choked. Tracey's picture came up. What the hell! He clicked back over to the flight manifest. It showed Tracey, using Dana's name, departing the U.S. for Paris on September 6th. There was no return to the U.S.

After clicking on a few more buttons, Bell found April's flight information.

She had a more recent flight, however. A planned departure from Paris non-stop to the U.S. What? Why would she be in Paris? Bell kept digging. April had a seat on a plane to the U.S. and would depart in the next eleven hours. Her layover was in Washington, D.C., before she headed to Miami. Bell looked at the clock on the wall. He had to get folks on this.

It was time to tell the director. Turning on his blackhawk, Bell typed out his text.

"33 still missing - possibly overseas w/daughter - daughter arriving DCA from Paris - Delta #2711 – will need a debrief." Bell hit send.

Bell leaned back in his chair. He let out a big sigh and rocked back and forth in his chair. All he could think of was Tracey's plan is headed for a bad ending. Maybe April could give them some insight into what her dad was doing. At least Bell knew from Trina that April had traveled for a new lease on life, and Bell was happy about that. A son or daughter able to grow up healthy was all any parent could ask for. Maybe that had something to do with Tracey going off the grid. Good Lord. Hopefully, the InCit program was still a secret.

Bell's drop phone beeped. He had a text. The message was from Athan.

"Hello. It's Athan. Have you heard from Special Agent Tracey? He might need your help."

No shit, Bell thought. Tracey needed help, all right. Who else was going to help him? It was a hell of a spot Tracey was putting Bell in. And Bell wanted nothing more than to get his friend home. Safely. Whatever consequences Tracey faced when he returned to the U.S., he would have to suffer them alone. Bell decided not to answer Athan.

Bell was more anxious to receive a text from the director. After all the gaps in communication between Bell and the director over the past twelve hours, Bell figured it would be a while before the director answered his last text. He couldn't have been more wrong.

His blackhawk chirped within two minutes of Bell's recent text. He eagerly opened the screen to find a response from the director.

"Update received – New orders: head to Jafaire - small country in Africa - Tracey will need your help - his drone is finally offline - your undercover dossier is on the Gulfstream coming to get you - 11-hour flight - SITREP when you have more - good luck."

Bell read the message three times. How did the director find out about Jafaire? Bell would ask him. Someday.

But right now, Bell needed to beat feet.

Chapter 55
Safe Travels

Fifteen hours after Tracey's drone was scuttled
Lingos, Jafaire

Tracey opened his eyes. He must have been pretty tired to fall asleep in the waiting room. He began to turn his head and stopped midway as he felt the stiff pain in his neck. He had slept in a bad position. Looking at his watch, he realized he had dozed for eight hours, long past the two hours Dr. Embuke suggested they wait to see if April's oxygen numbers had improved. She had been in recovery for more than eleven hours now. Equally important to Tracey was his drone should arrive in less than three hours.

He looked over at Amir, who appeared to be playing a game on his phone and smiling. As Tracey adjusted his body in the seat, Amir looked up at Tracey.

"Hello again, Mr. Tracey. You fell asleep. Dr. Embuke said for me to call him once you were awake. I believe he has good news."

Tracey sat upright. He looked at Amir as he wiped his eyes to wake up. He heard Amir say the doctor had "good news."

"Okay, let's give Dr. Embuke a call then."

Amir stood up and went over to the wall phone. He called back to the doctor. He spoke in Arabic and quickly hung up. Tracey stood up and began to pace slowly. He was anxious. He was more antsy than anxious, he convinced himself. Approximately five minutes later, the door opened, and Dr. Embuke walked out. He held the door open and smiled as Nurse Mariama pushed April through the door in a wheelchair. Tracey thought he had never seen anything so wonderful. April gave him a huge smile. She was the first to talk.

"I think I'm breathing better than you are, Dad," she said. Tracey gave her a broad smile and chuckled.

"Thanks to Dr. Embuke, I'll bet you are," Tracey said.

"April's oxygen level is almost at 90% effectiveness, given the additional time you were sleeping," Dr. Embuke stated emphatically. Tracey smiled.

"It was good that you rested, Mr. Tracey," Dr. Embuke said. "It will make your journey home easier for you and your daughter."

Dr. Embuke looked intently at Tracey, which reminded Tracey that Dr. Embuke knew of the plan to send only April home. The doctor knew what to say.

Amir, meanwhile, had been on his phone speaking to the general. He had just hung up as Tracey finished speaking with Dr. Embuke.

"Your ride will be here momentarily," Amir said to the group. "We have arranged the flights home as we talked about earlier."

"I'm glad to be going home," April said. "I feel so much better. Maybe I'll sprint down the runway onto the plane!"

Tracey could tell April was excited. He'd have to make sure she didn't sprint, though.

"Yes, that will be good," Tracey said.

"If I can assist you once you arrive home, please call me anytime, Mr. Tracey. For now, I will leave you in the hands of Amir to get you both safely to the airport. Here is my business card with my direct number. Safe travels."

Tracey accepted Dr. Embuke's card and casually put it in his pocket. He didn't want the nurse to think receiving the doctor's number was anything out of the ordinary.

Dr. Embuke and Nurse Mariama walked back into the clinic, locking the door behind them.

Tracey only had a small window now to explain things to April.

"Okay, sweetheart. There has been a slight change in plans."

April sat up a bit straighter in her wheelchair. "Okay," she said, furrowing her eyebrows and looking at her father with a pained expression.

"I'm not traveling back with you."

"You will get on a plane that will take you to Paris. It should take you approximately eight hours to get to Paris. You'll have a forty-five-minute layover in Paris, followed by a nine-and-a-half-hour direct flight to the U.S. One stop in Washington, D.C., and then you'll head home to Miami. To be sure you're safe, an employee of the head of the military here will escort you to Paris and then return to Jafaire. Unfortunately, I will remain behind and work with the general on a project. Your transfusion wasn't the only reason I was traveling here. I had a few things I needed to complete for work."

Tracey felt bad lying to April. For her safety, this was the only story she needed to hear.

"I should be home in a few days." Tracey put on a bright smile, and April reciprocated with a smile of her own.

"Your ride will be here in five minutes," Amir said as he waited at the door. He remained there while Tracey sat back down and held April's hand. And then, right on schedule, April's transportation to the airport arrived.

"Ah, here we go," Amir said as he unlocked the door and motioned for Tracey and April to follow. Tracey stood and grabbed April's wheelchair. He pushed her through the door and onto the sidewalk, where they boarded the same van Amir drove from the airport. They slowly left the doctor's clinic and headed to the airport.

Tracey noticed the two cars behind them as they turned the first corner. They were hanging back about 200 yards. And they were following them. Tracey guessed the general wanted Tracey to know he was sticking around. Tracey didn't care. He just wanted to get his daughter on the plane and on her way home.

Amir pulled up to the airport thirty minutes later.

"Mr. Tracey, I'm going to get you through security, and then we will go directly to the plane. Once we clear customs, a nurse will meet us to provide April with several backup oxygen tanks. We will use the wheelchair to take her to the plane if that is alright?"

"Sounds like that will work," Tracey said. April nodded as she looked outside.

Once at the airport, Amir displayed his ID, and they all moved past security very quickly. Tracey was allowed to push April through the airport as they made their way to their gate. The Jafaire airport was not very large and only had five gates. Once they arrived at gate number three, Tracey immediately picked up on two men sitting in casual attire. Tracey assumed they were both intelligence officers and belonged to the general's staff. After taking a quick look at them, Tracey paid them no more attention.

Tracey then caught sight of a woman, who was probably a nurse, pushing a cart toward them. The cart contained several bottles of oxygen. She stopped and spoke to Amir. As they talked to each other, the captain of the airplane appeared. He shook hands with Amir and the nurse, and they spoke for a few minutes while glancing over at Tracey and April several times. He nodded his head in agreement with what they were saying. Then, the nurse and the captain departed through the gate to the plane, with the nurse pulling the oxygen bottles behind her.

Amir walked over to Tracey. "Okay, Mr. Tracey. The plane is ready to depart now."

Tracey and April said their goodbyes, and she was wheeled through the gate to board the plane. The two men Tracey assumed were intelligence officers stood up and followed April through the gate. The general lied about having only one escort for April. Tracey moved to the window and watched as the plane backed away from the gate and began to taxi toward the runway. After a brief wait on the runway, the plane took off into the Jafairian sky.

April's journey home had begun. Tracey had at least saved his daughter.

Tracey turned from the window and followed Amir as they began to walk back towards the van.

It was now time for Tracey to find his way home.

Chapter 56

Set It Up

As Tracey and Amir drove back to the general's headquarters, Tracey wondered where his drone was. It should only be three hours away now. Had it traveled safely over all the terrain it had to cross? God, he hoped so. Once the drone arrived, Tracey would have to use it to defend himself and possibly the president. If only he knew.

They pulled into the general's command center and headed to the rear. Tracey felt confident about his next plan. He might have to improvise as he put it in motion, but he thought he could make it work.

Tracey followed Amir and several soldiers up the stairs again to General Repuso's office. They entered to find the general sitting at his computer, typing.

"Mr. Tracey, I take it your daughter is now on her way back home?" the general said as he looked up, then immediately back down at his computer.

"She is. And thank you for agreeing to let her go while I stay behind. Do you want me to check in with my contact in the U.S. to see where the drone is currently located? I plan on upholding my end of the bargain."

"Yes, why don't we do that, Mr. Tracey."

The general picked up Tracey's phone from his desk and walked it over to him.

Tracey accepted the cell phone and typed out, "Updated location?" He handed it back to the general, and the general pushed "Send." As the general closed the phone, he never noticed the rotating circle indicating the message hadn't yet been received by Athan. And Athan wouldn't remember to turn the phone back on anytime soon as it lay plugged into the wall charging.

"Good," the general said. He placed the phone in his pocket and walked to his desk.

Looking over his shoulder, the general said, "Are you hungry, Mr. Tracey?"

"No, I'm good. Amir was kind enough to pick up some food at the airport for us to eat."

"Very good." His assistant appeared, and the general said a few words to her. She departed and arrived a few minutes later with food and drinks on a tray. The general grabbed a spoon and a bowl and began to eat.

Now that April was on her way, Tracey had to execute the second part of his plan: getting out of Jafaire. But he had to be careful since April still had eight hours or so before she was out of the reach of the general and his men accompanying her. April had to get off the general's plane and onto the plane heading to the U.S. before Tracey and, hopefully, by then, the president and the forces loyal to her could neutralize the general. Tracey needed to get a message to Dr. Embuke. And fast. He had an idea that might work.

"General, in my haste to be sure my daughter was safely out of her procedure and onto the plane, I never had Dr. Embuke completely explain my daughter's follow-up care. I only briefly saw the charts of what my wife and I should be doing back home as my daughter recovers. Would it be possible to call Dr. Embuke and speak with him or have him come here to accomplish the same thing and show me all the charts?"

"What charts are those, Mr. Tracey?" the general asked.

"I'm not quite sure exactly what the charts were, but they showed her expected progression and explained the times of day we needed to be most concerned with her breathing, in addition to other general care instructions. I wasn't paying attention to much of that, and we didn't get through all of it at the time. We can also do it by video call if that's easier. After getting this briefing from Dr. Embuke, I would like to text it to my friend to relay to my wife."

"Let me think about the best way to arrange this, Mr. Tracey." The general motioned to the pastries on the tray in front of him. "Please, have some dessert or a drink."

Tracey indulged the general. He selected a similar-looking pastry to the one he had eaten earlier and a bottle of water. He had to admit - the pastries were delicious.

Chapter 57

Two Meetings for the Price of One

Tracey and the general continued to sit on their respective couches in the general's office. Neither of them spoke.

Tracey was getting restless and needed to talk to Dr. Embuke to get his plan rolling. He didn't want to seem too eager, though, as he and the general knew Tracey's daughter wouldn't be home for quite some time.

The general looked up and waved his hand, saying something to his assistant. She disappeared through the doors and returned moments later with a piece of paper, which she handed to the general. He took in a deep breath before addressing Tracey.

"Mr. Tracey, I have decided you can call Dr. Embuke for the instructions you seek for your daughter's after-care. We have a few hours before your drone arrives, so this will be a good use of our time. But the doctor will not know I am on the phone. We will keep the call on speakerphone. Will that be okay?"

"That would be great, thank you."

The general dialed the number on the paper using Tracey's cell phone. He pushed the speaker phone button and handed the phone to Tracey. Tracey waited. After a couple of rings, the call was picked up by Dr. Embuke.

"Hello?" Dr. Embuke said.

"Hello, Dr. Embuke. This is David Tracey. I'm just checking back with you about April's charts and what we need to be mindful of as she recovers."

Tracey knew Dr. Embuke would assume he was with the general and that the general was listening in on the call. He would choose his words carefully. Tracey was counting on it.

"Happy to help, Mr. Tracey. Just a few things to remember. Most important is the first chart I showed you with April's oxygen levels. Do you remember the blue chart showing where her oxygen level was when she first came into the clinic?"

"Yes, of course, Doc. It looked like she couldn't even breathe!"

"Yes, indeed, that is the chart. Remember the controller cell, the one in the center of everything?"

"I do, yes." Tracey knew the doctor was either referring to the president or the general. The rest of the conversation would tell him which.

"The controller cell wasn't functioning properly because the right signals weren't coming her way." Her? Tracey now knew it was the president the doctor was talking about. "As a result, that controller cell gave incomplete instructions to the surrounding cells, expecting them to function as part of April's body as a whole. But April's body couldn't send out the proper signals, so the cells couldn't do their job, putting all the cells, even the controller cell, at risk. So, the controller cell began to build up its defenses by producing more white blood cells. " Tracey noticed the subtle change in pronoun. Her - feminine was now "it," neutral. He inwardly smiled at the doctor's caginess. "Yes, I remember you explained how April's oxygen levels were depleting, but in one particular spot, she was healthy as ever."

"Correct. After the procedure, the controller cell now knows what is going on. The controller cell recognized the serum we introduced to fight the anemia as a friend. The controller cell, in turn, then infected, if you will, all the cells around it. The serum was provided to the cells that weren't functioning properly. The controller started working more effectively than we'd even hoped. Which is why April was able to travel home faster than expected."

Tracey was inwardly relieved. By the sound of it, Dr. Embuke had gotten word to the president of the impending coup attempt. Tracey now needed to know how *he* would get out of Jafaire. He felt he also needed to end the call soon lest the general start to figure out what they were talking about.

"And the second chart showed how April's defenses were shored up, and she can fight off the disease?"

"Yes, that is correct. April's immunity was being reinforced by the controller cell."

Tracey got it. The president was securing the presidential palace. What other measures she was taking to fend off the general's coup, Tracey would have to find out about some other time.

"As we continue going forward, Doc, what do my wife or I have to do to make sure she continues to heal as planned?"

"Just be sure to check her oxygen levels using the little breathing instrument I gave her. She'll blow into that as if blowing up a balloon. Her readouts will be on the chart I will email you later today."

"Ok, great, thank you, Dr. Embuke."

"Are you both at the airport already and set to depart?" Dr. Embuke asked quickly.

That was good. It made it look like the doctor and Tracey had nothing to hide. Tracey looked over at the general. The general held up the number four with one hand and then the number eight using both hands. Forty-eight hours, Tracey guessed.

Tracey understood.

"There was a slight change in plans. April has departed. I'm sticking around for another couple of days to cover some other items that came up at work."

"That is a wonderful surprise! Why don't I treat you to dinner tonight? I promise I won't take you anywhere near my sister. If I did, she would want to know how I know you, and then she would find out about the procedure, and she would not be happy with me!"

Tracey looked over at the general again. He held up his finger, and Tracey put the phone on mute.

"Tell him you have to check when your work conference call is scheduled for tonight," the general said.

Tracey took the phone off of mute.

"Hang on one second. Let me check my calendar and see when my conference call is back in the U.S."

Tracey put the call back on mute.

"This might work out, Mr. Tracey," the general said as he rubbed his chin. After several seconds, he said, "Tell the doctor you will gladly meet for dinner tonight at 8 p.m. at a local restaurant so you can try our cuisine. I will have a wire on you to listen to your conversation, and I will have two of my men in the same restaurant to monitor it as well. You will help me find out where the president will be in the next day or so. She does not give me her schedule all the time. I will need that for my plans."

Tracey nodded his head and took the phone off mute once again.

"Hey, Doc. I don't have my conference call until 11 p.m. local time here. Do you know a good restaurant where I can sample your local cuisine? I would enjoy that. And I must insist on paying to thank you for all you have done for April and our family."

"No problem, Mr. Tracey. Let's meet at The Offering, a wonderful little restaurant just around the corner from your hotel. It is within walking distance, or I can pick you up?"

Tracey looked at the general. He was using his two fingers, indicating Tracey would be walking.

"I could use the exercise, Doc, so I will walk and meet you there at 8 p.m."

"Great, see you then." They both hung up their phones.

Tracey sat back on the couch. He felt like he had just gone three rounds with George Foreman. He felt pretty good, though, and hoped the doctor had a plan for getting him out of the country.

Tracey would have to figure out how they would communicate this plan at dinner while being wired up and in the visual vicinity of two of the general's soldiers.

Chapter 58
Definitely Not a Chew and Screw

The Offering restaurant
Lingos, Jafaire

Tracey stepped out of the Humvee. He was two blocks away from the restaurant. It was hot. It had to be more than ninety degrees. He began walking as the Humvee rolled away, thinking about what he needed to get done at this dinner with Dr. Embuke. He had to make sure the president knew about the impending coup attempt. From his phone call with Dr. Embuke, it appeared like the president was aware and ready. And Tracey had to make sure his daughter was safe. Her flight was expected to arrive in Paris in about four hours. He would need President Embuke to intercept the two men on the plane when they landed. Then April would be home free on her way back to the U.S.

He also had to get word to the FBI that his family was in danger, as was Athan's, without letting anyone know he was in Jafaire. And he had to escape, hopefully, with the help of his drone. If Tracey's calculations were correct, the drone should arrive in an hour. What a nightmare this had become, Tracey thought.

Tracey arrived at The Offering at 7:55. He remembered his friend Bell telling him once: if you aren't early, you're late. Tracey was always early. He pulled open the door and was immediately confronted with wonderful aromas and a packed restaurant. He walked over to the hostess' station and asked for Dr. Embuke. He was led to the back of the restaurant.

After passing several tables, Tracey noticed the doctor sitting at a table in the back of the restaurant. Tracey also picked up two men sitting just to the left of Dr. Embuke. The general's men. They had their menus up, halfway covering their faces. They had watched too many spy movies.

Dr. Embuke stood as he approached. "Mr. Tracey," Dr. Embuke said as he extended his hand to shake Tracey's. Tracey shook his hand and gave a half hug of gratitude with his other arm.

"Hello again, Dr. Embuke. I have been looking forward to sampling the cuisine in Jafaire." Dr. Embuke replied, "Please, let us sit down and enjoy the food." After they were seated, Dr. Embuke folded his napkin and placed it in his lap before he spoke.

"So, April is on her way home?" Dr. Embuke asked as he motioned to the waiter to come to the table.

"She is, thanks to you, of course. I couldn't be happier for her."

"I am glad God has given me a talent to help people, Mr. Tracey. Even though I was reluctant to use the serum again after -" Dr. Embuke stopped when Tracey raised his eyebrows in silent warning.

Dr. Embuke continued, "- let's say all the experiments that didn't work. It makes me feel good that this worked for your daughter." Tracey nodded in agreement.

The waiter arrived and stood just off Tracey's left shoulder, blocking the view of the general's men behind him. The waiter presented Dr. Embuke with a menu. He quickly ordered several Jafairian foods he wanted Tracey to sample.

For one particular item, Dr. Embuke suggested the item was spelled wrong on the menu. Both Dr. Embuke and the waiter good-naturedly went over the spelling. Dr. Embuke finally asked for a pen and a piece of paper from the waiter, which the waiter obliged him. Doctor Embuke wrote down the name of an item on the menu and showed it to the waiter. This went on for a minute or two. Tracey was unsure of Dr. Embuke's plan, but he just kept watching.

Finally, Dr. Embuke tried to write a word down and suggested the pen was out of ink. He asked the waiter for another pen. The waiter left for a moment and returned with a new one. Dr. Embuke had already slid the first pen under the menu as the waiter filled Tracey's water glass. The waiter didn't give the pen a second thought.

Dr. Embuke pushed the menu and the pen underneath it to Tracey as he pointed to several items on the menu and laughed a little.

They continued to talk about the weather and other trivial matters. The waiter reappeared with their drinks, placed two cocktail napkins on the table, and then the glasses. Deftly, Tracey took his drink off the napkin so it wouldn't get wet and slid the napkin closer to himself. The doctor and Tracey lifted their drinks and together said, "Cheers to April!"

Once the waiter left the table, Tracey reached with his fork and placed several hors d'oeuvres Dr. Embuke had ordered on his plate. In the process, he grabbed the pen and nestled it against the fork. While Tracey sampled the hors d'oeuvres and spoke of how good the food was, he scribbled a note on his cocktail napkin. It read:

"General's men - behind me - 6 o'clock. He is listening, too."

Dr. Embuke took his water and attempted to take a sip. He dribbled it like a two-year-old, clearly on purpose. Tracey quickly provided the cocktail napkin with the note on it. Dr. Embuke took the napkin and pretended to dab his pants as he read the note in his lap. He looked up at Tracey and subtly nodded his head while continuing to smile. He turned the napkin over on the table and placed his water on it, letting the condensation drip down the glass, thoroughly smudging the wording. Dr. Embuke then pointed to the food on the table and described the ingredients to Tracey.

They continued to enjoy their appetizers and dinner selections. As he alternated between eating and reaching for food with his fork, Tracey would grab the pen and write on his dinner napkin. Towards the middle of the meal, Tracey leaned and rubbed his stomach as he enjoyed the fine food. His note was finished.

Tracey pointed again to Dr. Embuke's face, indicating some food stuck on his face. He handed the napkin to Dr. Embuke, who laughed. Dr. Embuke wiped his face and looked at the napkin, continuing this motion until he had read the note.

"I need a plane at the airport. Can your sister help?"

Dr. Embuke wiped his face and crumpled up the napkin, keeping it in his hand. He picked up his knife and fork and said, "Your daughter's oxygen levels were exponentially improving the last hours she was here in Jafaire, Mr. Tracey, so I have to believe she is breathing quite nicely on her own."

"Thank you. That is what I am hoping for, Doc." Tracey cut up a piece of meat lying on the tray in the center of the table and plopped it on his plate. "Now, what is this?" Tracey asked as he pointed with his fork to his plate.

"That is a 'pap and vleis' dish, a corn porridge with grilled Impala and a fig sauce mixed with chocolate balsamic vinegar. One of the best selections in this restaurant. Make sure you get some porridge and the sauce as well."

After several minutes of discussion regarding how each dish was made, Dr. Embuke asked, "So, when do you leave, Mr. Tracey?"

Tracey had to choose his words carefully, but he knew he had to get a response from Dr. Embuke about securing a plane ride.

"I haven't selected a flight yet since I want to be sure my work here is done first. Some flights leave in about three hours, but I won't make those. I would also love to meet your sister, but I'm not sure if it will be possible on this trip."

Dr. Embuke also chose his words carefully. "I can arrange a plane for you," he said as he looked at Tracey and then back down to his food. Dr. Embuke had a ride for Tracey. Tracey was sure of it.

Dr. Embuke continued, "It is too bad you could not meet my sister tonight, as she is at the palace. If your schedule frees up, I can drive you there. Or I will leave your name at the palace gate if I cannot accompany you."

"Thank you, Dr. Embuke. That is very kind of you, but as far as the flight goes, I will have my work arrange the trip. Also, thank you for the opportunity to meet your sister. Who knows - maybe I will stop by and say hello to her tonight. It is not often one gets to meet the president of a country!"

Hearing this conversation, the general would think Tracey had done his job in identifying the president's location. And it appeared that Dr. Embuke had already alerted her that the general was attempting a coup. Hopefully, Dr. Embuke understood the reference to Tracey stopping by to say hello to the president tonight, meaning the general was making a run for the palace tonight. He wanted to make sure the president was prepared.

Tracey and Dr. Embuke finished their meal. They bickered like long-time friends over who would pay for the meal. Dr. Embuke informed Tracey he had already paid the bill, and they both rose to leave. Out of the corner of his eye, Tracey watched the general's men get up to follow. They were fifteen yards behind them.

Once outside, Tracey shook Dr. Embuke's hand and thanked him again for dinner. Dr. Embuke walked away, and Tracey turned in the opposite direction toward the place he had been told to rendezvous after dinner. The general's men had not yet exited the restaurant.

Tracey made it to the corner and took a right down the street. Twenty-five yards away sat the tan Humvee, which would be his ride back to the general. He reached inside his coat and yanked out the generals' wire, pulling the microphone off of the electrical connection. The wire was now dead.

Tracey knew it was now or never, and he had to make a run for it. His daughter was not quite safely on the plane to the U.S. but would be in the next thirty minutes. Right now, though, he needed to get to the palace and arrange his flight home.

He also needed to let the FBI know his daughter was on that plane.

Chapter 59
Better Training Gets the Job Done

Beads of sweat ran down the small of Tracey's back as he strode with purpose towards the tan Humvee. While he walked, he strained his ears, hoping to hear the familiar sound of his drone. Nothing. The drone should have arrived. Maybe it was just trying to find him and would regroup with him at any moment.

Tracey noticed a tan sedan parked behind the Humvee. It probably belonged to the two guys in the restaurant. They still hadn't reached the corner. It was enough of a distance for Tracey to execute the next phase of his plan. As Tracey approached the doors of the Humvee, a soldier stepped out of the driver's side passenger seat with a long gun slung around his neck. The driver remained in the driver's seat. Tracey gave the driver a thumbs up and walked past the driver's door and the soldier standing on the sidewalk. Tracey grabbed the driver's side passenger door, pushed it completely open, and put his right leg into the Humvee. The soldier began to follow Tracey into the Humvee, but he didn't expect Tracey to stop short of fully getting in.

When the soldier got within arms-length, Tracey reached out with his left arm and pulled the soldier across his lap and into the Humvee, striking him quickly with his right hand with an upward thrust to his nose, breaking it cleanly. The soldier groaned and reached for his broken nose. Tracey grabbed the soldier's long gun and, in one quick move, twisted it cleanly from around the soldier's neck. Simultaneously, while the soldier tried to figure out what had just happened to him, Tracey reached around the soldier and took his 9mm handgun from his holster. Tracey sat in the back seat, training the 9mm directly at the bleeding soldier and then, alternately, at the driver.

"Just sit there," Tracey said to the driver. "Don't even think about moving or doing anything stupid, or you will both die." The driver started to raise his hands.

"Put them down! Now!" Tracey barked. The two men from the restaurant had just turned the corner. They were still walking normally and hadn't seen what happened. The driver still had his hands up. Tracey used the gun to motion for him to put his hands down, which he finally did. Maybe he was deaf. Or didn't speak English.

"Now, open your door slowly, but stay in the vehicle," Tracey told the driver. As Tracey watched the driver, the soldier in the back seat then made a move which forced Tracey to hit him in the face again with the butt of the long gun. The soldier crumpled down to the back seat floor and remained there.

"Next move is a round into your pea-brain. Don't try me." The soldier merely closed his eyes.

The driver still had not opened the door. Maybe he didn't speak English. That had to be it. Both soldiers didn't speak English.

"Hey!" Tracey yelled to the driver while he looked at the door. Tracey made a hand motion to open the door. The driver did as directed. But he also began to step out of the Humvee.

"No!" Tracey barked out, and the driver remained in the Humvee. At least the driver understood what "no" meant.

Tracey leaned forward into the driver's seat. He took the radio clipped to the driver's side and clipped it to his belt. He grabbed the driver's cell phone lying next to the driver and put it in his back pocket. With his next move, Tracey also grabbed the driver's handgun. He then sat back in the passenger seat. Moving the soldier onto his side on the floor, Tracey took his radio and clipped it to his belt with the other radio. The men from the restaurant were now beginning to walk faster. Tracey positioned himself behind the driver's seat and lowered the handgun. The men were now 15 feet in front of the Humvee. It was time.

Securing the long gun around his neck by its strap, Tracey let the gun hang down by his side. He leaped out of the Humvee with the handgun pointed at the two men, using the driver's door as cover. They moved for their handguns under their shirts, but Tracey waved for them not to try it. He motioned for the men to get into the back of the Humvee. As each man passed Tracey, he stopped them and took their handguns. He tucked them into his waist. He reached into the jacket pockets of the first man. The keys for the sedan were there. Tracey pushed the unlock button, and the tan sedan responded to the request. Tracey shoved the men into the Humvee, and they made their way across the seat, stepping over the bleeding soldier.

Tracey then motioned for the driver to get out. He didn't move. Tracey motioned again. Frozen. God help this man before he had to kill him, Tracey thought to himself. As Tracey moved closer, the driver took a step out of the Humvee and lunged for Tracey's gun. Tracey was ready. He fired three rounds from the handgun, the third round hitting the driver in the neck. He was dead before he hit the ground. Tracey looked around. No bystanders. No witnesses Tracey could see.

Reaching inside, he pulled out the keys from the ignition. He closed the door and turned his attention to the three men in the back seat of the Humvee. Showing his phone to the men, Tracey motioned for them to give him their phones. They weren't responding as quickly as Tracey expected, so he shook his head and leveled his handgun at the first man. That worked. Tracey had all three of their phones inside ten seconds. Tracey shoved the phones in his front pockets. He then motioned for the men to pick up the driver and put him in the Humvee. They did as Tracey asked, pushing his body into the front seat and closing the door.

Tracey took the Humvee keys and closed the door to the Humvee. He walked backward to the tan sedan and kept his handgun ready. When he got to the car, he opened the driver's door and threw the radios, handguns, and cell phones into the passenger seat. Now, he had to get to the palace, and he hoped to have enough time before the general was alerted to Tracey's new plan.

Tracey backed up and quickly slammed the car into "Drive" as he headed to the first intersection. He looked in his rear-view mirror. One of the men had jumped out of the Humvee and was running down the street in the opposite direction.

One part of his plan Tracey was never worried about was the possibility of the general getting his hands on his drone. He had a little secret he never shared with the general about the drone, and naturally so. No matter where the InCit computer program instructed a drone to fly, its number one directive was to find the IA it was assigned to protect. Once Tracey's drone arrived at the general's headquarters, it would immediately seek out Tracey by searching for his DNA. The drone would continue to search in a circular pattern until it found Tracey. It wouldn't take long for the drone to regroup with Tracey. But Tracey was now worried about his drone. It had not arrived.

If only Athan had remembered to turn the drop phone back on. Tracey would know the drone wasn't coming to help him.

Tracey remembered seeing a sign for the palace while driving with the general earlier. After three kilometers at excessively high speeds, he saw the sign indicating the palace was only two kilometers away. He took a right onto a street neatly lined with beautiful trees and gunned the sedan as fast as it would move. Within a few minutes, he saw an entrance with gates and barricades stretching hundreds of yards out. It had to be the palace. As he drove closer, he saw a modest, four-story building, which he hoped was the palace. In front of the gate, more than a dozen gray armored Humvees and metal barricades were staggered in a pattern to slow vehicles. At least Tracey could tell the president's Humvees apart from the general's since his were all tan.

He began to slow down so he would not be shot, and the car came to a crawl in front of the guard post. He counted at least two dozen guns trained on him. He slowly put the sedan in "Park" and exited the driver's side. Tracey realized that he was driving one of the general's tan sedans. That would suck - getting this far only thinking he was working with the general.

One of the soldiers yelled at him in Arabic. Tracey only knew to reply, "Special Agent David Tracey, FBI! FBI!" Nothing.

The soldiers continued to yell at him as Tracey lowered to the ground. Within seconds, they had Tracey in zip ties and placed him in the back of one of their gray Humvees. They backed up to make a path to drive Tracey onto the palace grounds and out of view. The gates opened, and the soldiers parted like the Red Sea. Tracey was on his way to see the president.

Hopefully.

Chapter 60
Hello, Madame President

Tracey again found himself in the all-to-familiar situation of late - being escorted in and out of a Humvee. Tracey was glad the Humvee he was now in belonged to the president, however. Though the zip ties on his wrists were a little tight.

He could tell that the driver of the Humvee was intent on getting to the palace as fast as possible as they sped down the road. No one spoke. Approaching the front of the palace, Tracey could see an ornate entrance with two large columns. As they passed, the rest of the palace appeared average-looking, made of concrete and stucco. It was a simple, streamlined building and nothing crazy or royal-looking.

The Humvee made its way around to the back of the palace and came to a screeching halt. The soldier next to Tracey helped him out of the vehicle. Accompanied by two additional men, they ascended the stairs to a back entrance. One of the soldiers placed a key card against a panel, and the door clicked open. They all walked inside. A cool rush of air immediately hit Tracey in the face. It felt good. And he smelled pleasant odors. Tracey sensed a warm feeling about the palace. They continued down a short corridor and took a left, heading down the length of the palace interior. The walls were modestly decorated with artwork. Everything about the presidential palace was low-key and humble.

About halfway down the hallway, they stopped, and the same soldier used his key card outside an elevator bank. The elevator door opened. They entered and were quickly whisked up several floors. When they stopped, they exited and walked across the hall into a nicely decorated conference room.

The furnishings included a small round table with carved wooden claw legs, several chairs, and a few couches against the wall. A golden chandelier with thousands of small, diamond-like stones hung several feet above the table. Floor lengthed drapes in front of the two windows were sewn with gold leaf and deep crimson ribbons. Beautiful wooden bookcases lined the remaining walls, their shelves full of reading materials interspersed with African antiquities, including a spear, several stone tablets that contained hieroglyphics, and a footprint in stone of a human, certainly from centuries ago.

The soldiers motioned for Tracey to sit in one of the chairs at the round table. Tracey did as he was told as one of the soldiers cut off the zip ties. That felt good. Tracey rubbed his wrists and thanked them. The soldiers nodded their heads in response. Almost immediately, the doors opened, and a woman walked in with a tray full of water and other drinks. She placed it on the table.

"Special Agent Tracey. Please, help yourself. The president will be in shortly." The woman motioned to the tray and walked away. They knew who he was, so that had to be good. Tracey poured himself a glass of water and drank it. He refilled his glass. He could see through the windows in the conference room that it was completely dark outside. Certainly, the general was aware he had escaped by now. All Tracey kept thinking about, no, praying about: please let April be on the plane from Paris to the U.S. And where the hell was his drone?

Just as Tracey began to take another drink from his glass, the doors opened, and in walked Dr. Embuke. Tracey stood up to acknowledge his friend. All three soldiers reacted to Tracey's sudden movement and placed their hands on their side arms.

"No, no, it is all right. Show him some respect, please," Dr. Embuke said as he held his hands out to all the soldiers, motioning for them to stand down.

"Mr. Tracey! You made it. Thank the heavens." Dr. Embuke walked towards Tracey with his hands outstretched.

As they shook hands, Tracey said, "I could not have done it without your help. I got this far only because you are a smart man, and I knew you would figure out my cryptic messages at the restaurant. You would make a great FBI agent!" Both Tracey and Dr. Embuke laughed.

"We will have to work fast. My sister is just ending a call and will be right in to discuss where she is with her plan. She is fortifying the palace and getting everyone and everything in place. She is also making arrangements for a plane to get you home."

"That's great news. After everything you have done for me and my daughter, I feel badly, but I need to ask another favor."

"Yes, what is that?"

"I need to call a Bureau friend back home and tell him what is happening, especially with my daughter traveling back to the U.S."

"Of course," Dr. Embuke said. "Wait one moment." Dr. Embuke quickly left the room.

Tracey nervously glanced over at the soldiers and smiled. They smiled back. Hmm. Maybe he wouldn't get shot today after all. And he had made friends. His wife would be so proud.

Within a minute, Dr. Embuke returned. He opened the door and stood aside.

"Mr. Tracey. May I present my sister, the President of Jafaire." Dr. Embuke waved his hands as President Embuke walked into the room. She was followed by four soldiers and a male and female assistant. Tracey stood.

President Embuke was a beautiful woman. She was athletically fit, and her hair was very neatly manicured and up in a bun. She wore a two-piece gray pantsuit. With white sneakers. Casual. But she looked like she meant business. She outstretched her arms as she continued walking towards Tracey.

"Mr. Tracey or Special Agent Tracey, I mean to say. Welcome, though I am sorry it is under such distressing circumstances." She walked directly up to Tracey and embraced him.

"It is a pleasure to meet you, Madame President. It has been an ordeal, for sure."

"Please, call me Chiz. My friends do, and I consider you a friend, not only of mine but of all Jafaire. We now have a chance to defend ourselves against the general because of you. I still can't believe his plan, but we'll be ready for him. Please. Let's sit down." Little did she know, if not for Tracey's loose lips, the general would not be positioned to attack her.

Tracey sat back in the chair, and the president said something to her assistants, who then headed out of the room.

"Are you hungry, Mr. Tracey?" the president asked.

"Oh, no, thank you, Madame President. Your brother took me to The Offering, and I think we ate enough for six people. It was some of the best food I have ever eaten."

The president smiled at her brother. Doctor Embuke smiled back.

"I am sorry to get right down to business, but I believe time is of the essence," President Embuke began. "What can you tell me about the general's plans?"

Tracey sat up a little in his chair. "What I can tell you is I came to Jafaire so your brother could help my daughter who was suffering from DBA, similar to I believe -"

President Embuke cut Tracey off by holding up her hand. This was not a conversation for everyone in the room to hear. Tracey got it.

"Understood, Special Agent Tracey. I have spoken to my brother about this."

She looked over at her brother a bit sternly. He looked down at his hands and only gave a slight smile. Tracey figured Dr. Embuke got his ass chewed for helping April.

"Before my daughter could finish the procedure, the general confronted me. He explained how he had been exploiting an FBI agent in the United States. This agent worked on a secret program with me, guarding a technology we keep close to the vest. Because the general knew of it, he then held me and my daughter hostage in exchange for this technology. He wanted it to help him overthrow your government.

"I had to play along. I promised to have a piece of this equipment flown here to turn over to him. That promise is how my daughter was allowed to leave Jafaire.

More to the fact, General Repuso allowed my daughter to get on a plane with two of his men through to Paris. I don't think she is safe yet."

President Embuke kept nodding her head. "Let me give you some good news. April is safe. She landed in Paris and departed for the U.S. approximately an hour ago." Tracey briefly closed his eyes, sighed, and eased slowly back into his chair. That was the news Tracey wanted to hear. He felt somewhat relieved now. He could die happy. He didn't want to die any time soon, however.

"When my brother told me about the coup and your daughter's plight, I contacted Interpol and gave them most of the story, only what they needed to know. They assisted by shutting down the cell towers just before the general's plane landed so they couldn't make or receive any calls. Interpol then used a ruse to get on the plane while on the tarmac. They were all taken into custody after your daughter was safely off the plane. Your daughter was told there was a technical issue with the plane and never knew what happened."

"Thank you, President Em – sorry, Chiz." President Embuke smile. "I am grateful for your help."

"On a separate note, I asked your brother for a cell phone to call a colleague in Washington, D.C. I need to make him aware that my daughter is on that plane. He had no idea she was overseas for this procedure. He may have figured out by now that I am here, but I need to tell him exactly what has happened."

The president motioned to one of her assistants, who left the room and quickly returned carrying three cell phones. "My brother mentioned your request. I hope one of these phones will work." She presented them to Tracey and explained they were all Google Voice phones with accompanying VPNs tied to them. He chose the phone with an Iowa VPN number.

Out of courtesy, the president cleared the room so Tracey could make his phone call.

As he opened the phone, he thought about what he would say. He then dialed Bell's number.

Please answer.

Chapter 61
Let's Go

The Gulfstream smoothly moved like a bullet through the air. Bell had been in the air for almost eleven hours. He would land in Jafaire in the next few minutes. He hadn't expected to fly anywhere today except maybe into D.C. to brief the director, not to get Tracey back with the drone from a foreign country. And to get it done quietly.

To hide Bell's identity, the Bureau arranged for him to fly undercover as a Coca-Cola employee on a Coca-Cola jet. His story was he was traveling to the country to work on Jafaire's Coca-Cola marketing program. The Jafairian authorities wouldn't suspect otherwise.

Coca-Cola's corporate office in Jafaire was located in downtown Lingos. At least, it appeared that way. It was simply a storefront set up and run by the CIA. They would provide Bell with an armored vehicle when he landed and help Bell locate Tracey.

On the flight to Jafaire, he poured through many databases to gain an understanding of the political and military structure of Jafaire. He also tried to make sense of Tracey's plan and why he would put his job and life on the line like he was. Bell couldn't come up with a reason just yet.

The pilot came over the intercom and notified Bell they would be landing within two minutes. Bell looked outside and watched as they flew over the last hundred yards of the mountain range surrounding Jafaire. Seconds later, the plane broke free of the clouds, revealing the country of Jafaire.

Bell looked off on the horizon at the city of Lingos. Buildings in downtown Lingos could be seen as they descended. It looked like any other city he had flown into over his career. Bell also noticed a lot of folks running around on the ground at the airport as they narrowed their approach to land. He couldn't see what they were doing, though. They all looked to be wearing military uniforms.

Bell checked his injured hand and the dressing. It looked good. No further bleeding and it was starting to feel much better. He squeezed his hand into a ball. It was painful but manageable. Just in case, he took one of the 800 mg ibuprofen the doctor gave him.

The plane banked slightly to its right, straightened out, and smoothly landed. They taxied to a small hangar where several cars were waiting for him. Bell grabbed his Pelican case with his drone and bounded down the stairs and off the plane.

Five feet onto the tarmac, he was met by a man in his forties wearing a pair of dress pants and a golf shirt. He had the standard CIA-looking sunglasses, so Bell had no problem identifying who he was meeting with.

"SA Bell, welcome to Jafaire," the man said as he reached to shake Bell's hand. "Steve Bantore. Your station contact here."

"Hey, Steve. Nice to meet you, and thank you for the assist," Bell said as they shook hands.

"I was planning to get you up to speed on Jafaire's government structure, all of it, as we drove, but we have a more pressing matter, so I'll brief you on that instead. The country is about to blow up from the inside."

Bell turned his head in surprise. "Really? What's going on?"

"Looks like we have a coup attempt about to come to a head, and we need to get the hell out of Dodge. Your guy Tracey appears to be planning his escape route. He killed at least one soldier outside a downtown restaurant several hours ago, and he is now at the president's palace. We're trying to let her know you're here and to offer our assistance to stave off this coup."

"Well, Tracey, the agent you referred to, is in some kind of hot water, and I'm here simply to get his ass back to the U.S. If you guys can handle the coup, we'll get out of your hair as fast as we can find Tracey."

"All right then. Let's get a move on and head towards the palace. We're only about five minutes out."

Bell and Bantore jogged towards a group of CIA personnel standing by four cars inside the hangar. The engines were running. Bell aimed for the open door of a black SUV and jumped into the back seat with his drone, closing the heavy, armored door behind him.

The cars sped away from the hangar. They moved out one at a time, each separated by fifty yards to eliminate the possibility of all four vehicles being taken out by any one weapon, such as an RPG - a rocket-propelled grenade. Bell's car was in the lead as they left the airport and headed towards the presidential palace.

Suddenly, Bell's phone rang. His Bureau phone. Not his drop phone. Bell squinted his eyes for a moment. Des Moines, Iowa? Who the hell would be calling him from Des Moines? He waited to see if the call would automatically be shuttled due to the Bureau tagging it as spam. After three rings, Bell knew it wasn't spam.

"This is Bell," he answered.

"Call me back." That's all Tracey needed to say.

Bell looked at the phone again. It was Tracey. Bell knew it.

Bell grabbed his drop phone and dialed the number. It took longer than it should have taken to ring through to Des Moines, Iowa. That was for sure. That's when Bell realized the number was most likely routed through a VPN, and God knew where Tracey was calling from. Bell assumed it was Jafaire, though. On the second ring, Tracey picked up the phone.

"Okay, look, I know you have a ton of questions, but please just listen to me for a moment, and then we can talk at length."

Bell covered the mouthpiece of the phone and spoke to Bantore.

"It's Tracey. Can you track this call?"

"On it," Bantore said as he opened a Pelican case lying on the floor between his feet. It contained a small laptop computer and antenna, which Bantore moved to the side and turned upright. Bell showed him the phone number Tracey was calling from. Bantore gave a thumbs up and began to type into the laptop. Bell listened as Tracey continued.

"My daughter is on a plane and scheduled to land at Reagan National in the next hour. You need to get to her and make sure she's safe. Please. She was being watched by two men loyal to the General of the Armed Forces of Jafaire. They were on her flight from Jafaire to Paris. Neither of them is on her flight now, but they could have placed someone else on the plane to the U.S. and didn't tell me. You'll need to take her into protective custody. And all of my family is at risk. Okay. Go." He shut up so Bell could speak.

"I know about April. I found out about her flight from Paris to D.C. and sent agents to the airport several hours ago to escort her off the plane and onto her flight to Miami. I also have agents at your home, and your family will leave there shortly for a safe house. April will join them.

"And I spoke to Trina. Don't worry, Trina and I worked it out so no one heard our calls. We were careful. She doesn't know April is on her way home, but the Bureau will let her know. She also doesn't know where the hell you are. But the Bureau does, David."

"Wow, that's more than I expected. I'm grateful you've stepped up to help me, Elliott. Thanks, bud. Also, I have another favor."

Bell interjected. "A lot of demands for a man on the run," Bell said with increased aggravation.

"I know. But this is the last one. My neighbor, Athan -"

Bell cut him off again. "Kratos, yeah, I know he's helping you, but I don't know why. What about him?"

"You have to get him and his family into protective custody. The general has operators in the U.S. - oddly, some of whom have been through our National Academy - who will try to take them out."

"Okay. I'm on it. We know about the surveillance teams and their capabilities. In the last few days, however, we've seen no one at your or your friend's house, within two miles as near as we can tell. All I want to know from you is this - is the program safe? And do you need to be helped out of whatever situation you're in?" Bell wasn't going to tell Tracey he was in Jafaire. Not until he had to.

"The program is safe. I swear the general will not get access to it. The general believes the drone is being delivered directly to him. It's cloaked, so he won't see it. He also doesn't realize our drones will ultimately seek us out by searching for our DNA when we program them to go somewhere, and they can't find us. The drone will find me pretty quickly. I'll use it if I have to. As for flying out of here, I think I'm all set."

At that moment, several helicopters flew past Bell in the opposite direction of the city. Simultaneous with Bell looking at the helicopters, Bantore grabbed Bell's arm. Bantore was shaking his head. Bell covered the mouthpiece again.

"Bad news?" Bell asked.

"I'd say so. Looks like the coup has begun. We just received intel that General Repuso has begun to attack the presidential palace. And it looks like your boy is at the palace as well."

Bantore turned the computer towards Bell. He could see a bright red dot, which he assumed was Tracey's cell phone. It was stationary inside the outline of a building that said "Presidential Palace." Bell nodded at Bantore and returned to his call with Tracey.

"Okay, bud, is this going to be your comms to stay in touch from here on out?"

"Yes, I'll keep this phone with me. I can't thank you enough, bud, and I'll -" The phone call abruptly ended. In an instant, several explosions could be heard towards the entrance to the palace. There was a spattering of gunfire as well. At least Bell got the message.

"We've got to go! I lost the call." As Bell looked outside, he saw smoke just off to their left. The general was close.

"Push it!" Bantore said to the driver. They accelerated and rounded a street corner that led down the same tree-lined parkway Tracey had driven down earlier. Halfway down the street, an RPG round landed harmlessly within twenty yards of the car behind Bell. The general's men knew they were there. Undeterred, the four-car caravan continued towards the palace.

As they approached the front gates, they could see the president's soldiers engaged in a gunfight with the general's soldiers.

"We've got to take out some of the general's men. The president's soldiers have got to see we're on their side, or both sides will be shooting at us soon enough," Bantore yelled out.

"Agreed," Bell said. "Let's do this."

The driver swung the SUV sideways in the road and came to a halt. He popped open the back doors, and everyone slid across the seats and out the driver-side doors. Bell grabbed his Pelican case as he got out. Bantore grabbed several RPG launchers from the back.

They started to draw gunfire from one of the general's Humvees forty yards to their left. Bantore wheeled around to Bell's side and got down on one knee.

"Clear!" he said to everyone so they knew to move away from the blast that would come from behind the launcher. He fired. The RPG struck the Humvee and sent it several feet in the air, killing three of the general's soldiers at the same time.

Bantore dropped the empty launcher and moved again to the back of the vehicle. He grabbed another RPG launcher. The other CIA agents were engaged in a gun battle with a second Humvee just past the one Bantore had destroyed.

"We're going to need some help and soon," one of them yelled, as a soldier in the general's Humvee began to turn the turret-mounted fifty caliber gun towards them.

While the CIA Agents remained occupied defending their position, no one noticed as Bell unpacked and powered up his flying friend. He was a little nervous. He remembered the first time he directed his new toy and had a few technical difficulties with the commands. He prayed he had it worked out now and would take out the right people.

"Cloak," Bell instructed the drone, and it immediately became invisible. "Secure Perimeter," Bell instructed. The drone took off. A perimeter was defined for the drone as a circle 150 yards out from the IA. Within five seconds of flying off, the first rounds from the drone rang out.

The CIA agents didn't know where the rounds were coming from and nervously looked around for a sniper. The drone, meanwhile, continued with its order, killing fourteen soldiers who were in a position to take out Bell or the CIA agents long before they could get to the front gates of the palace. And most importantly, it eliminated the fifty-caliber gun.

With a clear path in front of them now, Bantore told everyone to regroup in the SUV.

"Let's go. Head for the front gates," Bell shouted.

Bantore reached under the seat and came up with a white bulletproof vest. He held it out the window. As they slowly approached the palace gate, they drew a few rounds until the president's soldiers realized Bantore was waving what amounted to a white flag out the SUV window. The soldiers stopped shooting at them. But no sooner did the president's men stop shooting at them when a Tiger HAP helicopter belonging to the general's troops fired a barrage of rounds into the guard post, taking out a number of the president's soldiers. The Tiger HAP turned towards Bell's SUV. Before the helicopter gunner could get off a round, one quick invisible burst of gunfire six feet away from the helicopter killed the gunner. Bell smiled. Good dog. The pilot veered off. Bantore scrunched up his eyes as if he saw something he didn't see. He shook his head and looked again. He'd never see the drone.

"Hit it! Get inside that gate," Bell yelled out. The driver stepped on the gas and barely pushed past a burning Humvee and several dead soldiers. As the driver barreled towards the front of the palace, another Tiger HAP helicopter flew in front of the SUV. The pilot saw Bell's vehicle and banked sharply while the gunner inside began to fire at Bell and his group. The helicopter only turned several degrees before an RPG fired from somewhere inside the palace grounds struck the back of it, sending it spinning toward the ground outside the palace.

"Okay, let me out here," Bell said as he tapped the driver on the shoulder.

"What? No, we're with you until the end," Bantore said as he turned to Bell.

"Guys, you have been a lifesaver, but we have an asset with us that should be able to get us out of here. Can you secure my plane for us at the airport? I'm not sure if my guy has a ride lined up."

"You sure?" Bantore said again as Bell exited the SUV and closed the door.

"Positive, thank you. Get out of here. Plausible deniability." Bell smiled. Bantore chuckled.

"Keep your head down, Bell. We've got your plane covered. Good luck." Bantore tapped the driver on the arm, and the driver spun the car around and floored it towards the palace gates.

Now, where the hell was Tracey?

Chapter 62
Surprise, Surprise, Surprise

President Embuke jumped up and looked out towards the front gates and the walls around the front perimeter of the palace. She could see a helicopter belonging to the general's forces on fire and losing altitude as it headed over the palace gates. A second helicopter was banking sharply to its right. It had also been hit by her forces returning fire and crashed to the ground. A dozen more of the general's Humvees had arrived and were attacking the palace forces at the front gates. The president immediately went to the phone on the desk and barked out several orders. She hung up and quickly returned to the window, just in time to see two U.S.-made Apache helicopters make a beeline to support the front gates. Nice. They would get the job done.

"I wish we could have met under different circumstances, Mr. Tracey. I cannot express enough my gratitude for alerting us to this coup attempt. I'll hold the general accountable, as will the rest of the world. I need to get you out of here so no one knows you were ever here. At least that will be my official statement if anyone asks."

If only Tracey could tell her that he was part of the reason the coup was happening. Maybe if the general hadn't heard of the InCit program, which he now realized was surely from his big mouth, the general wouldn't be trying to overthrow the president. Or maybe the general was hell-bent on taking over and would have continued with the coup attempt without Tracey's drone. Either way, Tracey didn't feel as joyous about his role in warning the president as she did.

The president again gave out orders to several of the soldiers in the room. One of them departed with a quickened pace. The president turned back toward Tracey and her brother.

"Henry, you may stay here, of course, and we have secured our family, as you know. We are safe. Now, let's get you to the airport, Special Agent Tracey. I am giving you three soldiers to drive you there. At the south end of the airport, there is a small Gulfstream airplane with a black and white tail. The identifiers on the tail are EC471. There is a pilot and crew onboard, all of whom I have handpicked. They are several of my finest soldiers. They will protect your life with their own and get you to Paris. Once in Paris, you will be on your own to book a flight home. You should be safe then."

"Present Embuke, I can't thank you enough for assisting me. You and your brother have been extremely kind to me and my family." Tracey stood up, and President Embuke began to turn and walk out, but Tracey stopped her with his words. "Madame President, I have one more thing to tell you."

President Embuke turned in her tracks.

"There is that FBI technology I talked about. I can clarify somewhat, and I have a small request as well. If you clear the room, I will explain it to you."

President Embuke waved everyone out. Dr. Embuke also left. She looked at him expectantly.

"I am all ears, Special Agent Tracey."

"I have arranged for a piece of equipment to fly itself here. It is more a military piece of equipment than anything else. This equipment of ours operates with .223 caliber ammunition. It will protect my every move and assist me in getting to the plane. The general's men will never see this piece of equipment or be able to anticipate the rounds they will take. If you could spare some .223 rounds to replace any rounds I'll most likely use, I would appreciate it greatly."

The president looked at Tracey and smiled. "Say no more, Special Agent Tracey. We'll stop on the way out, and I will get you those rounds. And my lips are sealed. After we eliminate the general's threat, I think your secret will be safe."

The president motioned for Tracey to follow her, and she opened the doors to the room. They both began to walk down the corridor. And Tracey was now more than worried about the location of his drone. It should have made it to Jafaire and found him by now. But it hadn't.

Along the way, a soldier was instructed to provide Tracey with four boxes of fifteen rounds each of the .223 ammunition the drone required. Tracey placed a box in each of his pant pockets. The president shook Tracey's hand and thanked him again.

Before Tracey could completely walk away, the president said, "I never did get a chance to apologize for placing you in zip ties when you arrived. I had to make sure it was you. So, I hope you will forgive me."

Tracey waved his hands as if to say, "No big deal," and said, "I would have done the same thing, Madam President. No apologies necessary."

She nodded in approval, and Tracey turned and began to jog with the three soldiers the president had assigned to him.

They ran down the stairs and out the same door they had entered. Just as they opened the door, a Humvee parked just next to the palace in front of them exploded, having taken a rocket from a helicopter that had made its way past the Apache and onto the palace grounds. Tracey and the three soldiers were blown directly back into the building. Before they could even stand up, the helicopter took a rocket blast of its own and came careening down in between the burning Humvee and the building. It crashed directly into a Humvee idling by the door and continued into the side of the building. *Damm it,* Tracey thought. *There goes my ride.* Two of the soldiers got up. The third one wasn't moving. Tracey didn't have time to check on him. The other soldiers hastily motioned for Tracey to follow, and they raced to the door. Seeing no sign of the enemy troops outside, the two soldiers ran out the door towards the back of the palace. Tracey followed and called out for his drone. "Close Distance." And then, "10 Feet." He listened. There was no hum. There was no drone. Shit. He continued to run.

He made it about fifteen feet when suddenly, the sound of several .223 rounds rang out behind him. Tracey glanced back and saw two of the general's soldiers laid out on the ground, dead. The general's soldiers had come from the front of the palace. That's when Tracey saw a familiar friend. But not his flying friend. His human friend. He watched as Bell sprinted past the dead soldiers and headed towards him.

"What the – – ?" Tracey said as Bell reached his side.

"Don't ask. Let's move. And by the way, it's my drone, not yours, so try not to piss it off so it won't shoot you." Bell gave Tracey a quick smirk and smacked him on the back.

Tracey gave a half-smile, confused about how his friend had made it to Jafaire. And for the last time, he wondered where his drone was.

Chapter 63
Adios, Mother-Truckers

"Follow me," Tracey told Bell.

Bell, Tracey, and the two soldiers rounded the corner at the back of the Presidential Palace. Bell could see the president's troops storming out of military vehicles to shore up the perimeter of the building. Some were fighting with the general's men throughout the palace grounds. The president would be safe so long as there were no traitors loyal to the general within the group of her closest guards. Bell looked over at the front of the palace and noticed the metal shades had been lowered inside for all the windows. The president would be hidden somewhere inside.

The CIA convoy was nowhere in sight. They had disappeared. No one would be the wiser. While there would be talk the CIA had helped, no one would be able to ID them. They would ditch their cars and get replacements soon enough and still be Coca-Cola Company employees when the sun rose the next day. The Bureau's closest ally would remain in place for future operations in Jafaire and the region.

"Elliott," Tracey said, tapping him on the shoulder. He handed Bell the four boxes of .223 rounds. "Seeing how my friend is missing, I got yours a few extra rounds in case we need them." Bell grabbed the rounds and put them in his pockets. "Thanks much."

Bell could see several gray Humvees in the back of the palace. The two soldiers sprinted for one of the Humvees. Bell and Tracey waited a few more seconds.

"Let's go," Tracey said. They sprinted from the side of the palace. Bell could hear the faint hum of his drone following them as they ran.

Bell wanted the drone close but behind him, for now, as its ability to sense danger was more acute the closer it was to Bell. He wanted to be sure it could hear his every command. Tracey needed to eliminate the close-range targets before the drone picked them up as a threat. That way, they could save the drone's rounds for a threat they couldn't see. And Bell still had no idea how many rounds the drone had left.

"Close Distance. Rear," Bell barked louder than he probably needed to, as his drone was always aware of Bell's voice. Bell could whisper, and the drone would respond. It moved within fifteen yards of Bell and hovered behind him.

Bell and Tracey reached the Humvee without taking any fire. It appeared the general's reinforcements had not yet made it that far to the rear of the palace courtyard. The soldiers jumped in. Bell and Tracey did as well. The drone maintained its distance behind the Humvee.

The driver floored the gas, and the Humvee shot out of its parking spot. He turned left and out of the interior courtyard, then barreled down the long, straight drive leading away from the palace and towards the front gates. Government troops loyal to President Embuke, in their standard gray Humvees, whizzed past them in the opposite direction, evidently hell-bent on protecting the president and the palace. So far, so good, Bell thought.

"Where are we going, Tracey?" Bell asked.

"To the airport. I've got us a ride. We're getting out of here," Tracey said quickly. Bell remembered the ERT training at Quantico when Tracey surprised Bell with his ingenuity and ability to think fast. Bell would give Tracey the benefit of the doubt. He'd wait to tell Tracey he had a ride lined up as well.

After a short drive, the driver reached the main entrance to the palace. A dozen or more of President Embuke's soldiers had taken up a defensive position behind their Humvees, engaged in a firefight with the general's troops. The driver didn't hesitate and pushed his Humvee out onto the road, swerving to the left and continuing on past one downed helicopter and a number of the general's dead soldiers.

The driver continued towards the city center. Tracey seemed to be deep in thought.

"You good?" Bell asked as he swatted Tracey on the arm, knocking him out of his trance.

"Yeah, just a lot on my mind."

"Snap out of it. We're not out of the woods yet."

I know, I know," Tracey said as he looked out the window.

Bell looked at the two soldiers in the Humvee with him. They couldn't have been older than twenty-five. They looked scared to death. If the soldier in the passenger seat gripped his rifle any harder, his fingers would burst.

"Do you speak English?" Tracey asked out loud to neither one of the guards in particular. Both soldiers said, "Yes, sir," almost in unison.

"Okay, good. And the president told you where to go?" They nodded in agreement, and the driver replied.

"When we arrive at the airport, we will head to the far end where there is a runway and the plane the president has waiting for you. There should be guards in position who have cleared a path."

"That should work," Tracey said. "Do either of you have a radio on you?"

The soldier in the passenger seat reached over to his side and produced a two-way radio.

"Very good. When we get within a couple hundred yards of the airport gate, call out to the soldiers to let them know we're close. We will -" Tracey never finished his sentence.

A large explosion blasted off to the right side of the front passenger door of the Humvee. The blast forced the driver to his left, where he swerved before recovering and turning back to the right. The Humvee almost flipped over when he corrected back to his right. Bell and Tracey grabbed the door handles and hung on. Somehow, the driver managed to keep all four tires on the ground. He stepped on the gas and continued onward. Everyone in the vehicle was now on high alert.

Bell and Tracey looked back and saw several soldiers running into the road. One knelt with an RPG launcher in his hands. He was about to fire at them again.

"When I tell you, swerve to the side I tell you to," Bell said while still looking behind him. The driver nodded in agreement. And then the RPG was out and headed their way. Bell waited. And he waited some more.

"Swerve right!" Bell yelled as he hunched down in the Humvee, just in case they got hit. The driver swerved quickly and managed to keep the Humvee upright. Again. The rocket missed by a foot or two and continued into a grove of trees, where it exploded.

"Let's keep a look out for any more incoming fire," Bell shouted. "RPGs can take us out. I'm not worried about the small-arms fire. It won't get through this Humvee." Tracey nodded.

Just as Bell finished explaining what he thought could happen, several rounds hit the side of the Humvee and deflected off. More of the general's troops appeared behind them in a tan Humvee. The drone did not fire. The drone sensed it couldn't stop the general's Humvee or the shooter protected inside so it wouldn't shoot.

Their young driver stepped on the gas again, pushing the Humvee up to ninety miles an hour. Bell didn't think these vehicles could go that fast. He hoped the driver didn't kill them.

They were now within sight of the airport, but the general's men in the Humvee behind them continued to shoot at them. Bell scanned the airport. No planes were moving, and Bell didn't immediately see any military troops. A couple of civilian cars passed them as they sped towards their ride home. They were now only several hundred yards from the far end of the airport.

"Okay, let's get in touch with the plane," Tracey shouted.

The soldier grabbed his radio and called out to the pilot. No response. He tried again. Nothing. Bell and Tracey looked behind them. No one was following them. The general's Humvee behind them had veered off to fight in another direction.

Both soldiers were visibly nervous. Tracey patted the driver on the shoulder to calm him down.

"It's all right, nothing to worry about. Let's slow down and call out again."

But Bell was a little worried.

The soldier gave it another try. This time, chatter could be heard coming over the radio. Gunfire as well. Lots of gunfire. And screaming. But no response.

Jesus, Mary, and Joseph, Bell thought to himself. *Can't any of this be easy?*

Bell looked off to his left and saw an ongoing battle between soldiers at different ends of several hangars. How the soldiers could tell each other apart was beyond Bell's grasp. The challenge was how Bell and Tracey would figure it out.

"Guys, how do we know the soldiers we're working with aren't loyal to the general?" Bell asked.

The driver responded. "The president sent a text message to her loyal soldiers and gave them this secure channel with a password. We are the only ones on this channel."

"That's a good call by your president. What if the radios fall into the wrong hands, and the general's soldiers lure us in?" Bell asked. The soldiers looked at each other. Great. Their faces gave Bell and Tracey their answer. That could still be a problem for them. They would have to take it one step at a time.

Now, the passenger spoke up as if he remembered something important. "All president's soldiers have this gray armband sewn into their shirt," he said, motioning to his right arm. Bell and Tracey leaned forward and noticed a five-inch-thick armband woven into the uniform. That was better than nothing, Bell thought. Hopefully, no one would think to take the shirt off a dead soldier.

The driver barked a few more instructions into the radio. This time, he received a response. He then turned to Bell. "The president's soldiers near the plane are taking heavy fire from a reinforced group of the general's men. We may be outnumbered."

Bell leaned into the front seat. Tracey turned his head for a better view of what might be in front of them.

"By outnumbered, what do you mean?" Bell asked.

The soldier looked back at Bell. "Maybe five to one."

Bell gave a little twist of his head to the side as he thought about these odds.

"I'm okay with those odds. How about you guys?" Bell said with a straight face. Tracey smiled.

Neither one of the soldiers responded. Okay, they weren't good with those odds, but it would have to work.

They rounded the corner and almost drove directly into a gun battle between the president's and the general's soldiers. The general's soldiers had formed a blockade across the road with a half dozen Humvees. Two of the general's Humvees were on fire.

"Don't stop!" Bell barked out. The soldier floored the Humvee and maneuvered around the front end of one of the burning Humvees. He didn't turn quite hard enough, however. The front bumper clipped the front bumper of the Humvee and spun their vehicle around almost one full turn.

Once they stopped, Bell yelled again. "Go, Go, Go!"

The driver shook off the effects of the impact, righted himself in the seat, and cranked the ignition of the Humvee. He tried several times to get the engine running. Rounds from the general's soldiers were now splattering the Humvee. The driver kept cranking the ignition, and finally, it started again. Good 'ole American ingenuity, Bell thought to himself.

The driver floored the Humvee again and made it through the destroyed gate and onto the airfield. He drove around and between two hangers and headed directly towards the plane sitting at the end of the runway. The plane's lights were on, and he hoped that indicated the engines were running.

Bell nodded as he looked over at the plane. Okay, Tracey had an escape plan. Good.

No sooner had Bell contemplated slapping Tracey on the back for a job well done when, out of the corner of his eye, he watched as the bright streak of an RPG flew past the back side of a hangar and continued towards their waiting plane.

The RPG struck it head-on, engulfing it in flames and sending debris fifty yards in every direction. Everyone in the Humvee ducked down in response. The driver slammed on the brakes.

"Fuck. Are you kidding me?! There goes our ride," Tracey said as he pounded the front seat. He then threw his head onto his arms. They all watched the fireball continue to burn for several seconds. It didn't look like anyone survived the blast.

Bell took a deep breath and then reached over and grabbed Tracey by the arm.

"Hey," Bell said while he looked at Tracey. Tracey turned his head and looked over at Bell. Bell was pointing outside his window. Tracey looked past Bell's finger. His eyes opened wide as he took in the Bureau's Gulfstream.

"How about if we use the horse I rode in on?" Bell said.

"Oh, thank God." Tracey sighed and looked down.

"Head to that plane," Bell said as he tapped the driver and pointed to the Bureau's Gulfstream.

Bell hoped his pilot was ready to take off. At about fifty yards out, Bell told the driver to stop. The driver slammed on the brakes, and the Humvee came to a stop.

"Turn the Humvee around and face the other way," Bell said. Both soldiers' faces screamed, "Why?!?" Bell saw it in their eyes.

"You will have an easier getaway. Don't worry about us. We'll run the last fifty yards. We will all be okay. Including both of you."

The soldiers looked at each other with disbelief.

"You *will* be okay. Just believe in yourselves." Bell slapped both soldiers on the shoulders. The driver was still hesitant, but he turned the Humvee towards the direction they had just come from. More than a dozen of the general's soldiers were advancing on their location. Both soldiers in the Humvee looked even more nervous now.

"Thank you, guys. I pray you will be successful and for Jafaire's prosperity. Adios."

Bell and Tracey jumped out of the Humvee. They slammed the doors shut and ran to the back of the Humvee.

Bell yelled out three quick commands. "Close Distance". "Uncloak." "Ground." The drone appeared at Bell's feet and shut down. He turned the drone on its back. He quickly reloaded it with the rounds given to him by the president and yelled out, "Armageddon!" Each InCit agent could create certain commands for their drones. Bell chose Armageddon as the command to "protect-me-at-all-costs-the-shit-is-about-to-hit-the-fan." The drone would move out to 100 yards. It would take out anything it perceived as a threat, even if that threat couldn't logically kill Bell from that distance.

"I like it. The shit-is-about-to-hit-the-fan command, eh?" Tracey said, smiling.

"Yeah, I thought it would be a cool word to yell out, even if it is the last word I ever got to say." They both chuckled.

The drone cloaked itself as Bell and Tracey heard the soft whir of the drone take off towards the soldiers. Boy, would they be surprised. The drone was a calculating specimen of tactical perfection. It would shoot then move ten feet before engaging again, never giving away its clear location for the enemy to target. That was if they ever figured it out at all.

Bell and Tracey weren't waiting around to see the firefight. Bell hoped the drone now had enough rounds to help the two soldiers. Bell and Tracey sprinted for the plane. They had run about twenty feet when they heard the first shot from Bell's drone. The president's men would be okay as they were firing in the same direction the drone was. At the general's men. They wouldn't be viewed as enemies.

As they made it to the Gulfstream, Bell stopped to look back. The two soldiers were firing from inside their Humvee with their doors open. There weren't many of the general's soldiers left. The president's soldiers were beginning to close the doors to Humvee to make their way out of the airfield.

"Let's go, Elliott," Tracey yelled as he bounded up the stairs and into the plane. He looked down at Bell and waved his hand for Bell to get a move on.

Bell motioned with his index finger to hold on one moment. Bell moved back and underneath the plane, crouching so the pilot couldn't see him. He didn't have the Pelican case for his drone. He needed to get the drone on the plane without the pilot seeing it.

"Retreat!" Bell barked out. He waited until he heard his drone buzz overhead.

"Close Distance!" "Uncloak!" Bell yelled out. Two feet behind him, the drone reappeared, shedding its invisible cloak.

"Ground," Bell commanded as he walked towards the drone. The drone quickly touched down on the ground and shut down. Upon reaching the drone, he grabbed it and turned it over. Working swiftly, he removed the bottom of the drone and pushed the buttons necessary for the magazine containing the rounds to extend from the drone. Only one round was left. Bell reached into his back pocket and reloaded the drone with the remaining rounds. Bell immediately said, "Cloak," and the drone became invisible again.

"With Me. Quiet Mode." These would be the last commands Bell would give the drone for the foreseeable future. He hoped. He stepped out from under the plane and walked towards the stairs again. He knew the drone would be right next to him. Bell hurried up the stairs.

Once inside, he paused and gave the drone enough room to fly past him. No one would have felt its presence. It was pinpoint accurate when it maneuvered. Just as it was when it fired its weapon system. When Bell moved out of the way for no apparent reason, he and Tracey exchanged smiles.

Bell made his way to Tracey and took a seat across from him. The door wasn't completely closed as they taxied into position to take off. The door finally closed as they began moving down the runway. Bell looked out the window. Some small skirmishes were happening in the distance, but as near as Bell could tell, their plane didn't take any fire from the general's troops as they climbed out of Jafaire. Thirty seconds later, they were safe. Thank God, Bell thought.

He prayed the president was safe as well and that the world would condemn the general for his coup attempt. He was also happy his drone listened to him and did what he asked. It was quite a formidable piece of equipment.

Bell started to close his eyes for a moment, then remembered he had to send a text to update the director. The fighting in Jafaire was probably on the news now, and the director would already know what had happened. After finishing the short text and giving an ETA for when they would arrive in Virginia, he closed his eyes. He'd noticed Tracey's eyes were already closed. Tracey needed a respite. Bell wondered when Tracey last relaxed, even a little bit.

He knew the next twenty hours could be Tracey's last as a free man.

Chapter 64
Protecting a Friend

Bell and Tracey slept most of the flight home. They woke almost at the same time. The plane would land at the Stafford Regional Airport in Fredericksburg, Virginia, in approximately two hours.

Bell yawned and stretched out his legs.

Tracey yawned, too, and looked around. "What, no flight attendants? How do we get service in this cabin?" Bell laughed.

"Your flying friend sure saved our asses," Tracey said as he looked away.

Bell nodded and looked out the window at the clouds they were passing through.

For the next minute or so, they said nothing to each other. They both knew they were treading on dangerous ground, with Tracey being wanted by the Bureau for possible treasonous crimes and Bell tasked with bringing Tracey in.

Tracey spoke first. "I guess you should be able to make section chief after you turn me in, bud," Tracey said with a slight chuckle.

"Oh, you know me so well. I've always wanted to climb the corporate ladder. Hell no!" Bell exclaimed.

Tracey seemed content not to say anything. Bell would have none of it, however. He wanted answers, and he was going to get them from Tracey. He casually looked over at Tracey, who had his head turned.

"You feel like talking a bit?" Bell asked.

"Sure. I know I owe you an explanation for a lot of things." Tracey turned towards Bell.

"That's putting it mildly," Bell said without looking at Tracey.

"I never intended this to get out of hand, especially with what happened in Jafaire. That was supposed to be a simple 'in-and-out' to help my daughter. That was it. I know I should have had a Plan B in case something went wrong, but I couldn't ever have imagined General Repuso was planning a coup. Not in a million years."

"I agree you should have had a Plan B. There may have been rumblings in the intelligence community that the general was up to something devious, but I never heard anything. Not that I'm wired into the intel community at the moment anyway, so there is that."

"Yeah, that does make sense. They probably learned about the general's coup attempt on short notice. But they wouldn't have seen it coming either."

"You'll be answering a boatload of questions when we land. You know that, right?" Bell said as he looked at his friend.

Tracey nodded. "What do you want to know before we get there?" Tracey asked.

"As for why you did it, I imagine it was for your daughter. I know you wouldn't purposely put the U.S. government on the defensive by trading technology with Jafaire. You can tell me some other time how that went completely sideways."

"That is correct," Tracey said, slowly nodding.

They both immediately said, "Plausible deniability," simultaneously and laughed.

"I am curious about a few things I couldn't figure out. Take ERF. How did you subdue everyone, and why wasn't I left unconscious, too?" Bell asked.

"If I hadn't run into you earlier, you would have passed out as well. I didn't know you were going to be there." Tracey half smiled. Bell squinted his eyes.

"I suspect you figured out I have a sister who works in ERF?"

"I know now, but I didn't figure it out. A doctor in InCit did. That was a shocker to everyone."

"My original plan was to get the gas from her lab and knock everyone out. I needed time. If I could subdue the director, I knew they would put him in isolation at the hospital to make sure he was okay. He wouldn't be able to coordinate with InCit or take out my drone, at least not until he was medically cleared. That would give me enough time to get out of the country. When I saw you making your way to the meeting, I decided to take a chance and hoped my old friend would be an ally if I needed someone to hear me out or help me. And we both know how that decision turned out."

"How'd you get the gas, and why didn't I didn't get knocked out as well?" Bell asked.

"When we met outside the InCit conference room, I placed a tracker on your coat to keep tabs on your location at ERF. Then, I ducked into my sister's lab for a few minutes to avoid the Red Ladens and grab the gas. The whole time, I knew you were sitting in the InCit conference room. Once the coast was clear of Red Ladens, I headed to the InCit conference room.

"My sister showed me many different gases and explained how they worked. So I knew how to introduce it to the conference room. I also learned many of the gases had antidotes. And you could add any specific DNA directly to the antidote, and only the person or persons assigned to that DNA would be spared. I located the antidote for the blue gas I used and added your DNA sample. I needed you to be conscious to explain what I was doing, and I might need your help. The rest of the folks would wake up with a headache, but they would be all right. I think I'll be fired, at the very least, simply because I knocked the director out." Bell looked at him and nodded.

"Yeah, I found that tracker stuck to my coat when I left ERF." Tracey nodded. "Go on," Bell said.

"I put on my gas mask outside the conference room, inserted one vial of the blue gas with the antidote into the sprayer, and let it rip. It traveled quickly and undetected. Once a person breathes it in, they are 'urged' to lay down." Tracey chuckled. So did Bell.

"You may have felt lightheaded for a minute. Once it was released, you were almost immediately given that antidote instead of being put to sleep."

"I appreciate that," Bell said sarcastically.

"Then - everyone was out. They would remain that way for twenty to twenty-five minutes, depending on how much they weighed. Smaller people would remain unconscious longer. One thing I didn't realize was the super-sensitive oxygen level sensors would shut off the lights when the atmosphere around you changed. I'm not sure why."

"Where did you get my DNA sample?" Bell asked.

"All the DNA samples for agents in the Eyes Only program, even older samples, are kept in my sister's lab. Your sample was easy enough to locate.

"I wanted to brief you in the InCit command center, but I saw several folks head down there while you were in the meeting. I knew I couldn't go there or I'd be found. So I stayed back and watched as you stumbled into the hallway and accidentally hit the Hirsch Pad by the elevator leading down to InCit. I was going to grab you then, but once I saw you accessed the InCit command center from the hallway, I knew you would be in good hands. So I bolted out of there. I no longer had to show you where InCit was."

Bell shook his head, trying to take in all he was being told.

"What about the drone and your DNA? I know InCit command sent the kill code removing your DNA from the InCit database. Your drone should have just stopped functioning at that point. How'd you manage to keep the drone online?"

"Everyone *thinks* they sent the kill code to my DNA," Tracey said, smiling. "In essence, they did, but only to one strand of my DNA.

"Once I had access to my sister's lab, I removed her DNA profile from her medical file and replaced it with a copy of my DNA profile. So now there were two of my DNA profiles in the system, in separate files. When they sent the kill code, I knew they would target my DNA profile by selecting my medical file, not hers.

"Before they could shut down the drone, I had already sent it on its first mission. Don't ask. It was safely on the ground when they shut it off a few days after I went missing. As you know, the kill code only works once when sent. I waited a few hours and remotely turned the drone back on. Because our drones are connected to the InCit database, my drone quickly located my DNA strand in my sister's file. But they must have ultimately found that copy of my DNA as well, seeing as how my drone never made it to Jafaire, its second mission."

"Yeah, that would be Dr. Parker over at InCit. She's one tough cookie and smart as hell. She found your sister, so she was the one who probably figured out you exchanged your sister's DNA with yours. Your drone is probably at the bottom of an ocean. When she learned you tricked her, she probably fired everyone in the lab because they didn't catch it sooner." They both chuckled.

"Okay, switch gears for a minute. How did you manage the ID to fly out of the U.S. without us finding you?"

"Remember back when we were brought into the Eyes Only group? We had to get undercover IDs. Remember that fun admin crap we had to do with the State Department, driver's licenses, etc.? Back then, I was still a smart ass, so I decided to use my newly found twin sister's name for my undercover passport. The Bureau ran the name through the Department of State and didn't locate a similar passport for a "Dana Tracey," so I was good to go. If I were questioned, I'd say I was confused and thought I was typing in "Nearest Relative" and forgot to change the last name to hers. I figured it was a good bet I would only be slapped on the hand for using her name, so I just went for it. On the State Department books, I was now Dana Tracey. It had a nice ring to it."

Bell turned to Tracey. "I found your travel under Dana Tracey, but I didn't know how you had managed it."

"I'm impressed. Good job. The best part was the State Department never followed up with my supervisor to let him know they were sending me the undercover passport. No one in Bureau management knew I had this passport in the name of Dana Tracey. From there, I got a driver's license using my passport, and voila! I had two pieces of undercover ID that were off the books. After that, it was easy to book my flight and board the plane using the undercover passport and driver's license."

"You talk to Trina recently?" Bell asked, looking out the window.

"Not since I left. I told her it could take a few weeks and to sit and wait. I'm sure it's killing her not knowing. But wait until she hears April is cured. She should know by now, I suspect."

Bell shifted in his seat. Tracey pointed to the bandage on his right wrist. "I noticed that earlier and meant to ask you what happened."

"I ran into an InCit drone," Bell said, half-smiling. "Seems like you weren't the only IA using their drone in a personal matter. IA24, an agent named Cranset, was blackmailed by the general's men here in the U.S. They threatened to kill his family in the event he didn't do what they told him. And for his family's sake, Cranset told no one."

"Where is he now?"

Bell looked over at Tracey. He frowned and then looked back out the window. "Dead."

Tracey twisted his head and squinted in disbelief. "Who killed him!? One of the general's guys?"

"Unfortunately, it was me. He tried to kill me at your lake house. Pretty sad scenario," Bell said. "The place is torn up a bit. Sorry. Not my fault."

Tracey let it slide. "How about his family?"

"I sent a text to InCit command just after it happened. They were securing his family. Let's hope they're safe."

"Good Lord," Tracey said as he stared ahead, somewhat shocked. "And Athan's family?" Tracey asked just as quickly.

"They're safe as well." Bell left it at that. He didn't want to know more about Athan and why he was involved.

Tracey sighed, relieved. They both just stared out the windows.

When they were approximately twenty-five minutes from landing, they continued the conversation, albeit a bit more somberly.

"When we get to Stafford, several agents will drive you to ERF. This is being kept hush-hush, of course. They'll escort you down to the InCit command center without handcuffs. Besides the director, I'm sure department heads will be there who want answers, and you'll have to explain yourself." Tracey nodded. He couldn't have expected any better treatment from the Bureau. So far.

After a moment, Tracey spoke, "I just want to thank you for believing in me. I want you to know I never gave away any of the InCit secrets, and neither the general nor the President of Jafaire has any idea how the technology works. No one does outside of InCit. Even though your drone helped us out of Jafaire, I don't think anyone was the wiser. All the subjects the drone killed can't speak." They both chuckled.

"Hey, I'll let Trina know you're back in the U.S. That way, she can still say she never received any calls from you, and I'll find out how April is doing."

Tracey reached over and shook Bell's hand. He held onto it a bit longer than Bell anticipated. Tracey looked confident but scared. Weird. Bell had never seen that look in his friend's eyes before.

The Gulfstream eased its way down from the clouds and landed smoothly on the small runway. After taxiing for a hundred yards, the pilot turned into a hangar at the end of the runway. The pilot shut the engines down and exited the cockpit. He opened the door, walked down the stairs, and continued walking through the hangar.

Inside the plane, Bell watched as Tracey stepped out of the plane and headed down the stairs. Two FBI agents dressed in jeans and sneakers waved Tracey towards the black BuCar waiting to take him to ERF. Tracey slowly walked to the car and got into the back seat. He never turned around.

Then Bell walked out the plane's door and down the stairs with his drone still cloaked. It was following several feet behind him. Bell whispered, "Reconnaissance" when he hit the last step. The drone flew to the other side of the plane so no one would hear the soft hum of its rotors.

Bell shook the agents' hands. Without any further pleasantries, the agents quickly jumped in the car and sped off.

Bell's mission was complete.

Epilogue

For the next several months, Tracey underwent lengthy debriefs at both ERF and FBI HQ. The director removed Tracey from the InCit program. And he wasn't removed "pending a full investigation." He was summarily removed from the program for good. He was also suspended for three months without pay.

Tracey passed all of the mandatory polygraph tests. The Bureau concluded that the InCit technology was still a secret. The director was especially relieved of that fact. He didn't want to be the first director to tell the president of the existence of the InCit program.

While he was suspended, the Bureau continued to look into every angle of possible espionage and found none. Before Tracey's suspension was up, he was also removed from all the Eyes Only programs. It was too bad. Tracey was a good agent. He brought it on himself, however.

Back in Jafaire, General Repuso was captured as he tried to flee back to Vista Porto to gain support for his coup attempt from his former military colleagues. In his possession was a laptop and the blackmail photos he had shown Tracey. President Embuke seized and destroyed all of it. Some three hundred of the general's soldiers were either killed or captured. Those captured were imprisoned in Jafaire. The U.N. and world leaders condemned the attempted coup the general orchestrated against President Embuke. General Repuso was subsequently tried by a U.N. military court for his crimes committed against a peaceful nation and sentenced to life in prison. A psychiatric prison. He was deemed mentally unstable while trying to convince the world he knew about a secret FBI program that commanded invisible drones. He didn't have any proof, however.

For her part in decisively leading the defense of Jafaire, President Embuke received accolades from numerous world leaders. One positive outcome of the attempted coup was an influx of new military items from several countries to help protect Jafaire from any future military attacks. First-world countries sent more sophisticated small arms weapons and mechanized vehicles, including tanks and fully tactical Humvees.

Dr. Embuke continued to ponder whether or not he should reveal the success of his DBA treatment program and possibly a cure for cancer to the world. He would have to discuss his treatments outside the lab, and he was not about to give up April or discuss Tracey's involvement. Nor could he speak of his sister. He wanted to, but he had no plans yet to approach her.

His clinic continued to prosper. He did make some employee changes, however. The general's daughter was arrested shortly before the general was, and she was given a lengthy prison sentence. Nurse Talia was promoted to nurse administrator and immediately assisted with the hiring of new nurses to assist Dr. Embuke. And she received a raise. In the future, Dr. Embuke promised himself he would only hire professionals unknown to anyone in his family.

Tracey's and Athan's families were insulated from any liability. After remaining in protective custody for three months, they returned to their homes with updated security systems. FBI HQ was able to identify three groups of Jafairians who traveled into the U.S. on fraudulent passports and who were also identified as being loyal to General Repuso. They were located, arrested, and deported back to Jafaire to face charges. To be safe, the Bureau maintained surveillance for several months around Tracey's and Athan's houses to ensure they hadn't missed any of the general's men.

Athan's family was interviewed many times, as was Athan himself. The Bureau diligently tried to uncover why Tracey involved his neighbor in the scheme. The thought was that there always had to be something in it for people to get involved. Athan stated he was helping out a good friend and was only given access to a program to send equipment to Tracey. He denied knowing anything about

Tracey's drone or the Bureau's technology. Surprisingly, he was able to pass several polygraph exams.

Fully six months after the fallout from Tracey using his technology for personal use, Athan was removed from surveillance protocol from the Bureau. He was no longer being followed, even though he never knew he was in the first place.

Athan also never forgot the protocol for destroying all evidence of their plan when they were finished: wait six months and get rid of it.

One Saturday afternoon, Athan made his way to work. Of course, his wife figured he headed to work to run numbers on oil production and other corporate minutia. Arriving at his office, Athan found the small laptop Tracey gave him with the drone program. Although he could not see the explosives left in the polar ice cap, he *could* detonate them. Or he could take the explosives offline and destroy the program written for those explosives, and no one would be the wiser. Before Athan decided, he leaned back and rocked in his chair. He then agonized over the decision for almost half an hour. He compared the pros and cons of destroying the program versus setting off the explosives and possibly saving his company.

Athan concluded he'd find another way to save his company.

He rolled his chair back to the computer, clicked a few buttons, and the explosives were disarmed forever. Athan then executed several commands on the program, and the program deleted itself. Someday, maybe thousands of years from now, if the polar ice cap lasted that long, someone might find a package of explosives and a drill bit and wonder what they were doing there.

What Athan didn't know yet was the five o'clock news that afternoon would report that a massive oil gusher erupted within a previously non-performing oil well belonging to the Kratos Oil & Shale Company in the Gulf of Mexico. Athan's research donation to the Seattle Children's Hospital could now be written off. The company would make its way back to profitability and survive.

Bell, in turn, completed a "hot wash," an after-action evaluation of how he performed his duties. He provided a full timeline of the work he had completed in traveling to the portals, getting shot, killing IA Cranset, traveling to Jafaire to secure Tracey and the country itself, and arranging to transport Tracey to headquarters to answer for what he had done. For his efforts, Bell was offered a section chief position, just as Tracey said they would. Bell politely turned down the promotion. He wanted to remain an Eyes Only agent who could work in the field on difficult cases, as an IA and elsewhere.

In the end, the Bureau concluded that although Tracey acted against the interests of the Bureau, the InCit program wasn't compromised. That was the main reason he was not fired or arrested. Tracey had not intentionally subjected the U.S. Government to any threats, and any threats found were eliminated without the world knowing. If the Bureau had prosecuted Tracey, the Bureau would have had to identify exactly what treasonous acts Tracey had committed. Then, the InCit program and all the hard work put into it over the previous fifty years would be identified, and the InCit program would be dismantled.

It was better this way for both sides.

Six months after squashing the attempted coup, President Embuke was sitting at her desk in the palace, typing an email of no significant importance, when her assistant called her. The president's brother had arrived for a family meeting to discuss where they would vacation that year. She dreaded the conversation. She was a workaholic and didn't like to take time off. Dr. Embuke was there to convince her, yet again, that life was too short and they would be traveling somewhere to unwind and relax. No excuses.

The door opened, and Dr. Embuke entered with a wide grin. He came around the desk and hugged his sister. She looked up and smiled but remained in her chair and kept typing. Dr. Embuke headed for the couch, and the drinks and snacks spread on a table nearby. His mother and father would arrive shortly, so Dr. Embuke figured he'd get the best snacks first. The president continued typing.

Outside the president's office, the two soldiers who gave Bell and Tracey a ride to their plane were standing guard. They were both promoted and now serve as President Embuke's security detail. They went wherever she went. They stood looking at their phones, laughing and giggling like school girls.

While they were on their phones, one of the soldiers' facial expressions turned to a look of confusion. He had opened an email with an attached video. He thought the video would be from the ceremony following the coup attempt. At that ceremony, they were both awarded medals from the president for bravery in the face of overwhelming odds. This video was not from the ceremony, however. His eyes widened as he suddenly remembered just what this video was.

On the day of the coup, the soldier readied his M4, checked that he had a full magazine, and placed his two extra magazines on the dashboard in front of him. He anticipated they would be in for an extreme firefight. He turned on the GoPro camera attached to the front windshield and hit "record." He wanted the world to know he died fighting as a hero if he was killed. He was so thrilled they survived that he forgot all about the video. But the GoPro did its job and emailed the video to the soldier.

During the firefight, the soldier questioned where all the rounds were coming from, which killed the general's men in front of them. He and the driver of the Humvee killed their fair share of the general's soldiers. However, he remembered firing and cutting down one soldier and watching two other soldiers fall just behind him or next to him. He didn't concentrate too much on that at the time. He was just happy the general's soldiers were all being put down.

Now, the soldier stared in disbelief at what he was seeing. Or, more accurately, not seeing. Just off his one o'clock, the video captured short flashes of light, indicating a weapon was being fired. And then, a few seconds later, a flash would appear some ten feet away from the last flash. This continued for approximately fifteen flashes or so. What the hell was he looking at?

He leaned over to his friend and showed him the video. They both stared at the video for some time. They would have to tell the president. They waited until after the meeting with the president and her family members.

President Embuke reviewed the video with the soldiers. She asked if anyone else had seen it. They advised no, not anyone they knew of. The only other people who may have seen what happened were dead. The president took the soldier's phone and forwarded the email to herself. She then deleted the email and the video from the soldier's phone, retrieved the GoPro from their Humvee, and destroyed it. The soldiers were sworn to secrecy.

Meanwhile, the president edited the video, removing the flashes, and played that version at many subsequent appearances while explaining how she handled the coup.

President Embuke then texted the original video to the drop phone she gave Tracey during the coup attempt.

Back in D.C., Bell sat on his back deck drinking a beer. He was startled when he heard a notification inside his home office that he had received a text message. Bell got up and headed into the house. He sat down at his desk and flipped open the phone. He clicked on the text. And then the video.

Bell almost spit out his beer. He watched the video of *his* drone in action. The message from the president was succinct:

"Now we both have secrets to keep. Peace ..."

Acknowledgements

I never had to stop and think twice about who I would acknowledge first once I finished this book. My entire career in the FBI would not have been possible if not for the love and support of my wife, Lynn. For more than 40 years, she has supported me in every way imaginable. I have been fortunate to have her as the solid foundation for our family. I love you.

I also want to thank my close friend and excellent copy editor, Katie Daly. She generously poured through several versions of this book with several red pens. Okay, more than several. She was honest and upfront about difficult topics, such as changing the book's name on the first day we met or mentioning that my attempts at comedy were commendable but needed help.

To my wife's ten-member book club, thank you! While I struggled to find time to read simple literary masterpieces such as the monthly AARP Bulletin, their insight into what they liked about the inside of any book was invaluable as they beta-tested my story before publication.

Finally, to MEB, your developmental edits and gentle suggestions that I should try sixth-grade English instead of fourth are genuinely appreciated. I couldn't have finished this book without your help.

Made in the USA
Columbia, SC
16 January 2025